# ENCHANTING HER MONSTERS

## BEWITCHING MONSTERS BOOK THREE

# YVE VALE

# ENCHANTING HER MONSTERS

## BEWITCHING MONSTERS
### BOOK THREE

YVE VALE

Published by Entraverse Publishing

Sedona, AZ 86339, USA

YveVale.com

# AUTHOR'S NOTE

*T*his is book <u>three</u> in the Bewitching Monsters series, a dark yet often humorous paranormal why choose romance.

Books one and two **must** be read to enjoy this novel.

PLEASE NOTE: This series also contains several dark elements that some readers may be sensitive to. For more information, visit: ValeRomance.com

---

# INTERRUPTED

## JADE

*A*fter being chased into the forest surrounding Amira's home, I'm covered in dirt, marked with scratches from branches and werewolf claws.

Through his dangerous teeth, Arran pulls me closer. "You are mine. My mate."

I crave for Arran to claim me with his bite. "Yes, make me yours."

There's no hesitation on his part. His razor-sharp canines pierce the juncture of my neck and shoulder.

The threads of a mating bond immediately snap into place, linking our souls.

*Wholly. Completely. We are one.*

The feeling is like nothing I've experienced. It's as though I've discovered a lost piece of myself I didn't know was missing —like I've come home.

Then my body glows with sigils and strange writing, just as Maxum described before. The unidentifiable magical symbols over my body dissolve like they're evaporating into the ether. Have they vanished for good? Or is this how they always appear and disappear?

*"Oh, Jade..."* a woman says in my mind. She sounds completely mortified and distraught. *"What have you done?"*

I shake my head to clear my confusion. "Abuela?" I call out to the dark woods.

*"You made the same mistake I made."*

Mistake? What mistake did my grandmother make?

After hearing my grandmother's disembodied voice, I instinctively push the spirit away. I don't want to hear more. Not now.

Arran's grip around my waist tightens, if that's possible, and he growls at the surrounding darkness.

Since it's only a spirit who spoke to me, I know he doesn't understand what the threat might be. I'm sure he's feeling over-protective and vulnerable because we just sealed our mate bond. He's still locked inside me, so if we were attacked, this could get awkward fast.

Given my current circumstances, I don't want a conversation with my dearly departed grandmother right now. Although her ominous words about making the same mistake she did echoes in my head.

Did she mate a wolf shifter? Is my grandfather a supe?

*Oh, my goddess. My grandma is watching me get busy with my mate...*

That's it. I'm calling this experience a new level of embarrassment for me. If I didn't finally have someone—correction, *someones*—to live for, then I might just die from mortification. As it is, I must live and endure this. My guys had better appreciate this gesture.

I'm not embarrassed by sex. I mean, I write this stuff for a living.

Well, the steamy romance part, not the 'grandma watching

them bump uglies with a legit monster with special equipment' part.

Yeah. I'm burning with flushed skin in more ways than one.

Arran just rocked my body, then my soul. I feel our spirits intertwining. It's the magical equivalent of a marriage, but a heck of a lot more permanent.

*It hits me again. We are mated.*

I was so caught up in the moment that I begged him for his bite.

When I check in with my emotions, I don't regret it. I only regret my grandmother's ghost for an audience. Now, if Maxim, Flint, or both of them, were here watching, that would be hot.

Arran's berserker gives the darkness another snarl for good measure before he licks the fresh wound on my neck, tending to his mating bite. I feel it sealing closed as he administers the aftercare.

My other, more permanent ghost, Osen, slides forward in my mind, but I don't want to deal with him either, so I throw up a mental wall and demand, *"Is this a life or death conversation?"*

*"Uh, no,"* he mutters.

*"Then fuck off... for now, okay?"*

Thankfully, he fades into the background again.

Forgetting my ghostly audience for now, I turn my attention to the person who should have it.

My berserker is slowly grinding into me, giving me his entire release so his knot will subside.

I glance over my shoulder and watch as the berserker version shifts into his human form.

"Jade!" he shouts.

"Arran!"

He fists my hair and guides my mouth over my shoulder to meet his lips. He claims me all over again. Our tongues tangle, and his shallow thrusts become more urgent.

Breaking the kiss, he nuzzles the spot where my neck and my shoulder meet—where he bit me. "Goddess, Jade. I never thought…" His voice cracks with emotion. "We're really… Is this real? Are you mine?"

"Yes, my sweet Arran, my wolfy, my Serky."

He chuckles lightly. "Serky… for berserker?"

"He deserves a name, too."

"I suppose he does. Thank you, my sweet witch." His duller human teeth scrape over my flesh. "For the first time in my life I feel blessed." Deft fingers slide down my soft stomach and then find my sensitive bundle of nerves like a heat-seeking missile.

I cry out with pleasure as he works my body.

"My perfect love," he mumbles over and over. "I will never stop claiming you, Jade."

My body quivers with his words and his ministrations. The bliss he's driving me toward barrels at me.

I shatter into the universe. Stars go supernova. I'm blasted to the far ends of time, then I'm reassembled around Arran's perfect instrument of mass pleasure. I coalesce as someone who has their person.

I arch into Arran's powerful body as he shouts through his release.

He collapses against my back, breathing hard.

Fortunately, his arm braces me against him, while the other props us up from the forest floor. He leans back on his heels and slips free.

Arran turns me on his lap and cups my face with his other hand.

"Sorry," he laughs, "I made a mess of you. You're covered in dirt."

"Worth it." I smile wide, and I'm sure I look dreamy eyed. "Mud wrestling at its finest."

"I don't want to return to the others, but I know you need your rest after all you've been through lately."

"I understand your possessiveness, but I doubt I'll get much rest out here."

Arran doesn't let go of me. Instead, he lifts me in his arms and carries me back.

I silently call out again to see if the ghost is still lingering. *"Abuela, was that really you?"*

I hear a long-suffering sigh. Great. Now I know it's my grandmother. Other than Osen, who would sigh at me like that?

*"Mija, I warned you not to become attached to these males."*

I answer her in my mind so I don't upset Arran. *"Uh, well, damage done and all that. I don't want you ruining this for me."*

I hear a feminine grunt of disapproval, and I feel her presence slip away.

My heart aches. I wish I could have talked to her more, but this isn't the moment.

We quickly see our cabin ahead of us.

I bark out a laugh. "Geez. It felt like forever when you were chasing me."

When we get close, I give Arran another kiss and study his eyes. "Do I need to be careful about touching the guys until the bond settles?"

"You'll know if I can't handle it, but I think we should be okay. My wild side sees them as pack."

I sigh with relief.

Coming into my magic for the first time in my life must be enhancing my eyesight, because I can clearly see Flint, Maxum, and Calder standing outside, watching us return.

First, I wonder if something's wrong. Then, I worry I've frightened them.

As soon as I'm close enough to not shout, I ask, "What's wrong?"

Maxum chuffs and smirks at me like I'm a naughty child. "You just played a dangerous game of roulette. Thank the Fates, you won."

"Serky wouldn't have hurt me." I squeeze Arran and gaze adoringly at him.

Calder throws his hands up in exasperation. "You didn't

7

know that for certain. A primal chase with a werewolf is dangerous, at best." It appears he's concerned for me, not just for the body attached to his ghost love.

Flint rushes forward and wraps a warm blanket over me. "It's too cold for you to be out here."

My eyes snap back to Calder. I don't believe he's seen me naked before and perhaps never wished to. Although he might have accidentally caught a glimpse when Maxum had Arran lick me clean. I thought Calder had been in the cabin when that happened, but when it was over, he wasn't around.

I reach out to give Maxum and Flint a soft touch. "I'm sorry if we worried you."

Maxum quirks an eyebrow. "You're living for more than just yourself now. You have us. So, keep that in mind, stunt devil."

"You should have seen me run!" I say proudly.

"Sweet witch, I did." Maxum shakes his head. "I loved watching your juicy bottom bounce and jiggle, but you weren't as fast as you think you were."

"I was scared," Flint says. "Please let us know when you plan to do something spontaneous again."

I suppress a laugh at his comment. He's so protective, and I don't wish to squash his need to be the protector he was created to be. "I will plan all my reckless behavior from now on."

"Good." Flint pulls a twig from my hair. "I've realized that my danger-compass is broken around you. It's very unsettling."

"Oh, shit," I say, and think about it. It really is broken—he hasn't felt his spidey tingles when I'm in danger. "Why is that happening?"

"Could be your magic?" He shrugs.

"Or the wards your grandmother placed on you, scrambling his senses like it does with your legal documents to hide you from the world," Maxum suggests.

"Or his heart is always on alert, worrying about you." Calder throws out like a bomb. But as he says it, I feel the truth of it.

"Calder might be right on that." Flint frowns. "Not reassuring."

"But my sweetheart, it's so romantic," I point out.

"I will have to find a new baseline so I can protect you."

"Speaking of your grandmother, uh, why did you call out to her during our mating?" Arran asks.

Maxum goes on alert and demands details with a growl. "What happened?"

"I felt her pushing on my senses when I was playing out my primal chase fantasy, and I put up my wall," I explain. "But when Arran bit me, I lit up with symbols like Maxum said he's seen on me. Then they sort of dissipated into the air. Almost like they dissolved in the wind. Is that how it happened before?" I ask Maxum.

"No. They lit up and then faded back *into* your skin."

"Oh. Hmm. That's weird." I don't know if this is a positive twist, but there's not much I can do about it now. "Then my grandmother's voice popped into my head and said, 'You made the same mistake I made.'"

"What the hell does that mean?" Calder hisses. "Are you part supe?"

# 2

# AFTERCARE

## JADE

"*A*re you a supe?" Arran and Flint echo Calder's question.

"I don't know. I didn't ask her, I was in the middle of mating so I told her to bugger off." I bite my lip, wondering what I am. "Do you think that might be why you all are attracted to me? Because I'm not really a witch?"

"You're a witch," Maxum says with certainty. "However, it appears you might have something extra. But just so you know, that's not why we like you."

"But—" I argue.

"No. Stop trying to find reasons we don't just like you for you," Maxum says with his bossy tone.

"Okay…" I rub a hand over my face, feeling self-conscious. "I'm not usually this insecure, but—"

"Rob made you feel worthless," Calder interrupts with no malice. Damn, this guy is hitting the bullseye with all his comments tonight.

"Yeah. You're right." Magically suppressed and conscious memories trickle back. "He did say horrible things to me about my body and personality, especially toward the end. I now remember when he had me under his hypnosis spell to channel spirits, that also he used that time to degrade me. He tried to make me feel like I was unlovable. Probably so he could control me."

"But it didn't work, not completely," Calder reminds me with a sympathetic smile. It surprises me that he's saying such supportive words. He isn't exactly my biggest fan. "You broke up with him. That takes strength when you're being manipulated and beaten down on all levels."

Maxum cups my face with his large hand. "He's correct. You're strong. Stronger than they know how to control. I believe those witches and warlocks are afraid of you."

"Of me? Why?" I ask.

"I don't know, but we'll find out. Together." Maxum's gaze turns to my hair, his fingers comb through the strands. "Your hair... it's silver."

I roll my eyes. "Yeah, I have gray hair."

"No. *Silver*. Like an elf might have," Arran agrees and then stares into my widening eyes. "And your irises... they're glowing green."

I need to see this.

"Jade green," Flint adds. "Like the beautiful, powerful stone."

"They are no longer hazel." Maxum touches my hair reverently again. "Silver. That spell broke whatever was hiding your more obvious fae traits."

"We'll figure it out, but first we should bring our sweet witch inside. It's cold out here," Flint says and picks me up, clutching me to his chest. He braces the back of my neck with his large hand and it feels like polished marble. His thumb skims the bottom of my jaw, and he whispers in my ear, "Are you sure you're alright?"

I give my protective gargoyle a kiss on the lips. "I'm fine, sweetheart. I'm sore between the legs from the knotting, and I have some minor scrapes from tree branches and Serky's claws, but nothing serious."

Flint gently places me on the bed and makes me lie back. He pulls the blanket off me and inspects my body for the injuries. His smooth, thick fingers trace over my collarbone, over my breasts and stomach, to my thighs. I'm covered in drying mud and debris from when Arran's berserker claimed me and fucked me into the ground.

Flint pulls another twig from my hair.

Without asking, he spreads me wide for Arran and Maxum to inspect my abused pussy, running a thick finger over my center. "The werewolf made a mess of you."

*Holy Geezelbub.* Does this gargoyle know how hot he is?

Calder hangs back behind the partition in the living area and sits on the couch out there. He wants no part in this. Not yet. Maybe not ever. No. He only longs for the trapped ghost inside me, his former beloved, Osen. I shouldn't be greedy, but I want him to be with me, too.

"Eyes on me… Stay with us, my mate," Flint says as he strokes my thighs. I'm beginning to wonder if he's been reading my books for spicy inspiration. But I realize he's sensed with our budding mate bond my wandering thoughts about Calder.

Our gazes lock, and I'm drawn into his pale gray eyes.

"All in good time," he whispers, reading my mind.

"Arran, your tongue might soothe her cuts now that you're bonded," Maxum suggests.

Arran snarls at Maxum, nudging both males out of his way. "I planned on taking care of my mate. Thank you very fucking much. I came back here to do just that." My wolf shifter picks me up and carries me into the tiny bathroom in our hideaway cabin.

I'm thankful Amira took us in and offered us this haven, but

I miss Maxum's beautiful lake house and his spacious luxury showers.

Arran turns on the water to warm it up and presses his forehead to mine. "Goddess, I can barely stand not touching you. I was ready to rip Flint apart for carrying you inside."

I clasp his cheeks. "Will you have a hard time, then? Me being with them?"

"I think it's only since the claiming bond is still settling. As soon as it solidifies, I should be fine." He looks me in the eye and strokes my cheek. "Don't worry. I won't keep you from your other loves."

I smile sadly. I'm happy to hear this, but also worried about how he feels about the arrangement. "Are you sure you're okay with sharing me?"

"As Arran, yes. I mean, would I prefer to keep you all to myself? Fuck, yes, I would. But I see how you are with them, especially what you did for Flint." He whispers, his lips brushing over the shell of my ear, "And how you have already healed something in Calder."

I frown, worried about how Calder will handle things now that I have officially bonded with Arran and I'm forming a bond with Flint and Maxum. They are his people, his pack. Then I came along and turned his world upside down. Although I suppose his world was already screwed up when Osen died just before I stumbled into the picture.

My thoughts are brought back to my new mate when Arran licks over his mating bite.

*Holy macaroons.* The sensation travels like a lightning bolt directly to my clit. I shiver and press into his firm, naked body.

"I'd love to rut you again, but I'm worried that you won't be able to take me so soon. You aren't a wolf shifter. You weren't made for taking knots."

"Does it bother you that I'm not a shifter?"

"Not at all. Actually, I'm a bit surprised how well you took my knot and how rough... Serky was." He gives me another seductive kiss that makes me tremble with arousal. "But if you have supe blood, perhaps that's why it feels so natural for you to be with us."

"What if I'm some sort of freak supe-witch hybrid?"

"Then I will love and protect you just as much." He shrugs playfully. "And apparently, we love freaky."

I release a heavy breath, feeling less stressed about my mysterious background. "How did I get so lucky?"

"I'm the lucky one. I stalked you and tricked you into believing I was a dog. I never thought you would forgive that lie."

"I don't blame you for protecting your pack. You didn't know if you could trust a witch taking sneaky pics of you."

"I'm glad you were a bit of a perv and horrible at being sneaky." Arran chuckles and lifts me into the shower now that the water is warm.

He runs his fingers over my neck, prompting me to ask, "Do I need to bite you now to complete the mate bond? Or is that not how it works in the real magical world?"

The corners of his lips pull down ever so slightly. "You can try to bite me, but I doubt it will do anything more for our bond because you aren't a shifter."

It doesn't matter that he says it's not a big deal. I wish I could offer him what his kind can—the way I sense he *wants* it to be.

Arran lifts my chin with his finger and makes me look into his eyes. "I love you, Jade. *You're* all I need."

"Okay." I hate that I'm so worried, but they are all so special to me, and I don't want to disappoint them.

Osen's voice breaks through my barrier I've learned to create to block him out. *"Just be you, and you won't disappoint them. They picked you because you're perfect the way you are. You don't need to change or be more. You just need to remember the confident version of yourself before Rob hurt you,"* Osen speaks in my mind, then pauses. *"We will help you get there."*

I take a deep breath. I used to be more confident before Rob the Worm infiltrated my mind.

*"You want to help me?"* I ask.

*"As best I can… considering what I am."*

*"You feel stronger,"* I say, trying to change the subject. His kind offer makes me want to leak water from my eyes (as Flint might say), and I don't want to get emotional over something he's said since I'm still irritated with him.

*"Your mating powered me up. But we can talk more later. I'll let you have your time with Arran now."* He pauses and I feel the tension inside me brewing. *"We must talk about the situation with your grandmother."*

*"Okay."* I send him a mental wave goodnight to let him know I appreciate his support and care.

"Talking with Osen?" Arran asks.

"Uh, sorry."

"It's okay. I could see that you were somewhere else."

"It's weird to have your former friend and lover inside me, isn't it?"

"It's all weird, but it's what it means to be with you." Arran leaves a trail of kisses from my shoulder, up my neck to my mouth. Then he claims me with a fierce kiss. "For now, I'm going to hoard your attention, because to do otherwise might kill me." Arran licks over the bite again, and I moan with need. "I need to be inside you again… soon."

# 3

# FAMILY BINDS

## CALDER

*T*hankfully, after Jade showered off her mating dance dirt, the guys initiated nothing more with her.

I'm not jealous. Okay, maybe a bit. I wish I could enjoy someone's touch again. Now that Flint has overcome his aversion, it's given me some hope, but he was never broken like I am. He didn't lose a huge part of himself because he died a horrific death.

I will never be the same. Though, perhaps I don't have to be completely healed to endure being close to someone again?

Remembering the moment with Osen, while he was inside Jade's body, I mull over how I was able to share a kiss with my old love.

That's something, isn't it?

But if I had to listen to my entire pack fucking that sweet witch while basically in the same room? *And* I couldn't join in? Nope, that's a whole new torture.

I might be over the possible evil witch thing with her, but

that doesn't mean I'm ready to pursue something with Jade. Besides, I don't expect that she would be into me. Not after what an ass I've been.

I wouldn't want her to think I liked her just because Osen possessed her, either. For some wild reason she confessed to me she worried about that with the other guys, and it struck me hard in my gut. If I'm honest, I don't want to make that mistake with her if it really is Osen's energy that attracts me to her. It wouldn't be fair to any of us.

In the morning, I wake to discover Jade's magical creatures sleeping on me—Sage, the rabbit, and Trouble, the guinea pig. I'm scratching the bunny behind the ears when Jade shuffles into the main room and finds me snuggling with the little ones. Her sexy curves are barely contained in her skimpy sleep shorts and tank top. Not that I'm looking.

When she sees her creatures with me, her eyes soften and the corners of her mouth lift in a small smile. She takes a step toward me, but then thinks better of it and asks, "Can I pet them too?"

"They're your familiars, so yeah," I say in hushed tones, not wanting to wake the other guys. I flick my chin for her to come over.

"Uh, I didn't want to encroach on your space." Jade kneels down beside my makeshift bed on the couch and strokes Trouble's soft fur.

We share a quiet moment where it feels like the terrors of the realms aren't pressing in on us. I watch her gentle fingers gliding down the guinea pig's fluffy coat and find myself enchanted by her delicate hands. Loving hands. She isn't at all like the witches that have hurt my pack and me.

Jade hasn't looked at me since she knelt down to pet her animals. She bites her lip then says, "I'm sorry."

"About what?" I ask, skimming my finger over the rabbit's incredibly soft ears.

"You're stuck here like *this*. It must be uncomfortable."

"The couch isn't too bad," I say. I know what she really means, but I want to avoid the topic. What can I say about it anyway?

"No, about having to share this small space with me. It was probably bad enough when I was invading your pack's huge lake house. You had your beautiful room to avoid me." She swallows down the emotion bubbling up. "And now, you're forced…"

"Hush," I admonish her with a tender yet firm voice. "We're good. Okay? You're pack now. Arran officially claimed you. Flint and Maxum are already bonding with you. Osen is…" I choke up a bit despite myself. "You're literally carrying his soul inside you. Don't worry about me. If I need a break, I can take a walk."

Her hypnotizing green eyes finally meet my gaze and I swear there's a glow behind them, like a supernatural being might have. I wonder what she might actually be besides a witch.

The bunny wakes up and licks my hand. Then she says happily to Jade, "You lick birdman now. He likes it."

Jade's eyes go wide, and she covers her face in embarrassment. "Sage, he doesn't want me licking or petting him. *Please* stop saying stuff like that."

Even my face heats, feeling self-conscious. I swear this rabbit fancies herself a matchmaker.

Of course, Trouble pipes right in. "I think Birdman might like it more than he says."

Jade frowns at both of them and gets to her feet, stepping back. "No more of this talk. You will *not* pressure us anymore about me touching him. He's only comfortable with you guys. It's not nice."

"Sorry," Sage and Trouble say.

Jade looks at me, worry written on her face. "I'm sorry about all that."

"Not your fault." I sit up and set both creatures down on the floor so I can get breakfast ready when I hear the others rolling out of the huge bed they've all shared inside the small cabin.

I sense that they've been awake since Jade got up and approached me. I suppose they didn't want to make her think they're going to hover over her as much as they want to.

Flint enters the room and nods at me. We set things out on the counter and table for us to eat as Arran and Maxum join us.

Dressed in only sweatpants, Arran sits down at the kitchen table and pulls Jade into his lap. She squeaks as he does, and a blush creeps into her cheeks.

This woman confuses the hell out of me. We watched her come back filthy and naked from the woods last night after a werewolf knotted and claimed her, and *now* she's embarrassed sitting on his lap?

Maxum and Flint give her glances filled with longing, their hands clenching as if they are resisting the need to snatch her up and into their own laps.

I'm jealous for my own reasons. I wish I could get over my touch aversion and be comfortable, like Arran is with his mate.

I had always wanted a mate, but do I want that anymore?

With a heavy sigh, I place a couple of chocolate muffins on the table and some fruit for us to eat.

Arran grabs a muffin and lifts it to his mouth.

Just as he's about to take a bite, Jade screams, "No!" Then she smacks it right out of his hands and to the floor.

We all stare at her in shock.

"What the hell?" Arran asks, more in confusion than anger.

"It's chocolate!" she says, pulling away from him a bit.

"So?" He shakes his head, puzzled by her behavior.

"It could kill you," she explains, like he's daft.

Then Maxum lets out a booming laugh.

Her eyes dart to him with a snarl. "What's so flippin' funny about killing my mate?"

Dang, she's fierce. It's hotter than it should be.

"He's not a damned dog, little witch." Maxum wheezes with laughter. "It doesn't poison him."

"Oh, whoops." She turns bright red again and sinks down into herself, burying her face in Arran's chest. "My bad."

Arran chuckles and strokes along her back. "I appreciate the sentiment, but please never try to choc-block a werewolf," he jokes and kisses her temple.

"Arran has a sweet fang, but he won't admit it," I add, and I'm rewarded with Jade's laughter.

Flint picks up the damaged muffin, pulls off the crushed side that impacted the ground, and eats the rest.

Jade offers Arran her muffin as an apology. After a bit of fuss, he accepts, then feeds her a few bites when she finishes eating the sliced apples and peanut butter Flint gave her.

She licks Arran's fingertips clean of crumbs, and I imagine her licking something else... Dang, I need to get my shit together. Maybe I should go buy a tent and rough it outside of this cabin.

"Amira wants me to meet with her soon." Jade appears apprehensive at the idea.

"Hopefully, she will be able to help you control your new magic and understand how you connect with spirits," Flint says, taking Jade's finished plate from her to clean.

"I hope so too," Maxum agrees. "And I'd like to chat with Darius about our home realm. Find out what's been going on lately in hell." He smiles at Jade. "I'll walk you over to the main house."

"I'm going to do a sweep of the area," Flint says and hurries out the door. He doesn't like new places or situations, and he's on edge, being at the mercy of another witch's protection. No doubt he's worried about Jade being attacked again.

Jade pouts while she watches him run off. The big oaf didn't even give her a hug or kiss goodbye. He's going to need some pointers on how to be in a relationship with a mostly human woman.

I see the angst clearly written on Arran's face. He doesn't appreciate the idea of being separated from Jade so soon after their mate bond. Goddess, I have no idea why he bonded with her with all that's going on.

He should have waited until Jade's ex wasn't a problem anymore.

Maxum pulls out a sheet of paper with a sketch on it and places it in front of Jade.

"What's this?" she asks, studying the page filled with sigils and glyphs.

"These are the markings I saw on your body. I thought we could show Amira to see what she recognizes."

Jade's eyes widen in shock. "Do you have an eidetic memory?"

"Mostly… for the things that interest me." He smirks. "And you interest me."

I roll my eyes but lean over to check out the designs. "Strange. They almost look like fae sigils, but not quite. Are you sure you got them right?"

The demon gives me a pissy glare. "I got it fucking right, bird brain. That's why they confused me. But I had hoped it was some sort of secret witch thing and maybe Amira would tell Jade about them."

Maxum leads Jade away toward the main house and Arran huffs out a breath just like his wolf might.

"Get a grip, buddy," I tease and finish cleaning up our morning meal. "She's going across the field, not to another realm."

"It's the bond. For a little while, every time she leaves the room, I'm going to be a pathetic mess." Arran sets his golden gaze on me, and I know he's wondering where I stand with this development. "Well?"

YVE VALE

"Well, what?" I ask, just to drag it out. I don't want to answer him.

"Dude, really?" Arran shakes his head. "Out with it. Tell me I'm a dumbass for claiming Jade."

"You're a dumbass?" I say with zero conviction and as a question.

"So you're cool with us?" Arran cocks his head like a confused dog.

"I'm not pissed at her anymore, but I think your timing is a bit screwed up."

He runs a hand through his thick, cropped brown hair and frowns. "I know. I don't want to admit it to Jade, but her grandmother's disapproval is worrying me."

Sighing, I focus on him and empathize. Relationship stuff can suck ass, but when a disembodied voice offers him an ominous statement during the most vulnerable and fulfilling moment of his life—claiming his mate—it had to have rocked his world.

"We don't even know if it really *is* her grandmother," I say with a shrug. "And… uh, I am happy for you. It's no small thing to have a bond with someone you feel you have a mate match with."

He nods, but still looks a bit off-center. "I'm going for a run."

"I'm going to track down the other phoenix here."

Arran strips down, shifts into his regular wolf form, and races off to the woods. He's chasing his personal demons. With the image of his terrifying monster form in my mind, I still can't believe he didn't hurt Jade during their mating. She really did tame his berserker werewolf.

I fuss a bit in the house, delaying my talk with Raithe. As I open the door, I find him standing outside, ready to knock.

"Hey," he says with a wide grin.

Raithe is so much more easygoing than I am. I wonder how many times he's died and regenerated. I doubt if any of them could be as bad as my last rebirth. He wouldn't be so smiley if he went through the torture I did.

"Hey." I try to relax my shoulders and appear calm, but being around another phoenix stirs up a lot of emotions for me. Loss, anger, longing, and jealousy. "I was coming to see you."

"Good to hear. I didn't want to push myself on you if you weren't up for company." Raithe glances behind himself and then suggests, "Would you like to take a walk or maybe stretch our wings?"

I consider my emotions right now. "Uh, walking is probably best." I shut the cabin door behind me and step out into the sun. We are on the earth plane, I can sense that much, but nothing beyond that. However, I haven't been trying too hard to pin it down. If someone were to mind probe me, then I don't want to give up our secret location. And I really don't want to bring down the witches and warlocks upon Raithe and his mates.

"I know the cabin is cramped, but I hope you're able to make it work. When Darius and I shared it with Amira, it was tight. I can't imagine adding two more large males to the coven and staying in there."

"We aren't a coven," I correct him. "Well, *I'm* not one of Jade's mates."

Raithe's eyebrows rise with disbelief. "Oh? I could have sworn I sensed something between you. Sorry."

"Uh, yeah… it's complicated." I rub the back of my neck and feel my heart racing. How much do I tell him? Maybe I should tell him everything and get an outsider's perspective. I'm all turned around and twisted up.

Raithe nods and walks toward the woods. "I understand complicated. I hadn't expected to be with a witch… or a woman, for that matter. I'm usually attracted to males. But then Amira came along and captured my heart *and* my balls." He laughs, shaking his head, likely remembering falling for his mate.

"I'm bi with a leaning toward males. But I don't think I can be intimate ever again," I confess.

His gaze darts down to my crotch, probably wondering if I've lost my *dangly bits* as Jade would say and why they didn't come back in a regeneration.

"No. Not *that*. My last death fucked up my head pretty badly."

"Sorry to hear that, brother." He reaches out to pat my shoulder and thinks better of it, dropping his hand to his side.

I don't tell him it's okay, because it's not. A stranger's touch makes me want to scream. Sure, I allow my pack to occasionally buddy-pat me, but even that doesn't bring me any comfort.

Oddly, Jade's touch during our mental shield training didn't seem to bother me. I wonder if Osen being inside her was the reason. Then I remember I didn't enjoy Osen's touch since my last incarnation.

There's something different about her. But I still don't know if it's wise to pursue it when so much is unknown about her origins and who she may be.

I can't risk it.

"So... you left a big piece of yourself behind last time?" Raithe asks.

"Yeah. You know how it is. We always lose memories or some bits with each death. After the last one, I wish I didn't come back."

"Fuck," Raithe hisses. "My flames feel your pain."

We start on a path in the woods that appears well traveled. The forest swallows up the morning light, but my eyes quickly adjust to the darkness.

"Have you ever had a death like that?" I ask.

He nods slowly.

Goddess, it feels strange talking about this with another phoenix. My father is long gone, his magic was snuffed out when I was just a fledgling. I didn't get much guidance from him since he was taken when I was so young. My heavy heart feels as though it's been lifted as I realize I finally have another phoenix to help me.

But quickly, my anger swells inside again at what the witch who killed me did to me. Memories of her torture fill my mind.

Then what's been eating me up since that death finally comes out as I shout, "I can't shift!"

After a long silence, where I see his concern on his face, Raithe asks, "At all?"

I can't believe I admitted that to him. I've never even told my pack.

I want to punch Raithe for the sad look of pity on his face.

I want to scream.

*I want to fucking shift!*

Turning my gaze away so I don't have to look at his pity, I admit, "I can only manifest my wings and fire."

"I understand now that your last death wasn't an ordinary one. But if you have your wings and fire, your phoenix is still inside you."

I fall to my knees, emotion overcoming me, covering my face with my hands in shame. "But I'm broken. It's like a piece of my soul is missing, not just my memories."

Raithe kneels next to me and says quietly, "My last death was the worst yet." He sighs heavily. "Without going into a long ass story, I'll say I only survived it emotionally because of Amira. Because I finally gave in and trusted her, she saved my soul on so many levels. And I'll never be able to pay her back."

Scraping together my dignity, I get to my feet, considering his words, and we continue down the forest path.

"So you truly don't have a problem with Amira being a witch?" I ask with no small amount of skepticism, but my voice comes out as small and weak—it matches how I feel.

Raithe stops abruptly and looks at me. "She has essentially given up being a witch, and chose Darius and me as mates. If it weren't for her, we'd be dead or still being tortured. She has done more for supernaturals than most supes, so no, I don't have a problem with her." He levels his gaze at me, and I feel the weight of his focus like a threat. "Jade is in your pack, whether you like it or not. So you better figure out how to drop your prejudice or leave them."

My feathers are ruffled, but the asshole isn't wrong. "I'm trying. It isn't easy."

"Maybe, but it's not as hard as you're probably making it." Raithe turns and continues back on our walk. "What everyone seems to forget is that we are all individuals. We are more than our species, or magic, or lineage, or sexuality, or whatever the fuck there is to see on the surface. More importantly, we are the choices we make every damned day."

I think about his words. Who have I been if I only considered my choices?

I don't like the answer.

And Jade? She has only been kind, accepting, and giving.

I just hope I can repair any damage I might have caused and develop a friendship with her.

Because no matter my hang-ups, she's in my pack now.

4

---

# TRAINING

JADE

"I'm nervous about talking with Amira," I admit to Maxum as we walk up to the main house.

"How so?" His voice is calm and filled with authority, like a hot professor might sound in one of my novels.

"Uh, well, she's a witch. And probably a powerful witch to be able to protect and ward her vast amount of land. Besides, she doesn't seem to be overly fond of other witches. I feel like a burden."

Maxum stops and turns me to face him. I look up into his dark obsidian eyes and sigh. My gaze travels over his crimson skin and horns, admiring what a handsome demon he is. Not that I've met other demons, but it doesn't matter.

He's my demon. And he's gorgeous.

His hand cups my cheek. "Amira has an ugly past with other witches, just as our pack has. She doesn't like being a witch. So don't take it personally. Learn whatever she can teach you, and we'll figure out the rest together."

"Thank you." I lean into his palm. "It means a lot that you're helping me."

His expression turns fierce. "How else should I act? You're my mate match. Even if you rejected me, I would help you in any way I can. I would die for you."

My insides melt into goo, and my eyes widen. "You really think we are meant to be? What about my abuela's warning when I mated with Arran?"

"We don't know what that was about. And honestly, I don't care." Maxum steps closer until I'm flush with his body. He pulls me up by my ass, and I wrap my legs around his hips. "*You. Are. Mine.* And no one can tell me otherwise, except for you."

His lips crash down on mine, and by the time he's done reminding me I belong with him, I'm panting and grinding on his growing bulge.

"Understand, little witch?" he growls.

"Yes," I breathe out. Damn, he just erased my worries with a mind melting kiss.

We hear someone clearing their throat, and snap our eyes over to the porch of the main house.

"You going to hump on my lawn all day?" Darius asks with his gruff, gravelly voice.

Darius and Amira are standing side by side. Amira looks slightly amused, and Darius appears his standard irritated. I haven't seen him with another emotional setting yet.

He must have one, right? I mean, Amira loves him, he can't be one dimensional. Perhaps he doesn't let anyone but Amira and Raithe see another side.

Reluctantly, Maxum allows me back down to my feet and gives me a peck on the forehead before swatting my ass as I walk toward Amira.

I throw a dirty look over my shoulder. He's being a brat in front of them. "You'll pay for that," I threaten.

"I've already paid dearly for my time with you," Maxum says with a laugh.

I turn around and try to hide my hurt about that statement. I cost him two of his safe houses, one of which was his special secret home he had hoped to have for his pack. Guilt doesn't even cover it when I think of what he's lost since I came into his life. Hell, one could even say Osen's death is on me. Rob might not have killed him if I couldn't channel his spirit. And now, we are on the run because Rob and Galiana are hunting me.

Huge arms wrap around my waist and Maxum hugs me to his chest. He leans down and whispers in my ear. "Sweetheart, no. Stop this. I was talking about my heart. You own it now. Don't blame yourself for the houses. They mean nothing compared to your safety."

I lean back into his arms and look up into his handsome face. "Thank you."

He gives me another kiss and Darius grumbles. "Can we bring the public displays of affection down to a fucking minimum?"

With a blush on my cheeks, I pull away and hurry toward Amira so I don't get lost in Maxum again.

"Morning," I say to the witch, and we watch Maxum and Darius wander off together around the house.

"Never mind Darius. He likes to give people a hard time," Amira says.

"I understand why he would want me to leave. I'm a witch invading your territory, and possibly bringing trouble with me," I add, feeling bad about the whole thing. I didn't ask for my magic and all this drama. I only like drama in my books, thank you very much. If I could have all the yummy monster love and not be chased around by an asshole ex who wants to magically fuck with my head, then I'd be a happy little witch.

"Most witches and warlocks are a problem." Amira ushers me inside her home. "If they would drop their prejudice and work with the supernaturals, we might be able to figure out what to do about the loss of magic."

"Do you think that's why they are after me?" I ask.

She studies my face and then her eyes lose focus and I suspect she is reading my magic and aura. "Maybe. You have an unusual magic." Then she motions for me to sit down on a meditation cushion near the large picture window overlooking the rolling forested hills on her property. She takes up the seat in front of me.

"Can you figure out what I am?" The desperation in my voice is clear.

It truly is disconcerting to become the FMC in my story and receive weird powers.

*Will I answer the call to adventure?*

Well, I suppose I answered the call to monster cock adventures. That hasn't killed me yet, so I'm on a roll.

"Can you tell me what you know about your lineage? Your gifts?" she asks.

I swallow down my nerves and give her the quick summary. "As I mentioned before, my grandmother told me she was a witch. She implied I would have powers as well. She was odd, so I thought she was playing pretend with me. My mother didn't seem to have any magic powers, and she didn't like my abuela saying things like that to me. When I was a kid, I saw what I thought was my wild imagination—auras, monstrous forms under someone's face, and sometimes energy swirling around me. Then it all disappeared after my grandmother gave me that necklace when I was around ten years old. I was told she died not long after that visit. The only thing that didn't fade was my strange dreams. It felt like I was experiencing other people's dreams. It turns out I might have been channeling spirits this whole time. And my ex took advantage of this ability."

"Yes, your mates mentioned you can channel the spirits of supernaturals," she says thoughtfully. "I've never heard of that ability. It might be why the Anti-Supernatural Organization wants you."

"Yeah, I have the spirit of my guys' former pack member permanently tied to me now. But I don't know how to control this gift, and we were hoping you could help me figure it out."

"I know some things about channeling, but I'm far from an expert." Amira frowns. "I'll share what I know."

"I also believe I have heard my grandmother's spirit a few times now." I bite my lip, feeling nervous to admit what happened. "Uh, when Arran claimed me last night, she said that I made the same mistake she did."

Amira's eyebrows rise in question. "So, you're wondering if your grandmother had a supernatural mate and if you have supe blood..." She nods to herself and says, "That would make sense. Usually, only humans and supernaturals can mate and create offspring. If you have a witch-supe combination in your lineage, that might explain your unique ability. Did you ask her what she meant?"

"She sort of interrupted us during the mating, so I told her to go away," I admit with a blush.

"Oh, well, yes." Amira barely suppresses a laugh. "Do you have a process to connect with the spirits? Maybe you should try to ask her about it now."

"I don't have a process. It's one reason we came here—so you could teach me," I admit. "Do you have any suggestions on how to call on spirits?"

"Being a witch, I'd suggest meditation and some sort of focal object."

"I had my grandmother's pendant until we realized my ex used it to shove spirits into my body so he could question his victims after he murdered them." My hand automatically touches the now empty spot at my throat. "But we left it behind because of the tracking spell."

Amira watches my gesture and frowns. "I would offer you a

focal object for a replacement, but I don't think you need that—not if supe magic enhances your power."

"It's so strange to think I lived almost forty years with no clue that these other realms existed and that I might have magic."

"Unfortunately, magic isn't as wonderful as some humans might imagine." Amira studies her hands as if she is contemplating her power. "I did some terrible things because of magic and my struggle for power—for control. I hope you never have to do something you'll regret."

I swallow that comment down with all that it contains. I can tell by the haunted look in her eyes that she's seen some shit. Maxum told me she is older than she appears. I idly wonder how long I will have with my guys if we can survive Rob and Galiana.

"I'll teach you some meditations to help access your magic," Amira says and then guides me through some visualizations.

They are nothing profound, but I expect they will help me focus and center my thoughts.

I've used exercises like this before, especially when I first started writing professionally. But over the years, it only takes me sitting down at my computer with my tea to trigger my brain to enter the proper wavelength to write and create.

I realize as I allow my mind to wander that it seems channeling or using magic will probably be similar to my writing process.

I will have to create a mindset or mental space—a trigger—that I can use to access my gifts.

Osen's spirit vibrates gently, letting me know I'm on the right track with this idea.

At the end of the meditation, I open my eyes and find Amira staring at me.

"Is something wrong?" I ask when she appears a bit disturbed.

"No. I've been using this time to study your magic. It truly is odd. I've never sensed anything quite like it, but it also feels familiar."

I hum to acknowledge her statement, but I don't know what to say. "I don't need to try now, but I was also wondering if you would know how to release a spirit from my hold. Eventually, I expect Osen will want to move on. Or I might have another spirit try to attach to me."

"I did some research already in this area. Darius is a high-level hellhound. He said that there are many ways to separate a possessing spirit from a host. One is a complex ceremony mostly used by normal humans, since they rarely have magic. You're a witch, so there is a spell I have written out for you. However, it may not work since Osen is not a normal human or witch soul. Darius says for the demons and hellhounds dealing with supernatural souls, they use their intent to handle souls. Often seeing a severing in their mind's eye."

"So... just imagine it?" I ask.

"Yes, but with *intent*, with your will and magic."

"Oh!" I remember the sketch Maxum made. "I have something we wanted you to look at." I pull the paper out and hand it over. "We're hoping you can give us an idea of what this is."

Amira studies it for a while before her eyes snap up to mine. "Where did you get this?" her voice is almost accusatory, *threatening*. "Where did you see these symbols?"

Instead of answering, I ask, "Why? Is there something wrong?"

"Answer me."

I can't refuse her, but I rationalize it won't hurt me to tell her. She already knows too much. "They were magically embedded in my body. But they're gone now. They disappeared after I bonded to Arran."

"Hmm." She narrows her gaze at me. "Who was your grandmother?"

"Patricia Jones."

Amira tilts her head and her eyes widen as if something's clicked into place. "No, not Jones, it's Rosethorne," she states confidently and chuckles without humor. "I thought you looked vaguely familiar. I should have recognized you right away, but it's been a long time since I've seen her face."

"You knew my grandmother?"

"Not well, but yes." Amira looks back down at the paper but does not really focus on it. "Patricia disappeared around forty years ago, from what I understand." Her gaze snaps up to meet mine to gauge my reaction. "She was a member of the ASO."

"How do you know?" I ask, feeling like an ass that my grandmother was part of the witch-warlock organization whose goal is to destroy supernaturals.

Amira must see my disappointment. "I worked with her a few times. She was a powerful lust witch… not that she didn't have other talents."

"Lust witch?"

"They mostly used her as a *spy*."

*Spy* likely means she was used as a seductress that slept with targets to obtain intel.

"Does that mean I'm a lust witch too?" I gasp when I realize I'm probably attracting the guys with my powers. Is it why I write steamy romance?

"Powers are often passed down, but I don't sense that lust magic is what is strongest inside you." Her eyes seem to lose focus as she gazes at me, like a scryer would over a crystal ball. "No, there's other magic in you that's more prominent, and it doesn't feel like witch magic. That's why these unusual sigils and your grandmother's warning about making mistakes concerns me."

"So you think I'm part fae?"

"Yes, and perhaps something else. As odd as it would be, I suspect you could have some demon in your family tree." She hands the paper back to me. "If I had my guess, your grandmother was mixed up in a lot of trouble in all the realms.

She had someone from the hell realm working with her, if this mishmash of concealment and containment sigils are any indication. It appears to be long forgotten arcane spell work from all three realms, blended to form its own unique casting. Only the creator of this masterpiece *or* the person it was cast upon would have been able to break it."

"But then, what was the necklace for if I had this binding on me?" I ask.

"A necklace can be torn away. Besides, I believe the pendant's purpose might have been more to syphon any magic that leaked out of you, if the sigils weren't maintained over the years."

"So my grandmother meant to lock away my magic forever?" Sadness fills me as I conclude my abuela kept part of what I am from me. I've been living a half-life because of her.

"Don't assume the worst," Amira consoles me. "She might have believed she would come back and train you in your powers when you were ready."

My heartache and betrayal must be written on my face.

With everything that's happened, my entire being is suddenly exhausted. "I appreciate your help, but I think I need to rest now."

"Of course. Your magic is coming in. It will take time to adjust in your body. And if it's as unusual as I sense, then it might be even more challenging to manage at first."

Amira hands me a slip of parchment paper with the exorcism spell written in Latin on it and I walk toward her front door in a daze.

## 5

---

## TEAM SPIRITS

JADE

*I* thank Amira for her time and information about my grandmother, my sigils, and the meditation techniques. Then I wander back toward our cabin so I can take a nap.

In my mind, I sense Osen push forward to catch my attention.

"Yes?" I ask with a bit of irritation. I still haven't completely let go that Osen has highjacked my body twice.

*"I don't sense your grandmother right now,"* Osen reports.

*"And you sensed her before?"*

*"Uh, yeah, that's why I was bothering you when you were mating with Arran. She was trying to stop you from doing that."*

"Did you get any idea why?" I ask, curious to what he picked up from her.

*"She didn't wish to interact with me. However, I did get a few flickering images from her. I swear I saw Galiana. I believe she knows that witch. It makes sense since they both were in ASO together."*

I absorb that information, but until I talk to my grandmother, I won't have any answers. *"If you pick up her presence again, can you let me know?"*

*"Of course, sweet witch."*

I roll my eyes at his kiss ass nickname. He knows he fucked up, but I need him to sweat it out a bit more before I forgive him... again.

*"Amira isn't wrong about you having strange magic. Now that it has been unlocked, it feels like fae-born to me. The electric bolts you can innately summon aren't a witch's ability. At least not without training and a spell. And the soul magic you demonstrate with me is more akin to some types of demons or a hellhound."*

"Could that mean that I have demon blood? Is that why Maxum thinks I might be a mate match?"

*"Maybe. But until we get answers about your lineage from your grandmother or elsewhere, we won't know for sure what you might be."*

"Which means it will be probably harder for me to learn to control my powers until I know," I say aloud.

*"Not necessarily."*

"What do you mean?"

I sense Osen is delighted and proud that I'm interested in what he has to say, and that he can help me.

*"We are all built to control the magic within us,"* Osen explains. *"Some might need more guidance than others. Some are more inclined to abuse their power. But ultimately, we have an instinct to use it. Just like how birds fly and snakes bite, we innately access that part of ourselves if nothing is blocking our way."*

"Like how my grandmother's pendant blocked me."

*"Yes, but now, you'll likely find your powers come to the surface with little thought."*

"That seems dangerous."

*"It can be. That's why magic schools and tutors are mandated to teach supes control. But you have us to help you. You have me."*

His offer to help would mean more if he hadn't betrayed my

trust. "I remember you tried to steal my body to use that power."

*"Not my finest hour."* Osen sighs. *"I promise I won't make that mistake again. I'm feeling more like my old self. More complete. More in control over my reactions."*

"Why would that be?"

*"Maybe your mating bond fed my incubus magic. Or it could be our connection. Your unleashed magic is healing me and strengthening my soul."*

"I'm happy you're feeling better," I say and mean it.

*"I won't go rogue again. I realize how my stupid, impulsive decisions have hurt my pack, most significantly Calder and you."*

Entering our empty cabin, I shuffle to the enormous bed and flop down. My mind wanders over all the things I should be doing now for my author career. I have promotions to run. Books to write and edit.

"Do you think I can set up my computer stuff and check my accounts?" I ask Osen.

*"I think there might be too much interference with Amira's cloaking magic. Besides, it's probably best to ask Maxum to portal you somewhere else far from here, just in case Rob can track you somehow."*

Not being a computer expert, I don't know how likely that is. But I've seen spy movies that suggest if Rob has someone skilled in hacking, they might be able to ping my location. "You're right," I say with defeat in my heart. Things may never be normal for me again.

*"Rest now, Jade. We can get all that figured out when you wake up."*

As I close my eyes and drift off, Osen's presence shifts from just a disembodied voice in my head to a fully formed male in my dreams. He's standing in front of me in what he calls the shadowscape—where an incubus' magic resides.

He hasn't bothered to render imagery of the surrounding setting. We stare at each other amidst the darkness. There's only enough light to see each other. I study his handsome face since it's the first time he's appeared in a highly detailed human form. Before, I've only seen him as a shadow person, each time with increasing detail.

He's also completely naked and my eyes dip down to appreciate his toned and well-equipped body. But it's his intense gray eyes that draw my attention. His shoulder-length, wavy brown hair frames his masculine face in a casual, yet stylish, way.

Seeing him how he was in life assures me that Osen never had an issue feeding his magic with sexual partners.

He's fucking gorgeous.

Even his dead body was beautiful, since it hadn't decayed at all. The only thing that took away from his allure was the obvious lack of life in his body as it rested in a glass coffin.

Too bad that true love's kiss couldn't wake his sleeping beauty.

But then part of me wonders if anyone tried. Calder probably didn't attempt that with his aversion to touch.

"Your mind is somewhere else." Osen smirks. "I thought seeing me naked like this would at least amuse you."

"My mind has more than one track," I tease. "Horny isn't the only setting I have."

It's strange that he can't just read everything going on inside my mind. But I'm grateful for that now. My chaotic, wandering author's mind would likely baffle him.

"We need to ask Maxum about your body—why it looks so well preserved," I say with a frown of concentration. This has been low-key bugging me since the bunker when I saw his body in person.

"Yes, I hope now that things have settled, we can unravel that mystery," Osen agrees, then opens his arms.

I don't fall into his embrace even though his gorgeous naked form is acting like a magnet to my nether regions. "What if I'm a lust witch? You heard that, right? Isn't that what you thought I was when we first talked?"

"I was worried that you were seducing my pack, yes."

My heart squeezes with fear. "What if it's not really me—"

"Shush." Osen's face becomes fierce. He steps closer and places a thumb on my lips. "If you even have that ability, it isn't why they like you. I should know. You aren't the only one who has dealt with this bullshit."

That thought shuts me up. He's an incubus. I imagine that's a far more powerful influence over others than a lust witch.

I move my trapped lips to talk. He slowly drags his thumb away as he stares at my mouth with interest.

I resist the urge to bite my lip and force myself to remain focused. "In your life, you've worried about whether your intimate partners actually cared for you, too."

"Constantly." His jaw flutters with the emotions raging inside him. "*Always*."

"How did you deal with it?" I ask.

"I didn't. It's only now I realize that Calder really cared for me."

"*Cares*," I remind him firmly. "He *loves* you."

"I didn't trust it when I was alive. Not completely."

"Do you want to talk to him again?" I offer.

"I might take you up on that soon, but that's not what I want at the moment." He opens his arms again, inviting me into his embrace.

I hesitate, since I'm not sure how to proceed with this enigma. Osen is wrapped up inside me in a way no one else has ever been. If we pursue something deeper, the chances of it ending horribly are an enormous risk. The consequences could be devastating if he were to take over my body again in spite or in a rage over a fight we had. I hate to say I've been a victim of that too many times to not consider it a real possibility.

He can deliver an incredible sexual experience, but I'm not ready to engage with him that way again. Not yet.

"What are you expecting from me?" I ask.

"In general or right now?" He smirks and part of me wants to kiss that damned look off his pretty face.

"Now."

"I wish to do something I never tried before." He shrugs, but I sense it's a bigger deal than he's playing it up as.

"What's that?"

"Cuddles." He lowers his smoky gray eyes and drops his arms. "With your power released, I sense you're able to resist my incubus paralysis. So you would be the first person I could really do that with."

"You mean you freeze everyone else up when you're intimate? Even with snuggles?" I ask. I'm still shocked this is a default thing for the incubus.

"Well, I've only known high-born demons to resist my power. Maxum can. Until you came along, he wasn't a cuddler. And yeah, my incubus power feeds on emotion. My mother was a succubus and didn't care for children." Osen glances up to see my reaction. "It feels nice when the guys hold you. I wanted to try."

My heart turns to mush.

"Dammit. I'm too soft for my own good." I curse and pull him into a hug.

The next thing I know, I'm on a bed with him. He curls into me, placing his head on my chest. His muscular arms wrap around my waist.

I stroke my fingers through his long silky locks, and he hums with contentment.

"Goddess, this feels good." He murmurs over the swell of my breast. "I wish I could have done this when I was alive."

"I'm sorry you didn't get this experience." I kiss the top of his head. "Just ask if you want to do it again."

"Every night?" he practically begs. "We can meet when you fall asleep and hold each other and talk."

"I'd like that."

Eventually, I fall into a deeper sleep and dream of my guys holding me... even Calder.

# 6

## OH, HELL

### MAXUM

*E*ven for a hellhound, Darius is a grump. Sure, I can be a surly pain in the ass, but I also know how to have a laugh. Obviously, he's irritated by my pack invading his sanctuary, but I suspect this is his usual personality. It's likely why Amira didn't think to ever introduce us before. Not that I've interacted with the witch in a few decades.

I completely understand why he doesn't want us here.

Raithe probably doesn't either, but he seems to be the peacemaker of the bunch.

I can't say I would be happy either if their coven had knocked on my door, potentially bringing trouble to my pack.

"If my affection for my mate bothers you, I'll tone it down," I offer. It's the least I can do as a thank you. And some people are more riled by displays of affection.

Darius grunts and continues to lead me toward his hothouse. "If you think she's your mate," he says without judgment, "then why haven't you claimed her? It's not like our kind to wait. I sensed the wolf did so last night."

"Don't bring up what our kind normally does," I warn. "We both aren't like most of them. We don't just take without permission."

He nods, then he arches a brow. "Seems like she gave you permission from the way she was about to rut you on my damn lawn."

"Yeah, well. It's been a wild ride. She didn't know about the other worlds just days ago. She's... not what I expected. Not that I ever thought I'd find my match." I don't know why I'm rambling nervously. It's unlike me.

"You didn't expect her to be your mate match because she's a witch or because she's Ms. Klutzy Sunshine?"

I chuckle at his name for her. "Both. But even though she isn't what I imagined, somehow the way she fits with me and my pack makes sense."

"Hmm." Darius opens the door to the small structure and some of the heat escapes.

We both sigh contently at the searing temperature that only hell-born are comfortable with. Our shoulders relax, and we sink onto the wooden benches.

"There's something off about your little mate," Darius says, breaking the silence.

Protective instincts rise inside me, expecting I will have to defend my witch's honor. "Explain," I demand as a cold threat.

"Don't get your tail in a knot." Darius waves me off. He's more relaxed now and maybe that's why he feels like he can say whatever he likes about my love. "She's not just a simple witch. My nose can pick up that."

"We suspect she might have fae blood. Or something supernatural."

"Maybe... but doesn't she seem like she has a bit from home?" he asks.

With his suggestion, I recall how she passes through my

demon portals with no side effects. That rarely happens to non-hell beings. The rest of my pack doesn't react anymore because they've gotten used to it in the countless times they've used one. It didn't even phase her the first time. She also didn't seem affected by being in the hell realm on our way to Amira's. Curious.

"I don't have your acute sense of smell for our kind," I say. "But yes, there's evidence to suggest she has some hell-born blood in her."

We sink into silence again, and I ponder my connection with Jade. If she has demon blood, that will make the idea of being fated mates more reasonable. Not that I needed validation for how I feel about her.

My conviction to wait to claim her until Rob and Galiana are removed as a threat wavers. I don't know if it will be better or worse if I bond with her immediately.

No. I *should* wait. She's still coming into her magic. She accidentally mated with Arran during this delicate time. I don't want to mess with her balance further.

She needs to get control over her energy before I add a bond to it.

Although everything screams at me to claim her. To sink my sharp teeth into her flesh and feel the connection snap into place, linking us forever. Then I'll claim her pussy, marking her with my cum.

I'll declare to all and the fires of hell that she is mine.

"You realize if you mate bond with her and she has demon blood, you will probably send a ripple to the hell realm and the high lords will be alerted to her."

Ice pours through my veins at this devastating reminder.

Demon females are rare and the high-born lords may come to kill me so they can claim her for the hell realm, even if she is only part. She could end up as a caged, broodmare since she could potentially carry a demon child.

"Fuck!" I bellow.

"We don't know for certain if she has a drop of demon blood in her." Darius attempts to console me. "And maybe Amira can create some sort of protection spell to mask your female."

That eases a bit of my worry. Amira might not like to use her destructive magic anymore, but at least she still makes an exception for her superior protection, healing, and cloaking abilities.

"I also know you aren't the simple demon you claim to be." Darius gives me a knowing look and I snarl. He holds up his hands and assures me, "Don't worry, I won't be outing you to anyone."

I should have known a high-level hellhound would sniff out my secret. Not even my pack knows.

Why do I have a bad feeling that they will soon find out who I really am?

# 7

# MEMORIES

OSEN

*T*his sweet witch is breaking my shadowheart.

Jade's soft touch—physically and emotionally—has me on my metaphorical knees. Even though she has fallen into a deeper level of sleep beyond the shadowscape where I can interact with her, she is still somehow manifesting here with me. She's snuggled into my arms with her head tucked under my chin.

The shadowscape is an extremely convincing representation of real life. An incubus or succubus can create our surroundings and lure in our next target and feed, making our food source believe they are somewhere safe or terrifying, depending on our fickle moods. We can mimic almost anything, but it falls short in many ways. Mainly, that it *isn't* really living. I can't freely interact with my pack, and I can't help make the realms a better place for those I care about.

And Jade? I can't truly enjoy her the way I want to. Every

time I bring her here, I feel like I've trapped her or forced her to be with me.

In a way, I have. Though not on purpose. My soul being stuck inside her body and mind isn't either of our faults. But I feel more like a leech than I ever did in life.

When she spoke about releasing my spirit earlier, I panicked. I shouldn't. I *should* just accept that my reckless actions finally caught up to me in that alleyway.

But now that I've found her and I realize how much Calder feels for me, I don't want to move on from this life. I want to find a way to live—with them.

Jade hasn't said it, but I sense she would allow me to remain with her forever, as long as I behave myself.

I'm tempted to go along with that, but for my sanity I need to materialize in a tangible way or let go somehow and move on beyond the veil.

I don't want to move on though. I want to become a real member of this pack again. More than I was before.

I want Calder. I want to help heal him as I should have done before. Like Jade is doing now.

I can see it. He's changing. I'd love to claim it was about me. That my death shook him up enough to come out of his unhappy existence. Except that would be a lie.

Jade is our savior—for the entire pack.

I stroke her soft cheek and wonder how accurate my illusionary shadowscape is.

Closing my eyes to this imaginary place, I focus on Jade's energy and how she truly feels intertwined in me. In some ways, this bond we have is more intimate than what the others have. Not that I deserve it. Not yet.

I sink into the darkness and fall deeper into the place where Jade dreams.

I open my eyes to find myself inside her dreamscape.

A shiver goes through me when I realize where I am.

The wretched alleyway where I died.

I'm standing next to her. Jade has taken my spot, reliving what I remembered from that night and what we saw together right before Rob attacked us.

"Jade?" I ask as Rob's cloaked figure appears at the end of the alleyway.

She tears her gaze away from his ominous presence and looks at me in confusion. "Osen? Why are you outside of me?"

"You're dreaming, and I'm along for the ride."

"Oh, lucid dreaming. I do that." She bites her lip, looking a bit confused, and glances between us. "I'm just not used to seeing your memories with you beside me."

"Same for me." It's strange. I've been her ghost since I first died and possessed her. But I'm more aware now. More myself.

Jade takes a nervous step back, glancing around for an escape. "We should go to a different memory now," she says with a shaky voice.

I capture her arms and make her focus on me. "I don't relish the idea of reliving my death moment, but I wonder if maybe we should both witness this again with an analytical lens. Maybe catch something we didn't last time. A clue."

"Yeah, okay." She nods vigorously, regaining the courage I know she possesses. "It's just that when we were both in this alley... everything fell apart. I almost lost you, and I almost died."

"I know now that you aren't my enemy." I brush back a lock of her hair and caress her cheek. "We are remembering in your mind, okay?"

Her lucidity returns, and she turns to face Rob again.

I snatch her hand in mine, and we create a united front to experience this horrible moment together.

She squeezes my hand in solidarity. "I know this will be

hard for you. Just remember, I'm on your side. I will fight to avenge your death," she promises.

"Thank you, sweet witch. But now, I only want to focus on answers."

We both turn our attention to the warlock Rob walking toward us, silhouetted by the light of the moon.


*"You shouldn't have pushed," Rob says. "I warned you to walk away."*

*"You expect me to heed your message from the lips of my dying ally? You truly didn't expect that I'd seek justice for what you've done to my kind?" I counter.*

*"I thought you might be smarter than the rest since you're the only one who's gotten close to discovering what's truly going on."*

*"I know the Witch Council members are behind the ASO."*

*The man laughs—genuinely amused.*

*Suddenly, I'm hit with a blast of magic from behind, along with a chant.*

*This energy doesn't feel like anything I have experienced before. It's a new magic filled with dark intent.*

*My body trembles on the ground. Someone is stealing my magic, and my soul is detaching from my body.*

*"I told you he'd come," Rob says with an evil smirk.*

*Then someone who looked very much like Jade appears from the shadows.*

*I die.*


Both Jade and I float above the scene. It's an unnerving sight to see my dead body on the ground. Thankfully, Jade is floating beside me and not splayed out below.

I freaked out last time when I saw her appear, but now I'm much more rational and intend to find out the rest of this situation.

Astral Jade glances over at me, and I reach out to pull her closer. Her nervous energy about my reaction settles.

*Rob leans over my body and chants a strange spell. Dark shadows escape my body and Rob absorbs them. He's grunting and whimpering as he's stealing my magic.*

*The witch's face shifts, revealing it's actually Galiana, not Jade or her grandmother. Darkness swirls around her, too. They both have incubus magic.*

*But how?*

*"Send his soul to the abomination and get answers about what he knows," Galiana orders. "Leave the body here for his kind to discover."*

*"Can I kill the bitch after this one?" Rob asks, looking eager.*

*"No," Galiana snaps. "Jade's mine to destroy. And she will be useful for a bit longer."*

*Rob chants something new under his breath, but I don't recognize the language. It's not Latin or the other common magical languages. It sounds like an odd mixture of demon, Elven, and something else.*

Then both Jade and I clutch onto each other's spirit forms, flying through the city to her house, and we fall into Jade's sleeping body in her home. We are back in the early morning when I first possessed her.

I hear Jade speak as a spirit to me. "This is the morning before I saw the guys at the bar. I woke up feeling strange, worrying maybe Rob broke in again to harass me."

*Jade's body jerks to sitting, and she glances around her room. She's filled with fear.*

*She gets up and grabs her gun, checking around her house before relaxing after finding herself alone.*

. . .

"I'm sorry you had to live like that. Afraid your ex was going to hurt you. And now to discover he actually was hurting you."

"I'm not the only woman in the world dealing with an abusive and manipulative man," she says, sounding both angry and sad.

"Still. It makes me feel horrible for any damage I've caused being an incubus. But if I'm sticking around longer, I will do my best to not harm you anymore. If I do it without realizing, please tell me so I can be better."

I sense her agreeing to my request.

We observe as the front door flies open, and Rob rushes in already chanting a spell.


*Jade drops to the floor.*

*He hovers over her. "Osen? Incubus?"*

*I let out a wheeze through Jade's lungs. Being freshly dead ghost, I am unable to do much more.*

*"Good. You're in there," Rob says. "I'll be back in a few days to have a chat." He sneers at Jade's body and then reluctantly tosses her on the couch. Likely, he wants Jade to come out of the spell like she only fell asleep, so she doesn't wake up on the floor and become suspicious.*

*After a chant, he closes the door behind him. Jade is none the wiser.*

*She shifts on the couch and mutters, "Weird. I must be more tired than I thought."*


The memory fades, and we are left standing in the shadowscape once again.

"I was so off that day. I forgot to eat. I couldn't write worth a damn." Jade recalls from this memory. "Now I know why."

I wish I could comfort her, like she deserves, but I feel like I will fall short in every way. I don't really know how to comfort.

I've never done something like that before. I've only offered a sexual release for my partners. I wasn't the one people went to hoping to ease their worries or to be their pillar of strength.

Maxum was our strength and courage. Flint was our rock bed foundation, never wavering. Arran was often our confidant and comfort before he was cursed. Calder was our passion and spirit until he was damaged in his last life.

And now, Jade is our heart. She brings compassion and understanding. She brings the group together in a way I never did.

Moving forward, what can I offer? Even if I could return whole and in my body, I don't see what I could contribute.

I know one thing. I won't do anything to hurt her. Never again. If it comes down to it, I will sacrifice myself to ensure her wellbeing and her happiness with our pack.

"Osen?" Jade calls me. "Are you okay?"

"I will be," I answer, and then ask, "Will you do everything you can to help Calder?"

I sense her unease, and she asks with an uncertain tone, "What are you saying? Are you moving on?"

"No. Not yet. However, when I go, I want to ensure that you'll be there for him."

"Of course," she hesitates. "But you're still here. Maybe you could help too. I'm out of my depth with him."

Wondering how to respond to her worried expression and reaction, I ask myself, *What would Jade do?*

Then I pull her into an embrace. "Whatever you need. Whatever Calder needs, or the pack needs, I will do my best to deliver."

# 8

## REVEALS

JADE

*I* refuse to wake up from this delicious dream. An eager tongue is skillfully licking my center, and both of my nipples are being sucked.

Pressure builds in my core, but an orgasm is just out of reach.

I wonder if this is one of those dreams where I wake up to find myself incredibly horny and have to bring out Ole Faithful to vibe me to completion.

Then I remember I have three guys who'd likely be *up* to help a wanton woman out.

The soft, insistent swipes of a tongue remind me of Flint.

And the two hot mouths on my breasts make me think of Maxum and Arran. Both guys run so warm. I imagine it's their hot hands wandering over my skin.

This dream feels so realistic that I wonder if it's Osen making this fantasy come to life in the shadowscape.

Without opening my eyes, I reach down to work my clit, but find an entire head between my legs.

My eyes pop open with surprise, and I see all three of my guys tending to me.

"Oh!" I gasp.

The noon sun filtering in through the window lights up Flint's fully gargoyle form with his broad shoulders, horns, tusks, large wings, and heavy brow. The sight alone almost undoes me. Maxum has his wings out for good measure, and I just want to grab one of his horns and yank him back to sucking my breast.

Arran almost seems out of place in his human form. But if Serky comes out to play, I'm worried no one else will get a chance to be with me.

Maxum uses my shocked, opened mouth to kiss me dizzy, delving inside with his forked tongue and exciting me more. Then he pulls back and whispers over my lips, "You mentioned you wanted to be woken up like this. And Flint told us you gave him permission to touch you whenever he wanted to."

I gape at them all. "Yes... but..." I shudder with pleasure when Flint goes back to sucking my clit. "Okay... yes, yes, yes, I did say that. Why am I fighting this?"

Arran chuckles. "Don't know, but if you want us to stop, we will."

"Please, keep going," I beg, trembling. "I want you, and I need a release." Then I catch Arran's glowing golden eyes, seeing Serky is just under the surface. "You're okay with them touching me like this?"

Arran bumps my nose with his. A shifter's gesture of affection. "I'm keeping Serky in check. He seems to be happy enough to see you pleasured even if it isn't him doing it."

Flint pauses his ministrations to look up at me with his otherworldly, light gray eyes. "Maybe one day we can wake you up with our cocks inside you?"

"Yes, please, and thank you." I smile mischievously and my body undulates to show them how much I crave them.

"You and I need to complete our bond, my little mate." Flint says and slowly slides two thick fingers into me. "When would you want to do that?"

His eyes shine with his eagerness, but it doesn't feel right to bond with an audience.

I wink at him. "How about we talk about the details tonight?"

Flint smiles and pumps his thick digits into my pussy at a faster pace. "Yes, I can wait for the perfect time to have you all to myself. Now, come on my tongue so Maxum can have his turn."

"Holy fuck, Flint." My cunt clenches around his fingers. "I almost came just with your naughty talk."

"I'm about to as well." Arran chuckles and nuzzles into my neck.

"Make our woman scream your name," Maxum orders Flint. Then he fists my hair and claims my mouth again.

My once-shy gargoyle feasts on my pussy as he adds yet another thick finger inside me. I'm stretched so wide the thought of it ramps up my excitement.

Arran uses his partial shifting ability to elongate his teeth and his wolf's sharp canines pinch my hardened nipples.

I squeak and thrash, losing control. I'm flailing, feeling too much.

"That's it," Maxum breathes. "Come for us, our love."

I fall off that cliff and soar with bliss. Each clench of my pussy around Flint's hand feels like a flutter of imaginary wings that takes me higher.

Then I slip back into my body with a silly grin plastered on my face.

Flint licks his lips, tasting my juices. "If you'd let me, I'd live between your soft, pillowy thighs."

I might have taken offense for calling my legs *pillowy*, but that was when I was with Rob. My hard-bodied gargoyle thoroughly adores softness. He craves my soft, squishy body. I reach out to him. He answers my summons, leans over my flushed body, and gives me a possessive kiss before moving aside.

Maxum strokes his hands over my knees and then spreads my legs wide. "Ready for my monster cock, little mate?"

My demon rubs his unusual member over my slick center. He slides inside of me, and I feel every one of his soft spikes that run along the top and bottom of his cock and around its base. It only takes a few strokes until he's fully sheathed. His textured cock stimulates my clit and outer lips when he grinds his hips into me.

I'm gifted with a unique sensation deep in my pussy as he hits the spot that makes my toes curl.

Flint's hand grasps my breast, and he flicks his tongue over its peak.

At my other side, Arran's hand shifts into his werewolf's claws and the tips dimple my flesh. "I love your body. Pliant and thick, so we can grip onto you and hold on as we fuck you."

"It's perfection," Flint murmurs as he sucks and nips. His tusks scrape along my sensitive skin.

Maxum moans. "I love watching them monster-handle you."

I flick my gaze back to Maxum as he spreads out his giant wings that take up the entire width of the bedroom. He pounds into me, getting more excited with my moans.

I'm launched toward an orgasm and my body spasms.

"I want to make you mine," Maxum grits out through his sharp, clenched teeth.

"I want you. I want *all* of you!" I shout. Right now, I really, really need them. I need them as my bonded mates.

*All of them.*

There's a tug at the very core of who and what I am.

I sense the others' energy… their souls. I don't mean to, but I'm pulling them to me. Yanking their souls, their spirits reaching for me as well.

Even Osen glows in my inner eye.

Despite the unusual sensations, my orgasm hits me like cannon fire, making me shake and buck. Maxum spasms with his climax, gripping me like he might fall off the edge of the world.

Maxum crashes onto me as if someone's shoved him. Fortunately, he's able to brace himself with his arms. He appears dazed.

I hear a thump and a curse from the main room.

Calder must have been lurking there, listening to our lovemaking.

I pulled on his soul so hard he fell.

*Am I hurting them?*

I feel it when their souls are released from my strange hold.

"What was the hell was that?" Calder hisses from the other room.

Maxum's broad shoulders press into me. Grasping his upper arms, I encourage him to move back so I can see his face.

He shifts away slowly, and I glance over at both Arran and Flint, both look a bit bewildered and confused.

Did I hurt them? What have I done? Panic wells inside me. I worry, but wonder if this could be a mate thing? It happened when I wanted them.

*"I'd like to know what that was too,"* Osen says in my mind.

"Get in line," I mutter.

*"If there is a queue for your affection, I'll gladly buy tickets for that train,"* he retorts in a frisky tone.

I roll my eyes. But his joke relaxes me, just as he intended.

Flint recovers first and cups my cheek. "Are you alright, my mate?"

"I think so." I cover his hand with mine. Well, what I can cover, given his hand is so much larger than mine.

Still on top of me, Maxum braces himself on his elbows to relieve most of his weight from crushing me. "It felt like you tried to pull my soul out through my dick."

I wince. "Sorry. I didn't mean to."

"I'm not complaining." Maxum slides backward, but only enough so his hips are between my ankles.

"What was…" A disheveled Calder appears in the doorway and doesn't finish his sentence when he sees me between my three guys. His striking blue eyes hungrily take in my naked, recently fucked body.

I'm splayed out and exposed. I have an urge to cover myself, so I move to pull my knees together.

Calder growls.

*Okay.* Apparently, he doesn't like that.

"I thought you didn't want—"

"It doesn't matter what I want. I *can't.*" His hand drops to cover the tent in his pants, then he hurries away to the outer door.

I lurch to go after him, but all three guys place a hand on me to stop me.

"Calder, wait!"

He's already opened the door, but I hear him pause and sigh heavily. "I just need a moment. I won't go far."

"Okay," I whisper and settle back on the bed. When I hear the door shut behind him, I ask, "Is he going to be alright?"

"I expect Calder is overwhelmed with a lot of emotions he's finally having to deal with," Maxum says with a frown. "Let him work some of them out." He kisses my inner thigh. "He'll come to you when he's ready to talk about how he feels."

"I wish I could do something so he didn't hurt so much," I say.

Arran kisses my neck. "He has to meet you at least

halfway... like I did. You helped me just by being you and accepting me with all my broken pieces."

"You're not broken," I protest.

"Not anymore." He grins widely, then kisses the hell out of me.

"Arran's correct," Flint says. "Your very presence seems to be enough to heal. And Calder has the worst past of us all."

"But he's not what I'm interested in right now." Maxum gazes at me, his obsidian eyes glowing with a fire I've not seen before. "We need to know how you almost took our souls right out of our bodies."

"I didn't mean to!" I gasp, sitting up and leaning against the headboard. "Did I hurt you?" I grab a pillow and hug it to my chest.

The guys all grumble when I cover myself.

Maxum realizes playtime is over and slips his pants back on. "It felt odd but didn't hurt. I don't think you were trying to kill us."

"It felt more like a bonding to me." Flint stands at the side of the bed, revealing he never took off his pants.

Maybe he's still shy about his special equipment. I'll have to ask him about what his comfort levels are in group situations, so no one pushes him.

"Would that be something a lust witch can do?" I ask. "Or a... demon?"

All three guys stare at me in shock, quickly understanding what I'm implying.

Maxum goes unnaturally still. "So, you know?" he asks cautiously.

His guarded behavior unnerves me. I debate for a moment what to say, but I'd rather be honest than skirt around this. If he has a problem with what I am, then we should get to the bottom of it now.

"Uh..." I realize we know nothing for certain. I will need to contact my abuela to know exactly what I am and what happened. I clear my throat and clutch the pillow to my nakedness. "Amira suspects that I might have a bit of demon blood because of the sigils we discovered embedded in me. She also knew my grandmother and said she was a lust witch. That might mean I have some of that sort of magic."

Maxum reads the worry on my face and quickly races to embrace me, pinning the pillow between us. "Oh, shit. I'm sorry if you thought I'd be upset. I was worried about you. That the news would unsettle you. I've suspected the demon part. I sense a little lust witch energy around you. Just a touch, but in all the right ways." He pulls back and winks at me. Then he caresses my face and kisses me. "Whatever blood you might have, I know *who* you are… my loving mate."

I throw my arms around his waist and bury my face in his chest. "Thank you. But I probably should find out about my family's past. It's so odd that I never even considered it before."

"Not odd at all," Arran says. "The spell your grandmother put on you masked your presence to authorities, and I believe it probably made you uninterested, so you wouldn't go digging, either."

My stomach turns thinking how much I've been manipulated and controlled by magic my whole life—mostly because of my grandmother. If she hadn't put a spell on me, then Rob might not have been able to use me. Or it would have been harder for him to do so. If she only had stuck around or found some fairy godmother to come along and teach me if she was no longer around, then I could have had my power all this time. But no, I was hobbled and forgotten for decades.

Anger stirs in my heart. Even if her intentions were good, she harmed me.

And now, I'm blindly trying to discover my way and survive.

At least I have my guys. I reach out my hands to both Arran and Flint. For a moment, I fear they won't take the plea to be close to them. But within seconds, I find that concern is only my programmed bullshit raising its ugly head again.

With help from my guys, I hope to rid myself of the insecurity my mother and my ex created in me. My memories of Rob telling me under the spell over and over a hundred times that I was unlovable, echo in my head.

Tears fall, my mates grasp onto me, blocking out the negative thoughts until they are only a faint whisper.

9

---

# MIC DROP

JADE

*I* feel much better after our snuggle session, like I can conquer anything.

I highly recommend monster snuggles. At least *my* monsters. I can't speak for other monster scenarios. But embracing my demon has been a very therapeutic exercise.

"I need to find Calder," I say after we get dressed.

"I'm not sure that's a good idea," Arran hums. "He likes his alone time to cool down and center."

Osen's energy comes forward, and he asks, *"May I speak to them for a moment?"*

I give him the okay.

His spirit takes over my body. This time it's different from before. I sense I could claim it back with little effort. Is it because I'm stronger magically? Or is Osen not trying to be as controlling?

*"Both, sweet witch,"* Osen says in my mind.

Then he addresses the room. The guys all freeze when they

see the shift in my presence. Arran told me before that my eyes change from my green eyes to dark shadows of an incubus.

"Osen?" Arran moves to block the exit. He must think Osen is ready to force me to run off again.

"Yes, it's me. And don't worry. I asked for permission. Jade is aware of everything that's happening right now."

Arran, Flint, and Maxum lose some of their tension.

"I know I've fucked up. Partly because I'm a reactionary asshat. Partly because my spirit was damaged, and I couldn't think straight. I'm stronger now. Clearer."

"You aren't going to take off again?" Maxum crosses his arms.

"Not unless Jade wants it. She is also stronger. I don't think I could just take over anymore, even if I wanted to try. But I don't."

"Did you have a message for us?" Flint tilts his head, studying us. He doesn't like Osen possessing and talking through me—not at all. I don't blame him.

Osen turns and smiles at Flint. "Always to the point. I never admired that enough about you when I was alive." He sighs and looks at all of them. "Yeah, there are a few things. I'd like to talk with Calder. But I also was feeling cooped up and isolated. Jade's been a gracious host, but it isn't the same as having a body of my own. Speaking of which, I'd like to understand why my corpse hasn't appeared to decay. We need to investigate what Galiana did to me when she killed me."

"So it was her?" Maxum asks.

"Yeah. Jade and I had a memory of it. They seem to have cast a spell to pull out my magic and absorb it. Then they yanked out my soul and sent it to Jade."

"That isn't a normal death. Perhaps that's why your body is hanging in a sort of stasis?" Maxum guesses.

Osen paces the room, something I sense he used to do when he was alive. "We know magic can be stolen, but this is a new method... it's a different magic. It was as if they had used a supernatural being's magic, but as a witch. That isn't possible, is it?"

"Just because we haven't seen someone successfully use it before doesn't mean it's impossible." Arran motions to me. "Jade shouldn't have both sorts of magic, but she does."

Osen stalls our pacing, and our mouth falls open with the revelation. "It felt a lot like her magic. I didn't realize before because her power was suppressed."

*"Perhaps they used the pendant to siphon my magic and wield it?"* I suggest.

"Oh, shit." Osen falls heavily into a chair. "Jade's necklace was a two-way conduit. Sending souls to her and channeling her magic for Galiana and Rob to use."

"Thank goddess we got rid of the cursed thing." Arran looks about ready to shift and go seek vengeance for me.

My protective gargoyle frowns. *"That's* why they are after our mate. They've lost their power source."

"Which means they won't give up easily," Maxum adds.

"Osen, did you remember anything else important?" Flint asks. "Like why you were in the alleyway that night?"

"I was on to them. I dug up some secret. Sounds like they killed my source," Osen recounts. "Or they just lured me in to steal my shadows. Now that Jade and I are stronger, we might be able to see more from my last days."

Flint grunts and then nods toward the door. "Go. Talk with Calder if you must, so I can have my mate back."

Osen hangs our head in shame. "Sorry. It must be upsetting to see her like this."

"Mostly because you have hurt her," Flint interrupts, glaring at Osen.

Dang. I don't enjoy being on the other end of that anger. Thank goodness it isn't directed at me.

"I promise that's over." Osen raises my hands in surrender. "But if you need to, you can keep an eye on me while I talk with Calder. Just give me some space. Okay?"

"Fine." Flint ushers us to the door. With a gentle hand, he stops us as we get to the threshold. "Jade?"

My consciousness moves forward so I can take the reins. "It's okay, sweetie. I'm right here."

His eyes soften as he gazes at me. "I'll be watching."

I sense Osen wilt with Flint's distrust of him, unhappy he damaged his relationship with his pack.

*"Prove to us you can be better,"* I mentally say to my ghost.

Flint lets us go, and I don't have to look to sense him flying over our heads, watching as we walk across the yard. Through our own special telepathic link, which sounds weaker than it has before, he tells me, *"Calder is by the creek."*

Osen leads us in that direction, but he sits down to watch the water instead of chasing down his phoenix.

*"Letting him come to us in his own time?"* I ask.

*"Yeah. I don't know if it will work being in your body, but that's how we used to connect. I would have to wait for him to come to me. Especially since his last death."*

*"Are you okay?"*

*"As much as a dead guy can be,"* he chuckles, but I can sense his joke is forced.

He's not alright.

*"It's okay not to be okay,"* I let him know.

*"Same goes for you. This can't be easy, dealing with all of us. Your life turned upside down."*

*"No. But it's weirdly easier than I thought it might be. The biggest hurt has been that my life was a lie. My abuela squashed my magic. She was an ASO spy, and who knows what other awful things she did. I need answers from her. I want to know what I am."*

Just as I say this, I fall back against the boulder we are sitting on. I feel Osen being forcibly shoved deeper in my body and another presence appears in my mind.

*Abuela.*

"What are you doing?" we both demand at the same time.

"No." I throw my hand up for her to hear me. "You don't get

to demand things from me until you give me some damned, long overdue answers."

Her mouth purses with irritation, but then she slowly nods. "I suppose you deserve some… after everything."

"Let's start with why you mentioned the mistake you made when I bonded with Arran. Am I part supe?"

"Yes." She glances down at her hands, avoiding my eyes. "I've kept far too much from you. But know this: I never meant to harm you. I thought…" Her voice cracks. "I thought I was protecting you."

"From Galiana?"

"Yes, and others." My grandmother straightens her shoulders. "I'll start at the beginning. I was a powerful lust witch. Galiana told me that supernatural beings had killed my parents. Right away, she recruited me into the ASO, using my hatred so she could manipulate my magic. I worked various jobs for Galiana and the anti-supe cause. During that time, I conceived Jadeana Ruth with a mortal male who I met for a one-night stand."

"Wait, if my mother was half mortal and half witch… where does my supe blood come from?"

"Ruth isn't your mother… I am."

I stagger back, and my world spins.

"Ruth is your older sister by almost twenty years. We put a spell on her mind to make her believe she was your mother. Although the spell faded quickly once I died."

Thinking back on the time of my grandmother… my *mother's* death. Ruth had suddenly shifted in her personality. Not for the better. She was angrier than she had ever been and was harder on me. I had chalked it up to the loss of her mother. It was, but not in the way I had thought.

"So, *you're* my biological mother?" I shake my head and frown. "Why did you do that to us? To Ruth?"

"For your protection, I could hide you with a normal human like Ruth, since she didn't inherit my witch magic. I put a spell in place to mask your presence to those searching for you. If I didn't, Galiana would have killed you as a baby."

"Why didn't you just tell Ruth or me the truth?" I ask.

"I was going to do that when you came of age. But I was murdered before I could—tortured to death by Galiana in her attempt to get information on you and your whereabouts. Unfortunately, a couple of decades later, she found you anyway."

My heart sinks. She died to protect me. "I... I didn't know."

"How could you know, mija?" Her voice softens. "I wanted to teach you about your powers when they developed when you came of age. When you were born, I had hoped I could kill Galiana right away and we could be a true family. But it wasn't meant to be."

"And my father?"

"He was my target on an ASO job. I had to seduce a special individual, learn his secrets, and then eventually kill him. He was highly unusual, as he was a product of a demon and Elven mating. Both lines were from powerful, high-born blood. He was a double spy for the two realms. Brilliant and talented."

"And I was an accidental pregnancy from that job? A fucking mistake?"

"No." She smiles wistfully, her gaze far off, remembering. "As I got to know him, I soon discovered he was immune to my lust witch magic. We fell in love anyway—*true* love. Lust witches never get to experience actual love. So you can imagine how overjoyed I was to find him. But our circumstances made it so we had to hide our relationship. I fed Galiana lies. And he told me the truth of my family's murders—that Galiana was behind them all and used it to turn me against supernaturals."

"What the hell is wrong with her?" I blurt out.

"Broken. Angry. And power hungry. Power is all that's ever mattered to her."

"What happened between you and my father?" I ask.

"When I found out I was pregnant with you, we knew

Galiana would want to kill you just for the fact you were of mixed blood. He helped me create the binding and concealment spell that was embedded in your body. We brainwashed your magicless adult sister since she would be the perfect hiding place for you. Then I had to disappear and only visit when I believed it to be safe and to reenforce the spell work."

"No wonder Ruth hated me—hated you."

"I don't blame her." My mother frowns, and I sense she isn't as callous as I've imagined. "I'm sorry I couldn't be there for you growing up... or now. I wish I could train you, but it's taking all I have to communicate for this long."

"What about my father? Is he still alive?"

"I never saw him again. He had to go into hiding too, so Galiana couldn't kill him. And to protect your existence."

"He might still be alive?" I ask, wondering if I want to find him or let it be.

"It's possible."

I refocus on what's happening now. "It doesn't appear Galiana's goal is to kill me anymore."

"No. She's found another use for you—your unique powers. But if she gets you back in her clutches and you don't prove useful or under her control, she will end you."

I'd rather die than allow Galiana to harm other people, and especially not my mates, with my power. "You don't want me with my mates, but they are protecting me. So what *are* you suggesting I do?"

"Go back into hiding... but not with them. They will attract attention. They are easier to track. They will compromise you."

How dare she screw with my life and then expect me to give up the only people I trust and who actually care for me?

"No. I'm not making the same mistake you made. I'm keeping my loved ones near me. Look at what you sacrificed. It was all for fucking nothing." Tears threaten to pour from me. "You ruined my life. You lied to me. How can I trust a fucking thing you say? I can't talk to you anymore. Unless you can give me information that can *really* help me right now, then I don't want your—"

"Jadeana!" my mother snaps. "You need to…"

Her voice fades, reality pressing in on me. Someone shakes me to bring me out of my trance.

"Jade?" Calder calls me, panicked.

I blink against the bright light of the sky and raise my hand to shield my eyes. But no, when I look, it isn't the sky, but Calder's wings alight with a blazing fire. He's kneeling over me and appears frantic.

Osen pushes forward when he sees his lover. "Calder," he says with my voice sounding rough and concerned.

Calder sees it's Osen in charge of my body and not me. He leaps back to his feet in surprise and snarls at us. "What have you done?"

"Me?" Osen says in shock. "You woke us."

"Us?" Calder shakes his head in confusion, then glowers. "If you took Jade's body against her will, I won't forgive you this time."

"I didn't!" Osen shouts.

I take control and ask, "What's wrong?"

"You were passed out and non-responsive," Calder says, indignant but less upset. His flaming wings die down.

I grimace. "I was talking to my grandmother… uh, mother."

"Huh? Your mother's dead now, too?"

"No, well, yes. But my grandmother is really my mother. Turns out the woman who raised me was my older sister."

Calder sits down next to me and studies my eyes. I can sense they are my normal green and not Osen's gray. "You're okay? Osen didn't take advantage of you?"

"It's very sweet of you to worry, but I'm okay. And Osen has my permission to talk to you." I reach out to pat Calder's arm to comfort and thank him. Just before I make contact, I remember his touch aversion and pull back.

He catches my hand and holds it, giving it a little squeeze.

My eyes widen as I stare at our clasped hands. "Actually, Osen wanted to talk to you. We came out here for that. My mother showed up to drop some crazy secrets on my ass." I look up into his pale blue eyes. "You have my permission to do whatever you need to do together. Just no leaving Amira's property."

His thumb traces over mine. "I won't put you in danger." Then he grins. "I appreciate the offer, but I won't take advantage of your generosity."

I shrug. "It's not like it's a hardship kissing you." I didn't mean to say that. My mouth clamps shut, and I blush. "I, uh… I didn't mean I'd be…"

"Jade, stop." He chuckles. "I get it. You don't have to be so cautious around me. I know you aren't like the witch who hurt me."

"I wish I could undo what she did." I feel my eyes sting with emotion, hating that he was so damaged by my kind… or half of what I am.

Hell, I'm going to have to adjust to the idea of being more than a witch, and so soon after I wrapped my head around being a witch.

Osen presses forward, and I give Calder a little finger wave goodbye. He seems to understand and returns the silly gesture.

# 10

# THE TALK

## CALDER

*M*y heart aches when Jade's spirit fades to the background.

I bite back a curse. I wouldn't mind more time alone to get to know her now that I'm not hung up on her witch heritage.

Maybe part of me doesn't want to deal with Osen either. He's never been particularly talkative, so I know he has something significant to say if he's pushed to come forward.

I brace myself for what's coming as I watch the eerie change from Jade to Osen. Her face takes on an entirely different expression, one I've never seen her make. It's almost as if she's a shifter.

Her inquisitive and kind green eyes become the swirling smoky gray of an incubus.

"Calder." Osen frowns when I stare at him without emotion or response.

"Osen," I finally say.

"Why are you upset with me?" he asks.

I suppose he has a right to understand, but I'm still trying to understand what's got me riled. "It feels wrong for you to be inside her like this."

"You'd rather have me gone forever?" he asks, with a pained strain to his voice.

I sigh heavily and look at him. "No. It's just confusing."

"Tell me about it." He rubs his face like he used to, over his eyes and then over his non-existent beard. "Jade and I are getting along. We hope to discover more about what happened to me... to her."

"I'm glad you aren't fighting her anymore."

"I'm glad to see you're accepting her as well." He gives me a knowing look when I raise my brows. "I've been paying attention. More than she probably has."

"Don't—" I warn. I don't want him to push me into anything. I need to set this pace. *If* I set a pace.

He smirks playfully. "I wanted to tell you I'm falling for Jade."

Their body jerks as if Jade was surprised by this information enough to animate her shock.

"And how is that my business?" I bite my lip. I figured he was becoming infatuated. How could he not? She is his entire world—literally. And she has mind blowing sex with our pack. Jade is an incubus' dream girl.

"It's your business because I still love you, and you're part of our pack. I'm still here, watching. I see how Jade is healing us. I was hoping I could take her lead. Help you like I should have done the last time you died. I was scared and too caught up in myself to help heal what that witch did to you."

"You couldn't have helped," I argue. But is that true?

"Maybe, maybe not. But I know now why I didn't try. I felt rejected when you no longer wanted my touch. Selfishly, I made it about me... that I wasn't good enough. Wasn't lovable enough. I believed *you* should have fought your trauma to be with me again." He curses himself. "But I should have done more to fight for you. *With* you."

"*You...* were insecure?" I say in disbelief.

"Are you kidding? Behind all my swagger, I'm a fraud. Sure, I can make someone orgasm just by a snap of my fingers, but that doesn't equate to real love. Or being worthy of love. A fucking vibrator can do the same thing I can."

"Not quite." I chuckle. "But I get your point. Although it was a wonderful bonus how you could make me feel sexually, I didn't love you and want to be with you for your incubus magic."

"Why did you love me?" he asks, sounding more vulnerable than I've ever heard.

"Yeah, there was the physical aspect, but there was also the laughter. The loyalty. I loved how your mind worked, your passion for life, and your protectiveness." My voice comes out strong and with conviction, but I can't look at Jade while I talk. It feels like it would betray my feelings for Osen by gazing at her beauty when I did. And my budding feelings for her might get mixed up in all the emotions I have for him.

"I feel the same," he whispers, modulating his voice lower, likely picking up my reservations about talking through Jade. "I love you."

"I love you too." I gaze at the creek, watching the water cascade over the smooth rocks. "But I don't know what you want from me right now."

"I want you to be happy—whatever that looks like," Osen says earnestly.

Daring to look at them, I demand, "What? You want me to fuck Jade and pretend it's you? Because it's not you. Not really."

"Then maybe you should give in to your feelings for her. See if you can touch and be touched again."

My eyes flare with irritation. "Stay out of my relationship with her!"

"Fine. But I know for a fucking fact that she would let you take her right now if it would heal you."

"I don't need to be a thing of pity!" I jump up and clench my fists at my side.

"Neither of us thinks that." Osen jumps to his feet to match me. "She wants you, you idiot!"

I shake my head, confused. "No. That can't be true. I was an asshole. She's only getting mixed up because of you being inside her."

"Believe what you want." Osen gives me a dismissive wave.

"Osen!" Jade shouts, cutting through to take over her body again. Her face instantly softens, and she says quietly, "Calder, I like you. And I care about you. But I won't ever pressure you into anything."

"What are you saying?" I take a step closer. Is it hope bubbling in my heart? Could she really see me as someone she might desire?

"I want to be there for you in any way you'd want me to be," she says.

I charge forward. I need to set her straight. She *can't* want me. I grab her by her wrists and pull them behind her back. I clasp them together in one of my hands, pinning her so she can't move—or touch me.

My other hand grasps her jaw, forcing her to look at me.

She gasps that I'm suddenly towering over her—manhandling her. Her eyes are wide with shock.

"Is this what you want?" I demand, searching her face, taking in her beauty and her strength.

Even though I'm sure she wants to, she hasn't tried to pull away and run. Maybe she understands how dangerous that is to do with a predator.

"All I can offer is to tie you down so you can't touch me," I confess with an edge to my voice that bleeds with my pain. "Then I'd take your body. I'd be rough. Maybe violent.

Uncaring if you enjoyed it. I can't say you'd walk away uninjured."

"Is that how you want it to be with me? Painful?" she asks with all the calmness in the world. "Do you want to make me pay for what happened to you?"

I jerk my head back and blink. How can she be so calm? "I don't want to hurt you. Not really. But I'm broken, so I might." My thumb brushes down over her pulse that is thumping wildly.

"I get it. You don't want me to touch you. You need to be in control." She licks her lips. Is the subtle act from nerves or interest? "But do you even want to be with *me*?"

"My cock has woken up for the first time in years. My hands itch to reach out for you. My heart aches to truly feel again." I skim my nose over hers. "My lips are so close I might die from holding back. "Because of you."

"Me?" Her green eyes seem to glow electric. "If I let you tie me down so you're in control, would you want to see what happens?"

"I can't... but goddess, yes. One day, I want to get beyond this." I bury my face in her silky silver hair, inhaling her sweet, addictive scent. "You'd do that?"

"It's on my bucket list. Osen did something similar in the shadowscape, and I enjoyed it. And if you need to feel safe, I'm willing."

"We'd need someone there, so I don't go too far."

"Maxum," she offers. "Flint and Arran will be overly protective and possessive."

"Are you sure?" I ask, pulling back to watch her expression. "And what about Osen's power?"

"It hasn't been triggered when I'm with the others." Jade blushes. "And... I'm sorry for earlier. I didn't mean to tug on your soul when I climaxed."

"Why did that happen?"

She drops her gaze and chews her lip for a moment. "I, uh, wanted you. I didn't mean to upset you and make you run off."

"I ran off because I wanted to come into your bed and offer my soul to you."

Jade sucks in a breath. I'd be lying if my ego didn't inflate along with my cock at the look in her eyes.

Something primal takes over and, still clasping her hands behind her, I pick her up and crash us against a huge sycamore tree.

"Keep your hands there!" I growl as my hand fists the hair at her nape and the other is at her throat.

She whimpers deliciously, her pupils blowing wide with lust.

My mouth slams down on hers, consuming her like she is the air I need to survive. Tasting her like no other being can, I brush against her soul. She is my key to regaining my life.

She *is* life. Personified.

I don't know what she is exactly, but it feels like she could heal me just by being close.

Our tongues tangle, and I want to be inside her any way I can. If I could crawl inside her, I would. I will have to make do with my tongue, fingers, cock. And when we make love, I'll give her my magic—a magic I thought was long dead.

I grind my body against hers. She's being such a good witch, keeping her hands to herself. Part of me wants her to give in and run her hands over my skin. But I'm unsure if I can truly handle it if she does.

I suck on her tongue, pulling it into my mouth. She goes willingly.

Then I'm ripped away from her warmth, being thrown clear by twenty feet or more.

The ground shakes as heavy footsteps draw closer to where I've landed. "I won't let you hurt her!" Flint snarls in my face.

"I wasn't!" I hold up my arms, waiting for a brain bashing blow that will probably kill me.

"Flint! No!" Jade cries, jumping on to his shoulders to get his attention. "He wasn't hurting me. I liked it."

"Calder threw you into the tree. He threatened you, telling you to keep your hands to yourself! He held your head and was forcing himself on you!" Flint kneels and easily moves Jade around to his front. "He…"

"Sweetheart," she coos as she cups his massive, angry face that should terrify her. "It might have appeared he was rough, but I won't even have a bruise."

"You promise?" Flint softens and strokes her face gently, as if she were a delicate flower that will be destroyed if he looks at her the wrong way. The expression she wears shows she loves his tenderness. "If I had handled you the way he did, I could kill you."

*He's right… Am I a brute? Do I even deserve to work through my issues? What if I can never have a sweet exchange like this? What if I remain broken?*

"Flint," I call. "*If* Jade and I do anything again, I'll have Maxum watch to make sure I don't hurt her. Okay?"

He turns a glower at me, then he must see the sincerity in my eyes. "Fine. But she is pack. She is my mate. Our mate. If you fuck this up, I will deliver to you your final death."

For the first time in years, I don't welcome a threat like that. I have a reason to hope. I have a reason to live.

"Understood."

# 11

# FLESH AND STONE

JADE

*M*y mind is still whirling from my kiss with Calder when Flint pins me to his chest and says to the phoenix, "I'm taking my mate to cement our bond. Tell the others I won't be back until morning."

"Oomph," I breathe out as we launch into the sky. His massive wings flap effortlessly, and I envy his ability to escape so easily.

His thick fingers lace into my hair and feel my scalp, likely checking for injury since he thinks Calder pulled my hair. "Are you sure you're alright? You can tell me the truth now."

"I told you the truth. Calder was excitable. Yes, he was pinning me to the tree, but I enjoyed his kiss. Remember when I told you I don't mind it a bit rough sometimes? Calder needs to get to where he can be gentle. Until that day comes, I'll make sure he understands my limits. He didn't really hurt me anyway, although it was surprising he even kissed me."

"I didn't think he liked intimacy with women, especially

witches," Flint says as he banks right and soars toward a hill that might be classified as a mountain in some flatter terrains.

"I suppose I'm the exception?" I grin at myself.

My gargoyle picks up on my delight. "You want him even though he is damaged?"

"He didn't hurt me. Maybe he isn't as damaged as he thinks. He definitely needs boundaries so he can feel safe, though."

"You need to feel safe too. But enough of the phoenix," Flint says succinctly.

Yes. Our bond. With each wing beat, I feel his hardening cocks rubbing against my center. "Is that Mount *Shafta* in your pants? Do I need to get my hiking gear?"

Flint gives me a lopsided smirk. "Don't worry, I'll fly you to my peak."

I love that he's picking up my humor more.

Then his face falls back into his stoic gargoyle mode. "Jade, if we don't complete our bond soon, I fear it might slip away. I can barely hear your thoughts anymore."

"Our bond can fade?" Fear shoots pain right through my heart. "How?"

"We initiated, but I haven't been able to commune with you since then. Not with the attacks and travel and the others getting in my way."

His endearing possessiveness makes my pulse flutter. Though I don't like to hear he feels I've neglected him.

"Flint, you should have told me. With this whole arrangement, you'll have to be forthcoming if you need my attention. I'll try my best, but I wasn't very good at having one boyfriend, let alone several mates."

"Oh, I…" He stutters on his next thought. "I'm new to this as well. You just seem so naturally gifted at relationships and feelings. But you're correct. I shouldn't expect you will always know what I'm feeling or need."

"I can't assume you'll know either, even if we have telepathy. We need to be clear with each other." I squeeze him tightly around his waist with my thighs while I take a moment to admire the view he's given me of the surrounding wilderness. "I'll have to do better. I'm sorry."

"Do not feel bad. Any other week and any other situation, I could wait for my alone time. But bonding is special and time sensitive for gargoyles and their mates."

Flint dives right at the hill, and I screech a bit when he only slows down a fraction before a hard, jarring landing. "Sorry." He rubs his huge hands down my back to calm me. "I've should have warned you. Gargoyles aren't known for their graceful landings. I'll have to work on that too if I plan to carry you around more."

Keeping hold of me in his arms, he walks over to a mouth of a cave.

With a little giggle, I have a flashback to the monster story I was trying to write about my characters, Goliath and Nora, right before I met the guys.

Oddly enough, when we enter, it looks eerily like my scene from my unfinished book. Except my sweet gargoyle has soft blankets laid out neatly in the center and several unlit candles in a circle around the perimeter of the cave.

"When did you do this?" I ask as he places me down on the pallet of blankets.

"I scouted the location when we first arrived. And I've been modifying the structure to make it bigger and smoother inside, so it will please you." He returns to the opening and places a thatched handmade door in front of the opening.

"What!" I gasp as the cave is cast in darkness. "You carved this cave?"

"Yes, I asked the mountain to shift for us."

"Holy boulders! That's fucking amazing." I shake my head in disbelief and watch while Flint uses a long match to light the candles in the space.

"I suppose I forgot to mention my ability to connect with

stone. It's easier when the land holds magic. I believe the witch Amira has helped keep this land alive in that way."

Flint finishes with the candle lighting that gives our hideaway a romantic vibe. "I thought you would be more comfortable if you could see during our communing."

"Communing?" I ask. "Is that what a bond is called for gargoyles?"

"The process is done through communing, but the bond is known as a merge." His thick fingers slide under my shirt and skim over my waist, leaving goosebumps in their wake. "Are you cold?"

"No. Excited," I admit. "Nervous."

"Are you nervous about bonding with me? Do you not want to?" He leans down and his beautiful pale gray eyes search my face for the truth. "I will not force a bond on you if you're uncertain."

I snatch his horns in my hands and pull him to me, kissing the heck out of him. He moans and meets my passion with his.

"I want you. I'm nervous because I don't want to mess up," I explain. "And I guess I'm worried part of the reason our bond is fading is because of my bonding with Arran, or what I am now that my magic-containment spell has been undone."

"Arran's bond shouldn't affect our bond." He strokes his thumb over my cheek. "I will guide you through the process so you can't mess it up. Or do you worry that being a witch will make our bonding impossible?"

"Apparently, I'm half witch, a quarter Elven, and a quarter demon."

His thick brows rise. "Demon?"

"Oh, no!" I shake with anxiety. "Is that going to ruin things?"

"It doesn't ruin things." To ease my fears, he pulls me to his broad, hard chest. "Only surprising that you have such an unheard-of combination." He shucks his pants and kneels on the blankets in front of me. "My sweet love, will you be my mate?"

He's so large in his full gargoyle form that he's now my height when he's on his knees.

I wrap my arms around his neck. "Yes, I want that very much."

Slowly, he lifts my shirt over my head. His hands slide down my arms and over my bra covered breasts. I help unlatch it at the back. He drags the shoulder straps forward and intently watches the show as my full breasts are revealed.

"I'm very lucky that my mate is so beautiful," he murmurs as he dips his head to suck each nipple. His large tusks brush over my sensitive skin, and my pussy becomes slick with need.

He slides my pants down along with my underwear, and I help him by stepping out of them when they get to my ankles, kicking off my shoes as I do.

His hands move up to cup my ass. "So soft." Then one hand slides to my front and dips between my thighs. "Open for me?"

I move my feet apart and give him better access.

He slides a finger through my wetness and rumbles with happiness that I'm already needy. He bends lower, lifts my left thigh, bracing me from behind. His long tongue snakes out to fondle my clit.

I suck in a breath. With his solid hold, I can tilt my hips and grind into his face. "Flint," I whisper on a moan.

"Come on my face, sweet mate," he purrs, and it's better than any vibrator I've procured in my many years of flying solo. "You will come again on my cocks as we commune."

He takes me right to the edge, then I'm falling, clenching on nothing, but imagining his thick length inside me. I'm still panting and whimpering as he pulls back and shucks his pants.

With a grace I don't expect from such a huge male, he sits back cross-legged. His large wings are unfurled at his sides, taking up the width of the cave.

He offers his arms for me to fall into. His hard, thick cocks are standing at attention and begging for relief.

I step over either side of his thighs and prepare to sink down onto him. But before I can near his cocks, he captures me by my waist and hovers me over them.

"With this body, I merge with you, my fated heartstone, my center. I will protect you from harm. I will be the bedrock to bring you stability. I will devote my life to bringing you joy. I offer you all that I am. My body, my soul, my love."

Tears flow from my eyes as I hear his sincerity and devotion. I take a moment to absorb his vows. Then I panic because I didn't know I had to prepare for a ceremony.

"That was so beautiful. Do I repeat it? Or am I supposed to make up my own?" I ask, feeling silly and unsure.

"Whatever you say will be perfect."

"With this body, I merge with you, my fated heartstone. I will also protect you from harm. I will be the softness you crave. I will devote my life to bringing you joy. I offer you all that I am. My body, my soul, and my unconditional love."

Still bracing me, Flint's huge hand cups the back of my head and pulls me forward for a loving kiss. Gawd. My heart is always melting around this giant sweetheart.

The apex of my thighs presses against his ten-pack abs. I don't mind if I do as I grind along his sculpted washboard on the way down to my impalement. The friction is delicious.

He uses one arm to hold me in place while he lines up his second cock with my vagina. The one that juts out closest to his stomach glides over my drenched clit. I groan with relief at the contact.

Inch by thick inch, Flint slowly guides me down his shaft that's hard as stone, filling me up until I'm panting again.

He lifts and sinks me down on his massive cock a few times before I'm fully seated. I shift and grind against his second cock and feel myself heading toward the orgasm I've been waiting for.

Large wings close around us until we are fully encased. Candlelight filters in through the space at the bottom of his webbed wings and the floor.

"I feel like a butterfly in a chrysalis," I say in awe, running my fingertips over his wing.

He groans with the intimate touch that apparently is an erogenous zone. "We are like them in many ways. We will leave the safety of my wings changed forever."

I swallow down the strange emotions this idea stirs in me. I don't know how many more transformations I can handle. I've gone from lonely author to psychic medium to witch to wolf-mate to part-fae to part-demon, and now to a heartstone mate to a gargoyle.

Or is it I'm only revealing more and more of my true being, and I haven't changed at all?

"I need to come inside you," he whispers, then rocks me on his cock.

I sway with him to create the most friction. The cock outside of me gives me the perfect sensation over my clit.

His hand slides down around my ass, helping to lift me up and down his dick. He moves his hand lower and stimulates my rosebud, taunting me with his fingertip.

With his size, he has to crane down to kiss me.

I claim his mouth with my tongue, licking into him and making him moan with need.

"Goddess, I love you." His free hand grazes over my breasts, kneading them. Then, as if cherishing me, he smooths his palm over my heart and sternum before going back to pulling on my hardened nipples.

"I love you too." I don't know how it happened in such a short time, but it did. I look forward to feeling that grow with time as we deepen our relationship.

With the perfect amount of stimulation on my clit and breasts and the rhythmic stretch of my pussy around him, I'm close to coming.

"I'm about to…"

"I know, Heartstone. Milk my cum now."

"Fuck, Flint," I curse with his naughty talk as I feel the tingle up my spine and my cunt contracting around his cock. My body spasms, and I'm floating in bliss.

Flint floods me with his release, and his top cock splashes cum over my chest.

Then, as I focus back on him, I watch as he turns to stone.

*What the fuck?*

"Flint! Are you okay?" I ask.

*"I'm okay,"* he answers inside my mind. *"I should have mentioned this. I'm locking my essence inside you."*

I feel his cock swell at the base, much like a shifter's knot.

*"We now must commune via our telepathic link to solidify our bond."*

I have no idea what communing might mean to a gargoyle during this ritual. My pussy is still clenching and fluttering over his cock. Shouldn't that be enough?

*"Commune?"*

*"I will share with you my emotions and thoughts. We might be able to share images too."*

I take a deep breath and press my forehead to his broad brow.

*"I'll go first,"* he says and then a flood of images and emotions hits me like a semi-truck.

I'd fall back on my ass in shock if it weren't for me being locked in his embrace and cocooned in his wings.

After a moment, the dizziness passes.

*"Oh no. I was too excited when I shared."* I sense he feels like he's messed up.

*"It's okay, sweetie, just give me a moment to process that download."* I stroke his sides and he seems to relax, although it's only a feeling since his body is currently stone.

I sift through what is four hundred years of longing. Pain, both physical and emotional. Loneliness. I know that even though he had a pack, he always felt like the odd one out. He didn't participate in their sexual explorations and bonding. He'd risk his life for them without hesitation, but otherwise, he was distant.

He had no one to share his emotional side until I came along and shook his heart. He began to fall in love with me the moment our eyes inadvertently locked when he was invisible and guarding my home. He felt seen when I sensed him beyond the mask. I brought back his curiosity and joy at just being alive.

I blink and feel tears dropping off my cheeks.

"Did it hurt?" he asks.

"No, not like that. I just feel badly that you were lonely for so long." I sniff and wipe away the tears off my face. "I'm more than honored I helped awaken something in you. Your happiness. It feels like a big responsibility."

"I don't expect you to do anything but be yourself. I am responsible for my happiness. Although you're the one who inspired me to live again. And I will love you no matter what you do."

I sense I'm meant to share my feelings now. What do I share? How do I do it?

In my mind, I think about my gargoyle and all the sweet moments, our late night chats, and snuggling. I love his sincerity, earnestness, and his nurturing nature. With his solid strength of character and loyalty to his pack, I feel myself healing. His absolute acceptance of me that embraces me by just being in his presence. The unconditional love he offers is a cure to all the assholes who rejected me before him. His virtuous and brave nature stirs in me a desire to be the best version of myself. I treasure his immense trust in me, and I vow to never betray it. I think about how he had made me feel like the most beautiful creature alive when we first made love. He makes me feel that way every time he's looked at me since.

I take all that and visualize offering it to him through our telepathic link.

He mentally gasps when it enters his consciousness.

*"Goddess, I can feel your feelings for me,"* he says in awe. *"You really do love and accept me."*

And now I'm fucking crying again. Damn the big sweetie.

"I do," I confirm.

A powerful pulse of my love radiates out from my body and meets his. Our bond swirls like a tangible thing between us, glowing and tying together in an intricate pattern. My body lurches to meet his, my soft flesh molding to his hard muscles.

Then there's a strange ache in every one of my bones. It's almost painful. I whimper, wondering if something has gone wrong.

Has his gargoyle magic rejected me?

I want to ask what's happening, but I'm overwhelmed, and I sense he is, too.

The pain increases until finally it breaks just as Flint returns to his non-stone form.

We both gasp and grasp onto each other. Asking at the same moment, "Are you alright?"

Something feels off. I grab his sides, and I'm able to grip more than I could before, like his skin is softer—more flexible.

More human.

"Flint!" I cry. "I think I made you weaker!"

"No. Softer," he whispers. "What I've always dreamed of."

"It's a good thing?"

"Yes." His huge hands palm along my ribs. "You... your bones... I sense they took my stone nature. They are stronger— less likely to break or weaken."

"I'm... unbreakable?"

"Close enough."

"I'm Wolverine," I say with utter delight. "I'm an X-*woman*."

He shakes his head in confusion. "No. I didn't make you into an animal shifter. And you're still a woman, just reinforced with *stone*."

I suppress a giggle because I keep forgetting like most of these guys. He doesn't have a clue about most pop culture.

"Wolverine is a character in comic books who has bones plated with the strongest metal."

"Oh, then yes. You're like this Wolverine." He strokes my cheek and then cups my jaw. "Are you alright that I changed you? I didn't know that could happen. When gargoyles mate, they share part of their stone, but I didn't think it would work like that for us. I thought it would only be a sharing of the hearts and minds."

"I don't mind. But I'm worried that you will be more prone to injury with softer skin." I run my hand over his massive arms. "I don't want you to get hurt because of me."

"I heal fast, and I'm still hard."

I wiggle on his engorged cock. "Yeah, you are."

He blushes peach. I notice it's a deeper shade, as if he is more human because of me. "I *am* hard, and I want to make you come on my cocks again."

As an answer, I lean forward and kiss him while grinding into his massive knot inside me.

# TRIPPING

### JADE

*T*he following morning, I'm close to limping. Flint catches me as I exit the cave and we fly back. Fortunately, he lands softer this time.

He sets me down but doesn't lose contact with me as we enter the small cabin, as though he can't stand to be even an inch away from my skin.

Maxum and Arran observe us with avid interest.

"We bonded," Flint announces proudly, puffing out his already enormous chest.

"I can see that." Maxum smirks and waves a hand over his face. "She has that just-bonded glow."

He's playing it cool and lighthearted, but I sense he's a bit envious. I wonder what's holding him back. Perhaps he isn't ready emotionally. I get that. I'm not sure if I'm emotionally ready for all this.

Arran gives me a serious look. "But how do you feel? Something's different."

"During the bonding, I got an upgrade on my armor package," I joke.

"Huh?" Arran tilts his head.

"You can fuck me as hard as you like. I won't break."

From behind, Flint quickly covers my mouth with his huge hand. "Heartstone, don't make that a challenge. You still might break."

I lick his palm, and he jerks his hand away in surprise.

He then cups my chin and makes me tilt my head back until I'm looking up at him. *If you want to lick something, I have other appendages for that,* he says via our mind link.

I chuckle and lean into him and feel his appendages poking into my back. "I'll take a rain check. I'm pretty tired and sore."

I glance around when I feel what's missing. "Where's Calder?"

"Haven't seen him since he ran off yesterday." Arran shrugs.

"He didn't let you know I was bonding with Flint?" I ask.

"Didn't need to," Maxum answers. "I saw Flint take you in the cave and figured as much."

Panic rises in me. "But where is he? You aren't worried that he's been missing since yesterday?"

"Should we be worried?" Arran asks, standing at attention now that he sees my concern.

"Uh, yeah! Guys, you know as well as I do, he hasn't been okay for a while. Osen's death was hard on him. I thought you were supposed to be a pack." I shake my head and turn around to race out the door to find him.

*He's a big boy,* Osen chimes in.

"No, he's someone who's hurting," I argue aloud so all of them can hear. "And there are evil murderous assholes on the loose!"

I storm outside and crash into the broad chest of a phoenix. I hit him with such force that we both go down to the ground. He makes sure that he takes the brunt of the fall and cradles me in his arms with me laying on top of him.

Once I realize it's him, I lift my arms up and try to roll off like a fucking worm.

But he doesn't let me go. "Crap. You hit me like a tank."

"It's my upgrade. Sorry!" Not only am I reenforced with stone, I'm faster and more powerful. Dang, I could hurt someone. "I hulked out."

Calder captures my face and has me look at him. Concern flashes in his eyes. "Jade, why are you upset?"

I'm basically planking off his body, trying not to touch him. I don't know how much longer I can minimize my contact. Besides, it feels awkward as hell. I'm pretty sure it looks stupid, too. I never thought of myself as the klutzy heroine, but dammit if the guys don't bring that out in me. Although I'm impressing myself with my record-breaking plank time.

"I heard you didn't come back after we talked," I tell him. "I was worried."

I'm surprised he hasn't thrown me off. Instead, he sits up, holding me to his chest. My legs automatically fall to the sides of his hips.

"You didn't have to worry."

Keeping my arms tight to my sides, I lean back, but that only makes my sensitive pussy rub against his groin. I ignore that heated sensation and say, "Of course I'm going to worry."

His warm hands are on my upper arms. Are they there to help me balance or keep me in his lap? I'm not used to this touchy-feely side of him.

"I was keeping an eye out for you, guarding the cave while you had your bonding time with Flint."

"You were?" My mouth hangs open in surprise.

His eyes drop to my lips, and I nervously close my mouth.

"I knew you'd both be vulnerable and preoccupied." He finally lets go of my arms and rubs the back of his neck. "I tried to give you your space."

From his blush, I figure he heard my cries of pleasure. But

he's been around that before. Maybe it's different since it was a bonding ceremony.

In one fluid motion, Calder stands and easily sets me on my feet in front of him.

I'll never get over how strong these guys are by handling me like I'm a feather.

Turning, I see the shocked and strange expressions on the guys' faces.

Osen chuckles in my head. *"This is going to be interesting to see how this all unfolds."*

"They aren't jealous, are they?" I ask.

*"Not really. But we were never great at sharing, even if most of us shared our bodies at various times. We were never intimate at the same time."*

"Oh, so I'm a wild card?"

*"And I love everything about that."*

Calder's warm hands drop away from my waist. Instantly, I miss the connection. If the tiny sigh that escapes his lips is any indication, he misses it, too.

Arran clears his throat and waves us in. "Let's feed our woman breakfast."

Flint snatches me up before the others can and carries me inside and sets me on his lap. Then he feeds me the sliced fruit Arran places in front of me.

Arran cocks a brow and Flint shrugs. "What? You did it after your mating. Seems like a nice tradition."

I lock eyes with Maxum, and he smiles at me. But I sense an uneasiness behind his carefree gaze. I wonder if it's about me or that we haven't taken that step yet in our relationship. That's something to talk about next time we're alone. When I glance around the room, I wonder if I will ever be alone again.

I don't mind being by myself, but I hated being lonely, which happened often even when I had a boyfriend.

With these guys and the bonds, I won't be lonely again.

Though I will have to carve out some time soon to be alone with my thoughts so I can finish my book.

I suspect Maxum would say I don't need to worry about making money. But my career isn't only about that, not really. I want to write. I love to write. However, I could do without dealing with ads and all the promotional stuff.

Will I write again?

If I only cared about making money, it isn't an easy career. There are a thousand other jobs I could have chosen instead. It isn't easy for authors to rip our hearts open, expose all our insecurities, agonize over every word choice and plot point. We bleed our deepest thoughts and fears into a book. Then we must sit back and watch as reviews come in. Hopefully, sales too.

Some reviewers aren't just unkind, they are brutal. I wonder sometimes if they realize there's a human being on the other side.

Fortunately, I developed a thick skin. And not every book is meant for every reader. Instead I focus on the lovely people who reach out to me and tell me how much they enjoy my stories. That gives me the fuel I need to keep at it—knowing we all can escape together into a world that once only existed in my mind.

Then I wonder…

Do these stories only exist in an author's mind?

Or have we been channeling another reality?

Because now I'm living in one of these alternate universes.

I get dizzy with the idea that the stories we make up all have a truth to them. We could stumble into any of them at any time. If it's true what scientists say about the multiverse, perhaps all these worlds we write about actually exist.

"Heartstone?" Flint calls me out of my haze of thoughts. "Do you need to rest?"

As he says it, I feel the fatigue hit me since we were up the entire night bonding.

I nod, and he lifts me from his lap and carries me into the bedroom.

He places me in the center of the huge bed and crawls onto one side, pulling the covers over us.

Calder appears at the doorway, looking tired and lonely.

If he kept a lookout the whole night, I understand why he was.

"There's enough room." I scoot into Flint some more. "I'll do my best to keep my hands to myself."

He gives me a half smile, and after a moment of hesitation, he joins us, but on top of the covers.

Maxum peeks in and tosses the blanket that Calder has been using from the couch at him.

Calder thanks him and lies on his back, appearing uneasy.

"I'm going to turn away from you, but just so I can make you more comfortable." I say to Calder and then nuzzle into Flint's chest.


I wake hours later with a warm palm on my hip over the blanket and someone's face buried in the hair at the back of my neck. It slowly dawns on me it isn't Arran or Maxum, but Calder snuggled up to me.

Opening my eyes, I see Flint watching him. There doesn't seem to be anger or jealousy, just curiosity.

Using our mental bond, I ask my gargoyle. *"Have you been watching him the whole time?"*

*"Yes."*

*"Does Calder touching me upset you?"*

*"No. I now understand what happened yesterday. I also see you're good for him. I sense he's tired of being broken... to the point he welcomed my threat of death if he hurt you. It makes my heart weep for him. Especially since I know how wonderful it is to feel healed and loved by you."*

My eyes sting with tears, thinking about how they have

lived just getting by. Flint and Arran now have happiness, and I helped open that door for them. Calder and Osen are still hurting. I know it's not my job to heal them, but I want to do what I can.

Thankfully, it seems Maxum has only been lonely. Unless there's something else hidden in his heart. Could that be why he hesitates in bonding with me?

I hear Calder suck in a breath when he wakes, realizing where he is. Yet, he doesn't move away like I expect. No, he pushes his nose deeper against my scalp, inhales my scent, and hums.

"What do I smell like?" I ask quietly, letting him know I'm awake.

He jerks ever so slightly. "Uh… you smell like hope."

"Is hope a musky scent, or does it have more of a flowery note?" Maxum asks from the doorway.

I glance over and see him casually leaning against the door frame with his muscular arms crossed over his chest.

Has he been watching Calder the whole time, too?

It makes me nervous that both Maxum and Flint were so worried they couldn't let him sleep next to me without monitoring.

"Shut up, asshole," Calder grumbles at Maxum, but when I look over my shoulder to gauge his mood, he has a relaxed expression. His eyes are soft and hooded as he returns my gaze. He rolls out of the bed and rubs the back of his head, ruffling his auburn locks into more disarray. "Taking a shower."

Maxum smirks and waggles his eyebrows.

Calder punches Maxum's arm on the way out.

When the bathroom door closes, my demon crawls up next to me and whispers in my ear. "He's going to abuse himself in the shower while thinking of you."

I smack Maxum on the shoulder. "Don't tease him."

"What?" Maxum grins wider. "It's good for his mental health."

"Harassing him is good for his mental health?" I roll my eyes.

"Yeah, because it's how we used to be. Before." Maxum strokes the hair away from my face and smiles. "I'm taking this all as a good sign."

"We shouldn't push too hard," Flint adds.

*"I agree with Maxum. I'm encouraged by his new energy today,"* Osen says in my mind.

As I relax back into Flint's embrace, I feel a psychic urge to leave the safety of Amira's sanctuary. I've been compelled to do things before, and my intuition hasn't led me astray yet.

Will the guys refuse to let go so they can keep me safe?

## 13

# FUNISHMENT

JADE

*I* fill everyone in on what happened with my grandmother-mother and who I really am.

With the confirmation that I'm part demon and fae, Maxum says, "If you wish, I can reach out to a few demons I'm still in contact with and see if we can find your father." Something in his demeanor tells me he doesn't think this is a good idea.

"No. Not yet," I decline his offer that feels too dangerous to pursue. "We would only bring him into this mess *if* we found him."

"He might be able to help," Arran suggests.

"I doubt it." The bitter pang of abandonment hits me hard in the chest. "If he wanted to find me, I'm sure he could have found a way around his own spell. After all, Galiana got to me. Besides, I don't want to waste energy if he's not even alive."

Maxum grimaces as if he's upset by my negativity, but ultimately agrees. "And we might be also drawing unwanted attention if we put feelers out."

His energy seems to fold in on itself.

I need to get Maxum alone so we can talk about us and how he feels. I don't think asking him around everyone else around is a good idea.

Although I'm always stuck with an audience for my most private moments. Osen is around for everything since he's conscious and aware, probably even when I'm not.

That brings up a good question. *"Osen, are you paying attention, even when I'm asleep?"*

*"Yes. If anything were to go wrong when you were sleeping, I'd wake you. And if I couldn't wake you, I'd get you to safety and wait for you to come around."*

I'm relieved and reassured that someone is always looking out for me. Then I chuckle to myself—Osen is the ultimate stalker.

I glance at Calder and force myself to hold his gaze. I vocalize the strange urge I've had. "I need to go to your death spot."

"What?" He jumps up, and his eyes go wide. "Why?"

"Because I feel guided to do that. Drawn there." I soften my voice and check in with him. "Do you think you can handle going back?"

"I... I don't know. Maybe." He runs his hands through his hair and pulls on the strands. "Do you think it will help me?"

"I don't know. But when I've had feelings like this, they usually lead to something big."

*"Okay,"* Calder mumbles and paces. Then he regains his nerve and straightens his shoulders. "Yeah, let's do this."

"Hold the fuck up. Not so fast." Maxum puts his hands up as if we're bolting out the door already. "You aren't going anywhere right now."

I don't like being told what I can do. It feels too much like Rob controlling me again. And my finding out how my mother and father manipulated and controlled me... And with

Maxum's strange energy since he found out I'm a demon... I'm not in the mood for this bossiness.

"I'll do what I need to do," I snap.

"You *need* to explore your powers a bit more before we run off into the world." Maxum clenches his jaw in irritation. "If Galiana or Rob show up, I won't have you completely unprepared."

Dammit, he's right about the threats I face. But I'm still going to push for this since I don't want to become someone's puppet again.

"You can't just order me around. My gut tells me going there is a part of how I figure out how to use the magic I have."

Maxum strides over to where I'm perched on Flint's lap. He cradles my chin and leans down, staring into my eyes just inches away. "I'm not rushing to leave our safe haven if we don't have to. As much as I want Calder to be healed, I won't risk your well-being, running off half-cocked."

I nod with a smirk, feeling extra spicy. I cross my arms and sass, "Come on, I've recently been *fully* cocked. So stop arguing with me and get on board. *We are going.*"

"No."

My hackles rise. "I will do whatever the fuck I want."

Maxum narrows his obsidian eyes, fire burning in their depths. With a calculated, even tone that sends chills up my body, keeping his eyes zeroed in on me, he says, "Flint, your mate needs a bit of punishment to remind her who the leader of this pack is."

My gargoyle holds me tighter. "What kind of punishment?"

"A spanking." Maxum grins wickedly. "She wants to act like a brat, then I'll meet that accordingly."

Why does his fiery gaze send a thrill down my spine? I've forgotten what I was arguing about.

Flint must sense my interest because he releases his hold. "Then we should all watch," he says with a glint in his eye.

Maxum breaks my gaze to eye him appreciatively for a moment. "I'm loving this new side of you, brother."

I pout at Flint since he's offered me up. But I'm blushing, thinking about how I love the new dynamic too. "You're just making up an excuse to punish me."

"That's not it," Maxum breathes in deeply and adds, "well, not exactly."

My demon sits down on one of the dining chairs and pats his knee. I feel the bond thread between us flare back to life. He enjoys me challenging him, but I sense his worry too.

Sure, I've written and read plenty of scenes like this, but I never had more than a sloppy swat on the ass during sex. I never had a lover I trusted or wanted to play with before now. My heart is pounding more than I expect.

Glancing around the room, I see Arran leaning forward, his corded forearms braced on his thighs. By the smirk on his handsome face, he is highly interested in this display. Even Calder has heat simmering in his eyes. Although his head is lowered and he's looking through his eyelashes as if he shouldn't really be watching.

When my gaze lands on him, he nods to the door. "I can leave."

"You don't have to." I walk over to my crimson demon. Before I surrender to my funishment, I say, "Unless you aren't comfortable."

Calder shakes his head and the auburn locks fall forward and over his brow, giving him a roguish appearance.

I take the last step to Maxum. He's looking deadly serious now as I stand between his muscular thighs.

"You think this is going to be a sweet, little punishment, don't you?"

I swallow and take a half step back.

He snatches me by the waist and has me face down over his lap before I can blink.

"It's gonna hurt, little witch."

"I'm not just a witch anymore!" I huff. "And I didn't do anything wrong yet!"

"Oh, I heard your admission of insubordination." He pulls down my pajama bottoms along with my underwear, exposing me to the room.

His hand comes down swiftly over my right cheek.

"Ow!" I jerk and instinct has me squirming to get away.

His thumb sweeps over my ass. "Oh, yes, I knew you'd mark beautifully." He rubs the sensitive sting out and says, "Do you know why you're being punished?"

"Cuz you're a meanie," I answer.

*Smack!* Dang it, that really smarts.

"Try again," he orders.

"Because you're a grumpy demon?"

"No." *Smack!* "You're willing to risk yourself for some intuition. I'm not just your potential mate, more importantly, I'm your pack leader now. You accepted that by bonding with my pack members. And *none* of us can run off without thinking through our actions. Look where that recklessness got Osen? Killed."

"But I want to help… Do something." I'm frustrated now. "I won't be controlled. Not anymore."

His hand soothes me up and down my back. "I understand. And your voice is important and valued as much as the rest of us. And you *will* help, but when the time is right. When we all agree. When we are prepared." Maxum's voice is cracking with pain. "Do you know what I would do if I lost you? If *we* lost you?"

I didn't think asking to go to Calder's death spot was completely impulsive and ridiculous, but was it? I refocus to answer his question, "Uh… you'd be upset."

"No." *Smack!* "We'd be devastated. Without you, we would die."

"I…" Tears are gathering in my eyes, partly from the sting of his swats and partly thinking about how they would suffer without me. Then another level of pain slams into my heart. "No one really cared about me before."

Not even the woman who raised me really cared. My mother—or rather, my older sister—never showed me much affection or concern. And now, looking back with my new knowledge, when the spell was lifted, she resented and despised me. When I left home at eighteen, that was it, there was no more contact.

Maxum must sense my shift in emotions. Instead of giving me another swat, he curls over my body and hugs me. "That changes now. You have me. Flint. Arran."

*"Me,"* Osen whispers in my head.

Calder clears his throat and says, "And me."

My head whips up to look him in the eye. What I see surprises me—adoration. How did he change his feelings toward me so quickly? I guess after I stopped being his enemy, his hate shifted into something else.

Maxum sits back, and his hand caresses my ass. "Did you learn your lesson?" He asks.

"Yes."

"Then I'm going to make you come now."

Relief overwhelms me and I almost come with his promise. "Yes, please," I say, still gazing into Calder's eyes.

*Smack!*

I whimper with the burn.

Maxum's fingers slide down over my crack to my exposed pussy. His fingers sink into my folds, then inside me. "So wet for us. And so perfect since you're healing like a supe now."

With his observation, I realize the soreness I should feel from Flint's cocks and our bonding ceremony is non-existent. Well, this solves a significant problem that having a harem would cause.

Magically resilient pussy... check.

*"Just have to remember to stay hydrated,"* Osen chimes in with amusement.

*"Then that's your job,"* I quip back. *"Water boy."*

I hear his chuckle.

Calder kneels in front of me. I brace my forearms on Maxum's thigh to look him in the eye.

His gaze drops for a moment to my cleavage. My tits are about to fall out of my shirt. Then he searches my face for a moment. "I crave to capture and swallow all your whimpers and moans." He brushes away a stray lock of hair and tucks it behind my ear. "But I don't feel I've earned the right."

"You saved my life twice now. Once in the alleyway and then hiding me from Rob in the bunker. But if you're with me, you should know it isn't about owing you favors or earning my affection. I want you to touch me... kiss me..." Should I say it? "I want more when you're ready."

"And I want more with you... when I'm ready." Calder then glances at Flint, Arran, and Maxum to judge their reactions. He must see something in their eyes that gives him the encouragement to lean forward and claim my mouth.

His kiss consumes any worries I might have. Calder is passion and fire, pent up need just like my other mates and desperate to channel into someone.

Fuck yeah, I'll be that for them.

Maxum's long, thick fingers sink into my cunt, and I clench around them.

There's some movement in the room, and then I feel a tongue fondling my clit, working around Maxum's hand. I'd know that talented tongue anywhere—Arran.

"Why do you taste like rock candy?" I hear him whisper when he pulls back.

I'm about to break my kiss with Calder to answer, but right next to my ear a deep voice of my gargoyle says, "That would be my cum." Then he frees my tit, squeezing and rolling my nipple.

"Goddess damn." Arran frantically laps at my inner thighs and pussy.

I groan happily into Calder's mouth.

"That's it, baby," Calder whispers over my lips. "Let me hear your pleasure. And I told you Arran had a sweet fang. He won't ever leave your pussy alone after Flint cums inside you."

A shiver runs down my spine and my pussy flutters around Arran's probing tongue that has replaced Maxum's fingers.

Maxum reaches around and works my clit, and I detonate.

My body spasms and arches against Maxum's lap. I cry out in bliss into Calder's hungry mouth. Arran's clawed hands clamp down on my ass as he licks up my release.

I tremble for a few minutes before I collapse like a wet noodle over Maxum's strong thighs.

"See! Birdman likes licking faces!" my bunny Sage yells out in triumph.

"She's not wrong," Calder says with a blush and a wink.

My demon lifts me up and carries me the short distance to the bed, setting me down in the center. "You need more rest."

I yawn and feel the hazy contentment and exhaustion hit me again.

I hear Flint, Arran, and Calder whispering out in the main room, but I don't pay it much mind. I'd pay more attention, but I don't think they'd give Calder a hard time about kissing me and joining in.

Arran slips into the bed next to me, fully back in his human form. He smiles that megawatt smile that could ignite panties. Pulling me to him, he kisses me sweetly.

Flint curls up against my back.

"Everything okay?" I tilt my head toward the main living area.

"Yeah. Calder was just checking in with us." He skims his thumb over my cheek. "And I was demanding some snuggle time. I missed you last night."

"We're going to have to set up a schedule." I chuckle when everyone grunts a yes.

"I'll get on that, my sweet witch," Maxum says and pats my foot before heading out of the cabin with Calder.

Flint tucks a blanket over us.

In the safety of my two mates' embrace, I instantly fall asleep.

## 14

## BONKERS

ARRAN

*I* feel guilty for wanting to abduct my mate and hide us away like Flint did. Though the others would track Jade down to demand their time with her. And she'd be pissed too. We wouldn't really be alone since Osen is still haunting her. So there's that.

Oh, well. That plan is out.

But I will put my foot down after our matings are completed. We can't just run off unexpectedly like Flint did with her—hoarding her all night.

My berserker was going nuts.

Okay. It was me. I was going bonkers, but he was pissed too.

Taking her without warning set Maxum and me on edge. We don't want to make Jade feel like she is some sort of captive, so we won't make a big deal in front of her.

However, the guys need to know we can't do that to each other. Unless it's life or death, we can't run off. No matter how much we want to.

It's another reason Maxum gave her a spanking... to remind us we can't just take off.

I'm not sleeping as Jade naps, even though I should, since I didn't get much rest last night. No, I'm watching her. The movements of her eyelids suggest she's dreaming. Her breathing is even and shallow. I memorize every freckle and line on her face. I notice how different her hair is from the day I met her. Instead of the look of graying hair, it's now a consistent silver and almost glows. Fae hair concealed by the spell that I broke when I mated her.

*My* mate. She's my gorgeous, amazing, loving mate. I wonder how I got so lucky after my shit show of a life. Then I remember I have the harrowing responsibility to ensure her safety. She's the target of the most dangerous witch we have ever come across.

Galiana knows Jade's family secrets, and likely knows more about Jade's powers. She killed Osen and who knows how many more supes. Plus, this evil witch has a way to use Jade's magic to drain and kill us.

Eliminating Galiana seems impossible. The only hope I feel is in the possibility that she's gone rogue and the rest of the ASO witches don't know about Jade's abilities. That means she's separating herself from her main support, and we can take advantage of the vulnerability that comes with that.

If Galiana hasn't had access to Jade's unique magic for a while, then it might be fading. Soon she will be the same as any other witch. Witches are normally easier to kill than a supe since they don't have the accelerated healing ability that we have. She's a powerful witch, but she's still killable.

Still asleep, Jade groans and wiggles her body closer to me. She tucks her face into my chest, and I kiss the top of her head.

Flint's gaze finds mine now that Jade isn't blocking our view of each other. I think he's frowning. It's hard to tell with a gargoyle. His face always has a stern expression, unless he's admiring our mate. He nods to me, finding the camaraderie in this moment alone with her.

I return the gesture.

Then, with a sigh filled with longing and fear, his fingers delicately comb through her soft hair. It's strange to see the awkwardly bulky male, so careful and attentive with her. He's come a long way out of his shell. It's a shell he's used to hide himself, even from us.

I realize now how much more there is to him that as a pack we all ignored or didn't even suspect. But Jade knew. She drew it out of him. Just like she drew the positive out of me.

Because of her love and encouragement, I'm finally feeling sane again after all these years. I've accepted my berserker and made peace with him. My wolf is calm after feeling angry that his nature was mutilated into a rabid monster.

Wrapping my arm around Jade's waist, I hold her closer, and she hums happily in her sleep.

Or at least, I think she's asleep... until she says, "Good puppy." Then she lets out a sleepy giggle.

I palm her lower back, but say nothing, hoping she rests longer. It's been a few hours since we had the little spanking scene, and I want to make sure she's ready for what Maxum has planned next.

I wish it was more sex. But he wants to see if we can figure out her magic before we leave Amira's sanctuary and rightfully so. He wants to please her and agree to her plan, but he needs assurances.

Since she feels a magical pull, we know we must take her to Calder's last death spot soon, but we won't do it completely ignorant of her abilities.

"Is it wrong that I want to stay snuggled up with you two?" Jade asks.

"I'd say I'd prefer it." I kiss her forehead.

She tilts her head back and peeks up at my face. "I wish I had more than two sides so I could snuggle all of you at once."

"We'd like our one-on-one time too though," Flint says and strokes his hand down her arm.

Jade hooks her ankle behind her and over Flint's leg. "I need to give you all enough love."

"Things will settle down soon," I assure her.

"Once we annihilate our enemies," Flint adds with a gravelly growl.

"You always say the sweetest things." Jade looks over her shoulder at Flint and grins.

Then her face falters, and behind her beautiful green eyes, I see the wheels spinning in her mind. Through our mate bond, I feel her sadness and sense her anger.

"You're angry," I say, hoping to get her to talk about it.

"I talk a big game in my books. Killing characters off with the only concern being if it serves the plot." She rolls her lips inward and bites them, thinking. "But real life is different. There were times I thought I'd have to shoot Rob if he broke in and attacked me again. I worried that if I killed him, taking a life would mess me up, even if it was his. But now, after what Rob and Galiana did. They killed Osen and used me. She tortured and killed my mother and mother's parents. Those assholes need to go."

"Yeah, killing in theory, killing in cold blood, and killing in war are all different. But this is war," I say. "It's either us or them."

"And you didn't ask for this," Flint reminds her. "The only thing you did was dare to exist and refuse to be used any longer."

She nods vigorously, as if she's shaking her fears away. "We have to be careful. I don't think I could stand to lose any of you. Like Maxum said, it would destroy me. Especially since you're all trying to protect me."

"Whatever happens, you can't feel guilty." Flint captures her chin and guides her face to look at him. "Understand?"

Jade doesn't answer. She won't lie to him and to promise this would be untrue.

"Would it make you feel less guilty in all of this to know we would fight Galiana and Rob, no matter what?" I ask. "They killed our packmate. And before that, they were killing our kind. We've been hunting them for years."

"Yeah, okay." She acquiesces, but still doesn't promise a thing.

Flint glances up at me, asking for my help.

I give my head a shake. *Not now*, I tell him with my look. If it comes to pass, we deal with the fallout then.

We can't live in constant worry over what may be.

I'm learning that lesson by allowing myself to open my heart and love my mate. Yes, many things could go wrong, but what if everything goes right?

15

# CAPTURING SPIRITS

JADE

*A*fter my nap, Arran joins me in taking a long shower. He dotes on me, shampooing and conditioning my hair and scrubbing my back. He doesn't fool around... much. He must worry that if he gets too frisky, then Serky will break through and take over. Or perhaps he's just trying to be a caring mate and not make everything about sex.

I could see how that could easily happen with a pack like this. I'd enjoy the hell out of it, but I need more. Deep conversations, laughter, and being there for each other in any way that we're needed.

Arran shuts off the shower, and we towel ourselves dry before slipping on some workout clothes.

In the living area, Flint has a glass of water and fruit and nuts waiting. "Eat. You'll need your strength."

As I finish the snack, I ask, "What do they have for me today?"

"Maxum has asked Darius to help," Flint informs me as he

gazes out the window. "If you have some demon soul magic, then he's the one to identify it and guide you."

I walk up next to him and stare out the kitchen window, watching Maxum and Calder chat with Darius in the clearing between our cabin and the main house.

The hellhound is still a bit scary to me, which makes me chuckle. *That's* what I'm afraid of? But my bunch of monsters are no biggie. Perhaps because I feel the connection between us. I have no sense of Darius. I doubt he'd try to hurt me, not while Amira's blessing of sanctuary holds.

Though I can't say he'd spare me another thought either way if we were to meet as strangers on the street. If anything, he might kill me just for sniffing out my witch blood.

*"You're not wrong,"* Osen agrees. *"He only has kindness in his heart for his mate and mate brother. He tolerates Maxum because he likely reminds him of the positive aspects of their homelands."*

Squaring my shoulders, I head out to join them, with Flint and Arran following behind me. Raithe and Amira come out of the main house to meet us.

"The gang's all here," Raithe announces happily, with a playful clap of his hands.

This phoenix is a sunshine to Darius' grump, although I don't think they're an item as well. And I suppose Amira's disposition lands somewhere in the middle. I make a note to write something like this in the future... if there is a future. *If* I ever have time to write again.

*Le sigh.*

I hope I find a way back to my passion for writing smut. I mean, I have all these guys to test out all the things. It seems selfish to not share my research.

But first, kick some magical ass.

"Maxum tells me you tugged on their souls," Darius says, narrowing his fiery eyes at me. That isn't a metaphor. He has flames blazing right out of his eye sockets. I've seen Maxum and Calder with what looks like fire behind their eyes, but this is full on roasting my marshmallows level fire.

Damn if this dude doesn't make me shiver with nerves. What if he doesn't like my answer?

I don't think he would try anything with my guys all around.

Swallowing my anxiety, I answer with a small voice, "It was an accident. I was in a moment of pleasure, and I wanted them closer."

Darius grunts, sniffs, and tilts his head, studying me. "I can smell it more now. Demon blood. High born." He flicks his gaze at Maxum and says, "She'd be too good for you if she weren't a mutt."

"Hey!" I snap.

"I wasn't trying to offend you." Darius waves me off.

"I don't care what you say about me, but I won't have you putting Maxum down."

Maxum pulls me to his side and kisses the top of my head. "Thank you for defending my honor, just remember you're talking to a fancy pants fire puppy."

Darius chuckles or at least that's what I think he's doing. It's hard to tell.

"If you pulled their souls, then you have a magic similar to mine. I can take a soul out of a body and then release it beyond the veil. You may be able to do something like this. Or perhaps what you did earlier was actually siphoning their life force."

My face and arms go numb. I stand stock still, panicking.

Is that the magic that Galiana and Rob were stealing from me and used to kill Osen? Did I almost murder my mates?

"Can you tell if I hurt my pack?" I ask, terrified to hear the answer.

"I don't sense any damage."

Relief fills me. I need to be fucking careful until I know what I'm doing. Maybe I should lay off getting laid. I could rip the soul out of my partner with a big O.

I'm a cumming black widow.

I hug my arms over my chest.

Maxum rubs my shoulders with his huge palm, and he comforts me. "It will be okay. This is why we are out here… to figure it out."

"But how do we *figure it out* without hurting someone?" I demand, snapping out of my paralysis.

"I'm here," Darius reminds me. "I can help you return a soul to its body if you start to pull it out."

"But what if I'm siphoning their life force?" I throw my arms in the air, ready to walk away and never use my magic again.

"I will see that and immediately alert you to stop." Darius steps closer. His hellhound nature is right on the surface. His skin is dark gray like charcoal with cracks that reveal lava like fire underneath his fur. His flaming eyes narrow in on me.

I gulp, but somehow stand my ground.

"All you need to do is do what you did before, and I will identify your ability. You need to know, so you then can use it properly. And I'd like to go about the rest of the day."

I wonder what the rest of his day might look like, but I'm pretty sure it has something to do with his mate. I get it. I'd enjoy being with my mates, too.

"Okay. I'll try."

I shake out my shoulders, and Darius steps back to give me space again.

"Target me." Maxum turns me to face him.

"Why you?" I ask.

"Because I'm more akin to Darius."

I hear an omission in his tone. He doesn't want me to yank on one of my bonded mates, or further injure Calder. That only makes me more nervous since he expects shit to go wrong. I tilt my head back and stare at the blue sky, trying my best to keep my wits about me. This is no time to lose it.

Recalling how I felt when I tugged on their souls, I focus on bringing Maxum closer, needing him. Wanting him to be part of me.

Energy swells around me, and I give him a tug.

Maxum lurches forward.

Darius barks, "Release him!"

I let go of the thought and energy. I fall backward, expecting to land hard on my ass. But Flint has me around my waist and keeps me upright.

"Well?" I demand.

"You're a soul sucker."

I choke out a laugh. "Well, I've been called a lot of horrible things, and that actually *is* one of them," I joke. I have to make light of this, otherwise I might collapse into tears. I don't want this kind of power. I could hurt my guys.

"It's not a bad thing. I have this magic," Darius explains.

"She's worried about hurting us," Flint says, likely reading my mind through our bond.

"Now you know what it is. You can control it." Darius shakes his head, confused. "I don't see what the problem is."

This guy has the emotional intelligence of a brick.

"Remember, she's new to magic," Amira says. "Not all of us want the responsibility over life and death." There's a heaviness to her words. She's had to make that decision in the past and regrets it.

"Hmm." Darius eyes me. "Doesn't matter if you like it. That's what it is."

I huff at his dismissive behavior. But what do I expect? "Fine. Tell me what I can do to make sure I don't hurt an innocent."

"I don't recommend calling their souls to you," he states simply.

"No shit." I grump.

Darius sighs wearily. "If your magic activates, and when you feel the tug, release your hold. Or if you want someone to die, pull harder and rip them from their mortal coil. With a thought, send them through the veil."

From what I'm gathering, supernatural magic is mostly innate. Instinct guides them. He makes it sound so easy.

Human born witchcraft often sounds more involved with spells or focal objects.

"What about my fae side?" I ask.

"From your magic display when we were in hell, it seems you're an electric mage," Maxum says. "Most fae-born mages come from Elven and human matings."

"And that's where a lot of the supernaturals come from, such as vampires and shifters," Arran adds.

*"And the incubi and succubi, among other species,"* Osen chimes in.

My head swirls, thinking about my lineage. I thought I was a plain ole human, but nope. I have DNA that comes from three different realms.

Who were my father's parents? Are they alive even though they may be centuries old?

There's so much I don't know. Sure, I've briefly traveled through the fae and demon realms, but what are their towns like? The people? I only have a limited picture from what my guys have told me and from Osen's memories. Yet his memories weren't much for daily living and seeing the cities and populations.

Will I ever be free to visit and travel to these places? Will I ever meet my father or perhaps distant relatives?

"What is the extent of your electric magic?" Amira asks, breaking my mind's wanderings.

"Uh." I look at my hands. "I threw a ball of energy at a hellhound that was chasing us and about to bite Calder."

"With no spell or training?" she probes.

"No. I just wanted to protect him, and boom—lightning fingers."

"With that affinity, you may have the ability to drain the power from a mortal's building," Raithe says appreciatively.

"Or restart a heart," Arran adds. "If an electric mage is strong enough, they could affect the weather."

Flint steps closer and strokes his thumb over my cheek. When our eyes meet, I know he's sensing my chaotic thoughts and worries. "Heartstone, can you call upon that gift now?"

"All I can do is try," I say with a shrug. "What should I target?"

"I recommend holding your hands out in front of you about a foot apart and try to form a ball between your palms," Amira offers. "But if you have to throw the energy, then aim for the lightning rod over the hothouse." She points to a small building near the tree line.

Maxum and Flint both step back to give me space. And Arran moves out of my path to the rod.

I ground my feet shoulder's width apart and hold my hands in front of me.

Electricity. Where to start? Is it as simple to summon as throwing a switch in a house? Or do I have to feel my people are being threatened to call upon it?

I concentrate on the space between my palms. I imagine a ball of energy glowing blue and white, since that's what magic looked like when I threw it to protect Calder.

My hands begin to itch. Encouraged, I focus harder, thinking about zapping the fuck out of Rob. Then Galiana.

A flash of light explodes from my hands.

A chorus of curses surrounds me.

I blink to see properly again and fortunately my accelerated healing repairs my eyes quickly. "Is everyone okay?" I ask with a wince.

Glancing around, I see nods and find everyone blinking as I am.

"Needless to say, you'll need to work on that," Darius grumbles. He turns and saunters away, throwing an offer over his shoulder. "If you have more soul questions, I'll answer them after you get a handle on your fae magic."

I'd growl at him if I thought it'd do any good. But he's probably right. I need to figure my shit out.

Why isn't it as easy as in books? Why can't I just wave my hands around and be the biggest badass magic wielder around?

*I need a montage!*

Then the words that I'm a *'good-for-nothing loser'* ring in my head, in my sister-mother's voice and in Rob's.

Why can't I instantly disregard all my emotional abuse and trauma from my entire existence? Why can't I get over my insecurities? And why can't I accept the kind words from strange, sexy monsters when they tell me I'm amazing?

Okay, I'm handling that last one better than I thought. But I have enough life experience to know my emotional hang-ups will rear their ugly heads occasionally.

I've been alive long enough to know I'll have days when I'm feeling vulnerable. Because the scars and effects of abuse don't just completely vanish because the source of the pain is gone. Even when the new people in my life are wonderful.

But I know with my guys at my side, any trauma will be easier to move past and conquer.

# 16

# ELECTRIC FIRES

## JADE

"*I can help you learn to control your electric powers,*" Osen offers. "*Calder could help too since he has fire affinity that I assume would be similar.*"

"I'd like to work on this without the pressure of an audience," I announce. As the crowd disperses, I hurry over to Calder. "Would you help me?"

He looks over my shoulder at the other guys, then back at me in confusion. "You want me?"

"If you want me to find someone else, I get it." I wave my hand, erasing the request. "Osen said your experience with fire magic might be helpful."

Calder uses his fingers to comb back his auburn hair, and I watch his arm muscles flex with the simple movement.

"Uh, I..." he pauses and waits for everyone to leave the area.

I wait patiently for him to tell me what he needs to get off his chest. Either he wants to help, or he doesn't. I will not force him.

"It's just… I haven't been able to work with fire magic since my last death."

"Oh." I cover my mouth, feeling regret for bringing it up. "I wouldn't have asked. I didn't know…"

"I don't think Osen or the guys have figured it out yet." He nods behind him, where his now hidden wings would be. "My wings light up. I guess they didn't think much about it."

"Is your magic gone forever?" I ask, then grimace. I probably shouldn't ask that sort of thing. "Sorry, ignore me."

Calder fiddles with his fingers. "No. It's okay. You can ask me anything. Weirdly, I don't feel defensive talking about it with you. I suppose I thought the guys would think less of me."

"How could they? You're a freaking amazing phoenix!" I say with enthusiasm.

His mouth turns up at the corners, and he lets a gorgeous smile out on his handsome face. "Thanks. This is what I mean. You're so new to all this, you're excited by the little things."

"You're definitely not little." I chuckle when I hear the innuendo. "But yeah, I try to be excited by life—even the mundane—which you, being a mythological creature, are not. Take the compliment, brat."

He smirks at my sass. "I suppose I can guide you through some things to get you going. I don't currently need magic to talk about it."

"And maybe you just have the yips."

Calder jerks his head in confusion. "Yips?"

"It's a human sports thing. Usually, it's thought of as a state of nervous tension affecting an athlete, making them freeze or spasm. They get all up in their heads and have performance anxiety."

He glances down at his crotch.

"It sounds like you went through a horrible experience. I'd be surprised if you didn't have some blocks from something like that."

He stares at me for a long time. I wonder if he's pissed and is trying to compose himself.

"I suppose it might be that. I lose part of myself when I die, and the last one was a particularly traumatic death."

I want to hug him and tell him it's all going to be alright. Fortunately, I remember myself before I leap at him and encroach on his boundaries.

Calder surveys the area and flicks his chin toward the hothouse. "Let's get away from prying eyes and go where it's a bit more private. You don't need the extra pressure to cause the yipping."

I grin to myself as we walk to our destination, loving how he's making sure I feel comfortable.

When we're in what looks like a more private location, I stop and stare at the small building.

Calder's powerful presence slides up behind me. It's closer than I expect him to be. I feel the heat from his beautiful body.

His hands cup my shoulders, and he leans down to whisper over the shell of my ear, "You can do this."

Goddess, how I want to press back into his muscular chest and feel his arms wrap around me. At this point, I'd settle for a friendly hug, just so he can get over his aversion to touch.

I wonder why I have such a draw to them, including Calder, other than the obvious. I've seen a lot of gorgeous guys in my life, but none has made me ache with the need to make them mine.

*"You're still denying this? They're your fated mate matches,"* Osen says wistfully.

*"I suppose I thought it only happens in books."* Then I ask him in my mind. *"But what about what you had with him?"*

*"Yes, I believe Calder and I were a mate match, but it seems you're matched with the entire pack."*

*"Well, that's not heavy or anything."* I had thought maybe the gravitational pull between us might have been a bit of Osen's influence. But what if it isn't?

"First thing to do is to relax." Calder brings me back to the moment. "I watched you earlier and your instincts are good. You rooted your feet in the earth with the intention of grounding yourself. I would suggest that before you call upon your power that you visualize what your goal is." He points over my shoulder at the weathervane, staying close. "Do you want to throw a ball? Or a lightning bolt? What does it look like in your head?"

"Yeah, okay. I understand." I suck in a breath and shake out my hands. Instead of holding my palms facing each other like Amira prompted, I lift them up toward the building's lightning rod. Then I call on my magic. I'm paying more attention since I don't feel like I'm performing for a crowd.

The magic doesn't flow until I think about how I could use it to protect my pack from Galiana and Rob. It must be triggered by the need to keep them safe.

Energy seems to gather from inside me and then draws from outside of my body.

"Very good," Calder encourages. "I can feel it. Keep going."

Excited that I'm a flipping mage and I'm doing this, I open myself even more to the magic.

My hair is rising on my arms and head.

Maybe too much? *Shit.*

I throw the energy like I did in hell, and it streaks out of me like Zeus' bolt, fully formed.

It crashes against the lightning rod and obliterates it.

Metal explodes out.

Calder grabs me, spinning. He protectively expands and curls his wings to shield us. I can feel his feathers slide across my arms.

Glowing scrap metal lands all around us, sizzling in the grass.

Calder jerks as though he's been hit with debris.

Then I realize his wings are on fire. I expect them to burn

me, so I recoil. But other than heat, I don't feel like I'm being hurt.

"Calder! Are you okay?" I ask.

"Fine," he grunts and yanks his wings away from me. "*Fuck*, Jade, did I burn you?"

I touch my arms and hair, then I turn for him and pat my sides. "I don't think so."

"How?" He keeps inspecting me for damage. "I swore my wings touched you, didn't they?"

"Maybe?"

He looks disturbed by that revelation.

"What the fuck?" Darius barks as he charges out of his house, staring at the scattered lightning rod pieces smoldering in his yard. "Woman, you owe me a new rod!"

Protectively, Calder moves in front of me and growls, "Back off, hellhound."

I peek around the phoenix to see that we've gathered a crowd again.

Amira waves her hand and mumbles a chant and the flames on the grass are snuffed. "You told her she could use it as a target."

"I didn't think she had *that* much juice." Darius shakes his head, studying the damage. "You better use that power to fight our enemies."

"I will."

He gives me a once over. "Not bad." With an approving grin, he spins and disappears back into the house as he takes Amira's hand in his.

My jaw drops in shock. I didn't know he could smile.

Calder turns and gazes into my eyes. He smooths back my hair as the guys approach to check on me. "She wasn't burned by my flame," he says. "Does that mean…"

"We don't know what it means. Your flames probably didn't touch her," Maxum cuts him off and grunts. He glares at me, probably reading the look in my eyes. "Witch, I'm not going to test to see if you're flame proof."

"It could be a small test... and you can heal me, right?" I offer. I should know this for any potential battles, shouldn't I?

"Absolutely not!" Maxum slashes his hand through the air. "I will not hurt you!" He waves his fist at the others. "And none of you fucking try it!" He storms off before anyone can argue with him.

This feels like more than just seeing if I will get a tiny burn.

I want to ask what it could be, but I understand if something is bothering Maxum, I have to talk to him about it alone.

Calder clears his throat to draw my attention away from Maxum's retreating backside. "Jade? Are you sure I didn't hurt you?"

I check myself again, but don't even see singe marks on my clothing. "I'm good."

"Guys?" Calder looks to Arran and Flint. "Can we have a minute?"

My mates give me a quick kiss to reassure themselves I'm okay before they leave me alone with the phoenix.

I stare up at him, curious to hear what he has to say. He appears nervous and sad while he studies my face, like he's trying to remember what he wanted to say.

When he doesn't speak for at least a minute, I say, "If you're worried about me, I'm okay. I'm fully aware I might get hurt playing with my magic. This isn't your fault."

"Well, it is. I was supposed to be teaching you control."

"And that doesn't happen the first try." I shrug, then tilt my head, attempting to read him. "What's really upsetting you?"

Calder drops to his knees in front of me, staring up at me with a pained expression. Surprisingly, he takes hold of my hands. I will myself to remain calm. Whatever this is, I need to let him process it.

"I'm so sorry," he pleads.

I can't stand to see him so torn up, so I drop to my knees to meet him where he is. "I don't understand."

"I've been such an ass—"

"You haven't been lately," I interrupt. "And I know why you were before."

"But I'm so fucking broken."

"I'm not asking anything from you." As I say the words, they feel like acid on my tongue and the pain of rejection stings my eyes. I want him more than I should.

"I curse the Fates," he mutters and turns his head away. "But maybe this isn't that…"

"Huh?" I lean over to catch his attention. I don't understand his erratic emotions. "Can you explain?"

"It might be nothing. Or perhaps my flames aren't the same since my death. But *if* my fire touched you and left you completely unscathed, it means we could be mates."

*"Told you,"* Osen whispers in my mind.

*"Not now,"* I scold, then refocus on Calder. I'm unsure of what to say to make him feel better. I struggle with every response I come up with, since I don't want to make his suffering worse. "I'm sorry."

That snaps him out of his torment. "Why are you sorry?" he asks softly.

"I'm sorry it upsets you this much that you might be matched to me."

His brow furrows. "It has nothing to do with it being you. Not like that. I wish I wasn't broken, and I could be a mate you deserve. You're everything I'd want in a woman."

I smile gently. "I will accept whatever affectionate companionship you're willing to offer. Even if it's only friendship." I glance down at our clasped hands. "If this is as far as you can take things with me, I understand."

Calder's glacial blue eyes pierce my soul and flame with heat. He lets go of my hand and grasps the back of my head and pulls me in for a bruising kiss.

I surrender to his passion and find I'm swept up in it. I return his kiss, swiping my tongue over his lush lips, and he draws it in to suck.

We are in a frenzy until we finally gasp for air.

He rests his forehead on mine and sighs. "Fucking hell."

"Good fucking hell?" I ask, biting my lip and gazing at his handsome face.

"Fantastic." He nuzzles my nose. "Jade, I don't know how this is going to work. But I will try to manage my damage. I'll do what I should have done for my other mate and failed."

I know he's speaking about Osen. My heart aches for them. I wish I could just write some better ending for them.

Then I wonder…

Maybe I can.

# 17

# THE PAST

## MAXUM

*I* feel Jade's presence before I hear or see her. I fear our souls are already intertwining, even without a bonding mark.

She approaches cautiously, unconcerned about the woods or what creatures might hide in the brush.

No. She's nervous about me.

That upsets me more than I would have guessed. Only weeks ago I might have reveled in giving her a fright, but I don't wish her to flinch away from me in fear again.

I'm sitting at the edge of Amira's boundary, and it gives me a view of the neighboring valley.

Jade picks through the brush and leaf debris as she comes slowly closer. When she's fifty feet to my right, she calls out in question, "Maxum?"

"Come." I wave her over.

She still appears skittish. "I understand if you need some alone time. We're a bit on top of each other in that cabin."

"And some of us are on top of *you* quite a bit," I joke.

My flirty smile eases some of the tension in her shoulders, which eases my heart. When she gets within arm's reach, I can't resist and pull her into my lap.

Jade lands with a surprised yelp.

I curl my body around her as we both face the view. My chin rests on the top of her head and my arms snake over her waist, caging her to my body.

She squirms a bit.

"Don't," I hiss.

"Am I hurting you?" she asks with alarm.

"No, but if you wiggle your sweet ass over my cock anymore, I might explode all over your back."

She chuckles, then sighs. "I thought I might be crushing you with my weight."

"Never. You're perfect."

We sit in a comfortable silence after that. My hand slips under her shirt, and I stroke my thumb over her soft belly.

Finally, she breaks the quiet. "Out of this bunch, I think you're the most like me."

"A psycho demon?" I ask with a smirk.

She shakes her head, and I pin her with my chin to make her squirm again.

"You aren't *that* psycho," she argues. "Besides, if I lived eight hundred years dealing with dumb douchebags, I'd probably be even more murderous than you."

"Yes, well then, I'm quite restrained when you think about it that way."

"And you're usually coming from a place of love, protecting your pack."

"I could see you protecting, killing for them as well," I say, knowing her electric magic seems to awaken with the need to keep her pack safe.

"For *all* of you," she counters with emphasis, squeezing my arm.

I sigh, thinking of the people I've failed to keep alive—most recently, Osen. "Maybe, but I'm not always good at protecting."

There's another lull in the conversation, and she breaks it again. "So, what happened back there?"

Here it is. I knew she'd call me on it.

I could just try to ignore her question, and she'd probably let me slide. She's good at giving us space to work things out. She's being a fucking saint with Osen's and Calder's baggage.

"I don't want to see you hurt," I say. It's the truth… just not all of it.

"Yeah, but in the scheme of things, it was about testing for a minor burn. I could easily get hurt worse in my kitchen." She tilts her head back on my shoulder and looks up into my eyes, her jade irises shining with magic. "It feels like there's more to it than that."

I grunt, but don't elaborate. Kissing her temple, I try to sort out my thoughts and emotions. "If you need to do any tests, then do them."

"I was going to anyway."

With my demon sense, I feel her need to set her boundaries with us. I can't blame her. We are possessive and protective more than she even realizes yet. I regret the spanking even though I know she enjoyed it. I want her to have a voice in our pack. To be free. I only fear that if we leave the safety of Amira's sanctuary that she will be stolen from us. Then she wouldn't have any freedom if taken by Galiana or the demon lords, if she survives at all.

"I also want to go to Calder's death spot. And before you ask, I don't know why exactly."

"Fine," I yield. I promised myself centuries ago that I'd never be a controlling mate if I were lucky enough to have one. "A quick trip should go unnoticed. And I doubt they'd think to look for you there."

Her soft fingers trace over my hands, as if memorizing my

flesh. "Is the reason you got upset about the fire the same reason you don't want to mate bond with me?"

"I never said I didn't want to mate bond."

"Is it because I have a haunted koochie?" she teases, trying to lighten the mood. I know she's driven by the same call I am to claim each other.

I chuckle softly. "The ghost vagina is not an issue." I pause, unsure what to say.

"Yeah, I know. You said you weren't ready yet. But—"

I lift Jade up and spin her so she sits facing me. "I will mate with you when it's the right time and if you still want me, once the dust settles."

"Why wouldn't I want you?" Her brow furrows, and she looks fucking fierce, like she's going to fight me.

I love it. Too much. And that's the problem. I'm a danger to her. And now with her lineage revealed, I'm the last demon she should bond with. They may take her just to spite me, and I can't protect her the way she will need me to.

I press my forehead to hers, my lips brushing over her mouth as I confess, "I want to possess you just as much as Osen is in your mind, or Flint's stone is in your bones, or Arran's bite etches your flesh. I want my mark burned into your skin like a brand that can never be removed. I want your love to reveal itself in my markings, branding me and announcing I'm bonded to the most beautiful soul I know."

She's panting by the time I'm done, and she claims my mouth. Her tongue sears my next protest into smoke. Our kiss is hard and almost violent, and it's *exactly* what I need from her. Any tentativeness she had before is long gone. I wouldn't be surprised if I walked away with her mark burned into my flesh by the time we are finished here.

Her nails dig into my shoulders, feeling sharper than ever. In response, my hands grip her hips so tightly that I'm sure I'll leave bruises.

Fuck. This is what I am worried about. Now that I know

she's part demon, I'm positive she'll trigger me into a rut. I can't guarantee her safety. Some fully demon females don't survive the mating process. I thought I could keep myself in control when she was a witch, but now?

Now unbound magic stirs in her veins. Her blood sings for mine, and I will answer with a brutal mating.

And if the demon lords sense her presence, they will come for her.

I break the kiss and guide her face to my heaving chest.

"Maxum?" she asks, sounding out of breath and confused. "Are you okay?"

"No." I should pull her off my lap and step away. I should run away, but I can't bring myself to do that. "I can't be intimate with you anymore."

"Why not?"

"The spanking? I was on the edge of losing my control. I shouldn't have done that." I sigh. "Or kiss you now."

"You never seemed to have a problem before. And I can handle it."

"Your magic... your demonness was bound—masked—before. I don't think I can resist the wild nature of a demon mating."

"Oh." Jade pulls back to look me in the eye.

I don't meet her gaze until she catches my chin and makes me look. Stars, how many times have I done that to her? How the roles have reversed.

"Do demons go into a sort of frenzied rut?" she asks.

"Yeah. I don't think your body could deal with what might happen. You're only a quarter demon. Maybe if you were half demon or more fae..." I run my hand down my face in frustration. "You're still vulnerable. You're only just coming into your magic."

"Okay." She coos, sadness lacing her words, "It's okay."

I dart my eyes back to her, searching for her meaning. Has

she already given up on us? Do I want her to fight for me? Should I be that selfish?

"Stop it," she says firmly. "I can see your thoughts spinning. I don't need your mind-reading power to glean that. I'm saying it's okay. We can wait until you're sure. This only makes me want to test my resilience more. If I'm able to take flames, magic, and hits, then I'll be able to handle you."

"We don't know that."

"Then we find out what I can handle." She clasps the sides of my face and stares right into my soul. "I'm not giving up on you."

She's so understanding it cracks my black heart. I haven't even told her the main reason I can't claim her. Not yet. Maybe never.

I've never felt the need to cry more than I do now. If only I were capable, she would know how deeply I feel for her.

But I can do something else...

"I love you more than you'll know," I whisper the phrase, like the sacred words they are.

"And I love you."

## 18

---

## MISSING PIECES

JADE

*T*here's more to Maxum's resistance, but I don't push him to explain. When he's ready to tell me the full story, he will.

A demon mating rut might be intense, but I'm sure there are ways to ensure my safety. Maybe we could chain him up... that would be hot.

But only if he's ready to make that commitment.

It's strange to have him wavering now. He was so confident about us until we found out about my demon nature.

Perhaps this has something to do with his aversion to the hell realm. Do I now remind him of what he left behind? What he escaped?

He holds my hand as we stroll back to the cabin. At least he hasn't completely retreated from me. I won't pressure him to be with me. He has to want this. Want us. If he's having second thoughts, I have to find a way to be okay with his decision. I hope if he doesn't want me, he will be my friend, because I don't want to lose him completely.

We're quiet, and I use the time to assess how my mate bonds feel with Arran and Flint. Separated like this, even if it's not more than a quarter mile away, I can feel the cord pulling thin.

I wonder what it feels like when mates travel to different locations. Does it pain them to be apart? I suppose I'll likely find out if we ever get to move on to a normal life.

I chuckle to myself.

"What's funny?" Maxum asks with a curious expression.

"I was thinking about my life in the future and realized I won't ever be normal again."

"You will find normalcy within this new reality," he assures me.

"I guess so." I nod noncommittally. "It might take a while since there's so much I don't understand about supes and demons and whatever else I don't have a clue about."

"We will help you navigate it." Maxum squeezes my hand. "You aren't alone anymore."

That simple promise hits me in the chest like a punch. I stumble with the emotions that come with it. He won't abandon me.

*I'm not alone.*

"Fuck," I mutter and grasp at my heart.

"Are you alright?" Maxum rushes to stand before me, holding my upper arms, fearing I might fall.

My eyes sting, and my throat closes up. "I never fully realized how alone I've felt all these years… my whole life, really. But now, it's all changed." I gaze up into his smoldering obsidian eyes. "I have you, and a pack to watch out for me."

Maxum presses a kiss to my forehead. "We are pack. We will care for you with every ounce of our being."

I collapse into his embrace and soak up his warmth.

We return to the cabin several minutes later. Flint and Arran collide with me bodily and I oomph out a breath.

What a weird, wonderful feeling to be missed.

For the next few days, I spend time with my guys, talking, kissing, snuggling, and magic training. At night, Osen and I spend my dreamtime talking, playing, and getting to know each other.

The guys take turns helping me channel my electric magic. I'm not perfect at it, but I can conjure a ball of energy to toss, and I've gotten pretty good at actually hitting a target.

Once Maxum is satisfied I can do that to protect myself, he agrees to take me to Calder's death spot.

Of course, the entire pack is going since no one wants to leave my side.

Amira guides us out to beyond her magical boundary. As we pass it, I turn to see the cabins disappear.

"I plan to be back at sunset," Maxum informs her.

"One of us will be here to cross you back over the wards," Amira says. She looks at me. "Good luck."

She must sense the strange weight I feel in my soul. The need to go to Calder's spot has grown over the last few days.

Then the witch vanishes before our very eyes, back in the protections she has placed.

"So cool," I whisper in awe. I'd love to protect my guys like this.

Although he's been brave about returning to the place of his nightmares, I turn to see Calder as pale as I've ever seen him. "Are you sure you can handle going back?"

"Yeah. It's just not the most appealing thing to do." He then nods to Maxum.

Our demon takes the hint and leads us away from the magical border, and when he feels it's safe, he opens a portal. We run through a few different portals before we end up with one that opens to the back of a run-down industrial building.

From the lack of cars midday, I'd say we're in a sketchy, desolate area.

Calder's breathing becomes uneven.

Knowing he will probably deny me, I offer my hand anyway.

Staring at it, he frowns and shakes his head. "I'm not sure that's a good idea. If I lose my shit, I don't want to hurt you."

"Okay. But if you want it, I'm here."

"Thanks." Calder pulls himself together and leads us inside after breaking a thick chain around the doors handles like they were made of paper.

I always forget how strong these guys are.

Before I can step inside after Maxum, Arran pulls me into his arms. "Not yet. Let them check for traps first."

Flint follows Maxum inside and Calder stands near us, scanning the surrounding area for threats.

After a few minutes, they come back. "Looks clear, and no one's inside, but stay alert," Maxum warns.

*"I can help,"* Osen says in my mind.

*"Okay. Let me know if you pick up on anything."*

I've noticed he's become stronger lately. As my magic grows, so does his energy in my body. He sounds more rational and determined to help. But he's also been quiet when we are around the others.

I worry about him and how hard it must be to be like this— living, but not.

I'm wondering if I should offer him freer rein with my body. Allow him to speak to the others whenever he wants.

I had been so worried about him taking off without my permission again that I've been hesitant, but he's trying his best not to be intrusive.

I no longer fear for my wellbeing.

I worry his mental health might suffer without an outlet. Who knows how long he'll be with me?

But now is not that time.

I follow Calder and Maxum through the messy, dusty ruins of the abandoned factory. Arran and Flint protect my back. Even though the place is creepy, and death seems to linger in the air, I feel surprisingly safe with my monsters.

There's trash strewn around, evidence of this place being used by the homeless, but it feels like it hasn't been used in a long time. I wonder if anyone has been inside since Calder experienced his last death.

I'm careful not to touch a thing. Can a supernatural being get tetanus? Probably not. From what the guys tell me, most supes are immune to human illnesses. Guess that's why I never even had a common cold before.

We can still be susceptible to magical ailments and poisons, so I make sure not to brush up against something or step into a trap. Fortunately, Maxum can sense stuff like that and is resistant to most witch curses.

That's mostly what they are looking for. The witch that killed Calder might have left a boobie trap behind in case his friends came to help.

I don't know what I'm searching for by coming here. Maybe a clue to the ASO's plans. Or perhaps some part of my subconscious hopes to heal Calder.

As we approach a corner of the large room, my skin tightens and goosebumps.

Calder stops his slow walk, and I see his fists clench at his sides.

Everyone else goes on alert and freezes, waiting for what Calder might do next.

I can't see his face from my angle, but I know he's glowering at the place he was tortured to death. There's a simple twin sized cast iron bed frame with no mattress on its support beams. Broken chains hang from the corners onto the floor.

Old blood stains the floor underneath and spreads out several feet.

*Fuck.* This is Calder's blood, and I want to cry out for the pain and injustice he suffered.

He's drawing in heavy, ragged breaths, his shoulders straining against his shirt. I expect his wings to spring free and light on fire, but they don't. I suspect he's too overwhelmed to do a damned thing.

*"Open up your senses,"* Osen prompts.

Taking his suggestion to heart, I open my psychic sixth sense as Osen taught me the first time we were on a field trip in the alleyway—at *his* death spot.

Another wave of death hits me hard. When I quiet the sensations, I see something I wasn't expecting. Shadows moving in my vision. Not in the physical realm, but the astral or spiritual level. But these aren't the shadows that an incubus commands.

There is a strange light flickering within each amorphous shade.

*Shades…*

Are these specters—echoes of some poor lost soul?

My gaze darts to Calder.

Are these fragments of his essence?

# 19

# FALLING

## CALDER

*I*'m unsure what I expect to find here. The memories of that witch flood my mind. How she tortured me. What she did.

While she demanded secrets about my pack and the supes I work with as she carved into my chest with a knife. She slowly pinned my wings. She sawed them off. Finally, she hacked off my malehood, letting me bleed to death.

It's no surprise I couldn't get it up for sex after I was reborn.

During the regeneration, my body was made whole again, but parts of my soul were missing. I lost my desire for friendship and love. I lost my phoenix form. At least my wings had returned.

I no longer had sexual desires. At least not until Jade showed up. She has stirred my needs both physically and emotionally.

I stare at the bed and chains, and I can almost feel the iron burning into my flesh. They were enough to keep my naked body in agonizing pain during my time here. Preventing me from healing properly. The witch thought she had exhausted my magic enough for me to never to be reborn again.

Luckily or unluckily, depending on how one looks at it, when I died, I exploded. I scattered into an ash so small and fine. The witch didn't see my remains as she escaped.

She left, thinking her job was done. But slowly over the course of a day, my ashes pulled back together, and I burst forth from a fire of rebirth.

I don't know how long I've been standing here staring at the evidence of my vicious torture, but Jade sidles up cautiously beside me.

Her gorgeous green eyes glow with magic. She isn't even looking at me, but staring up at nothing, like she's watching butterflies flutter in the air.

What does she see I cannot?

Finally, her gaze falls on to me. "Can you feel what's here?" she asks in a quiet voice.

"What?" I ask in a hoarse whisper, even if I don't mean to.

"I believe… its soul fragments." She waits for my response, but I'm so stunned, I can't react. "They feel like you."

I turn back to search the air above us but see nothing.

Jade holds out her arms, palms up, as if calling someone into an embrace.

She closes her eyes, and I feel that same odd tugging sensation she did when she climaxed the other day. Except it's not as strong.

After a few moments, she gasps and jerks backward.

Out of instinct, I catch her before she goes down to the floor and pull her to my chest.

Jade opens her eyes, which are now glowing like a freaking spotlight.

She rises to her toes and parts her mouth. Her hands grip my shoulders and guide me down to her lips.

I kiss her, but it's nothing like I expect. Instead of her tongue snaking inside my mouth, it's energy. Or maybe it's magic.

No… it's *me*.

My soul fragments fall into me. They ping and bounce into my body like a pinball machine.

I grab at Jade, then some part of me fears I might hurt her, so I push away, falling to the dirty floor and onto my back. My body spasms, and I erupt in flames.

Jade gasps, scrambling toward me on her hands and knees.

Arran snatches her up in his strong arms and carries her several yards away.

My eyes lock with hers, filled with fear.

My entire being feels like it's being ripped apart and jammed back together. It hurts worse than anything I've felt before—even in my last death. It feels like my last death on replay and amplified.

There's a blood-curdling scream.

It's me. I'm screaming. Tears leak from my eyes, and they evaporate with the heat of my flames.

Am I dying? It feels like I'm dying again.

My bones ache and snap. It's a familiar feeling that I never thought I'd feel again.

I launch into the air, wings spread, talons out, my beak snaps at the pain.

As Arran goes slack in shock, Jade stumbles out of his arms.

"Calder!" she cries, taking a step closer as she stares up at me in wonder.

I'm overcome with emotions that I haven't been able to deal with yet.

I dive toward her…

# BURNING UP

JADE

*H*oly firebirds. Calder is a magnificent, giant flaming phoenix. His bird form's wingspan is at least twenty feet. I feel the heat on my exposed skin as he flaps his wings, hovering over our heads by thirty feet. His flames scorch the high ceiling just above him.

He glances around, as if looking for a way to escape through a window. Except the windows are all too small for him to clear, even if he broke through the panes.

*"He appears out of his senses,"* Osen says.

Fearful he'll fly off and lose himself, I stumble forward and out of Arran's muscular arms. "Calder!" I plead for him to come down and return to us.

His piercing blue eyes watch me as if I'm prey. I can't say it's the same Calder I know behind these eyes. Even Arran's berserker still has more of him than this creature has of the man I've come to know. I sense Osen agrees with me.

The phoenix dives straight at me.

Shit. Is he attacking?

Flint is on top of me in an instant, moving faster than a gargoyle should be able to move with their bulky mass. I'm pinned to the floor. He curls around me the best he can with his body and wings, covering and protecting me from Calder.

He turns to stone just as I feel Calder crash into Flint's back.

Flames swirl around us.

I bury my face into Flint's stone chest in an attempt to avoid being cooked alive.

Blazing heat brushes over my back, but I don't feel the searing pain of being injured. More like standing in rays of a summer sun too long.

Shouts and sounds of scuffling feet surround me. I dare to peek beyond the safety of Flint's massive arms.

Calder is unconscious on the floor next to me in his human form. His flames are gone, yet his wings remain, but they're contorted in a mangled way.

My heart pinches. Are they broken?

Maxum and Arran are standing over him, their chests heaving with exertion.

Arran's face glints with sweat. His shirt is torn to shreds, and his skin is burned.

"Fuck!" I scream, as if I'm wounded. He must be blocking the pain from traveling through in our bond. "Flint, turn back! I need to get to Arran."

My gargoyle's stone form softens, and he falls a bit more into me before catching himself and pushing up onto his knees.

With my back flat on the concrete floor, I move to roll up and get to Arran and Calder. Flint grasps my shoulders to stop me.

Frantically, I turn back to him, fearing that I've missed something else. Is Flint okay?

My eyes search him as his hands grope to check me for my injuries.

"You're not burned," Flint says in shock.

"Are you alright?" I ask.

He gives me a quick nod. "He can't melt my stone."

I hold out my hands in a silent request for him to help me to my feet. He does without protest now that he's certain I'm okay.

I run to Arran, but quickly realize I could hurt him if I hug him like I want to. I'm still carried on my momentum, and Maxum catches me by my waist and pulls me to his chest. Flipping me around to face him, I see his shirt has been burned off... and his pants. My eyes search for damage.

He shakes his head in answer. "Demons are hard to burn. Not that phoenix fire doesn't sting like a motherfucker."

I spin in his grasp, almost clawing my way to get to my sweet wolf, Arran.

He holds his arms up to stop me. "Give me a little while to heal, my mate. I should probably shift a few times to speed up the healing."

I'm in shock that he didn't berserker out for this. But maybe he did, and now he turned back to his human form before I could check on him.

My gaze drops to an unconscious Calder. His chest doesn't seem to move with a breath. "Guys? Is he...?" I can't say the words.

Osen's ghost inside me stills, waiting for an answer.

Maxum drops into a crouch and feels his neck. "Alive. His body is behaving like he's in a regeneration. It slows down to nothing until he's ready to reanimate."

Flint moves so he's on the other side of Calder's body. Then he glances up at me. "What happened to him, Heartstone?"

"I think I put the missing pieces of his soul back inside."

"Stars, you can do that?" Arran asks with awe and concern.

I shrug. "I sort of did it on instinct."

Arran removes his fire-damaged clothes and shifts into his wolf. My heart breaks at the missing fur from his burns. Tears fall from my eyes, and I bury my face in Maxum's hard chest.

"I'm so sorry," I cry. "I didn't know he'd do this. Hurt you."

Turning back, Arran's muscular, naked body presses against

my side. "Baby, don't blame yourself. This isn't the first time the bird burned me. I'll be okay in a bit."

I turn to look into his beautiful glowing amber eyes and find he's telling me the truth. He's more worried about me.

Arran strokes a hand softly over my hair. "Besides, you helped fix him."

"Although he might be more broken until his soul's returned pieces come to terms with what happened." Maxum frowns. "He could be a mess for a while."

I just shoved unhealed, traumatized pieces back into the guy without thinking it through. What if I fucked up any progress he's made?

Flint gently picks up Calder's body. "Let's get him back somewhere safe, where another phoenix can help him through this."

Maxum glances down at his naked body and says, "We'll have to make a few jumps before we can return. Hopefully, he'll stay knocked out until we get back."

Thankfully, Calder remains unconscious for the entire journey to Amira's. We also stop by one of their old abandoned safe houses to grab clothes for Maxum and Arran.

Oddly enough, though my clothes and skin should have burned, I don't have any damage.

To my surprise, Arran is almost completely healed, too.

It's Raithe who meets us just outside the concealment ward of his coven's property. His eyes immediately snap to his fellow phoenix when we arrive.

"What happened?" He runs forward, looking Calder over. "Did he die?"

"No," Maxum answers. "Let's step over into a secure area before we get into it, if you don't mind."

"Yes, of course." Raithe rushes back to the boundary and

waves us through, inviting us all into the safety of Amira's magic.

Now that I'm more aware of my magic, I can feel her power wrap around me like a warm blanket.

Raithe doesn't press for more information as we head straight for our tiny cabin. Amira and Darius must have sensed something off because they appear quickly as we come to the large clearing between the two main buildings.

Amira inspects us all quickly, then her gaze falls back on Calder cradled in Flint's arms. "Were you attacked?" Her voice is firm. I assume she's ensuring we didn't bring more trouble.

Maxum shakes his head. "Apparently, Jade has the ability to return soul fragments to their bodies."

"Interesting," Darius drawls, giving me a once over. "Few can work with such a delicate skill."

"I don't know how delicate it was since he freaked out immediately afterward."

"Fractured souls have a tendency of panicking and reacting on primal instinct," he explains. "You'll need to monitor him when he finally wakes up."

"You can use my regeneration space. It won't burn down." Raithe nods toward a hill with a metal hatch. "It's as fireproof as I could manage."

Without question, Flint carries him over and Raithe helps him inside.

I bite my lip, wondering what I should do. I want to be with Calder, ease him through this process, but I worry he won't find my presence comforting. He might hate me. He might never forgive me.

*Fuckinggoddessdammit.*

"Maxum and Flint will tend to him," Arran whispers over the shell of my ear as his arms wrap around my waist. "Come, you need some rest."

I resist and take a step toward the underground shelter.

Arran growls and snatches me up in his arms, bridal style. I fight him, shifting in his hold, but I'm unwilling to hurt him to break free, so I'm left with few options against his strength.

"Please. He's going to hate me." I plead. "He'll think I've abandoned him."

I won't be able to live in this pack if he hates me. He will make all our lives miserable. I'd be guilty of ruining their family. I've already mated with Arran and Flint... What have I done? Rushing into mating when things are so chaotic?

This isn't like me. Do I even know *myself* anymore?

Dammit. I'm having an out-of-body experience. It's as if I can see my mind and body and some other rational part of me is helplessly watching on as I'm spiraling. I can't stop. Because things *are* fucked up. And I'm the reason.

Maxum appears suddenly in my field of vision, and Arran abruptly jerks to a stop.

My demon grasps my jaw and forces me to look him in the eye.

I'm instantly back in my body and alert. I almost recoil at his fierce glower. I know he's a force to be reckoned with, but I don't back down from meeting his gaze because in my gut I know he won't hurt me.

Not on purpose.

But the way he's peering into my damned soul rattles me.

"We will get through this. *Together*." He waits for me to acknowledge what he's said, but I only stare up into his beautifully heated eyes. "Don't do anything reckless. You belong here with us, and that means with Calder too. He just needs to wake up, settle down, and remember what's happened."

Maxum sears his words of promise into my flesh with a passionate kiss. When he's done, he storms off toward the cellar.

# LEVELED UP

JADE

"He's not wrong," Arran says, gazing down at me as he walks toward the tiny cabin. "I could feel your emotions reeling through our bond. Bastard just beat me to helping you settle. My only consolation is that I get to snuggle you while he's busy."

Arran sets me down on the edge of our bed and strips off his clothes before he lifts off my shirt. Before long, we are both naked, and I'm studying the remaining pink scars of Calder's fire. My finger tentatively skims along his shoulder when he leans over to place a sweet, chaste kiss on my lips.

"I'll be completely healed by tomorrow. No need to fret." He tucks a loose strand of my silver hair behind my ear.

"But Calder won't be okay. I messed up." I sigh and rub my face. "I did what so many FMCs do—something impulsive and screw it all up."

Arran doesn't let me brood. He has me by my thick thighs

and lifts me up in his arms, wrapping my legs around his waist. My pussy lands squarely over the length of his hardening cock.

My werewolf drags his luscious lips down my neck until he licks at his mating mark at the juncture with my shoulder. I moan, his attention to it sending a wave of lava straight down between my legs.

His cock grinds into me, his length slipping through my silky wetness. "Then what happens in your books?"

I loll my head back and surrender to my alpha. I grin up at the ceiling, realizing what he's done. "They somehow work it all out."

"Exactly. It's just like life. Shit happens, and we work it out." Arran moves forward and places me in the center of the bed. He gives me a brain melting kiss, stroking his tongue over mine and then pulls back. His eyes travel down my body, admiring all I have to offer.

Under his gaze, I feel like a goddess. Like all my feminine curves and softness are a blessing to celebrate.

Another pang of guilt for Calder hits me. "Maybe we shouldn't…"

"I'd argue that we should. Even Calder would say that life goes on and we have to hold on to the precious moments because we don't know when it all will be taken away from us. There's nothing we can do until he wakes up."

I suppose he's right. Calder is safe and recovering. Our lives are dangerous. This might be the last time I have Arran in my arms.

His glowing golden eyes slide down my body to my exposed pussy. My thighs are spread wide around his hips, and he growls low and hungry. "I'm going to eat you, diving my long monster tongue into your cunt. Then I'm going to fuck you until you come around my knot. Understand?"

I nod and bite my lip. His berserker is right under the surface. But even in the likely event Serky ends up being the one knotting me, I know Arran is right there too.

Arran dips his head down and licks over my nipple, and it hardens under his attention. With his other hand, he pinches and rolls my other nipple to a peak.

He licks and sucks, moving lower and lower down my stomach as he nips at my flesh. "So fucking perfect."

My hips rise and tilt to meet his tongue as he lazily brushes it over my clit.

Arran lifts and holds my thighs apart and hums as he gazes at my wet and needy sex. "It's eager for my knot, isn't it? So wet for us. You must have some shifter blood to make you slick like this."

"Please. I need you… your knot, too."

Light flashes in his golden eyes. He dives for my center and feasts like a man possessed. Which I suppose he is. Two fingers slip inside my clenching channel, and he pumps slowly. With a hard suck on my clit, I come undone and scream out his name.

He crawls up my body, and I feel the heavy weight of his cock rest against my throbbing pussy.

I wonder if this is when the man disappears, and I'm face to face with his werewolf. I now know Serky wouldn't really hurt me, but he's a monster and I expect a few scrapes. Yet, Arran craves to have full control of his body when we are in the throes of passion.

"I love you, my moon mate," he whispers over my lips and then ravages me with a kiss before I can return the sentiment.

I taste the tang of my release on his tongue and tilt my hips to meet his.

Without breaking eye contact, he pulls back and braces himself on his elbows. Then he sinks in slowly, enjoying the entire journey, inch by inch. "Fuck. I don't think there's a better feeling in the world than being inside you and gazing into your eyes."

He pushes all the way to his bulging knot. I lift my hand and brush away his mess of wavy brown hair, more out of the need to touch him, to make sure he's real. I don't want to wake up and find this whole thing with my guys was all just a fever dream.

Arran hums and closes his eyes in bliss for a moment, sliding in and out of me.

Then his eyes open, and they are bright with magic. He smiles, displaying Serky's sharp canines. His skin ripples, and I discover fur has erupted at his shoulders and chest. Arran is part Serky, and it's like they are sharing this experience.

He begins to pound into me, grinding his knot against my clit with every thrust.

I'm riding closer and closer to a climax.

"Come for us, mate," Arran purrs in a deep, monstrous voice.

It's all I need to fall off the precipice. I cry out and spasm around his cock. He uses the moment to force his flared base into my cunt and lock inside me.

I come again on the tail of the first. "Love. You!" I shout. My toes curl, and I grind against his deliciously muscular body.

"Mine!" he growls, dragging his teeth over his mate mark, ratcheting me higher.

Overcome, wild with my need for him, I shout, "Mine!"

I bite at his shoulder, getting a mouthful of fur.

But surprisingly, my teeth sink into his flesh. I taste the metallic flavor of blood, but also magic. Something snaps into place.

He jerks like… well, like someone bit him.

"Mate!" He pumps into me frantically, as much as he can, while still locked inside me.

Then I realize what's happened. As deep as Flint's bond, I've completed the mate bond like a proper shifter. Is this possible because the containment spell is truly broken now?

I don't care how as long as I can give this to my wolf-mate.

I'm winning this mate thing! At least with Arran.

After an hour of Arran luxuriating as he lazily pumps his knot into me with a fucking grin as big as I've ever seen, he finally slips free and pouts. "I wanted to stay inside you forever."

"I know, baby, but I gotta pee." I move to roll out of bed, but he snatches me up in his arms and carries me to the bathroom, setting my naked ass down on the toilet.

"Out." I wave him away.

"No." He crosses his arms. "If I can lick that spot, then I can watch you while you pee."

I huff. "Okay then, and you wanted me to watch you while you were taking a dump in my yard as a dog?"

His ears turn pink from embarrassment. "No, but…"

I can't hold it any longer, and I piss anyway.

He smiles smugly, like he's won the argument. "See? No big deal."

Rolling my eyes, I wipe and flush. As I lean over the sink, I see Arran gingerly touching the mark on his shoulder.

"You did it. We're fully bonded," he says in awe. He glances down at my ass, his hands land on my hips. "I need to be back inside you. Now." His cock comes to life and rests over my ass crack.

"My poor pussy is sore. Give a vajayjay a minute after all that knotting business."

"I can make your ass sore."

I spin and playfully swat away his hand. "I'm serious about needing a break. And I'm hungry." Right on cue, my stomach grumbles.

"Fuck, I'm sorry!" Arran's eyes widen as he panics, scrambling out of the room and to the tiny kitchen. "I need to feed you. I'm such a bad mate!"

I hurry over and soothe him. I can see his instincts are riding him hard. "You're doing a great job. Okay?"

He shakes his head and grabs a leftover bowl of pasta salad from the fridge. He pulls me to him by my waist with his other hand and sets me down on his lap.

"Food. Now." He rips open the container and lifts a forkful to my lips.

I grin at this caretaker's behavior and gladly accept. I'm getting used to being taken care of.

"I can't believe it. We're fully mated," he whispers, as if he doesn't want to wake from a dream either. He licks and nuzzles my neck where he bit me.

"Maybe I have shifter blood," I say with a glow in my heart. And I do the same for him, tending to the bite I gave him.

"Seems like the wolfboy likes licking, too." Trouble's voice squeaks out.

"Yes. Good mates," Sage agrees, bouncing beside him in their corner. "They will make a hundred million pups."

I palm my face. "Sage! I definitely won't be making a bunch of pups. I'm not a bunny."

"We can hope!" she says excitedly.

"Don't you dare start with that," I warn. "No more from you about licking or breeding."

"But that's all we have to entertain us," Trouble whines.

Arran nuzzles my neck. "We could get them some toys to play with."

"And treats!" Trouble grumbles. "You and Birdman haven't delivered what you promised."

"My wolf agrees we need more treats soon," Arran says with a straight face.

I hold back a snicker. "Then we need to go on a shopping trip soon."

## 22

---

# FUSION

FLINT

*I* thought my Heartstone was going to die by the flames of my pack brother, but she walked away unscathed. None of us have talked about what this means.

Ultimately, it's Calder who will have to decide if he wants to walk away from his misery, move past his painful death, and accept the bond with Jade.

Maxum and Raithe stare at Calder's unconscious form then we all give each other a worried look.

My heart goes out to our phoenix. I hope he can fuse his pieces back together and become stronger for it.

Stronger for her.

Through my mate bond, I sense Arran is easing our mate's stress with his attention. She's finding pleasure with him. I'm not angry or jealous, though I wish I could be there with her.

Maybe I should assist him. It's not like I can offer Calder words of wisdom like Maxum or Raithe can. I'm not eloquent like they are.

Besides, they are strong enough to subdue him if need be.

But before I can ask to be excused and leave, I feel Arran's presence through my connection with Jade.

*What? How?*

They've somehow deepened their mate bonds. I sense Jade's and Arran's joy, and realize I should give them some time to be alone and revel in their full bond.

It's the least I can do since I had an entire night with my Heartstone, making love to her. By the end, she had no doubt of my utter devotion to her.

She is my center.

Without her, I would lose my mind.

I stare at Calder, wondering if he will heal and find the peace and comfort to soothe his broken heart.

Finally, Calder stirs, still out of his mind. He mumbles unintelligible words until one rings out clearly, over and over. "Jade."

I cannot say if it's because he wants her there or because he's having a nightmare. I glance over at Maxum to see if he can understand with his mind reading abilities.

His lips are pressed into a flat line. That doesn't give me much to go on. I've never been great at reading expressions, especially the subtle ones. It's why I love my Heartstone so much. Jade doesn't make me guess because she is so open with her emotions. She doesn't seem to understand how precious that is to someone like me or in the supernatural world.

All supes seem to mask their genuine needs and feelings. I hear humans and witches are much the same. I often wondered why, until over the centuries, I witnessed many times how a person can turn that knowledge against another. Then that injured person turns wary and guarded.

It breaks me to think Rob could have done that to our Jade,

but she is strong. Stronger than she realizes for still being able to be vulnerable with us.

"Do you feel that?" Raithe asks.

"The room has grown warmer," I answer. "That's all."

Raithe pulls his gaze away from Calder, and it lands on me, then Maxum. "I believe, on top of everything else, that he's entering a mating fever."

I can deduce what that means from context, but I need to know more, "What does that mean for them?"

"If he doesn't consummate his mating bond with her, he may die…" Raithe pauses and frowns deeply. "With how weak he is, it could be the final one."

Maxum jumps to his feet and hits his horns on the low ceiling. "Are you sure?"

"You must pick up from his mind that he's craving Jade." Raithe eyes Maxum, waiting for confirmation.

"Yeah." He rubs his hand down his face. "I just thought… he's been that way for a while now."

"But his fire… it touched her? Tasted her?" Raithe asks. "It should have consumed her?"

"Yes," I say. "I tried to block his attack, but I don't think it was an attack per se."

"It was a call to be close to her," Raithe says. "I had something less dramatic, but similar when I met Amira."

"But he was out of his mind because he just had his soul fragments returned to him." Maxum sits back down, his shoulders slumped. "We thought…"

"He's out of his mind because of the tortured soul pieces, but he's also out of his mind because he's been denying his mate," Raithe explains.

"I should let Jade know how he is," Maxum announces. "Warn her what to expect."

Raithe explains how the phoenix bonds work and says, "Go. Both of you. I can keep an eye on him." He nods to the hatch's stairs.

Maxum and I are quiet on the short walk over to the cabin.

Before we enter, I hold out my hand to make him stop. "Whatever happens, whatever Jade decides, I cannot allow her to be harmed. I don't want Calder to suffer or die, but I *will not* let Jade die."

Maxum turns, facing me head on. "I love that grumpy bastard, but I will kill him myself if he hurts her. She is our heart now and her death means we'd all die."

I give him a curt nod and a grunt of agreement.

Maxum opens the door for us to see Jade naked and snuggled into Arran's lap at the table. He's feeding her chocolate, and she's licking it off his clawed fingers.

My cocks come to life and press uncomfortably against my pants. I hold my hands in front of my groin and enter, quickly sitting down at the table on the other side so no one notices. I'm not ready for their jokes about my body, and now isn't the time.

Maxum plasters on a playful grin to ease Jade's anxiety spike after seeing us return. I sense through our bond she worries something bad has happened to Calder.

"Is he okay?" she asks.

"He's still asleep," Maxum answers vaguely and then he notices the teeth marks on Arran's shoulder. "What have you been up to?"

"We're fully bonded," Arran says proudly.

Maxum whips his gaze to Jade. "But how?"

"Probably because I'm a mutt." She shrugs and winks at Arran.

Maxum kneels in front of her, taking her hand in his and daring to irritate the wolf with his new mate, but Arran doesn't react. The completed bond must soothe his territorial nature.

"You, my dear anomaly, are a designer breed." Maxum kisses the tops of her knuckles and Jade giggles.

Maxum sits down next to them and sighs heavily. His good cheer fades like the drop of a mask.

The blood drains from Jade's face, as she knows bad news is coming. "What's wrong?"

"I want to preface this with you promising me you will take time to think about what I have to tell you before rushing off to be the heroine."

"*Okaaay?*" Jade says, drawing it out as a question. She glances at me for some clue as to what's going on.

I don't shut down our bond, but I don't feed her any information.

Out of all of us, Maxum is the best to deliver news. His stone-cold killer instincts allow him to be rational when he needs to be, and over his eight hundred years, he has developed the ability to communicate.

During my long life, I've shied away from talking and connecting.

Connecting is something that I only want to do now, exploring it with my Heartstone.

Maxum leans forward and presses his lips flat. "I was hoping it wouldn't come to this. At least not so quickly. It's his place to tell you, but he's stubborn and messed up from his past."

"Is he not going to live?" she whispers.

"It doesn't look good."

"Because of what I did?" Tears fall down her face. "Because of the soul fragments?"

Dammit. Maybe Maxum *isn't* the right person to tell her.

"No," I say firmly, just below a shout, so she listens. I correct my volume, but I still am forceful when I finish, feeling angry at the birdbrain male. "Because he's rejecting his fated mate."

Her hand goes to her chest and she guesses, "Osen?"

"You," all three of us say together. Even Osen's voice chimes in through her mouth.

"I can't be his *fated*, can I? He was only starting to get past despising me because I'm a witch. He was fine before we left." The words fall from her lips like a chaotic storm. Her eyes are wide and frantic. "He said he didn't think he could be a mate. And I can't make someone accept me. He barely can touch me. How is this even happening?"

I'd find her rambling endearing if it weren't that she was so stricken with sadness. She wants to help him.

Goddess, she is a blessing—one that none of us truly deserves.

"His phoenix flame touched you, tasted you." Maxum takes her hand in his and rubs his thumb over her palm, calming her. "After that, it was all over. Raithe said Calder is now suffering from a mating fever on top of his soul mending."

Jade swallows down her nerves. With our connection, I can feel her fear and confusion. She doesn't understand how to fix this and is desperate to find a way.

"I can't just mate him without his permission. He doesn't want my touch. Any touch! And after the raw, tortured parts of his soul have just been returned, the likelihood he would want me around is less than it was before."

"I'm not suggesting you take him by force," Maxum agrees. "We will have to wake him and see how he responds to the fever. I needed you to know all the facts so you can decide about what's right for you. It wouldn't be fair to go into this situation blind."

"If he rejects the bond, could he die?"

"Chances are good that he might, especially if you say yes and he doesn't." Maxum then adds, "Only a few species react in such a dramatic way to rejecting a mate bond, so I don't think you would suffer from that fate. At least he won't take you with him and harm you and your other mates."

"What if he says yes, but I reject him?"

"His odds are better in that scenario, but not great." Maxum studies her face. "If there was no pressure, would you want him?"

Jade bites her lower lip. "I like him quite a lot, even when he was being a bit of a jerk. I haven't given myself much space to consider it since he can't handle me touching him, and he didn't seem very interested in me until just the last few days."

"My Moonmate," Arran breaks his silence. "You must think about it now. Just in case he asks that of you."

She nods, but then looks to Arran and then to me. "What about you guys? How do you feel about it?"

"If I'm being honest," I admit. "Nervous. Because I feel Arran through our bond. I suspect he feels me too now."

Arran grunts his affirmation. "When Jade bit me and I calmed down, I sensed your presence."

"Oh, wow." Jade looks at me again. "So you don't want Calder in our mutual bonds?"

"I don't mean it like that," I correct her assumption. "But I worry that because he is so broken, his energy will harm you."

"Aren't you worried about yourself?" she asks.

Holy stones below, she is so considerate—almost to a fault.

Feeling my face pull into a frown, I say, "I could shoulder it for my brother, but Calder and I have a history and loyalties whereas you do not owe him anything."

"I may not owe him anything," Jade says firmly. "And I might not have a history with him. But I want him to have a future with me… us… if he wants it, too."

Arran nuzzles into her neck and inhales. "You're too caring, my moon."

## 23

---

## CALDER, TAKE ME AWAY

JADE

*H*e's eerily quiet, but I sense Osen panicking inside my head.

Who am I kidding? I'm panicking too.

The guys laid out the whole Calder might die thing so matter-of-factly, there was no other choice but for me to help him.

I understand they didn't want to force me into mating with him.

I just hope he accepts me so he'll live, maybe even one day find happiness with our bond.

Then I think about what Flint said…

What if Calder harms us because of his fractured soul?

I can't think like that. If Flint and Arran can shoulder his pain, so can I. Calder saved me from Rob and Galiana. I don't believe it was only for Osen's sake.

He likes me. He is attracted to me, even though he fights it because of his trauma and aversion to touch.

I think about how Calder kisses me. His lips sizzled when he swallowed down the orgasm the others gave me over Maxum's lap. I think about how his eyes light up when he looks at me.

He's pack. And *I'm* pack. We take care of each other. That deep compulsion to make sure my mates are alive and well resonates in my bones.

Literally, since Flint has gifted me his stone to make me stronger. Unbreakable.

I won't be unbreakable if Calder or the others die. Or if I lose Osen.

Damn, how things change. A few weeks ago, I was lonely and aching for someone to share my love. I wanted to finally live out my fantasies—not just the paranormal ones—and find my soul mate and true love. I wanted someone who would do anything for me, and I would do the same for them. Just like the romance books.

I didn't want my heart to only exist in fiction anymore.

And here they are. Bigger than life and better than I could have imagined.

I won't let Calder just give up without fighting for him. Our story was just getting started.

I hope we're almost to the point where the book usually ends and the characters are finally happy. I want to experience when all the big bad antagonists have been conquered, but in real life, and we can enjoy lazy days in bed, and travel the world, or in our case, realms.

We just have to eliminate Galiana and Rob, and we'll be free to live our *Happy Ever After*.

Hell, I'd be good with having a *Happy For Now* for the first time in my life.

"Jade?" Arran nuzzles my mating mark.

"Yeah?" I blink and return my attention to the room.

Around the kitchen table, Maxum, Arran, and Flint are all staring at me like I'm about to lose it. Whoops, I guess I spaced out for a while there. I stir in Arran's lap and suddenly feel claustrophobic.

Thankfully, I don't have a panic attack because he doesn't resist when I slip out of his hold.

"I need some time alone." I glance down at my naked body and don't feel the urge to throw clothes on. "I'm going to take a bath."

"Of course," Maxum says, then rushes into the bathroom.

I follow him inside. I'm about to grumble and throw him out when I see he's wiping down the bath tub of any dirt and grime to make it clean for me.

It strikes me as one of the nicest, most thoughtful gestures someone has ever done for me. Screw saving my life. It's the little things, like making sure I'm cared for, that make me all misty eyed and glowing heart.

I realize I *am* crying by the time he's done cleaning and running the hot water for me.

"Oh, sweet woman, why are you crying?" Maxum asks as he scoops me up in his huge, muscular arms.

I've never felt so safe and cherished as I do in these guy's embrace.

A sob rips from some deep primal place in my soul and hits Maxum in his broad shoulders.

His warm hand strokes up and down my spine, comforting me. "It's okay. We'll get through this."

I nod, but don't answer. I sure fucking hope so.

But life isn't like books. People rarely get their happy ending.

When I'm all cried out, and the tub is almost full, Maxum dips his tail in the water to test the temperature and then lifts to place me inside. He holds my elbows to keep me steady until I've sunk down completely.

I sigh as the lovely warm water surrounds me.

"You still want to be alone?" he asks, bending down to study my eyes.

"Just for a bit." As he moves to leave, I grab his forearm to stop him. "Thank you."

He takes my hand and kisses my palm. "Anything for you, my love."

When he shuts the door behind him, I realize he's slowing down our courting. Is it for Calder's sake? For the fresh bond with Flint and Arran? Or is there something else?

I don't believe he's worried about hurting me during a rut. That's not the complete story.

I sense Flint and Arran through our bonds. They're worried about me. I'm worried about me too, but mostly about them.

The three of them slip out of the cabin, I imagine, so they won't disturb me with their conversation.

I lean my head back and give myself a damned minute to relax.

It then hits me. I have two mates, maybe a third soon, then another.

I'd pinch myself to see if I'm dreaming up this entire life. I know the test is bullshit. The only proper test is trying to read, and I've written while in this new reality.

Which reminds me... I need to finish my book.

But it seems so unimportant now. Between almost dying several times, my new mates, and the revelations about my origins, what does a preorder deadline mean in the grand scheme of things? Not much.

I don't want to disappoint my readers, but if they knew what was really going on, they'd likely understand. And then they'd want detail accounts of the sex.

"Jade?" Osen whispers. "I know this is probably a bad time, but I don't have anyone else to really talk to."

I'm not even mad that he's bothering my quiet time. It speaks volumes that I really do care about this incubus ghost.

"I'm sorry about Calder," I say.

"Why are you sorry?"

"Hurting him with his soul fragments. Being his mate."

*"I've known you're his mate for a while now. And the soul fragments returning are probably for the best once he settles."*

"I hope so." I sigh and skim my hand over the water. "When I returned his soul to him, I had a fleeting thought. I wondered if I healed him, then you and Calder could finally be together."

*"Through you? With your body?"* he asks.

"No. Not like that."

*"What do you mean?"* He sounds interested.

Does he sense what I'm about to suggest? Has he wondered the same thing? He's smart. I doubt it would take him long to figure it out.

"Osen," I hesitate. "I'm scared to even suggest it. Calder might not be okay. And that means you might not end up okay, either."

*"Jade,"* he presses with just my name.

"If your soul is with me and I can put souls back in their bodies…"

*"You mean… do you really think that's possible? But what about my magic?"*

"I thought about that too. If Galiana and Rob used me to steal it from you, that means I could steal it back. If you didn't have enough when you were put back together, that is."

*"I don't believe I would. Supes don't last long without their magic. That's what killed me. It being ripped out of me."*

"Then we need to go after them, see if we can steal it back," I say, worried that I won't be able to pull all this off.

*"No."* Osen sounds like a fierce leader right then. *"I won't risk you like that. Not for me. I made my mistakes. I won't make another to fix it."*

This version of Osen is a far cry from the one I knew that forced me to go to his death spot in the alleyway. He truly cares about me.

*"Don't you dare mention it to the others,"* he warns. *"I won't be the reason they lose you. I will find a way beyond the veil before you*

*can risk it. Do you understand? I will use that unbinding chant Amira gave you."*

"How?"

*"I memorized it when you glanced at it."*

"Fuck."

*"Yeah, fuck. You're too precious to lose over an asshole like me. Think of our pack."*

That's what stops me from arguing further. "Okay. But if we find a way that will work, hear me out."

*"I doubt it, but fine. First, we need to get Calder on his feet."*

Fortunately, Osen allows me the rest of my bath time to feel like I'm alone and stays quiet.

I sense he's thinking about what I've proposed. Maybe he's wondering if there's a way to make my plan work that won't risk everyone else.

I push those thoughts away. There are too many variables. And my mind can go off forever trying to anticipate all the variables and possible solutions until I'm exhausted. But I don't know enough yet to make it a reality. I don't know what I can do. I don't know how to do it, or even if I actually have that ability. And I don't know enough about how this universe and magic work.

I need to be prepared if we encounter Rob and Galiana. It seems likely that Galiana will hunt me down. She wants her weapon back.

A shiver races through me with that realization.

*I'm* a weapon.

Then a thrill zips up my spine.

Yeah, I *am* a fucking weapon.

If I can get a handle on my magic, Galiana and Rob will be afraid of me.

They *should* be afraid. They hurt me. They've hurt my pack.

My family. They're a threat, and I will do what I have to do to protect my guys.

When the bath water turns cold, I slip out and dry off with the fluffy towel Maxum left behind.

I stand at the vanity, staring at the reflection in the mirror. Cliché, I know. But I rarely ever looked at myself. Now, I see someone else, except what I see in me seems oddly familiar. It's as if I've been waiting forty years to unmask this version of myself that's lurked just under the surface. Under a spell.

I comb my fingers through my wet hair, noting how different it looks now. It's an ethereal silver that a fashionista influencer would kill to have. I lean in and study my eyes. No longer hazel, they shine, literally shine, a soft jade color.

My skin subtly glows too, but I could pass for a human if I needed to. Besides, most people don't really *look* at others. Everyone's too busy, distracted with their own thoughts or glancing at their phones to notice my minor oddities.

I flex my hands, thinking about my enhanced bones. With a thought, my fingertips crackle with magic electricity.

*Wild.*

I leave the sanctuary of the bathroom and find the cabin empty. On the bed, someone has set out a red slip dress with a skimpy pair of red silk panties.

I know it was Maxum who picked these out.

He's fulfilling his promise to replace all my destroyed clothes.

I slide on the pretty dress and find it fits perfectly. My nipples are hard and their outlines are clearly visible, but whatever. Time for these girls to be showcased a bit. And I'm certain that Amira's guys have zero interest me and likely wouldn't spare me a glance if I walked around naked. Not that I want their attention. I have enough with my own hulky males.

Instead of calling out to my mates with my bond, I go out to find them, slipping on my leather clogs as I leave the tiny house.

Maxum and Arran are standing by Raithe's bunker and talking in low voices. Using my bond with Arran, I reach out and pick up how worried he is.

They catch sight of me immediately, smiling and waving me over.

I can feel the heat of their gaze as I saunter toward them. Damn, I've never felt sexy in my life and now, with my mates, I feel like a goddess.

"Gorgeous," Maxum murmurs and slides his hand down my side to rest on my hip.

Arran does the same on my other side. I'm pinned between these devastatingly beautiful males, and I forget how to breathe.

How can they affect me like this?

My wolfboy kisses his mating bite mark and asks, "Feeling better?"

"A bit more grounded." I flick my chin toward the cellar door. "How's Calder?"

"He seems to be waking," Arran answers and steps back. "You want to see him?"

My nerves coil up tight and I worry I'm overstepping. "Is that a good idea?"

"Your presence might soothe his mating fever," Maxum suggests. "He'll need a clear head so he can mend his soul."

Squaring my shoulders, I gather my strength. "Let me see him."

## 24

FEVERED DREAMS

CALDER

*I* wish I'd just die already.

I don't care if it's my last death.

I hope it is.

The witch drags iron chains over my exposed chest, burning a trail over my flesh. The toxic iron of the bed sears into my back and legs. I hear the sickening sound of my blood dripping to the floor from my multitude of wounds she's inflicted. When I look over to the side, I can see the stain of my life marking the concrete.

"Tell me what I want to know and this can all be over," the witch falsely coos.

I doubt she will give me a release of death, even if I were to spill the secrets of my fellow supes. If I tell her what I know, she will keep me as a plaything.

No. I'll have to anger her and get her to kill me so I can burn to ash.

I've already been tortured for weeks. My mind spirals with

only moments of lucidity, as my fae blood allows my body to heal. My self-healing magic is almost exhausted now. Every time I regain my wits and realize my plight, I wish to fall back into madness again, so I don't have to consciously feel the pain she doles out.

My pack, my love Osen, and my allies haven't found me. I'm giving up on a rescue ever happening since this witch is clever and has warded our location too well.

Can I *make* myself die?

Just when I'm about to try, I hear a commotion. My vision is blurred, but I sense my packmates are near.

My phoenix instincts sense impending death.

*Please let it be mine. Not my pack.*

"In here!" Osen shouts.

The witch hovering near me, curses and begins a chant.

Other witches pour inside the building, battling my pack. Magic is flying across the warehouse, crashing and exploding.

Shadows swirl over the fray… Osen's incubus magic.

The witch screeches the last of her strange chant, in a language I've never heard before. She raises up her dagger and slams it down into my chest.

I hear something shatter.

But it isn't glass, it feels like my soul.

Before I can think about it, I'm consumed by my own flames.

The next thing I know, I'm hovering in the corner of the warehouse while the ash gathers and my body is remade. Osen and the others stand by in silent vigil. The witches and warlocks who fought them are piled in a heap, but I don't see the one who tortured me.

I don't understand why I'm seeing things this way, from above, out of my body. This has never happened before. When I see my body suck in a breath, I panic. I should be in there now.

Who is in my place? *What* is in my place?

After my body has completed its regeneration, the *thing*

pretending to be me leaves me behind. With my friends and my lover.

I rush to follow, but I slam against some invisible barrier.

I've been trapped.

I don't know how many days, years, decades that have passed. I've gone insane waiting for my body to return.

Like a whisper, I feel it. A call. A gentle caress over my spirit.

Then I watch as an angel walks in with the thing that kidnapped my body.

She can't be an actual angel. The Seraphim race is rumored to be long extinct. But she appears like one to my senses. Glowing brightly with perfect features and containing a powerful magic.

The angel looks up and *sees* me. Maxum, Arran, and Flint are with her, but they don't see me. Not even the being inside my body. I'm worried when Osen isn't among them. What happened to him? I don't want to entertain the thought that he's no longer alive, but that's the only thing that makes sense. He would be here.

Pushing that aside for now, I test my theory that she is aware of me by swirling around the warehouse. She watches my acrobatics in awe.

I'm tugged in her direction, and I go willingly. I don't know why I trust her, but I do. Besides, what do I have to lose?

I slide into her body and sense I'm not the only extra soul in here. Before I make sense of it, I'm moving again. It's like someone pulling a plug in a sink, and I'm sucked into my body.

Finally reunited.

"Calder?" a woman's voice draws me back to consciousness.

I fight to greet her, to answer her call, but my body doesn't respond to my wishes. I sense I'm in my phoenix form, which means I'm on fire.

Am I hurting this angel who has returned me to my rightful place?

That thought frightens me.

Why do I feel like I know her?

I don't know her name. Do I?

*Jade.*

I've been stuck in that warehouse for years, but I've also lived a life with my pack. I lost Osen. My heart contracts and spasms with the grief.

But I've not lost him completely. He still lives on inside her —my angel.

The urge to claim her love is overwhelming. Then all goes black.

Images flip through my mind—of her, my mate. Then I see flickers of the time between my torturous death and now.

I pry open my eyes. I'm no longer in the warehouse.

"Jade?" my voice cracks, hoping she isn't gone. That she isn't an enchanting hallucination.

"I'm here," she whispers.

My eyes dart across the small space to see her beautiful, expressive face lit by the glow of my skin that simmers with flame.

Maxum and Flint are here as well, standing like giant guards at her side. Their gaze is wary and protective, as if they expect me to lunge at her. Hurt her.

"Are you okay?" she asks. "Do you remember what happened?"

The answer formulates as memories merge in my mind.

My soul was fractured, left to rot. But now my phoenix form is back.

*I'm whole.*

"Yeah. The warehouse. You put me back together." I wipe

my brow and frown at the sweat I find on my forearm. "Why is it so uncomfortable in here?" I glance around at the strange room. "Did something else happen? Where are we?"

"We're in Raithe's regeneration cellar," Jade says, then glances at Maxum as if she's questioning if she should say more.

"Please, just tell me." I sigh, rubbing my face and scooting back to the wall to lean against it. "I'm horribly fatigued, and I don't have patience for anyone skirting around the truth." I stare into her eyes, like she's the only one I'm willing to hear it from. "Am I dying the final death?"

She bites her plump, crimson lip. "It depends."

Blood drains from my face. I don't know if it's from the dread or from how much I want to suck her lip into my mouth. Probably both.

"Your flames." She pauses, then goes on. "You dove at me when you were in full phoenix mode."

"Goddess!" My whole body goes on alert and my eyes search her for injury. "Did I hurt you?" Not seeing anything obvious, I quickly look at Maxum and Flint, wondering why they let me live if I did. Or maybe they've already killed me a few times to get it out of their system and I don't remember.

"You didn't hurt me. But that's part of the problem. Your fire engulfed me, and I didn't burn."

"And… that confirms… you are…" The pieces all fall into place. My feverish skin, my urge to worship her body, and her worried expression. I have mating fever. "No. This can't be happening." I yank my hair. I already knew it, didn't I? I *did* touch her with my fire during the first day of training. From the beginning, even when I thought she killed Osen, I felt the pull to mate just as much as my brothers did.

"I didn't mean to hurt you," she murmurs, her voice full of regret and heartbreak. "Or put your life in danger because of a bond you don't really want."

"What?" I gasp, realizing she's taking the blame. "No. I'm sorry that you feel burdened by my trauma."

"But you might die now… because I came into your life." Tears fall from her glowing green eyes.

"I'm the broken one." I scoot closer, craving to reach out, but I fear the emotions swirling inside. "It's you who shouldn't even consider bringing me into your heart and into your bonds."

She stills, eyes wide. "You're pack. And I want to be with you."

"No. I won't have you pressured into a mating bond with me." I shake my head vigorously and scramble backward until my back slams against the wall.

My heart screams in agony. It wants her more than it wants blood in my veins.

Then the broken, angry pieces stir in my mind. Confusion.

"Your soul is trying to reconcile these last years," Maxum explains, like I can't feel that slamming sensation in my thoughts, trying to jam everything together. "And Raithe said that the mating fever might be eased by being close to each other. Skin to skin, if possible. But if you use touch to defer the fever, and *then* you decide against mating, it will probably mean your death. No touching and furthering the bond, and you still have a chance to recover if you reject her."

My hands itch with the need to caress her soft skin. "I'm terrified I'll hurt you."

"And I worry I might trigger your trauma," she says.

"We can stay. Watch over you both," Maxum offers.

Jade fiddles with her thumbs nervously. "You could tie my hands behind my back so you'd know I couldn't touch you. Hurt you."

It pains me to hear her suggest that.

It unsettles me how my body reacts hungrily to such a thing. I want her tied down and writhing for my cock. I want my hands and mouth exploring her soft skin, making her wet.

Maybe she would enjoy that, too. She's been open to other things.

Maxum cocks an eyebrow, likely sensing my interest.

I glance around at the horribly wretched environment. A cellar? For my twin flame? I want to argue and demand better, but I don't want to burn down Amira's buildings. The bed I'm sitting on seems to be a flame-retardant bed pallet.

There is one quick way out of this—reject her and face the consequences. Every cell in my body revolts at the idea. I want her. But I shouldn't drag her and the pack down with me.

I'm fucking weak, because when I gaze into her eyes, shining with affection, I want it. I want to wake up with that face on the pillow next to me. I want to give her the realms. I want to be a better male for her.

"Okay." I scoot over and look at Maxum for his assistance.

Jade stands from her makeshift chair on a barrel and I finally take in her curvy body under a short, red silk dress. My cock aches even more with her beauty.

Her hands fall to catch the hem. "On or off?"

I bite my lip so hard I taste blood. "On... for now." I don't have the willpower to hold back and defer the mating if I see her tits and her round ass.

She turns for Maxum to tie her wrists behind her back. It does things to me I've never truly explored before.

I'm sexually submissive by nature. I loved when Osen would dominate my body. And with his incubus magic, he *completely* dominated me.

But that evaporated with what felt like a nuclear meltdown after what the witch did to me. Tied down, I was helpless to all her torture. And she was creative and utterly vicious, abusing me, then cutting off my malehood. Blood everywhere.

I shake that ugly memory away. I don't want it to cloud our moment. My flame offering herself to me, trusting me.

Jade is *not* that witch. She is the opposite.

Flint and Maxum assist and guide Jade to lie down next to me. On her side, she stares at me, a look of longing in her eyes.

"Are you comfortable?" I slip down so we are face to face.

"As much as I can be." She smiles weakly, sounding vulnerable.

Slowly, I reach out to tuck a lock of her beautiful silver hair behind her ear. My hand slips down to her cheek. I trace my fingers over her jawline, her brow, exploring and memorizing every feature.

Already some of my mating fever seems to dissipate. But I know I'm a goner now. If I reject her, I'm dead. And if I reject her, I'll want to die. Permanently.

"Hi," she says sweetly.

"Hi," I say with a smile. Leaning forward, I skim my lips over hers.

She sucks in air and her eyes glow brighter.

Encouraged by my response and hers, I move my hand down her arms, then the dip of her waist, over the swell of her wide hips. I drag the hem of her slip dress up her hip as my hand returns, revealing her fuck-me lace panties. I want to burn them away and slide my fingers over her seam. Dip inside her wet heat and make her cry out in pleasure. I want to give her the bliss the others do.

Fuck, even Osen has given her pleasure and he's dead.

Dead, but not gone.

I retreat a bit at the thought of him, as he's likely watching this whole thing through her eyes.

I clamp my eyes shut and hear Jade's voice change to signal Osen's control. "It's okay. I'm here, my love. She's our center. The center I could never be. She is the loving heart we all needed. We both knew we craved more. We were just waiting for her."

"But you..." I feel my eyes sting with sorrow. "You aren't really here."

"Not like I used to be, but I'm here. Let's love this beautiful mate as if we weren't broken. Because that is the very least she deserves."

When I crack open my eyes, I see the charcoal swirl of Osen's magic, but also the shine of Jade's.

They are both here... *loving* me.

We are all together.

My mouth crashes into hers... *theirs*. They return my passion, our tongues tangling. My hand grips her hip and draws her against me. My erect cock pokes into her stomach and I grind into her to feel some relief.

I pull her thigh so her leg curls around me. My hand slides up to cup her full breast. I squeeze and roll her nipples through the thin, silky fabric, and she lets out the cutest needy whimper.

She loves this.

I pull down the top of her dress enough to reveal her nipple. I draw it into my mouth and she moans, canting her hips into me.

"I want to taste you," I whisper over her wet flesh. "I've never gone down on a woman before."

"Whatever you need from me," she breathes out. "But don't do anything you don't want to do."

"Oh, I want to." I grin and kiss her again, stroking her tongue with mine. This action is all hers. She's so soft, so gentle. Nothing like Osen's demanding kisses.

Making my way down her body, I press my lips to the silk dress, feeling the heat of her body through the fabric. I kneel between her legs. Both of my hands skim up her thighs, pushing the material until I reach her hips.

Her panty covered pussy beckons me, and I hook my fingers over the elastic straps and draw them down slowly. Once they are off, I toss the pair to Flint, then turn back to admire my mate's cunt.

I lean over, adjusting my hard cock in my pants. I don't plan on fucking her today. I need to take this slowly. I'm still afraid of myself. But I do plan to make her come several times.

Taking her by the knees, I pull her legs open so I can feast on my woman.

I lick up the inside of her soft, thick thighs. Glancing up at her face, her pupils have blown wide with arousal. There's only a tiny ring of green.

"You enjoy being pleasured while your other mates watch on, don't you, my flame?"

Her eyes dart to Flint and Maxum. "Yes, but I like the one-on-one time just as much."

I hum my approval. As much as this is turning me on having them watch, when I can get a grip over myself, I want some personal time with her, too. Eventually, I hope to be able to have her freely run her hands over me.

Seeing her surrender to me, with her hands tied behind her back, is making my cock ache for her.

I get close and inhale her scent. Lilacs and blackberries and fire. My fingers slide through her wetness, and I use it to lubricate her clit and lips.

Then I swipe my tongue through her slick, my eyes fall closed to remember this moment.

"How does she taste, brother?" Flint asks, and his low, gravelly voice makes our mate shiver.

"She tastes like the thrill of an electric storm. Like the warmth of the hearth during a blizzard. She tastes like fate incarnate."

Jade gasps and stares down at me as I give her another long lap with my tongue over her clit. Her eyes roll back in bliss. I haven't even used my gift on her yet and she's already this turned on by my attention.

I explore her entirely. Kissing, licking, and sucking to find what makes her toes curl. To discover what makes her groan and moan with an impending climax.

I sink my fingers into her soaked cunt and pump into her, finding a spot that makes her lift her hips off the bed, and I suck her clit. She comes undone and shouts my name. My heart rejoices that I can give her this.

She's panting, completely limp in my arms. I crawl up her body and snuggle against her side. I study her face as she turns to study mine.

"Don't you want to come?" she asks, a flash of confusion on her face.

"If I pull my dick out, I will mate you right now," I admit. "I'd like to take the process slowly."

She nods and tries to suppress a frown, but a bit of it slips past her hold, tugging at the corners of her lush mouth.

"Maybe we can just talk for a while?" I ask.

Her eyes light up with the suggestion. "Would it bother you if my hands were untied?"

She must be slightly uncomfortable, and it will only get worse as the hours pass.

I sit up, with a smirk I roll her over on her stomach, then get a magnificent view of her plump ass. I swing my leg over her and straddle her upper thighs, essentially pinning her down. Her ass is like a gravitational force for my hands and eyes. I grab each globe and squeeze.

She moans into the mattress and wiggles her tied wrists.

I spread her ass cheeks and thumb over her puckered hole. "I'm going to fuck you here. And both you and Osen will feel me claim your submission."

"*Fuuuck,*" Osen and Jade hiss together—a strange dual tonality to her voice.

My thumb teases her tight hole, and she squirms, but not away, toward me.

"But not now, sweetheart. You'll have to wait for that until after I feel your sweet pussy wrapped around me, milking my cock."

She groans in need and disappointment, and it makes me chuckle. I swear I haven't laughed in years, since my last death.

Not until this crazy angel saved me… *us*.

I untie her hands and gently massage the red indentations.

How can something make me fucking hard and break my heart all at the same time?

I suppose when I've *hopefully* recovered from my PTSD enough to allow her to freely touch me, then it will be only for play to tie her up and make her come.

My hand pats her hip, and she rolls over onto her back. She stares up at me, waiting like a good girl for my next request, hands tucked at her sides.

With a tug on her dress and a look, I ask if I can remove it. She slowly raises her arms, and I slide the garment off and find my body is hovering over her naked glory.

Capturing her wrists above her head, I pin them in place. "Keep them there."

"Yes, sir," she says with a playful smirk.

"You *are* perfect for us, aren't you?" I grin at the blush that rises on her cheeks. She is still coming to terms with how much we want her. She has to erase all of the venom Rob programmed into her mind while she was both under a spell and their day-to-day life.

*Fucker*. I hope I'm the one to kill that bastard.

I was tortured, but so was Jade.

Instead of wallowing in the injustice, she's doing what she can to help me. So if I can rid the world of the assholes who hurt her, I'll give her the security to know her enemies have been vanquished.

I shake off my dark thoughts of death. Torture. I'm spiraling, my mind falling back to that warehouse where I lost myself.

I take in a deep breath, locking eyes with Jade, and center myself.

Then, letting my gaze wander, I admire her full breasts, licking my lips.

"I crave to bite and suck this sensitive flesh into my mouth."

Her back arches, inviting me to do just that.

She's begging for me to break my promise to wait. And I can't blame her one bit because everything inside me is screaming to claim this wonderful woman and make her mine —body and soul.

## 25

---

# THE LITTLE DEATH

JADE

*M*y fears fade when I see the way Calder looks at me. *Passion. Affection.* Perhaps he won't be irreparably damaged now that I've returned his soul fragments.

Sure, I expect he'll likely have a long road to a full recovery. But he's able to push his anger and pain aside to be with me. And Osen.

Maxum and Flint are standing quietly in the corner. If it weren't for my connections to them, I would swear they weren't in the room with us. I appreciate how they're giving Calder enough space to figure this out and letting me know I'm safe in case he loses his mind.

Our incubus ghost hasn't said much to me, but he's enjoying every second and every caress as much as I am.

*"He never got to touch me like this,"* Osen finally confesses in my mind as Calder hovers over my body and pauses to eat me up with a look. *"My incubus power took over too fast and*

*immobilized him. He always riled me instantly. A blessing and a curse."*

An idea occurs to me, and I ask Calder, "How does a phoenix claim a mate?"

His gaze snaps up to mine. He considers me for a moment, then answers, "We... uh, during the mating, our talons pierce our mate's flesh. Then, when we experience the little death that is a full body orgasm, I share my flame with you. My essence."

"So, with me being your potential mate, could you still have sex without mating me? Or could that happen without you meaning to?"

He cocks a brow. "It would be hard to resist claiming you, but yes, I believe I could deny the compulsion."

"Not that I'm asking you not to," I hurry to add. "You just mentioned you didn't want to yet."

"You really can't live without my cock inside you now?" Calder says with a smirk of pride.

I smile wistfully, wishing I could caress him. He must sense my need and leans down, kissing me, then rubs his cheek over mine. The light stubble of his beard only makes me want him more.

When he lifts back up, I find my words. "I want to feel you inside me. And Osen wants it too. Would you make love to... *us*?"

His eyes widen, and he swallows hard. His ice-blue eyes search my face as he thinks about my offer. "Jade, I don't want to dishonor you. Or what Osen and I had."

"I don't think of it like that, but do you?" I ask.

"I think I'm in love with you." He rests his forehead on mine and clenches his eyes shut hard, like he's expecting me to shove him away. "*And* I still love him, too."

"Hey," I call softly. "Look at me." When he does, I go on, "I love Flint, Maxum, and Arran. And I pretty sure I'm in love with a certain bratty ghost too."

Calder smiles, but then it fades.

"And I love you too," I add. When his blue eyes blaze with affection, I say, "I want us to have this, but only if you want it. Osen is part of me now, so you might as well embrace this situation as much as I am. I don't want to shut him out and pretend he isn't here when we're together."

"Okay, yes." His luscious mouth claims my lips and tongue, and I'm panting when he breaks away. His eyes flicker up to my unrestrained hands, appearing nervous.

"Tie me down," I say firmly so he won't second guess my request.

He bites his lip and grabs a long strip of fabric. Like a pro, he wraps one end around my wrists above my head, then he ties the other end to the frame of the pallet under the mattress. His finger grazes my binds.

"Comfortable?" When I nod, he says nervously, "If it gets to be too much or if I'm hurting you. Or the binds are hurting you—"

"I'll say yellow for slow down and red for stop," I interrupt. "And if you're fucking my mouth, then I'll mentally reach out to Flint."

"Stars, you *are* made for us," Calder whispers and stares at my mouth. "I want to feel your sweet lips wrapped around my cock."

I open wide and stick out my tongue, flattening it.

All three males groan, and even Osen does in my mind.

I remind him. *"I want you to be here with us. Maybe teach me a thing or two about sucking cock."*

Calder stands and shucks his pants. His cock is beautiful and looks painfully hard, already leaking pre-cum. With a firm hand, he gives himself a few casual strokes while gazing at my body. "Open those legs. Show me that pretty pussy I'm going to ruin."

I spread my legs, and he kneels next to me and takes a bit of his pre-cum to rub over my clit. My hips jerk with the sensation.

"Maybe I should take your ass now, so I can finally fuck Osen like I've always wanted to."

"Yes, fuck our ass," Osen says.

It feels like Osen and I have become one being now. Sharing this body for our pleasure, and for Calder's pleasure and healing.

Calder sees the swirling charcoal and green glow of our eyes. Hell, I can see the glow cast on his face.

The kiss he gives us is heartbreakingly sweet and somehow filthy all at once.

He pulls back and cups the back of our head and lifts. "First, I need you to suck my cock."

"Yes, sir," we say.

Calder guides the thick and weeping head of his cock to our lips. We use our tongue to flick out and lick the pre-cum from the tip and probe the slit.

"Shit, I don't think I'm going to last a minute." Calder moves away and drags in a ragged breath. "It's been a long time since I've been touched."

We open our mouth, inviting him back. He moves faster now, slipping his cock down into our mouth, and we swirl our tongue around his shaft.

He presses farther in, and it feels like he's going down to our throat. When he reaches it, he blocks our airflow and holds for just a second before pulling back.

Testing my gag reflex? Or testing his control? I'm not sure.

He pumps forward again, claiming our throat. We swallow around his tip, and he groans happily.

"You enjoy sucking cock, our monster fucker?" He smiles down at us, adoringly. "Yeah, I'm talking to both of you."

We hum our response and rub our tongue against his shaft.

"Fuck, I'm definitely not gonna last," he says, pulling out of our mouth.

He sits back on his heels, appearing as if he's in a daze. His eyes are locked onto our bound wrists, expressionless.

We know he's back in that torture chamber.

"Love, come back to us," we whisper. "You're here. *Safe*."

Our words crash into him, and he blinks hard, flinching. He then stares at us for a beat too long. Did he snap?

Calder shakes his head, flicking away the nightmare memories.

His hand slips into ours, holding them with a gentle touch. He places sweet kisses over our face. "You're so beautiful. Your hair is like an ethereal halo, marking you for the angel you are."

"Are angels real?"

"They used to be. No one has seen one in a long while." He bites our lip. "But my pack is mated to one."

He refocuses and moves down our body and slides his thick fingers into our cunt. "So wet for me." He pumps his digits inside our channel and curls against our g-spot. Pulling out, he uses the slick to wet the head of his cock and down around his shaft.

"I need to have your pussy. I've been dreaming about it since you first had Maxum and Arran at the safe house." Calder positions himself between our legs and grips his dick to run it through our folds.

We shiver with need, feeling empty inside. "Please, fuck us."

Instead, he takes one of our breasts in hand and rolls our nipple, then sucks and bites. We cry out, the pain delicious.

We thrash, our hips bucking to meet Calder's cock, begging for relief.

Then he slowly slides into our pussy, working his length inside with shallow pumps of his hips. He cradles our head, and we look up into his beautiful blue eyes and see the love that radiates like a blazing sun.

It's almost too much to look at directly. Like we might melt into nothing under the heat of his gaze.

We force ourselves to meet his eyes and fall deeper in love with him.

He seats himself fully inside, hips grinding against each

other and whispers over our lips, "Thank you. Thank you both for loving me."

He doesn't give us a chance to respond before his mouth is on ours, tongue thrusting past our lips and his hips pounding into our sex. His hand moves down, strumming our clit and bringing us closer to an orgasm.

"Come for me," he demands.

And we do. Our body shudders and pulses with the pleasure he gives us. We cry out and find ourselves lost for a moment.

"Holy shit." He pulls out, breathing hard, but he hasn't come yet.

Then we feel slippery lube at our back door. His thick fingers slide past the tight ring, and he hums while diving deeper, scissoring. "That's it, baby. Nice and ready."

"Please," we whine.

"Please what?" he taunts.

"Need your cock." A whimper escapes as the sting easily gives way to pleasure. We rock in time with his probing.

"Since you asked so nicely, I'll give you what you want." He keeps us facing him, and lines up his lubed dick, ping-ponging his attention between watching our face and as he sinks into our ass.

Calder gets to the hilt and groans, "Jade... Osen... feels so good."

He takes care with us, making sure our body can handle him. Satisfied by our moans that we're alright, he pumps with vigor. His face contorts, and he grunts, mumbling words of love and adoration.

It feels right that it's the three of us together in this moment.

And it's beautiful for both Osen and me to see our phoenix come undone in this way. He's a work of art. His skin is on fire as he gets closer to his climax. But the flames don't burn, they only tickle and stimulate us.

We pull against the binds, wishing to grab onto him and

anchoring ourselves as we spin out of control. He was right to tie us up.

Our orgasm rushes toward us like a freight train. We're sure when it hits us, we'll be obliterated.

Calder remembers our clit and pinches it hard as he shouts his own release. "Come with me!"

The pleasure shoots down our spine and crackles like electric magic.

I'm unsure why, but Osen and I seem to break apart inside my mind back into two beings. For some reason, he's giving me space.

Then an consuming urge takes over.

My soul reaches out and grasps onto my phoenix's soul.

My essence seeks to be bonded with my fated.

I sense Calder cannot deny his need any longer either.

His fingers become sharp talons, piercing my shoulder blades, the similar spot where Calder's wings erupt from his back.

His fire, like lava, flows into me.

I'm melting and reformed all in one moment.

The love that radiates from our combined emotions overwhelms me.

I shout with the unexpected pain of his talons, but it quickly shifts to overwhelming pleasure that seems to echo into eternity.

My bliss magnifies as I feel his bliss as my own. I even sense how my body clamps down and caresses his length. How my skin feels under his fingertips. The climax shooting up and down his spine. The release of years of pent-up tension. The warm embrace of his love.

I see the cosmos open in front of me.

I feel the fabric of life woven into my body.

I sense the many lives my phoenix has lived.

And finally, after what feels like an hour-long climax, I black out.

# BORN AGAIN VIRGINS

## JADE

*I* swear all I do is blink, and I'm untied. Osen has stepped back from the profound unification of our souls and is allowing us space to process this whole wild ride.

Calder has his muscular arm over mine, holding my wrists together in front of me, as he becomes my big spoon.

I jerk and freeze, assessing what's happening. Why did Calder untie me? Why are we canoodling like this? With only a tug of my hand from his hold, I would be free to touch him.

"Are you okay?" Calder nuzzles at the back of my neck.

"We… I thought… you didn't want to mate," I stutter to get out.

"I felt the pull, your soul… I couldn't deny you. You wanted that, right? Oh no, you didn't, did you?" His voice is full of worry.

"I did. I felt the call to bond too. My spirit reached for yours." I turn my body to look over my shoulder at him, so close I can see the swirling of blue flames in his eyes.

"I never expected to feel the completeness of a matebond. It's more profound than finding my fractured soul."

"I'm untied. What if I accidentally touch you?"

"I'm okay with holding you like this." Then a moment of uncertainty must come to him, and he asks, "How do you feel? Are you alright?"

"Yeah…" I check in with my body and sense Osen purring happily in the back of my mind. "That was intense, but in a good way."

"No kidding. It felt like I was a virgin again."

"But with mad hot skills." I chuckle, then tease, "In each life, aren't you a born-again virgin?"

He laughs easily. "I suppose so. Theoretically."

"Osen loved experiencing you being in control for the first time with him," I tell him.

Calder traces my fingers and lets out a long sigh. "I enjoyed being in control more than I expected. But one day, I hope I can handle you both dominating me."

My mind is swept away, envisioning that very thing. Calder on his knees with a collar. While I'm dressed only in a black leather corset and heels, my fingers clenched in his hair as I direct him between my legs to feast on my pussy.

Calder chuckles, bringing me back to now. "You did that steamy author dream sex sequence thing again, didn't you?"

I giggle and wiggle back into his firm chest. "Guilty. How did you know?"

"Probably the lusty haze over your eyes and the bit of drool here." He skims his thumb over my lips.

"Well, you're great writing inspiration." A strange, desperate longing hits me in the chest.

"Why are you sad? Did I do something wrong?" he asks, sensing the turn in my mood through our new bond.

"No. With everything… I haven't been able to write in a while. I miss it." I glance down at my fingers. "And now, with my magic free, I don't even know if I'll be able to use a computer to type anymore."

"There are a few spells and meditations you can use to make it easier. Or you could make Arran be your secretary and dictate to him. He can handle computers if he doesn't get too excited."

"I'll be writing smut…" I laugh, but it sounds tired and resigned. "He's going to be excited."

"We'll figure something out," Calder assures me and gives me a squeeze.

Because my writing career is on hold for the foreseeable future since people are hunting me, I change the subject, "How are you feeling?"

Calder kisses the back of my head. "I'm good as I can be. I think the bond is helping me stay grounded. And the fragments are working to line up with what my body has been up to since the split. I feel like I should be more fucked up, but it's also a relief for those lost pieces. For me too."

"How so?"

"I know why I didn't feel whole all these years—why I was missing my phoenix."

"It gives everything you felt context."

"I don't feel like I'm insane anymore," Calder explains. "Phoenixes never quite return the same, but it's usually some memory loss, loss of connections. Or, in some extreme cases, we can have significant personality shifts. But the last one felt bigger, more destructive than any other death before it."

"Why did it happen differently?"

"The witch used a curse on me right before I died. She fractured me on purpose."

"Fucking bitch," I growl. "If she isn't dead, I'm killing her."

He stills in surprise of my wrath. "I didn't think you were a vengeful sort."

"I suspect most people can be when you fuck with their mate."

Calder's hand guides my chin, so I'm looking over my

shoulder at him again. "You don't mind being my mate? My twin flame?"

"No." I blink back the tears connected to the vulnerability we are both feeling. "How do you feel about it?"

"Like I'm the luckiest male, besides your other mates, obviously. But also like I don't deserve someone as kind and beautiful as you are."

"I can start acting like a bitch, if it helps you." I smile playfully.

"Even your bitchy mode is far too kind to me."

"And I'm not *that* beautiful." I roll my eyes. "Besides, you're hot as fuck. You could just walk straight up to a random supermodel and hump their leg and they'd be cool with it."

"Arran's the leg humping dog, remember?" Calder jokes. Then he rolls me over onto my back, props himself on an elbow, and stares down at me. "And you need to release the bullshit Rob programmed into your brain."

I gulp at his intensity and nod. "I'm trying. Unfortunately, society offers the same bullshit programming for curvy women over twenty. And before you all came along, I didn't exude magnetic sex appeal. So I never felt all that attractive. The magical vagina is a new development."

He chuckles at my joke, then turns serious. "Your soul knew it had five mates out there and likely kept that magnetic appeal on lock down, waiting for you to find us. And now you're our gravitational force. Our center. Our nexus. You're the most gorgeous being. Even when I was being a bratty dick and resisting, I could see your beauty. I felt drawn to you. And honestly, it killed me to push you away. I didn't want to do that anymore."

Calder takes my hand in his, feeling the weight of it, like one might test the balance of a weapon. Then he lifts it to his face, placing in on his cheek.

He sighs, a painful moan that I'm not sure how to interpret.

When he opens his eyes, the blue flames of his love burn brightly.

I don't move, allowing him to get used to my touch.

A tear falls from his eye and lands on my cheek, melding with the salty tears I didn't know I was shedding.

"You're safe with me," I say. "I love you."

"I know, and I love you. I won't let anyone hurt you ever again. Not even me."

## 2 7

## PHANTOM MENACING

JADE

*A*fter Flint helps to clean me up, Calder and I snuggle in bed. His mating fever abates with our bond. He's clearheaded again. He confesses to me what he can stomach to tell me about the torture he suffered. How she violated and mutilated him. It makes my stomach turn, picturing him abused like that.

I'd say I wouldn't wish that on anyone, but it would be a lie. I wish that witch would feel the same pain she inflicted on him. I want her to experience how she ruined him all these years.

However, I suspect she's messed up because someone hurt her, but that doesn't give her a free pass to be a torturer.

"I'm sorry. I shouldn't have burdened you with all that," Calder says, turning his face away from me.

"No. It isn't a burden. I'm here for you, just like you have been there for me. Even when you didn't like me or trust me, you listened when I told you about Rob's abuse. I didn't feel so alone when you understood how much he had hurt me."

Calder's hand lightly strokes my cheek. "I hate that when you were under the spell that I asked you to remember it all."

"Are you kidding me? That was a brilliant idea. Now I understand why I felt the way I did. I was brainwashed." I search Calder's face, trying to read him. "Are you unhappy that I gave you back your soul pieces?"

"Of course not." He presses a kiss to my lips. "It will take some time for my soul to integrate. If I didn't have it back, I don't know what kind of a mate I would be for you."

Calder sits up and moves the pillows to the wall at the head of the mattress. Then he rests his back and opens his arms, inviting me.

I get to my knees and knee walk toward him.

My gargoyle moves closer, worried.

Calder nods to Flint. "Stay close."

"She enjoys this sexual position. Bouncing on top," Flint says and gives me a slanted smile when I blush.

"*Flint!* I didn't take you as a kiss and tell type." I pout, then laugh.

"I'm not planning on fucking… right now, but thanks for the tip, big guy." Calder catches me by my waist and easily lifts me onto his lap, my knees landing on either side of his hips.

Damn, these guys are fucking strong.

His cock perks up with my vagina's proximity.

I feel awkward, unsure where to put my hands, so I rest them on my thighs until I understand what's going on. I know he's trying to get over his nightmare experience, but I worry he's pushing himself too hard, too fast.

Calder's finger catches under my chin and lifts my face so I'm looking into his eyes. They no longer look as haunted as they did when we first met. "I want you to touch me, my flame. Explore my body. I need to get used to it. And I crave your touch. It's driving me insane."

Taking my hands in his, he places them on the sides of his face.

I don't move, waiting to see his reaction. Instead of fear, I see hope and affection in his expression.

"If it gets to be too much, tell me," I say, moving my fingers to trace over his fantastic cheekbones and his chiseled jaw.

His unshaven beard is softer than I expect. I've kissed him, but I was so overcome with desire that I didn't notice how unusually soft his whiskers are. I feather my fingertips over his strong brow, and he closes his eyes in bliss. I run my thumb over his plump lower lip, and he pokes his tongue out to lick the tip.

I move my hands down over his neck. He snaps his eyes open and shivers when I stroke my hand over his throat. He tenses, and I worry I've triggered him.

An image flashes in my mind. Osen's hand wrapped tightly around Calder's neck during sex.

Osen speaks to me, *Maybe one day we can play again like that, but not now. Not yet.*

I explore Calder's collarbones, his huge deltoids, and down over his pecs. My hands practically thump over his washboard abs.

I skim my hands up his arms, admiring his corded forearms and his defined triceps and biceps.

Looking for the next place, I ask, "How do you feel about me touching your back?"

He holds my wrists, leans forward, and slides my arms around him. I stroke up and down his spine and touch the place where his wings usually emerge. In response, he groans with pleasure. His arms wrap around my waist, and he pulls me flush against his chest. I fall into his embrace, my face nuzzling into his shoulder and neck, and he hums happily.

It becomes clear that he isn't likely to have an episode and hurt me. When he realizes this, Flint leaves to make us some food.

Maxum stays to monitor us. He sits in the corner, watching over me like my personal guardian demon.

I giggle at that thought.

"*Jade.*" Maxum narrows his eyes at me, likely sensing I was making a joke at his expense. "What did you just think?"

"Who needs angels when I have a demon to keep me safe?" I blow him a kiss and the sweet and sappy demon reaches out and catches it. Then he wickedly tucks it in his pants, then stares down wide eyed, like it's working some blowjob magic.

Calder and I bark out a laugh.

I'm still cautious and don't initiate touch. Calder's been holding my hands since our touching session and snuggling with me.

Hope fills my heart that we might get past this. If not, I will still love him the way he needs.

The cellar hatch opens, and Arran and Flint are carrying plates stacked with sandwiches.

"Guys, we don't have to eat in here," Calder grumbles. He looks at me with a frown. "It's bad enough Jade has to be down in a dark hole at all because of me."

"Yet you got down my holes anyway," I say and waggle my eyebrows suggestively.

Every one of my guys groans at my joke, even Osen.

"What?" I wave them off. "You all are joke snobs."

"I'm new to jokes and even I know that one was bad," Flint teases.

"Heathens!" I announce. "Want to get barbaric?"

"Not until you eat." Arran places a plate in my lap as I sit at the edge of the mattress. He lifts my chin gently and gazes into my eyes. "Missed you."

I grasp his wrist, moving his hand so I can snuggle into his palm.

After a quick glance to judge Calder's mood, Arran dips down and gives me a soft yet dizzying kiss.

He walks around the bed and then shouts, arching his back

and his body ripples with a shift. I'm freaking out. It appears something's attacking him.

"What's wrong?" I frantically ask my werewolf.

Arran grabs his crotch and doubles over. When he glances up at us, it's not pain but embarrassment written on his face. "I just came in my fucking pants!" he hisses in surprise.

"I believe that was my ectoplasm," Osen says through me. "Ecto-jism, if you will, that was floating in the room from having sex."

Arran scans the space, warily. "Your incubus ghost cum is hovering around like mines in the air, waiting to explode our cocks?"

Maxum swiftly rushes around the room with a wicked grin. When he doesn't cum, he says with a laugh, "Dammit, Osen. Can you jerk out another one?"

"*Haha*," Arran grumbles and uses some napkins to clean up his mess, but it's already soaked into his pants.

Flint shrugs and sits down on the ground next to me. His shoulder presses against my leg like a puppy needing his attention fix.

After the spontaneous ejaculation, we quiet down and eat, enjoying each other's company.

It's wonderfully pleasant except something's niggling at me. The situation is far from where it needs to be. We still must rid the realms of Rob and Galiana so we can stop hiding and find a proper place to live.

And Osen. I want him here, sitting next to me, in his own body.

As amazing as it was to experience a new way with him riding along inside me. I want him physically inside my body with his real cock. I want him to have a relationship with Calder, independent of me. The way they both deserve.

"Guys, I was thinking..." I hesitate, stalling as I try to figure out how to suggest it.

"*No. Don't*," Osen warns, sensing where my mind has gone.

"I have to, Osen," I argue aloud so the others can hear me. "If they shoot down the idea, then fine."

Calder shifts, turning on his perch next to me. "Tell us."

I focus on Calder as I explain. He'll give me the most honest feedback. "With what happened at the warehouse, I think there's a chance, maybe a slim one, to bring Osen back."

"Jade, doesn't it give you pause that fucking *reckless* Osen doesn't want to do it?" Maxum growls.

I look over and find my demon fuming. "Just because he's skittish now after he died doesn't mean it's a bad idea."

"Do you even hear yourself?" Maxum jumps to his feet, coming close to ramming his horns into the low ceiling. "No. We would need his magic back. That means putting you in Rob's path so you can attempt to snatch it from him. You don't even know if you can do that. Souls are one thing. Magic is different."

"But we're pretty sure he used my siphoned magic to take both," I argue.

"He might have, but he would have used a spell to manipulate it to do that." Calder makes a stupidly smart point.

I want to scream. Why didn't my grandmother—dammit, *mother*—leave me with someone who knew what I was and how to train me?

If she did, I wouldn't be starting my new career as a fucking magical freak at forty.

"Then maybe we need to see if I can steal magic," I say with a shrug. "Then if we just happen to wander across Rob, I can rip it from his body."

"Fuck." Maxum drags his hand over his face. "Fine. I can see you aren't going to back down. And we should know what a little monster you've turned out to be."

"We can hunt down some ASO witches and warlocks," Flint proposes. "And beat them to the edge of death, then they can't hurt our precious mate. She could test her powers on them."

"Aw, always thinking of me." I kiss his horn that's only a few inches from my face.

He smiles at me, looking pleased.

We finish up our meal, and Calder insists we return to the tiny cabin.

I don't argue. I could use another shower since the washcloths Flint used to clean me up after Calder fucked me could only do so much.

While we get ready to sleep, Calder gives me a kiss and hug. I soak up the affection and try to radiate it back out to him as much as I can. "I'm going to sleep on the couch since I'm not quite ready for a dog pile on the bed."

"You're welcome when you're ready."

"Hey!" Trouble grumbles at Calder. "I thought this was my bed now."

"You take up a tiny bit of this entire couch!" Calder argues. "I'll put you outside if you want your space."

"No need to get dramatic," Trouble squeaks.

"Yay! Cuddles!" Sage cheers as Calder sets them on his chest.

Seeing them snuggled up makes my heart glow, and I crawl into the middle of bed and what I expect to be another sweltering night of body heat.

Once we get settled in a new permanent home, I'll need Maxum to fork out the big bucks on an industrial sized air-conditioner so I won't suffer a heat stroke at night with them.

As soon as I'm horizontal, the heavy weight of massive arms and legs falls over me. My mind envisions I'm in a horror movie, being pulled down into a dark pit and slowly suffocated. It's not far off, but fortunately, it's like a warm, fuzzy version.

It's as if I'm drugged with happy endorphins, and I fall into a smothering oblivion with a smile on my face.

## STRANGER DANGER

MAXUM

*J*n the early morning, I find Jade in the yard between the two cabins, sitting in a meditation pose with Amira.

I wait patiently for their training session to be over, knowing Jade needs to work on her focus. It isn't horrible, but she allows her mind to wander if she's triggered with a new shiny thought or a problem to solve.

For her writing career, it works perfectly. In a magical battle to the death, not so much.

When Jade and Amira blink back to their surroundings, I give them both a nod. "Thank you for your help, Amira." Then I turn to Jade. "Darius is going to meet us in a bit, but I'd like a word alone with you first."

"Okay. Thank you for making me the magic containment talisman." Jade smiles widely at our host.

Amira slightly bows her goodbye and walks back to the main house.

"Ugh." Jade grumbles and hops to her feet. "That sounds a lot like *we need to talk* talk."

I know from reading romance books, that's the breakup talk. A bit of trepidation fills her eyes and her shoulders curl in slightly.

"No, darling. But you might not like it."

The statement has her shoulders straightening and her eyes narrowing. "Might as well get on with it then, instead of me imagining all kinds of random stuff."

To the point it is then. "Osen was correct to discourage you from the dangerous path of resurrecting him," I say firmly. "It's one thing to channel Calder's fragments, and quite another to hunt down our enemies and use your untested powers. We don't even know the spell they used to rip the magic out of him."

"Actually, we do." She crosses her arms, looking triumphant. "Osen heard it when they used it on him."

I thought he was against this plan! I guess he might change his mind now if he hopes it will work.

I swallow hard. "His memory was while he was dying. He might not have caught the whole thing or accurately."

Osen's charcoal eyes appear, and his deeper voice cuts through. "I see and hear your concern. I have it too. I won't let her do this if it risks her life."

"It *will* risk her fucking life!" I shout. "Not *if!*"

"Okay. Maybe it's better to say if it's too much of a risk." He shakes his head. "Jade's already argued for this, and she has a point. As long as those assholes are alive, she isn't safe. No one is safe. We should go after them."

"No." I throw my hands in the air in frustration. "She needs to work on her powers. *If* we get caught, she can fight back."

"Amira won't let us stay here forever. And you know as well as I do that eventually we *will* get caught if we leave. If we wait for our enemies to find us first, then they'll have the upper hand."

Dammit, why does he have to make sense?

Osen continues. "I'm not saying we go today or even this week. We need to test this spell and her magic. We all need to be ready to go on the offensive as soon as possible."

"Tracking down *any* witch or warlock is fucking dangerous right now," I huff.

"Don't you want your mate to be free of a parasitic ghost?" Osen snaps.

"Shush up, you aren't a parasite," Jade interrupts, sounding irritated, like she's had this conversation a million times.

I shrug, because he's not wrong about being a psychic leech.

Jade rushes to me. "I have to try to help him."

I catch her by the shoulders, and she gasps. I stare down into her glowing green eyes. "I know. But, my love, everything in me is warring against this idea. I wish I could burn the realms and keep you safe and properly fucked and sated."

"For fuck's sake, can you keep it in your pants for five seconds?" Darius snarls from behind me.

When I turn to scowl at him, I see a glimmer of mischief in his eyes.

He's a prick, but he also knows the need our kind has for our mates and is busting my balls about it. I doubt he waited long to mate with Amira once he found her.

I'm surprised I haven't given in and claimed her soul, but I know how dangerous that might be. I can't have us running from both witches and demons.

"Let's get on with it." Darius grunts and eyes Jade with a glower that would make a lesser being crumble.

Not her. She's studying him right back, like she's making notes for her next book. I'm almost jealous. I want to be her next main character. Though she could just as easily make him an irrelevant side character, so I relax.

With Darius's special hellhound sight, he evaluates her magic, her life force, her demon energy signature. "Good news is that even after her magic has bloomed, she won't come off as a demon right away unless they dig, so that's a fucking miracle."

"If she doesn't put up any wards, what *will* people sense?" I ask.

"I don't know what people will sense. But a hellhound will leave her alone. Unless she throws demon magic around and catches their attention."

Jade shivers. "And what happens if I do that?"

"They'll drag you down to hell."

He's about to explain the gruesome aspects of demon culture, so I stop him short. "Yep, let's avoid that!" I say almost cheerfully.

Jade cocks a brow at me, but doesn't press for answers. When I skim her mind, she thinks that I'm just sensitive about my ancestral roots. That isn't the half of it.

Thank fuck, Osen keeps his trap closed. I doubt he wants to worry her either.

"You have Amira's talisman?" Darius prompts.

Jade pulls the metal charm from her pocket and dangles it from the chain.

"It needs to be in contact with your skin to work," Darius explains. "Put it on, and I'll take another gander at you."

Jade slips the necklace on, and I feel her magic mute. Amira said she could make another more powerful one if this one didn't work, but it would take longer for her to create.

"I assume most supes or witches wouldn't give you a second glance with this in place," Darius says with a shrug.

"Agreed." I cross my chest and a growl escapes me when I realize Jade is set to leave Amira's wards.

"Cool!" Jade says happily. "Can we please go to the grocery store and maybe a coffeehouse? Oh, and I'd like to get some more clothes. Can we bring my computer so I can see if this talisman will allow me to use it for writing?"

Darius looks over at me as Jade rambles on. "I'm glad Amira's the quiet type."

Jade stops talking and pouts. She opens her mouth, likely about to insult his grumpy behavior, but I stop her with my comment.

"Jade is perfect for us, so I suppose it all works out as it should."

Her pretty eyes light up, and she crashes into my body in an all-consuming hug.

Fuck. I love this woman.

Of course, absolutely no one wanted to be left behind as we left for civilization. If you can even call most human cities civilized.

The plan is to wear our glamours and split up, blending in and keeping an eye on each other.

One beautiful woman with four intimidating males will draw unwanted attention. Hell, just one of us with her will probably get noticed. And the witches have eyes everywhere. We'll have to watch for fucking tattling familiars too.

Luckily, I'm paired with Jade since I have the innate portal magic. Not that Calder can't make one too, but it takes him a lot longer and drains his reserves. Seconds can mean the difference in life or death.

Jade is still fuming that she didn't inherit demon portal magic. She could probably learn the complex skill like Amira has, but again, it's magically draining for those without the gift.

Osen could create one in his own body, but he needs his incubus magic for it to work. He just doesn't have enough magic other than to seduce our mate in the shadowscape.

I've often wondered if the shadowscape was the final resting place for incubi souls. But with what we've learned about Osen's death, it seems like that theory is bunk.

We only got to visit a rundown haunted warehouse when we left Amira's sanctuary before. This time, Jade bubbles with excitement as we make the trek beyond the borders.

I don't like that we're leaving again so soon, but we're all going a bit stir crazy. We're used to fighting and hunting. Hiding is not in our natures.

After I create the first of many portals, I take Jade's hand. She swings our arms between us like we are human spawn on a school field trip.

"Don't use magic in front of humans if you can avoid it."

"Because the Supes Council will be mad I outed them?" she asks.

"Because we don't need the attention. You're unregistered, which is how we want it. If the magic world knew what you could do…" I trail off not wanting to say it.

"I'd be the new lab rat."

I grunt in agreement. "Don't talk to anyone," I remind her.

"Stranger danger, got it, sir." She salutes me and laughs at me when I roll my eyes. I appreciate she can be so lighthearted with all that's happened, but sometimes I worry she believes this is all some wild hallucination.

She's too brave for her own good.

Jade accepted five monsters into her heart and into her bed like it isn't a fucking big deal. She's pushing her limits to make sure we all get our individual happily ever afters. It makes me love her even more than I do. But damn if it doesn't irritate me that we aren't focusing on Jade's well-being. Although she's already argued that making sure the pack is happy also benefits her.

Thank goddess she has more than human and witch blood to keep her alive. Now that it's free inside her, the demon blood alone might offer some protection from most magical attacks. Jade's fae blood is already helping to speed up her healing. She needs that healing just to recover from all the sex she'll have with four and, possibly soon, five mates.

I portal us through several places before we arrive at our destination in the human realm—a coffeehouse that allows computer use.

I give Jade some cash to buy whatever she likes, and I order a black coffee to drink as I wait outside.

With her mocha and pastry in hand, she finds a seat where I can easily watch her from the sidewalk. She sets up her computer and tests out her magic containment talisman. I do my best to not look like a stalker, but my eyes can't help but snag on her every time I do a sweep of my surroundings.

She's so gorgeous, even in plain, baggy clothes and no makeup, my heart aches to be near her. I want to sit next to her and listen to her silly (and usually dirty) jokes as she giggles at herself. I want her to confess all her thoughts and dreams and share all my secrets.

I snap out of my daydream and scan the area again, finding the other guys just as transfixed as they watch her.

Jade blissfully is unaware of our possessive longing as she types away on her computer. Good. This will ease her anxiety about her future since she can continue her writing after we vanquish Galiana and Rob.

I allow myself to indulge in her fantasy, where we steal back Osen's power, kill them off, and then return Osen to our pack. Then Jade can claim each of us as mates.

I have no doubt he would be a better, more considerate member than he ever was before.

After a half hour goes by, Jade packs up her laptop computer into the lead-lined case to protect it from magic.

She gives me a wide smile as she sashays toward the cafe's main door.

Then all hell breaks loose.

# DRAWING THE DARKNESS

JADE

*I* smile to myself when I feel the gaze of all four of my guys on me as I sit in the cafe window, using my computer to check on my accounts and sales.

No surprise that my sales have slumped a bit, but not as bad as it could be since I'm not around to promote them. I resist the urge to pop onto social media and see what the latest situation in the book world is.

I take the last bite of my pastry and mouth-gasm from the treat. We've been living off some bland meals lately and I'm looking forward to stocking up on some groceries today.

I check my emails and find a few from fellow authors who noticed my absence. My virtual assistant, who creates graphics and promotes book releases, has inquired about the book I was supposed to release in a couple of weeks.

I'm definitely missing that deadline. I can't reach out to her right now, though because it could give away my location if someone is watching our interactions.

Damn, I swear there are nine flipping million emails in my inbox. I need to unsubscribe to the businesses that blast me every single day. It didn't feel that overwhelming before since I checked my email several times a day in my old, regular non-magical life.

My blood runs ice cold when I see a newer message from Rob. Sent right after his failed attempt to cast his hypnosis spell and abduct me from Maxum's lake house.

My cursor hovers over the email, debating if I should open the email with the subject:

RE: THIS IS YOUR LAST CHANCE TO CHOOSE
ME OR...

Like we had a real relationship, and he's giving me some ultimatum.

I doubt he will know if I read his email, so I click on it.

"YOU'VE HAD YOUR FUN, BUT YOU KNOW YOU
BELONG TO ME. COME BACK BEFORE IT'S TOO
LATE. YOU WOULDN'T WANT TO SEE HOW MUCH
IT COSTS YOUR LOVERS IF YOU REMAIN WITH
THEM."

I'll give it to the bastard. He didn't technically threaten them, but he did.

I turn off the computer and pack my crap up. Fuck him and his click bait. Taking a deep breath, I shrug off his threat. He wants to get me riled up, and I can't let him win yet again.

Remembering how he hurt me on so many levels, I force myself to take another deep breath to calm down.

I give Maxum a wide, unbothered smile as I saunter toward the door to join him.

A shout comes from behind me. Which is odd. There aren't kids in the cafe and it's been fairly quiet this whole time.

I spin to see what's going on and find a strange glow coming from the restroom hallway. A man flies from the corridor and slides along the tile floor.

Then someone else emerges—the attacker—and he's storming straight for me.

*Fucking Rob.*

Survival instincts kick in and I whirl around to run from my predator.

Maxum tugs on the glass door handles, which only warp from the force of his pull. The glass glimmers with magic, likely some sort of force field to keep my guys out.

Magic that feels like a giant fist slams me in the back and I fall on my face, knocking the wind out of me. I lay prone on the floor when something wraps around my ankles and yanks me, dragging me quickly toward Rob.

He begins to chant his spell to hypnotize me.

I throw up my mental shields to prevent him from controlling my mind.

Once I'm at his feet, I come to an abrupt stop.

Rob takes a handful of my hair, roughly lifting me up by it.

I scream from the pain in my scalp and try to hold on to his hand so it won't pull so much.

Once the shock subsides, I twist in his hold and swing my heavy computer case at his gut.

Rob grunts with the impact as I hear his ribs crack. I shove at his chest to break away and run.

Unfortunately, he hasn't let go of my hair. He swings his fist at me, aiming for my face.

Dumb move. Hitting someone in the head isn't easy on the knuckles. Maybe he thinks I'll have a glass jaw.

Guess again, sucker.

His hand collides with my cheekbone, and he screams as his hand shatters—my newly enhanced stone bones saving the day.

Just as Rob releases me to baby his broken hand, glass shoots across the coffee shop in an explosion. Thankfully, the few customers and employees inside have already sought shelter behind the counter.

Rob's eyes widen when he sees Maxum and Flint charging up behind me like they are going to kick his ass.

For a moment, I worry about Arran and Calder, but Osen assures me, *"They will have held back to surround anyone trying to flank you."*

Using my bond, I sense Arran is alive, and he's freaking out. But it doesn't seem he's in danger.

Maxum rushes ahead of me, grabs Rob by the collar, and opens a portal below Flint, Rob, himself, and me.

We fall through the floor and a scream catches in my throat.

Rob screeches as we free fall.

I glance down and see we're a thousand feet in the sky, falling fast.

Flint swoops under me. A gust of air leaves my lungs as I land in his arms and his wings completely unfurl to slow our descent. I glance back at the portal above us and see a dark feathered mass fly through.

Calder.

I panic. Where is Arran? Did they leave him behind?

The portal snaps shut.

Calder is diving toward us, tucking in his wings. When he gets close enough, I can see Arran in his arms. Relief washes over me.

Full demon version Maxum soars next to us with his wings out. He still has a solid grip on Rob's collar, whose head wobbles, his eyes closed.

I wonder if my ex is dead, but he jerks back to consciousness only to scream like a baby and pass out again.

"It's clear now that the only way this wimpy piece of crap could make you fall for him is to put a spell on you," Maxum shouts over the wind.

"I'm going to rip his body to shreds for violating you like that," Flint growls.

"Get in line," Maxum growls back.

Is it wrong I'm getting warm, tingling feelings?

It's easy for me to forget when they are so sweet to me, but this display of pure murderous rage keenly reminds me again that my guys are dangerous monsters. Thank goddess, they're on my side.

Calder and Arran catch up to us and Maxum nods to where he plans to land.

Maxum drops Rob to the ground about ten feet up and my ex grunts as he rolls to a stop.

Flint lands but doesn't let me out of his arms.

A half-shifted Arran jumps from Calder's hold before the phoenix lands and rushes over. Werewolf ripples over his skin. He still has on his sweatpants, but his shirt has been torn to shreds. His clawed hands clasp my face as he checks me for injury. "He bruised you," he snarls.

"He's done much worse than that to me," I say almost flippantly. I don't mention the missing chunk of hair from when he just yanked on it.

"If we weren't going to kill him before, he's definitely going to die painfully now," Calder grits out with barely restrained fury as he steps to where Rob has collapsed, opposite Maxum.

They both stare at the jerk warlock with a fiery glow in their eyes, their fists clenching at their sides, waiting for him to wake up.

I shift to get out of Flint's hold, but he grips me tighter.

"Sweetheart, this is my chance to use my power," I say, giving his firm chest a soothing rub. "I have to see if I can get Osen's magic back before you all kill him."

Reluctantly, Flint loosens his hold, and I slide down to my feet. I drop my computer case, because yeah, I held onto that mofo. I wasn't going to let this dickhead make me lose my stories.

Flint and Arran flank me as we all stare at the bane of my existence. Well, one of them. It sounds like Galiana might be the one who has ruined my life and everyone I care about.

But with Rob, it's personal. This asshole took advantage of

my good nature, my body, my mind, and my powers. He invaded my home and made me feel like crap. He wanted me to feel worthless so he could do any horrible thing to me and I'd beg for another scrap of his attention.

But Calder is right. I was strong enough to push him away. I broke up with him, even when he had the power of his magic over me. In a way, that makes me a badass.

*"You ready?"* Osen asks me.

*"Not really. You?"* I feel the heavy weight of this moment on my shoulders.

*"I'm excited and terrified,"* he admits.

I nod, feeling the same. I take a moment to center myself. The last few minutes have been bonkers, and my guys' aggressive energy is distracting.

I go inward so I can unleash my power.

After the feeling of calm washes over me, I open my eyes and focus my magic on Rob. I reach out with my psychic senses and feel energy writhing under his skin.

"I feel shadows," I announce. "I'm pretty sure it's Osen's incubus magic."

"It is," Osen confirms, moving forward inside our body to work with me, guiding me with the extraction spell.

*"What if I mess this up?"* I express to Osen in my mind. *"I don't want to rush this and ruin your chances."*

*"No matter what, I don't want him to have my power,"* Osen says. *"If we cannot bring me back, we'll deal with that later. I'd never blame you."*

Reassured by his words, all of my magic wells inside of me —fae, demon, and witch. I sense these parts make this ability possible. Like I'm the magical equivalent of a perfect cocktail that looks innocent but knocks you on your ass.

I reach out with my mind and dive into Rob's chest, feeling the angry lashing of Osen's shadowtendrils. Osen whispers the spell that I must recite.

I struggle with concentrating on both the words and the action, as I'm still new to wielding magic.

When the chant is done, there's a release of some sort. It's subtle, but there. I gently tug on Osen's shadows, his power, and it slowly leaks out of Rob.

It's working! Excitement fills me.

It also wakes Rob, and he cries out as he witnesses the shadows being taken back.

He chants to regain his hold on Osen's magic, but Maxum kicks him in the teeth, shutting him up.

Rob sways and falls on to his back again. "Bitch," he mutters.

Flint charges forward and places his foot over Rob's mouth, pinning his head down and applying more than a little pressure.

Rob squirms and flails.

"I wouldn't recommend insulting our mate," Flint growls, and the ground shakes with his anger.

I remember to focus on my task, coaxing and drawing out Osen's shadow magic.

It slinks across the ground and winds up my legs, finally sliding down my throat.

I panic as I sense the shadows taking over.

I can't move.

My mind goes blank, and I sink into darkness.

## 30

UNGHOSTED

ARRAN

The moment Jade inhales the shadows, she drops like a lead weight.

I snatch her up into my arms to keep her from hitting the ground.

When her eyes open, it's all Osen. No trace of Jade's glowing green eyes.

"Where is she?" I demand.

"Still here. Just overwhelmed by my magic because it's united with me again," Osen answers, finding their feet and standing.

I don't let go. It doesn't feel like Osen is unaffected, either.

"We should go, get my body," Osen says. "See if this works."

I snarl, hating that I can't see my mate when I look at her face. "Always thinking about yourself, huh?"

"No!" he snaps. "I'm worried that Jade won't be able to handle my energy for much longer!"

"Enough!" Maxum shouts over us, drawing our attention.

He looks over at Rob, clearly debating if we kill him quickly now or slowly later. "Let's go. We can bring this piece of garbage along for the ride. We'll take care of Jade and Osen, then we'll claim our pound of flesh."

We tie up Rob's hands and gag him as a precaution.

Maxum has us jump through a few portals before we end up in the partially collapsed tunnel under the lake house. We stand outside the bunker door as the final portal closes behind us. Maxum presses his palm to the door and unlocks the safe room. When the door swings open, all our eyes fall upon Osen's body inside the glass coffin set in the center of the room.

"You preserved his body?" Rob mumbles behind his gag in disbelief.

Calder shoves him forward and ties him to a cot frame.

No one bothers to answer Rob's question, but it wasn't us that did the preserving. Something about Osen's unnatural death froze his body in time.

Now we'll just have to see if he can be brought back to us in his full glory.

Jade needs to expel Osen's magic, whether it's to resurrect or to just release it into the cosmos. Rob shouldn't have it. Not that it would have been a problem for long, because that asswipe is going to experience a slow and painful death if we can control ourselves enough to make it slow.

I've been helping Jade and Osen make it through our journey here. Her body is rejecting the magic as if she's ill.

"Jade?" I call to her, holding her close, searching her face for a sign she'll be okay.

A faint pulse of green shines through from behind the shadowy gray of Osen's magic.

"She's here, just fighting to stay with us," Osen grits out.

Maxum and Flint remove the top of the coffin.

Calder looks ready to lose his freaking wits. I thought I'd be the mess with being a berserker and all, but no, it's the phoenix.

Tears stream down his cheeks. "Let's go, come on."

He has two mates on the line. In one fell swoop, he could lose both if this goes sideways.

Not that it means a fucking thing. If we lose Jade, then Flint, Maxum, and I will have lost our fated mate. Because that's what we are to her and she to us.

There's no coming back from that loss.

My beasts howl inside of me, and I'm having a hard time containing them. If this goes wrong, I won't contain them any longer. I will retreat so far back in my mind that I'll be completely feral. No one will be safe.

I don't expect much less from the others. Flint would likely turn to stone one last time and return to the earth, releasing his soul back to the cosmos.

Maxum will... I don't even know what he will do, but nothing good will come of it.

Calder will probably end himself with the final flame.

Osen? I suspect he won't forgive himself for allowing Jade to sacrifice herself. If he survived, he'd go insane. And if he died, he'd likely become a vengeful wraith.

I shake myself out of my dark thoughts.

Jade was born to do this. This *is* her power. It's what makes her a valuable weapon. If a hack like Rob can steal and wield her ability, then, even untrained, Jade should be able to figure this out.

And we're here. Not that I'm much help. What do I know about souls or controlling death? Nothing.

"Help us get closer," Osen asks.

With my arm around Jade's waist, I bring them closer to the coffin.

"Fuck, this is weird," Osen hisses.

"No shit," I grumble.

"I feel a tug," Osen gasps. "It's like my soul and magic *want* to return to my body."

"That's good, right?" I ask, excited to hear something might go our way.

"Jade?" Osen calls. "Come on, sweet witch, you gotta help an incubus out."

There's a long pause, and everyone holds their breath.

Well, except Rob. He's just scowling.

"I have to do all the work?" Jade mutters, sounding tired. "What's the point of having a harem then?"

"It's a polycule, sweetie." Osen smirks.

"No. I definitely signed up for a reverse harem with a MM side quest."

With their levity, my chest releases some of its anxiety. She can't be that bad off if she's joking around. Well, knowing Jade, that's probably untrue. Her last words will probably be something to make us laugh.

It's one reason I love her so much already. She's brave, sexy, and quick-witted.

"Hey," Osen says and glances at all of us. "I just want to say something in case this doesn't work out."

"Don't!" Calder throws his hands up. "Don't think like that."

"I won't risk not telling you all how I feel." Osen turns to Flint. "You're the rock bed that keeps us all sane. I'm sorry I didn't appreciate that enough when I was alive. And I have no doubt you will be the most incredible mate to our girl."

"I will do my best with that honor." Flint bows his head. "And may you live to see that happen."

"Arran, you have been the best pack mate. And seeing you heal with Jade has been a blessing in this situation."

I nod, biting my lip so hard it bleeds. "I love you. Try not to leave us again."

"Maxum, *dude*," Osen chuckles. "It isn't like you don't know how much I treasure our friendship since you can read my mind."

"I know, asshole," Maxum says with a playful smirk. "Now get the fuck back into your own body so I can have some alone time with my woman."

Osen shakes Jade's head with a wide grin. Then he turns to the phoenix. "Calder, I love you so much, it aches in my very soul." As Osen says this, Calder rushes forward and gives him a bruising kiss.

"Same." Calder presses his forehead to Osen-Jade and then drops away.

Osen doesn't offer Jade words, or perhaps he does through their mental connection and wishes to keep it private. Likely, since he usually isn't one for public declarations of affection.

"Focus," he guides her. "See in your mind what you want to make happen. Feel my soul and magic gather into your grasp and then coax it back into my body. This is your birthright. You can do this."

Jade closes her eyes. Through our bond, I sense she's calling upon her strange magic. Her skin begins to glow and when she opens her eyes to gaze at Osen's body, they shine like stars. Almost too bright to look at.

She opens her mouth and a bizarre combination of light and shadow flow from her lips. The shadows I recognize… Osen's incubus magic. The light must be his soul.

The cloud of energy slides into Osen's nostrils.

Jade falls backward when the transfer is complete.

I catch her, holding her close to my chest. Her eyes are half closed, and she's spent. Wielding magic this powerful, especially for new magic users, can be taxing.

I cup her head to my chest and expectantly watch Osen's body. I was hoping for a gasp of air or a wiggling finger. But nothing.

"It didn't work?" Calder asks, sounding heartbroken.

"Give it a minute," Maxum whispers. "He was dead for a while. I suspect the body will need to heal and reconnect to his spirit."

We wait and wait.

I don't know if it's been a minute or an hour. It feels like days as we wait for our friend, former lover, and pack mate to wake.

But he remains frustratingly still.

"Anything?" Calder asks as he leans over the casket, his hands fisting in agitation.

"I don't sense brain waves. I thought by now…" Maxum drops into a crouch and hangs his head, giving up.

"Jade?" Flint calls and strokes her hair. "Heartstone? Do you feel him? Or is he truly gone now?"

Jade blinks and rouses to the room, her eyes falling onto Osen's inert body. "He's in there. Feels stuck." She struggles to talk.

"Fuck!" Calder slams his fist into the wall. "We need to release him!"

"I could try taking him back inside me," Jade suggests.

"No," we all say in unison.

"He was hurting you." Maxum stands again and walks over to stroke her cheek. "His magic and soul together were too much for you to contain. I'm afraid he might take over and you'd cease to exist."

"We don't know that would happen," she argues, but I hear her concern that it could.

"He wouldn't mean to," I explain. "But incubus and succubus naturally drain other people's magic. That's how they feed. His magic would feast on yours."

"I believe that's what happened when you brought his magic inside you," Maxum adds.

"But it didn't hurt Rob," she argues.

She has a point there.

"Why is that?" I ask Maxum, because he's the most knowledgeable amongst us.

"Look at him, he isn't alright. His witch magic is drained. This whole time we've been down here, he hasn't even tried to attack us," Maxum points out. "He used Osen's shadows to attack Jade at the cafe. Besides, he didn't have Osen's soul also inside him. Only his magic. He used that to suck the magic out of others. We know from recent events that stolen magic has a short shelf life."

"Why?" Jade asks. "Is it because Rob's body isn't set up to naturally regenerate the magic energy?"

"Yes, exactly." Maxum smiles. "For example, a vampire needs blood from a magic user to replenish. Someone who steals a vampire's magic only has what was in that vampire at the time. The thief can't drink blood and extract what they need to keep the magic thriving."

"But if Osen's magic *and* soul were inside me, it would be different?"

"I believe if he has both, he *could* replenish, even in another person's body." Maxum nods. "Incubi are different. They are adaptable... existing in another plane as well as this one. He would overtake you."

"So then what?" Jade demands. "I'm not giving up on him so easily."

"I never expected you would." Maxum offers her a sad smile. "But we are *not* losing you for his sake. And he wouldn't want to hurt you again. He brought this fate onto himself by acting alone and outside of our pack."

I don't like victim blaming, but Maxum isn't wrong. Osen might have lived if he had kept us in the loop and had us as backup.

"Move out of my way." Jade waves Maxum aside.

I growl and grip her tighter.

She turns to face me, her face full of determination and irritation that I've prevented her from her objective.

"Let me see him. Now," she orders.

## IT'S ALIVE

JADE

"*L*et me see him. Now," I snarl.

I'm not sure why I'm so pissed. I had been dreaming and hoping that Osen would join us in our life together, but now, he seems entirely lost to us.

I didn't even get to say goodbye.

Arran releases his hold, but still has a hand on my back to keep me stable as I shuffle to the coffin. I'm not okay. Maxum wasn't lying about Osen draining me. I used up a lot of magic just to get Osen's shadows out of Rob and into his rightful body.

From what Calder has told me during our lessons, I will get stronger with my magic as I use it. Like a muscle. But there is a maximum capacity for every individual in what they can take on. I'm just beginning my training, so I have only so much strength.

I gaze at Osen's handsome face, wishing I had a chance to

kiss him in this life. To feel his strong hands hold my body. To feel him make love to me in this reality.

Is this really the end of what we have?

I'm fucking mad. I carried this guy around and was doing everything I could to make this right. But in the end, what I could offer was fleeting.

Calder will be heartbroken. Truly mourning his lover and mate.

I will have lost a potential mate and partner. Someone I was growing too fond of. Someone who I was spending my nights with during the sleeping hours. Talking and making love in his shadowscape world.

Tears stain my face. I've been so lost in grief that I didn't even realize I'm crying.

I wipe my tears from Osen's bare arm and find a current of something.

*Him. His magic. His soul. But sluggish. He isn't stuck as I thought. He needs something to stir his life force.*

An image of an old movie pops into my mind.

"Do you know one of the first science fiction books was written by a woman?" I ask.

"Mary Shelley," Maxum says confidently.

I eye him. "Knew her too, didn't you?"

Maxum shrugs. "Met her in passing."

This guy... acting like that isn't a big flipping whoop.

"We're talking about that later." I refocus back on the thread. "Frankenstein's monster was based on an idea at the time, bio-electric Galvanism."

"Don't they use a gigantic bolt of lightning in the movies?" Arran asks.

I hold up my hand, electricity sparks off my fingers. I reach down over with both hands, palms flat on Osen's broad chest, and send a bolt of electricity into him.

His body arcs and shakes. It looks more like I'm hitting him with a defibrillator than magic, but that's exactly what I'm hoping to do. Restart his heart.

I remember in medical dramas, they sometimes have to try a few times.

I stop the flow of electricity. "Maybe someone can breathe life into his lungs?" I look at Calder. Life-giving air from a phoenix seems fitting.

He rushes over and pinches Osen's nose, and blows a deep, intentional breath. He releases him, and I shock Osen's chest again.

Then we do it again.

His body arcs and rattles.

Then a gasp. An intake of air.

It's the most wonderful sound. I release my magic, and Osen flops back flat against the bottom of the coffin.

His eyes barely open. He takes in another ragged breath.

"Water!" Flint calls.

Maxum throws him a bottle from their stockpile down here. Flint splashes some over Osen's closed eyes and then tips the container to Osen's lips while Calder lifts his head.

They only wet his lips, then when Osen seems to be aware, they allow a few drops, then a mouthful into Osen. Finally, Osen swallows down the water.

His limbs don't seem to be working, but I'm hopeful about his ability to drink.

Osen blinks a few times, then gazes up to Calder's face, who's still hovering. He smiles, then turns his head toward me. Our eyes lock, and I feel the weight of the connection between us.

We have something few people, if any, have experienced. His hands lift slowly from his sides. One for Calder and one grasping for me.

"Thank you," he croaks out, his throat still horribly dry and his vocal cords unused.

"We have a modern-day Prometheus amongst us," Maxum

says as he comes up behind me, kissing the top of my head. "Good job, my little demon."

I just fucking brought someone back to life. Dead for weeks, then not dead. I *did* just steal fire from the gods.

I hope they aren't going to be pissed.

But then the room swirls. I fall back into Arran. "I over-magicked."

Arran scoops me up into his arms, bridal style, and I let the world fade away.

"Rest, sweet mate."

When I awaken, I see we aren't in the bunker anymore. I don't know where we are. It's dark, but I can make out that I'm in a bedroom. I've been stripped down to my panties and bra. And a thin blanket has been thrown over me.

Osen is asleep beside me. The moonlight filtering through a window reveals Calder's silhouette sitting on a chair near our bed. He's watching us like some dark protector, flames burning low in his eyes.

"What's wrong?" I ask.

Calder rushes to the side on the bed's edge near my hip. His warm hand grazes down my cheek, over my hair, and settles over my heart. "Nothing. Everything."

"That doesn't help to clear things up," I say with a hopeful smirk.

"I want to be here with you both, but I also want to have my turn ripping Rob to shreds."

"I'm surprised he isn't dead already."

"I'm sure he wishes he was. The guys have shown him no mercy."

"Why aren't you helping them?" I ask.

"I found the sight of torture… triggering," he explains, and I nod in understanding.

Osen hasn't stirred with our conversation, and I worry. "How is he? What happened after I passed out?"

"He rallied enough to sit up and wiggle his toes. So that's good." Calder frowns. "We gave him a shower and some food. He passed out not long after. He still needs more time to heal. Unfortunately, I don't have healing magic beyond regenerating myself. And Maxum believes his sex magic only works on his true mate."

Hmm. He didn't mention that to me. I suppose he hadn't wanted to scare me before when he used it.

Then I remember. "Hold up. I healed Flint after we were attacked at the lake house. Maybe I can help now."

"We'll have to see if that will work, but should wait until you recover more." Calder narrows his eyes. "You're completely spent. And we still don't know what replenishes your magic. Other than time and rest."

Being a late-blooming freak has more drawbacks than I expected. I will have to figure out the replenishing thing soon. But since I'm not quite a proper witch, fae, or demon, I may never know.

"Why wouldn't my healing work on Osen?" I frown, studying Osen's profile in the low light.

"You had initiated a mating bond with Flint when you healed him. Some demon and fae have a healing ability... but only with their mates."

"Oh." I bite my lip. "And I haven't mate bonded with Osen."

Calder rubs the back of his neck, thinking. "But we don't know if you healing Flint was that or not. It will be worth a try when you're replenished, my flame."

I grin at his mating nickname. With my depleted magic and overall fatigue, I feel more like a little flickering candle, and not a roaring bonfire.

Curling up against Osen's side, I place my hand over his heart. A heart that wasn't beating yesterday.

His shallow breathing instantly becomes deeper.

I try to recall how it felt when I healed Flint. The need to take away his pain and suffering was overwhelming. All-consuming.

While I concentrate on Osen, I stir those same feelings. It seems ridiculous that we'd get this far, so close to having it all, for it to fail now.

He deserved better than dying alone in a dirty alleyway. He died fighting to protect his pack, his people, and innocent fae children from being killed by a fanatical group of witches and warlocks.

"Come on, Osen. I need you here. Calder needs you. I want to know what those lips feel like on mine. I want to be with you, all of you. Don't you fucking dare slip away now."

The pain of losing him before I even have him stings my eyes. Love thrums in my heart. A wave, a pulse of magic so pure radiates out of me and into his chest.

His body twitches, like he's waking up from the deepest sleep of his entire life.

"Sweet witch," Osen murmurs. "You're not getting rid of me anytime soon."

I exhale with relief. Joy springs inside my heart.

"Besides, I need to claim you and Calder, my mates. And I plan to show your pretty pussy a good time."

I bark out a laugh. "Because, of course, that's what a naughty incubus would have at the top of his to-do list."

"I'm not apologizing for my sexual desires. It *is* how we power up. But I've been aching to connect with you since the beginning. Instead, I had to sit back, watching all these other punks give you pleasure in the real world." He chuckles, then he rolls over to stare into my eyes. His charcoal eyes swirl with need. "But truly, I just want to make love to you without my damned powers."

"Powers or no powers, I want you too. I'll be here when

you're ready." I pour more of my healing into his body because I can tell he's still suffering.

"I sense your reserves are low. You should stop giving me your magic."

I frown. I want him to be completely healed, but I remember touch and sex power him up, and I can do that. So I pull back my magic and sweep my hand over his chest.

"Do you think this healing means we're mate bonding already?" he asks, stroking my hand with his fingertips.

"We were bonded in a way. So maybe?" I shrug. "I'll have to try healing with someone who isn't a potential mate."

He hums thoughtfully. "Is it wrong that I don't want these beautiful hands on anyone but our pack?"

I roll my eyes. "I didn't say I was giving out hand jobs."

"Unfortunate, since that might help me right now," he says with a wink.

"How can I give you a hand job if your magic takes over and paralyzes me?"

"Oh, my shadows can keep your hand moving."

"That just sounds like fancy masturbation," I tease.

Calder laughs, and it draws our attention.

"Will you join us?" Osen asks, his voice cracking with vulnerability.

Calder gives me a sweet kiss. Then he goes around to Osen's other side and crawls into bed. His hand reaches over, stroking my arm, then he places his hand over mine that rests on Osen's chest.

Osen keeps his hands at his sides, not wanting to trigger Calder's PTSD.

Calder presses his forehead to Osen's temple and sighs. "I still can't believe you're back. I fear I will wake up from this dream and lose you all over again."

Suddenly, I feel like I'm invading their space. They deserve to have a moment for themselves.

I pull my hand free and roll over to get out of bed.

Hands are on me in an instant, dragging me backward over and between Osen and Calder's body. "Where do you think you're going?" Osen growls playfully.

"I was giving you a moment to reconnect."

"Why do you assume we'd want to do that alone?" Calder asks.

"Because I'm not so self-centered as to believe I should infiltrate the relationship that you have together."

"Too bad, because you're in it." Osen crashes his unyielding mouth over mine. He commands my entire being with a kiss. I know he isn't using his shadows, but it feels as if he's binding me to him, gripping my body and soul, drawing me to him. I'm being possessively dragged into his world. Claimed.

Now he possesses me from the outside, reaching in.

Osen breaks the kiss. Still cradling my face in his hands, he turns to claim Calder's lips. I have an intimate, front row ticket to the most passionate kiss I've ever witnessed before.

I don't feel left out. No, I feel my heart beating in time with theirs, sharing this moment of reconnection.

Calder then turns to me and gives me a consuming kiss like I'm the fuel to his flame. Our tongues stroke along each other, and it feels like the moment before an explosion.

Osen groans with delight.

My body is taut with need, and I rub my legs together to ease the searing burn of lust.

Osen slides his hand over my thigh and presses at the seam where they meet, running his fingers back up to my apex, grazing my sensitive lips through my underwear. "Fuck," he hisses. "I can feel how wet you are for us. Your panties are soaked."

"I need to check for myself," Calder says with a wicked grin. He runs his fingers down my stomach and over my mound. "Such a needy pussy. Maybe we should give it some relief?"

"Yes please," I beg.

Calder's fingers shift to talons, and he shreds my

underwear with a few swipes. I gasp as it falls away in tatters. He cuts my bra where it joins between my breasts and the fabric slides to my sides, revealing my already hardening, aching nipples.

Calder and Osen each grasp one of my knees and they pull me open, my pussy exposed and glistening. Osen slides his fingers over my sensitive flesh.

I moan with how delicious it feels, and I don't think he's even using any incubus magic on me yet.

Calder joins in. Their fingers work in tandem, brushing over my clit and inner thighs, and teasing over my entrance.

Both lean down, laving and nipping at my tits as they plunge their fingers into my pussy. I cry out with the sudden invasion and then tilt my hips, inviting them to continue. To give me more.

They play thumb war over my clit and they're ramping me toward an orgasm.

Then, right as I'm about to crest and fall off that cliff, they both pull their fingers free. Locking his heated gaze onto me, Calder sucks on his fingers and hums.

"I need to taste you," Osen growls into my neck. "From the source." He slides down the bed and plunges his face into my wet heat. His tongue delves deep inside, then he laps at my clit before inserting his fingers once again.

Calder squeezes my breasts, pinching my nipples so perfectly it's like he's been trained his whole life in how I enjoy it.

Osen whispers over my lower lips, "Come all over my face, sweet monster." Then he feasts on my pussy like a man possessed. Well, as no longer a ghost possessing me.

Calder claims my mouth as I whimper and moan.

I fist Osen's long hair, and he groans with pleasure. I had a feeling he'd like it a bit rough and passionate.

His fingers curve, rubbing along that sensitive spot inside me, and my toes curl in response. Then I'm shouting at the heavens with my release. I float through the cosmos, pleased that I've finally found my loves.

I'm quaking in their hold when I return to my body.

"Wait!" I gasp, realizing something that feels off.

I was able to move. Calder was moving, too.

"Why aren't you using your shadows? Why am I not paralyzed? Is your incubus magic not working?"

Osen smiles and his entire face lights up like the sun when the clouds finally part. "My magic is being fed, but not with intention."

I glance at Calder, remembering the frustration that Osen's magic always took over and Calder was immobilized during sexual encounters. "I thought if you were sexually excited, it just happened." Then that rejected part of me rears its head. It's one thing for him to sex me up when I was his only source, and he was only in my mind. But in real life, it appears the spark just isn't strong enough. "Oh, you aren't enjoying this very much?"

Feeling ridiculous, I try to close my legs and wiggle away, but Osen is solidly between them, his face hovering over my crotch.

"Stop," Osen growls, holding my legs open and my thighs against his shoulders. "Remember, I figured my incubus paralysis magic wouldn't work on you in the real world because of your demon magic. Believe me, I'm very much enjoying this and am fighting my release with all I have."

Still not one hundred percent believing him, I ask, "But what about Calder?"

"Your bond, our bond, when I was inside you, has given him immunity, too."

"Oh!" I smile excitedly. "So you can be together in any way you like now?"

"I believe so," Osen says, kissing my inner thigh, making goosebumps race along my flesh. "Thank you for that."

"Will you be able to use your shadow magic on us at all?" I ask. I sort of wanted to play with that sometimes.

Two shadowtendrils shoot out of his body and wrap around my wrists, pinning me down. It's just like extensions of his body, but I can still wiggle and squirm.

I grin, wanting to give in to this some more, but I also feel I have a responsibility to give Osen and Calder a moment to figure out what all this means for them.

I tilt my head. "Are the other guys here?" When they nod, I say. "I think I'm going to get something to eat and give you both a moment alone."

The shadows slip away. "What? You sure?" Osen crinkles his forehead in confusion. "We want you. Here with us. Between us."

"I want you both too. But I want you both to figure out how I fit in with what you have. You need to discuss your boundaries with me, with each other. I'm not going to assume that because we have bonds, it means a free for all. When you've decided how I fit with this, I will be here for you both in whatever way you decide."

"You don't have to leave for us to talk about this," Calder argues.

I kiss both on the lips and sigh. "Yeah, I do. I won't pressure you. And I don't want you to regret anything with me."

Osen captures the back of my head, pulling me to look into his gorgeous, haunting gray eyes. "How could I ever regret being with you?"

"You're not the only one in this room," I remind him and pull away, leaving them to work out how their new lives together will be.

## 32

# IT'S NOT ME, IT'S YOU

JADE

*W*alking out of the bedroom, I find myself in a cozy, small, unfamiliar house made of stone and mud, like an ancient building with old-world plaster.

Magic seems to flow around my body, caressing me, and I suspect we are in the fae realm.

The strong metallic scent of blood fills my senses. When did I get a detective nose like that? I suppose being a supe comes with its perks. Although I don't know if smelling blood is a perk.

I hear the thud of someone being punched. When I come to the end of the hallway, I discover Maxum, Flint, and Arran towering over Rob who's been strapped to a chair.

With all that's happened with Osen's return to the living, I'd almost forgotten about that asshole. I'm glad I put on Calder's shirt before I left the bedroom. Not that Rob hasn't seen all my merchandise, but I'd rather not have his eyes on me again, especially like that. Besides, I'm sure my possessive monsters would throw a fit.

Maxum swings his head around to eye me entering the room. His wild gaze travels up and down my body, lingering on my exposed legs.

He blocks Rob's line of sight to me. Not that Rob is even aware of his surroundings.

Maxum grabs a long robe and wraps it around my shoulders. Where the hell did he materialize that from? "I don't want you here for this. Though if you insist, we don't want him seeing your body."

I snicker to myself. Apparently, even showing my legs is too much for them to bear.

Maxum steps out of the way as I tie the robe at my waist and move closer.

The torture session is set up in the kitchen area. Tiled floors will make it easier to clean up the mess. My eyes scan Rob for his various injuries. His clothes are in scraps, dangling off him. He's missing chunks of skin on his legs and arms. One eye is swollen shut, and a couple of fingers have been cut off. His flesh is marbled with fresh bruises and lined with cuts and claw marks.

His head hangs listlessly to the side, unconscious.

I study the damage already done, and I don't feel one ounce of sympathy for him. In fact, I hope he suffers a bit more for all the damage he's caused. The pacifist in me is not reporting for duty, not for him. He hurt me for years, more than I ever knew. He had a shifter warlock masquerading as my pet. He used me, shoving ghosts into my mind and interrogating them through me. Abused me while I was under his spell, convincing me I was worthless and unlovable. Then he stole my magic to create dark spells to kill Osen and who knows how many others.

Arran's hands have shifted into his werewolf claws and his canines are poking out from his mostly human face. Serky is fighting to make an appearance and slaughter my ex.

On the surface, Flint appears calm, but through our bond his rage seeps through. I know he's trying to protect me, but he needn't worry about that. My rage is brewing to a pitch-black cup of revenge the longer I'm in this room.

I remember how Rob couldn't just let me go when I broke up with him and moved on and started dating Arran. Instead, he almost killed me in my home when trying to exorcise Osen. When I ran, he hunted me down in the alleyway, intending to expel Osen again and hurting Calder. Then he came for me at the lake house to abduct me, almost killing Flint.

There will be no mercy for Rob and no letting him go. He won't stop. It's us or him. He doesn't deserve a chance. He wouldn't give me one.

"Have you got anything out of this douche canoe?" I ask, my voice deadly cold.

"A few glimpses," Maxum answers, glaring at Rob. "He has strong mental walls. I'll give him that."

"We're trying to break them down," Flint informs me. "If Maxum pushes too hard, it will melt Rob's brain."

"We might only get one answer if I do that," Maxum adds, resting his hands on his hips.

Arran snarls at Rob, and I pick up that my wolf shifter is perfectly on board with melting my ex's brain.

I drag over a chair, place it about ten feet in front of Rob, and sit down, waiting for the show to resume.

"This will not be pretty, Heartstone," Flint warns.

"I understand."

We wait until Rob is just coming around. From behind, Maxum brackets Rob's head between his hands, his eyes gaze off to the middle distance as he dives into Rob's memories.

"If he wakes, ask him questions," Maxum instructs, hands still in place, but his lip is curled in disgust at having to touch the bastard.

Rob blinks his eyes open and lifts his head. His eyes land on me instantly, and he glowers. "I recognized you were trash as soon as I met you."

Flint and Arran growl, but I hold up my hand for them to stop.

"I knew you were about as useful as a cup of piss in a shitstorm, but you used magic to make me put up with your flaccid... *personality*. Besides, I wasn't the one pursuing the whole fucked up relationship now, was I? So what does that make you?"

"You think you're better than me? You're a mutt, an abomination."

"It's sure funny how worthless you claim I am, but you needed me for your little world domination scheme."

"Useless other than as a weapon."

"Weapons are often more important than those who wield them. You think Galiana will be upset when you're dead? No, she'll probably be relieved that a problem has been taken off her hands... well, other than losing Osen's magic. You're nothing but a pathetic pawn to her. A replaceable one at that."

"Shut your whore mouth," Rob spits out.

He gets a solid punch to the gut for that outburst from Flint.

I sense Rob is so filled with rage and focused on arguing with me that his walls are dropping, so I question him, hoping to make him think about the things we'd like to know.

"Do you believe Galiana was going to keep you around after she had me in her clutches?"

"She's figured out how to claim your powers permanently. Then she'll throw your dead body out with the garbage."

"And then what?" I demand. "She kills off all the supes? What's the point of this madness?"

"They're stealing our magic, so we're going to end them before they end us."

"We aren't stealing magic, you fool," Flint growls.

"We both know that isn't true. You think we didn't hear about what happened in the fae realm? We know that was just the beginning of the fae's plot to control all the magic in the realms. So we found a way for us to do it too."

"Stealing Jade's ability." Flint glances over at me.

"Fight fire with fire." Rob looks smug for someone with one foot dangling in the grave.

"How many others know about me?" I ask, worrying that I might never get to rest.

Rob bites his lip and refuses to speak, but I can tell by Maxum's raised eyebrow he's got an answer.

Then the question that has been burning in the back of my mind rises to the surface. "How did you and Galiana find me? I thought I was hidden by the pendant."

"You're so stupid." Rob laughs. "And so was your traitorous mother."

His insults bounce right off me. Why should he rile me with his hateful words? His actions prove he's only worth the time to make sure he's dead soon.

It irritates me that he knew my true origins before I did.

Great job, abuela. Ugh. It was so hard to get that she wasn't my grandmother at all. And although she was my biological mother, she wasn't really my mom. Even my sister didn't do a great job being a mom.

I sometimes wonder how I can be a kind and loving person when I didn't have a good example. Can't say I feel very loving right now.

*"It's in your nature, your soul, to be loving,"* Flint says through our mental link, reading my thoughts like a book. *"Sometimes it isn't nurture that makes us who we end up being."*

"Well, I want blood now," I say aloud for Arran and Maxum to hear. "It pisses me off what this bastard and Galiana did to me. And they hurt you guys."

"It's your revolting, violent fae and demon blood that make you a savage," Rob says.

I laugh heartily at that. "I wasn't a savage until you fucked with me. You prove witches and warlocks can easily be revolting and violent. Savage." I bite back a burst of fury from the injustices I've endured. "Do you think forcing a spell on me to be your girlfriend was anything less than sexual assault? And you call these guys monsters?"

"Believe me, I didn't enjoy being with you other than laughing about how I'd stolen your power."

I stand up, my limit reached with his bullshit. It stings even if I don't want it to. I wish I had thick enough skin that the thought of him touching me didn't make me want to scrub my flesh from my bones. "I'm done here. In case there's any doubt, you were so vile that I dumped your ass even while under your dark magic spell."

Rob opens his mouth with a rebuttal.

"We can kill him now," Maxum announces.

Rob's flustered, red face pales instantly. "You need me," he pleads to stall his fate.

"I *never* needed you," I snarl in his face.

Maxum grips Rob's head, and Rob screams.

"Keep your psychic guard up to block his ghost," Flint warns.

Rob's eyes bulge with pain and turn glassy as the life drains from his body. For a moment, I'm tempted to destroy his soul, but I don't feel like it's my place to go that far. I sense karma will come for him in the afterlife.

I see a gray wisp slip into the astral plane and beyond.

Finally, I'm free of him, but I know there's at least one more person we need to eliminate before we can relax.

"Are you okay?" Calder comes up behind me from the bedroom, his hand landing gently on my lower back.

Osen is right beside us, glaring at the warlock who stole everything from him.

"Not yet. But I'll be better when we take out Galiana." My jaw is set with my determination. Then I soften as I look at Osen. "You?"

He nods. "We can talk later." He presses a kiss on my temple.

"Jade's right," Maxum says as he washes Rob's blood off his hands in the kitchen sink. "We need to cut off the head of the snake."

"Did you get any intel?" Osen asks as he walks up to Rob's corpse and shoves his chair over, so the body crashes to the floor with a wet thump.

"A bit." Maxum frowns, drying his hands on a dainty tea towel. "The good news is that it doesn't appear that Galiana trusted many people with her plan to use Jade's magic. There is one other witch I saw briefly flash in Rob's mind. Not even Floofers knew all that was going on with you, just the mediumship, not the unique powers."

"But how did they even find Jade in the first place?" Arran demands, his werewolf quelled, relaxing with the death of the warlock.

"When you asked him about that, I saw your books," Maxum says to me. "Do you know why that might be?"

I shake my head, but I think about his question. How could my books lead them to me?

"Even before I met Rob, I had weird dreams. So I was probably seeing a ghost's memories. Maybe I wrote about something that happened in real life? But even then, I'd be shocked if witches are reading smut by an indie author. Besides, it isn't like I just wrote verbatim what happened in my dreams. Or... I don't think I did."

"We can't rule that out completely." Maxum gives me a grin and a wink. "It's a great excuse to take the time to read your books like I've been meaning to."

It's so weird it makes me jittery to think of him reading my work. Maybe because it's a whole different kind of vulnerability. Authors pour their souls into their worlds, often giving up a normal life. And for those keen enough to read between the lines, they can see past the words and right inside an author's being—their wounds, healed and unhealed.

I worry Maxum won't like my writing… that he won't like the parts that are me.

"Time to take out the trash." Osen bends to drag Rob's body out of the house.

"No," Calder snaps, catching his arm. "Go. Rest. We can deal with this."

Osen grumbles, but takes my fingers in his and gently guides me back to the bedroom. "You could use some rest too, sweet monster."

# 33

# TOGETHER SEPARATELY

JADE

*I*'m in a bit of a daze as Osen leads me back to the bedroom.

Watching Rob die was a mind-fuck. I think that's the first time I watched a human's life force leave their body. The effect was eerie, but oddly, I don't feel upset by it.

Now, an animal dying, especially a pet, would have me ripping my hair out and tears flowing until I was gasping for breath. Perhaps it's because an animal is pure, whereas Rob was corrupt.

A weight in my heart has been lifted. He was a threat to me and my guys, and to the supe population at large. I will no longer have to fear him breaking into my home and hurting me.

Osen leads me over to the bed, but stops me before I crawl in. I realize just how tall he really is as he towers over me. He's not as broad or as tall as Maxum or Flint, but definitely six-three with an athletic build. His long, brown hair drapes over the tops of his shoulders with a soft wave. His hypnotic gray eyes are light right now and not the dark charcoal of when he's feeding.

His fingertips trace the planes of my face as he studies me like I study him.

"It's strange to see you like this. In real life." He places a feathery kiss on my forehead. "You're more beautiful than you believe you are in your mind."

"And you look a whole lot better alive," I say with a smirk.

Osen's hands skim down my neck, and he slowly pulls the robe down and off my shoulders and unties the belt, letting it fall to the floor. He pulls the shirt over my head. Then his hands slide over my breasts, admiring me, then around my waist. He draws me close, dropping his head down to give me a soul searing kiss.

"I don't have the words to communicate how much I appreciate what you did for me. Being so kind to me when I was possessing you, then risking yourself to bring me back from the dead." He twists a lock of my silver hair around a finger. "And now, to be able to touch you and Calder... to love you both the way you deserve... it's beyond any fantasy I could have had about how this would turn out."

I'm blushing at his words. I suppose I've never been great with compliments. "I'm happy you're here with your pack." I pause, and then ask what I've been curious about. "Did you and Calder talk about what you both want moving forward?"

"We did." Osen steps toward me, further encroaching on my space.

I back up a bit. It's intimidating, having his commanding presence here in real life. My legs hit the edge of the bed, and my ass lands on the soft mattress behind me.

I look up, my gaze hungrily traveling up his bare muscular chest to his handsome face. I'm keenly aware that my mouth is almost level with the bulge in his pants.

His fingers comb through my hair and massage the back of my head as he gazes down at me adoringly.

I swallow as the silence continues. "And?"

"Do you really believe we wouldn't want you in any way you'd let us have you?" he asks.

I place my hands on his narrow hips and say, "That's not exactly what I was wondering."

"I think it is." Osen drops his pants, and his erect cock appears in 3D, not far from my face as I take in his thickness. "Calder and I don't want boundaries between us. Between all three of us. We'd like to continue our individual relationships, *and* we'd like to have a relationship that is all three of us being intimate together."

"I like the sound of that, but I'm worried. You already have an established relationship that I might intrude upon when I don't mean to."

"It isn't just about Calder and me together. We both will want alone time with you, too." His fingers tickle under my chin, and I smile. "We will need to make it clear if we need alone time with a certain person, such as a date or sex. And if there's no designated parameters, then the third person is free to join in."

"So if I stumble in on you fucking, I can just grab a dick and play?"

Osen growls with need. "That sounds amazingly hot. I might have to find ways to get *caught* by either of you."

My stomach gurgles, and I chuckle. "With the whole Rob torture display, I forgot to eat."

"I have something for you to eat." He waves his cock in front of my face.

"Uh, no offense." I smirk. "But I need more than a protein shake." Although I'd love to indulge in this, my shoulders slump. I'm feeling the fatigue again from all the magic that has been pushed through me. I wouldn't be able to actively participate in sex right now. I doubt I even have it in me to orgasm at all.

The bedroom door swings open, and Flint bustles in with a

food tray filled with all sorts of treats. He fully ignores the naked sexual energy of Osen towering over me. "In bed, both of you," he orders, then places the tray over my lap when I comply. "Eat." He folds his arms and stands there like a warden about to force feed us. "Osen, I remember you enjoyed almond butter and fig jam sandwiches." He points to the plate with two sandwiches stacked on it.

"Thanks, brother." Osen smiles widely and moans when he bites into it.

I eat some crackers and cheese, washing it down with some apple juice. Osen shares a bite of his sandwich with me, and I can tell by Flint's surprised expression it isn't a normal thing for the incubus to do.

*"Why do you look shocked?"* I ask Flint through our special mental link.

*"Incubi don't share food from their plates unless it's with a mate. I didn't realize his feelings for you were so profound. Even with Calder, he never shared before."*

*"So it seems I was meant to be with all of you."*

*"Fated, my Heartstone. I suppose I'm still surprised my entire pack is blessed with such a perfect mate."*

Not long after Osen and I finish our meal, Maxum, Arran, and Calder strut into the bedroom. The space isn't tiny, but it feels like that now with all the massive, muscly males crammed inside.

"Is he gone?" I ask, staring at my four beautiful guys standing in a line.

Arran rushes over and nuzzles into my cheek. "All gone. We've cleaned the house and our bodies of his slimy presence."

I wrap my arms around Arran's neck and breathe in his freshly showered scent of lightning storms and sage. "Where are we?"

"It's a property of an old friend," Maxum says. "He offered it to me as a safe house in return for a favor I did for his mate. It's good in a pinch, but we shouldn't stay here long."

"Why?"

"We're in the fae realm. There are too many nosey creatures that might sense your unusual magic since you're no longer contained."

I pat at my neck, realizing the concealment talisman is gone. It must have been lost in the fight with Rob at the cafe.

Then panic takes over. "What about my computer?"

"Right here, Heartstone." Flint points to the corner of the room. "I made sure to grab it."

"Thank you." My pulse returns to a normal pace.

I shift to get out of bed, and Maxum charges over, blocking me in. "What are you doing?"

"I thought we had to go because of my weirdo magic."

His large crimson hand palms my jaw, and he inspects my face and aura. "You're much more drained than you're letting on. Rest some more."

I throw out my lower lip in a pout. "I'm fine. I won't draw more attention than necessary if I can help it."

"Flint and I will create a few measures to dissuade anyone from coming too close." Maxum brushes his thumb over my still pouting lip. "In the meantime, you actually need sleep, no slumber party chats or playing hide the shadowcock with the incubus."

"Dude, don't shadowcock block me," Osen jokes and gives his friend a lopsided grin.

"Fine. I'll rest," I concede.

Maxum helps me slide on underwear and a large t-shirt that smells like Arran's.

Thankfully, the bed is enormous, and we have enough room for Calder and Arran to join Osen and me for a nap.

Because that's all it's going to be… a short, little nap.

# 34

# FEED ME, MI AMOR

OSEN

*I* hold my sweet savior and future mate, and she reluctantly falls asleep telling me, "Just a little, tiny nap."

But it isn't a little nap. Jade falls so deep, so fast that I can't even snag her subconscious to bring her into my shadowscape with me.

My magic is slowly replenishing with the intimate moments we've had since I was been brought back to life, but it's not quite enough to fill my magical pockets. I'm barely hanging on to my sanity and my life. I don't want to push Jade or Calder, and I definitely don't want to make them feel like they are only a meal to me.

It hasn't been easy. I suppose I've failed and pushed some already.

Instead of falling asleep and resting with her like I should, I study Jade's gorgeous face, and my heart swells with the gratitude I feel for her.

She didn't need to forgive me after I took advantage of her trust. Yet she helped me come back and made sure my relationship with Calder was going to survive.

I wouldn't have faulted her if she had turned her back on me or blatantly hoarded Calder for herself.

It's an incubi gift to sense the emotions of others, since we feed off powerful emotions, too. With my special sight, I can see this woman glows with magic but also from the massive amount of love in her soul.

I've never been one to feed from emotion, preferring the spicy flavors of sex.

Except now, my death seems to have changed me, and I'm just as willing to feast on experiencing the love that pours from this woman into our pack.

I want to claim her. I want to make her cry out my name as I make her come over and over on my cock. I *am* an incubus after all. The shadowsex we had in her mind was wonderful, but it isn't the same as feeling the warmth of her skin and the subtle, involuntary reactions of her body. I want to smell the fragrance of our combined releases. I want to taste the desire of her body on my tongue and in my soul.

I want her. Completely.

The guys have accused me of being obsessive, and they aren't wrong.

And Jade is my new obsession.

I'll have to remember to share. Just not today.

As soon as she wakes, I'm going to fuck her into oblivion. When I'm done, she won't remember her own name.

*Consent...* I must remember to get consent.

I haven't told her yet, but I need to. My shadows are already bonding with her. She is mine. If she were to reject that bond, I'd be torn into pieces and set adrift in the darkness.

I cannot live in darkness anymore. No, I need my lightbringer for my shadow. And she can truly be my shadowmate. I know a trace of my magic still resides inside her.

I didn't mean to leave it behind, but I don't think it's an accident. Maybe some part of her wanted to keep me with her.

I hope that's it.

Jade snores softly, and I chuckle like it's the cutest thing in the world. I suppose it's precious because of what it means. She trusts me—enough to have me inside her body and to be vulnerable with me. That's a big fucking deal. I don't even think my pack ever trusted me completely.

Calder didn't.

If he did, then he would have come to me when he was broken.

He trusted Jade more than me, even when he didn't know her to be anything other than a witch—a witch who might have killed me, no less.

Fuck. What *does* that say about me?

Guilt swims in my mind as I remember how I behaved before my death. I was secretive, stubborn, hotheaded, and reckless. I deserved to be the one cursed as a berserker more than Arran did, which is saying something.

I have to do better. For Jade. For Calder. For all of them. Earn their unwavering trust again.

I must fall asleep for a while. When I open my eyes again, the only light in the room is from the moon leaking in through the window.

Jade shifts against my body, electrifying me in a way that should be illegal. She groans when she wakes herself up. Her half-lidded eyes blink slowly, trying to remember where she is. "Osen?"

I squeeze her to my chest and kiss her forehead. "Here, my sunshine."

She grins sleepily and nuzzles into me. "What the hell is on my legs?" she says in a wary tone.

I glance down and see Arran in his wolf form, curled up and pinning down her feet with his huge body.

"Beast," I laugh. Then I see Maxum on her other side.

A hand slides over my hip, and I instantly recognize Calder's touch.

"Where's Flint?" Jade asks with a worried tone.

"Patrolling the area to make sure no one sneaks up on the house," Maxum grunts, and grinds his hips into Jade's ass.

"Who's going to guard my ass against your sneak attack?" she jokes.

"The only one with the authority to do so… *you*." He kisses her shoulder. "But go back to sleep for now. I promise I won't invade."

"I'm awake now." Jade sighs, rubbing the sleep from her eyes. "I'm overheated with the living wolf blanket."

Arran's wolf whimpers, but Jade sits up and gives his ears a good rub and coos over him like he's an innocent puppy and not the apex predator he is.

Beast is eating it up, thumping his tail against the bed, rattling all of us with the beat. I sense Arran isn't immune to her sweet talk, either.

"I'll get up with Jade," I offer.

Calder moves out of the way, and I drag Jade out from under a bratty wolf who refuses to lift off her legs.

I help her to her feet, and she says with a bit of amusement, "I've lost feeling."

"You can't lay on her like that," I reprimand.

The wolf covers his snout with his paws in shame. Fuck, even I know that's adorable.

"It's okay, sweetie," Jade says to him in a baby voice.

I lift her into my arms, and she squeaks at the unexpected action.

"I won't have you fall down on my watch." I carry her out of the bedroom and set her down on the long couch in the living area. I sit beside her and lift her legs into my lap and massage her feet. After a minute, I ask, "Better?"

She sits silently, staring at me with a strange look on her face.

"What? Something wrong?"

"No. It's just weird having you here. Really here." She quickly adds, "Not in a bad way."

I'm irritated by that comment, and I'm not sure why. Though when I think about it, I realize she's correct. It *is* weird.

I pinch my lips together, feeling awkward for the first time in my entire existence.

"What is it?" she asks. "Did I upset you?"

"I… I don't know how to be *me* anymore." I turn my face away, trying to hide my inadequacies.

"Hey?" Jade leans forward and with a gentle finger, she guides me to look at her. "You can talk to me. No judgment."

"I'm a selfish asshole most of the time. I fed off Calder and others only when it served me. And now…" I choke up and stop talking.

"What's different now?" she prompts in a soft voice.

"I don't want to be just a magical sex leech." I rub my eyes and feel the sting of tears. What the fuck? I don't cry. Shit. This must be the influence from dying and being trapped in someone who's actually in touch with their emotions.

When I don't go on, Jade says, "From what I've seen, you weren't *'just'* anything. Your pack meant more to you than a meal ticket. And they loved you too. You were a complex person with a full range of traits, both good and bad. Just like everyone else."

I sigh long and hard. "Jade, you don't realize that I'm the monster other monsters fear. I can destroy a person, get past any locks, and dive into any mind and bend them to my will. I have consumed people whole, leaving them an empty husk. I can rip the dirtiest secret from someone's thoughts or drive them to madness. I am *the* monster. And I'd understand if you broke the bond building between us now that I'm explaining this all to you." I look into her eyes, trying to implore her to grasp the truth in my words. "At my core… I'm just a monster who uses people for sex and magic."

"Are you though?" She frowns like she knows something I don't. "Tell me this, are your powers working?"

"Yes," I answer warily.

"Then why haven't you fed off me yet? Or Calder?" she asks. "If you were a mindless sex-machine monster, then you would have pressured me into sexual feeding or you could have *forced* us, as you say, but you haven't done that."

"Yeah, but…"

"No more buts. I need to hear what *you* want to be in this new life of yours. And don't tell me what you *think* I want to hear." She sits back and waits for me to answer.

I take a long moment to consider truly what I hope for. "I'd like to finally participate in life. During my death, I got a taste of how removed I really was. I had time to reflect on how I always pushed my pack away. But now, I want to be a proper mate to you and Calder. Sure, I was loyal to the pack, but I didn't participate. Engage. I mean… did I really know Flint at all? Not really. I want to truly know them. Be there for them." I shake my head, feeling like the asshole I am. "I'd like to be someone you come to for comfort and love. And I'd like it in return."

"And sex?"

"I mean, I'm not going to turn down sex with you and Calder," I confess. "But I don't want that to be the only connection between us."

"It isn't," she says, like it's a fact. Perhaps she's right. "We are connected through a freaking crazy bond of our souls and our experiences. We have spent hours in the shadowscape just talking."

I pull her into my lap and kiss her like she is my very soul that I need to merge with. Not for a feeding but because she's my mate.

"It's okay to ask for what you need in a relationship," she says, soothing me with soft strokes of her fingers over my brow and jaw. "Are you hungry?"

I growl with need. "Yes." My mouth crashes over hers, and I murmur as I claim her, pulling her to me. "I'm hungry for your body, but I also hunger for your love. I want to devour you so I can keep you safe inside me. I want to give you the worlds and share all the beauty in them with you." My lips brush over hers. "I love you, Jade."

"I love you too."

I pull her underneath me on the couch and cage her in with my body. I could use my shadows to pin her down, but I want her hands on me. Having her as a partner is a revelation. Only Maxum could thwart my paralytic power with his demon energy, not that we were physical very often. And now, Jade can give me that blessing and, by extension, give me Calder in a new way.

"How do you want me, sweet witch?" I ask, nipping at her lips.

"How do you want me?" she counters. "You know I can take pretty much anything you offer. Although I don't think I can deal with being whipped with a cane."

I chuckle darkly. "I might want to spank your plump ass, but I'll never want to chance leaving a permanent scar on you. Besides, I doubt this house is equipped with a full arsenal of toys."

My hand slips down between us and under her waistband.

Jade grips my biceps and squirms as my fingers find her wet center gliding over her clit. I press forward and sink two thick fingers into her cunt.

She lets out a tiny gasp, trying to be quiet for the others.

"Make as much noise as you need to," I growl. "I want them to know how much you enjoy me fucking you."

"Yes, sir," she says with a smirk.

My shadows slide around her throat, and her eyes widen. I hold her with enough tension for her to feel it, but not so much that she can't breathe.

My lips claim hers and our tongues stroke against each other. My fingers pump into her wet heat with an obscene squelch of how needy she is for me.

I lift up her shirt. Two more shadowtendrils slide under, winding around her breasts, squeezing in time with my thrusts. She undulates into my hand, taking as much as I'm giving and more.

Curling my fingers and circling her clit with my thumb, I bring her to a climax. Her body shudders and she moans, clenching around my fingers. "More. I need to feel your cock inside me."

"As you wish," I pull back, tearing her underwear from her body.

She pulls her shirt over her head, revealing her full delicious breasts, while I yank off my sweatpants.

My shadows seep out of my body, reaching for her, needing her.

She purrs with delight when she studies my muscular body and monstrous incubus tentacles in the moonlight. "You're beautiful," she says with awe.

I blush at her praise. I don't think I've ever had anyone say that about me before. Certainly never about my paralyzing shadows ready to pounce, claiming a victim.

Is she a victim?

I wasn't lying. I am the true monster in the pack. Yes, the others have killed and maimed, but they're also honest about it. I've manipulated and bullied. Even Maxum, with all his demon nature, wouldn't have blatantly used people the way I have. He just kills them by ripping them to shreds or scrambling their brains. But never for fun, always with a purpose.

When I was killed and shoved into Jade's mind, I changed.

Perhaps it had a lot to do with being separated from my magic and my body.

I don't want to be the monster I once was.

Can I learn to be giving and compassionate? I was able to when I was inside Jade. Can I do the same at her side?

"Um... should I call you handsome instead?" Jade asks, biting her lip and watching me with a vulnerable expression.

She is bare to me in every way. I spent all this time getting to know her. After talking and dreaming together every night, I know her better than the others do. She might even know me better than all of them put together, too.

Fear crawls up my spine and constricts my airway.

*Will I fuck this up?*

"Call me anything you'd like," I say with a lopsided grin, pushing past my insecurities. If I plan to make this work, I need to be honest. It's what Jade values above almost everything else. "Goddess, I don't deserve you."

"Because you've done bad things?" she asks, reading me like a damned book.

"Am I that predictable?"

"I know you, Osen. And yeah, you're playing hard into the '*Am I Redeemable?*' trope right now," she says with a wicked grin.

I cross my arms over my chest, and her eyes eat up the sight of my muscles. It makes my dick ache with pride and the need to satisfy her.

"Poking fun at the recently dead guy, huh?" I tease back, but with an edge so she can sense I'm not completely joking.

"You can poke me." She points to her vagina. "Right here is a good spot. Or here." She indicates her mouth and licking her lips. "Dealer's choice."

I bark out a laugh. Because yeah, she's antagonizing a monster incubus into having sex with her. It's ridiculous.

Without warning, I descend on her. My hands wrap around her thick thighs as I wrench them wider for me so I can dive

YVE VALE

into her wet pussy. My shadows capture her hands and hold her down. I kiss the living hell out of her.

I pull back and see her eyes are wild with lust. "Is this what you want? Me to fuck you like a madman? To lose my mind?"

"Yes!" She heaves her chest up to rub against my torso. "Fuck me like you need to."

I slam into her channel, and she sucks in a breath. Her cunt flutters around my length, adjusting to my thickness. I slide out slowly to the tip, then thrust back into her. And again.

Her eyes roll back into her head with each thrust as I grind against her clit.

She murmurs my name over and over, thrashing her head back and forth while I work her into a manic state, edging her with my calculated rhythm. My magic feeds on her sexual excitement. My shadows torment her with a mix of gentle and gripping touches, sipping her pleasure like a fine vintage.

"Please, Osen," she cries, panting beneath me.

My mate is a beautiful mess, writhing and sweaty with need.

"Please *what*?" I ask, biting her lip and then sucking the pain away.

"Please, let me come."

I release her hands, and they are instantly on my body, searching and exploring every hard plane of my flexing chest and arms as I pound into her. Nails dig into my back, carving her will into me.

My own desire unleashes inside me. I lose all restraint and fuck her with abandon. The couch rocks into the wall with each of my thrusts. It's as if I'm trying to crawl back inside her body through her pussy. I want to be one with her again.

"Jade…" I grit out as her body clenches around my cock, milking me.

As I spill inside her, I gaze into her glowing green eyes and discover a bliss I've never experienced in all my years. I feel truly, unconditionally loved.

My shadows soak up all the pleasure, the desire, the love we've created together. The energy around it is unmatched… like it's a work of art.

I absorb all her affection and feed that dark place in my heart that has been closed off for far too long.

My shadows intertwine with her soul's brilliant light. We bond. Light and dark. Yin and yang. The other side of the same coin.

She is my perfect shadowmate.

We are the two in one.

I just hope I haven't cursed her by being linked to me.

## 35

---

# GROUP DYNAMICS

JADE

*B*eing with Osen in real life is… intense.

I can't say if it's the merging of what felt like our essence, or if it's doing things that have only taken place in my mind, but the energy between us feels different. Binding.

His eyes swirl with dark gray clouds as he hovers above me. He hums and gives me sweet little pecks over my face, admiring me and cooing sweet *somethings*. Because they aren't sweet nothings. No. Nothing he does is nothing.

Especially when it comes to affection. In all my visions of him, he'd never shown this warm intimacy. But I had only seen him with guys. Maybe it's different because I'm a woman.

He lifts off me and sits back on his heels as he admires his cum leaking out of me. His fingers push it back inside.

"*Fuuuuck me,*" someone hisses in the room.

We both snap our gazes over to see Calder with his cock out, stroking himself and watching us. His eyes are filled with desire and angst. He wants to be smack dab in the middle of this.

"You enjoy seeing our mate well-fucked?" Osen asks as he sinks his fingers into my pussy, pressing his release back inside me.

"With all five of us, it's going to be her constant state of being," Calder says with a cocky grin.

"Looks like you could use some love too," I say, beckoning him closer with hooded eyes and a curling finger.

"Come here. Both of you. On your knees," Calder orders.

Osen and I share a surprised look because dom-Calder is fifty shades of hot.

"Wait," he says with a wicked grin. "First, lick that cream from her pussy and bring it over here and use it when you suck my cock."

I spread my legs wider, and Osen takes his sweet time, licking up his cum from my center. Then he knee-walks over to Calder. I follow right after, eager to see this play out and show them my love.

Calder presses the tip of his cock to Osen's lips. "Paint my dick with your releases."

Osen slides Calder deep inside his mouth and when he pulls back, Calder is slick with our essence.

Calder turns for me to take him in my mouth.

I taste the mixture of our salty, tangy sex and groan with the pure debauchery.

"Jade, up," our phoenix orders.

I stand, and Calder claims my lips and dives in, savoring all of us. He grabs the back of Osen's head and guides him to continue sucking his cock and taking him right to the root.

"Osen, you better feed off me, too. Understand?" Calder says with a commanding tone that sends shivers down my spine.

Osen swallows Calder into his throat like the pro he is and hums his agreement. His whole body swirls with shadows as his power is ignited by our lust.

Calder kisses me, running his hand down my body and

squeezing my tits. Then he smacks my ass before coating his fingers in my slick and plunging them inside me.

I whimper against his mouth, and he consumes the sound.

"Goddess, yes." He grunts. "I almost came when I was watching you together. But this is so much better."

I notice Osen's shadows aren't binding Calder. He's careful not to trigger his PTSD and keeps his touch light. And so do I. My hands are on his chest and bicep as he works up to his release.

"Fuck!" Calder shouts, thrusting into Osen's face. After his ridiculously long climax subsides (thank you incubus power), he pulls Osen to his feet and pants with such joy. "I love you both so much." And then we all three collide in a sloppy kiss.

As the sun rises, Flint returns from his patrolling and Maxum takes to the sky for his shift.

Flint smiles at me with my head in Calder's lap and my feet in Osen's as we relax on the couch. Calder's fingers comb through my hair. Osen skims his hand up and down my legs.

"You all look cozy," Flint says before dropping to his knees in front of the couch and giving me a gentle yet passionate kiss. "Hungry?" he asks as his finger traces along my neck to my cleavage.

"For food? Yeah." I give him a wink. "I don't have the energy to help, though."

"No need, Heartstone." Flint stands and walks over to the open kitchen. "We should be careful not to tire you so much that you can't even stand."

"I can probably stand, but I'd walk funny," I say with a chuckle.

Osen smacks my naked ass and growls with approval when it jiggles in reverberation. When I glance at his face, he snaps his jaws like he's going to bite it.

Arran enters the room and pops Osen on the back of the head. "Biting her ass is *my* job, shadowcock."

"I can bite her too," Osen pouts.

Arran growls and lies on top of me, crushing all three of us. "Missed you," he whispers over my lips as Osen and Calder try to extricate themselves from the couch.

Osen uses his shadows to lift both of us and then sets us down gently after he and Calder get to their feet.

Then Osen wraps his shadow tightly around Arran's throat, leans down, and says over the shell of Arran's ear, "You hit me again, and I'll hold you down and fuck that pretty ass of yours."

"Promises, promises." Arran winks at me. "Jade might like that too much."

Osen barks out a laugh and smirks. "Yeah, I can sense her arousal around that thought. But I'd rather have her or Calder now. No offense, puppy."

Arran launches off me and at Osen. They tussle for a moment, getting out some pent-up energy. They break apart, splayed flat on the floor with wide grins on their faces.

Looks like some good ole fashioned Greek nude wrestling.

"I missed you, dickhead," Arran pants out.

"Same." Osen gets to his feet and gives Arran a hand up.

Flint is filling the dining table full of fruits and pancakes. I roll up to a sitting position and barely have time to stand before Arran has me in his clutches and sits down, placing me in his lap. It's weirdly natural to be naked in front of them like this. And with Arran's shifter body radiating more heat than a normal person, I'm mostly warm in the slightly chilly house.

Arran grins with pride to be the one feeding me, but the others offer me bites from their plates as we eat.

With a bit of food in me, I find I'm regaining my energy.

Then I wonder what rejuvenates my magic. I feel some part of me charging up with the feeling coming through my bonds. Can love power me?

I muse aloud, "I don't have just one kind of magic in me, but three. Does that mean I have to use three different methods to charge each one?"

"Well, rest, time, and food will recharge almost all supes and witches." Osen explains. "But it's slow going and doesn't help if you're in a war zone."

"Witches usually charge by the nature of their magic," Arran adds. "For example, green witches need to be outdoors or gardening. Your witch heritage is from a lust witch, so you would be like an incubus—feeding off sexual energy and desire."

"Hmm. Do you think that's why I gravitated to writing smut?" I ask.

"Probably," Osen agrees. "We should ask Maxum or Darius what might fuel your demon side."

"And the electric mage stuff?" I ask.

"Lightning storms are the fastest, natural way," Arran answers. "My old Shadowcraft Academy professor said that electric mages can also use power outlets from the human realm in a pinch, but that can be dangerous."

"But any friction or spark of energy will do to some extent," Osen adds. "Like churning water or a spark of fire. Winds. Even the sun. Hell, maybe even fucking. It's one of the more versatile powers. Some of the more powerful mages have been able to pull magic from the ethers to recharge."

"Cool." I study my hands and wonder what kind of power I can channel.

"Speaking of which… How are you doing since you've recharged your magic?" Arran asks Osen.

"Surprisingly good." Osen flexes his hands. "Almost as good as before."

"I'm feeling strong enough to travel." I slide off Arran's lap and stretch. "We can head back to Amira's place now."

"First, we need to finish our errands and grab some more supplies," Flint reminds me as he comes up behind me and wraps his arms around my waist, holding me close. He's so solid that it feels like I have the strength of an entire mountain at my fingertips.

I glance down at my body and remember my clothes were torn in my fight with Rob, and then further destroyed by my passionate lovers. "Uh, I'll need clothing for a public appearance."

"Oh, yeah. Maxum grabbed some clothes for you from the lake house before we left." Arran guides me down the hallway, pulling me away from Flint. "I'll help you shower and dress you."

"*I'm* capable of doing these things." But I grin happily after my half-hearted protest, because doing them with Arran sounds much more fun than alone.

"Hmm." Arran rubs his chin thoughtfully, but with a mischievous gleam in his eyes. "Not sure if you've recovered yet. I should be there to supervise."

He herds me into the bathroom like a border collie. I can't stop laughing at his antics. I love this silly side of my werewolf. And I sense he loves the idea of playing and having me alone for a moment.

This brings up an issue that I've only had to deal with as a *Why Choose* author, but now I must juggle in my real life. How to make sure I give so many men my attention.

I worry again that I'm going to fail at this. I could barely handle one guy, even if he didn't really want to be around me much.

"Hey, sweet mate." Arran brackets me in with his muscular arms against the sink vanity. He presses his forehead to mine. "Don't fret."

"Do you know how I'm feeling?" I ask, meeting his golden gaze.

"Yeah. Mate bond and all that."

I avert my eyes, feeling crappy. "I should tune in more to

our bond. Also protecting you from my emotions. It's like I'm on a rollercoaster lately."

He places a finger over my lips and gives me a sad smile. "Don't hide your emotions from me. It's my role as a mate to be there through all of it."

"I'm messing up this mate thing."

"My moon, I only have you to focus on. You have five bastards with all our chaos and baggage. I'm happy you've been able to block out our possessive, violent minds over the last couple of days, especially as we dealt with Rob."

"But I didn't mean to!" My head drops to his broad shoulder.

"Sweetheart, we are all charged up with emotions and with our mate bonds clicking into place. Once we settle into them, we'll find our rhythm. Osen just returned from the dead. Calder just got the pieces of his soul back. Of course, you're going to be there for them. I suspect you'll give a big chunk of your energy to Maxum when you finally solidify things between you two. It's the nature of this dynamic."

"Logically, I know you're right." I say, and he puffs out his muscular chest. "But please let me know when you need me," I plead.

"Wolf shifters are very touch oriented. Even a brush of your hand or a snuggle will ease a lot of my tension. And when I need more, I'll just chase your plump ass down and fuck you in the woods."

I burst out in laughter. "Deal."

"And the same goes for you." He snags my gaze and holds me hostage with his golden eyes. "Come to me with anything you need. To talk, to snuggle, to fuck. Whatever it is."

Through my bonds, I sense Flint's love enveloping me, echoing Arran's sentiment. I idly wonder how it will feel when all the bonds are fully formed. Will I be overwhelmed? Or will it become as natural as breathing?

Arran turns on the shower to let it warm up, which is instantly.

"Wow. Fae plumbing is great!"

He guides me into the shower stall. "This one has a few great spells on it."

Arran proceeds to make me properly filthy and then ensures I have all my bits clean before we get back out.

# 36

COMEUPPANCE

JADE

*A*fter my shower, Arran and I discover Maxum pacing in the bedroom.

My handsome demon watches silently while I get dressed in leggings and a long sweater. He's uneasy.

I pull on an expensive pair of new boots that I definitely didn't buy, so they must be something Maxum purchased before we fled the lake house. "Thank you for grabbing some clothes for me."

Maxum grunts, obviously distracted.

"What's up?" I ask, stepping closer to grab his attention.

"I had time to think while being on watch." He pauses his pacing to hover over me like the towering possessive male he is. "I don't like that Rob found you so quickly. I'm worried about Galiana tracking you down. She will try to use you. Or if you no longer serve her plans, kill you. She's far more powerful than he was, and she has stolen cubi power, too. Maybe most of her witches don't know what exactly she's doing, but they *are* willing to die for the anti-supernatural cause."

I rest my hands on his forearms and stare into his obsidian eyes. They flame with anger, and for the first time since I've known him, I see genuine fear behind them.

Fear for me.

"After eight hundred years of being alive, you should know that worrying doesn't help," I tell him.

"This is the first time I actually give a fuck about what happens in my life. If we lose you..." He swallows down his strangled voice and can't continue.

"Maybe we should go on the offensive and hunt her," I suggest.

"No," Maxum and Arran growl in unison.

Dang, why do I love a protective male so much? Maybe because I don't want to be the only one fighting for my survival. It's the first time someone has cared like this in my life's history. Not even a few months ago, I would have scoffed at the idea of trusting someone enough to help me, but these guys have convinced me that sometimes we can have faith in someone other than ourselves. I not only have one guy to lean on after all the years of pain and loneliness, but five. Maybe because of this, I feel invincible. I want to end this shit so I can be happy with them.

"As smokin' hot as that growly moment was, I still think we should consider taking action and gain the upper hand instead of being at her mercy."

"Okay," Calder's voice chimes from the doorway, with Osen and Flint standing right behind him. "But hypothetically, how do we entrap her? Because we need a plan, not a prayer. Look at what happened to Osen because he went full gangbusters without thinking it through."

"Hey!" Osen protests, then frowns, rubbing his mouth. "Alright, fine. I deserved that."

After a brainstorming session, we pack up our things and leave via a demon portal. We travel through a few places before we end up near the edge of a quaint New England town. I can see the State Park not far in the distance. When we scoped it out earlier, we found it empty of tourists, a blessing if our crazy plan works.

"We stick together," Maxum orders, leveling his gaze at me.

"What?" I grumble. "When have I wandered off?" I rub his huge arm. "I'm going to stay real close to my big, meanie demon so he can keep me safe."

He growls and yanks me to his side protectively. "Fucking right you are, sweet monster."

I chuckle, but nod. "I'm not dumb. All this kicking ass stuff is way above my pay grade."

"That isn't necessarily true. You're powerful," Osen argues. "But as Calder pointed out, there's safety in numbers. And it's likely the witches will have them on their side."

In their glamour to make them look like your run-of-the-mill insanely hot guys, they crowd around me like fierce bodyguards. We get a few strange looks from people, likely wondering if I'm some celebrity with my entourage of supermodel bodyguards.

Alas, I'm only known in the spicy romance world, and apparently now I'm making a splash in witchy society, too. *Yay, me.*

We make our way through the streets, hoping to attract the attention of any local or tourist witches. Do witches go on road trips? Witch retreats? Do they have coven support group meetings with donuts and old coffee? Do they gather around the water cauldron and exchange gossip? Whispering, *"Did you see Martha try to substitute the eye of newt for gecko? Goddess bless her heart."*

Okay, plot bunnies are now officially loose. I want to write an office witch romance. Should it be enemies to lovers or billionaire boss? Both?

I need to refocus…

Maxum tells us there are rumors that indicate there are a few witches and warlocks from the ASO living in this area.

When our parading doesn't seem to get a reaction, we move to Plan B.

Without my containment necklace, I can't risk handling my computer. So the task lands on Arran's shoulders since his magic rarely affects electronics, and he has some familiarity with them.

Besides, he's familiar with my actual computer—the sneaky spy. I idly wonder if he did a deep dive into my search history. Geeze, I hope not. A smut author's browsing history is not for the faint of heart. Graphic sexual images, weapons, poisons, bondage, torture, how to kill someone with almost anything I can think of, and ways to dispose of a body are only a few of the nefarious topics. It suggests the makings of a very bad person.

At the park, I talk him through setting up my travel router and logging onto my computer.

All my guys are standing in a circle facing outward to keep watch for an attack.

Fortunately, we've already set up this place with magical booby-traps and other surprises.

With my enhanced vision, it isn't too hard to see over his shoulder from a few yards away. "Check my email. Rob sent me a message. When I opened it, not long after, he showed up."

Arran snarls when he opens and reads the email. "What? You *never* belonged to him! I wish that bastard wasn't dead, just so I could kill him all over again."

"Samsies, babe, samsies," I quip. "Any other emails?"

"Uh, nothing that looks odd."

My computer chimes with a notification from my social media account.

"Click on the messenger icon. And tell me who just messaged me."

"I see a bunch of unread messages from what looks like a few other authors," he answers. "And just now, it's someone named Minerva Marvin. It's a request to video chat."

"Odd. We've never done that before." I pace behind Arran, wondering what this means. "Decline the invite."

"She's asking what's wrong… why she hasn't seen you online. She's worried."

"Reply to her via text," I dictate to him.

> Jade: A lot has been going on lately. Turns out my ex is a psycho.

> Minerva: Are you safe?

> Jade: Yeah. Just had to leave town.

> Minerva: Where are you?

Warning flags are flapping wildly in my mind. But we are fishing to see if we can catch a witch. Maybe Minerva is one, or maybe she's just an innocent, yet naughty, paranormal author.

Telling her where I am is a test and a trap.

> Jade: I'm in a little town on the East Coast.

> Minerva: Oh, I know.

Suddenly, we're surrounded by witches and warlocks. None of us move, everyone waiting for the other to throw the first magical strike.

A pretty witch saunters forward a few steps, and an alluring energy floats off her and curls around us. I almost snarl. It feels like she's trying to sway my guys to her will.

"Hello, Jade."

"That's the fucking witch that tortured me!" Calder cries out.

Flint holds him by the arm, keeping the violence at bay. For another few moments at least.

My blood electrifies with his claim. I'll kill her for what she's done, but first, I want answers of my own.

"Minerva?" I ask. I've only ever seen her author logo online, but never her face. Many spicy romance authors don't show their faces, so I had no reason to think there was something odd.

"Yes, that's me."

"I don't understand... we've known each other for years."

"We have, because I was the one who discovered you." She smirks and cocks her hip out. Another wave of magic swirls out. She's pure sex embodied, and she hoping to attract my mates' attention and enchant them.

"How did you discover me?" I demand.

"You're such an ignorant bitch. Your mother did you no favors, leaving you in the dark. How fortunate for us." Minerva shakes her head with a self-righteous sneer. "It was your books, dumb dumb. You wrote about things that were too accurate. About actual events. When we hunted down the author, we found you, a witch who had no idea that she was channeling the dead. Not just any dead though... supernaturals. With details that no one else should know about our crimes."

I think back and realize Minerva had reached out to me as a fellow author just a week before Rob showed up in my life.

"So you sent Rob and the hamster to spy and manipulate me," I surmise.

"It was going so well for our cause until you got rowdy and took up with this lot." Her gaze slithers all over my guys, appraising them. "But I have to say, for supes, they are pretty hot. I can't exactly fault an ignorant lust witch from sampling these tasty snacks. I'm sure they fuck like monsters, too." She eyes Arran like she's tempted. "Especially this one. My coven gave him exactly what he deserved with the curse, but I'd love to tie him down and unleash the berserker." Then she spots

Calder and licks her lips. "And how could I forget how easily I *fractured* this tasty morsel?"

Anger flares inside me. How dare she minimize what I have with them and what she put Arran and Calder through? "They aren't fucking snacks, you piece of shit."

"My my. Someone is feeling protective over their lust meals." Minerva doesn't seem to sense my bonds, or she dismisses them as nothing. She takes another step closer.

I feel her power wash over me, but I suspect my lust witch blood allows me to resist her.

Her voice turns steely and cold. "Galiana is waiting for you. Let's not keep her waiting any longer, shall we?"

She lifts her hand, and her people rush forward to capture us.

Electricity cracks in my hands, but I hide the magic since I don't want to use it while my enemies are watching. These witches don't seem to know about my unique heritage and powers. Maxum has warned me that the more others know, the more dangerous it is for me.

My guys surround me, fighting in a protective circle.

I watch helplessly as our magical booby-traps are destroyed by a few witches.

Osen's shadows shoot out and knock people to the ground several feet away. I know from my visions of his ability that he's not even close to recovering his full power.

Calder is throwing balls of fire with his flaming hands, but his attacks bounce off some sort of witch-shields.

In full gargoyle form, Flint's huge wings are taking an onslaught of magical blasts to protect me. Through our bond, I sense he's weakening.

Arran slices his massive claws at our attackers, dodging and weaving. But he takes more hits than he dishes out.

Maxum takes a bastard down with his mind magic. The warlock drops dead, crumpling at our feet after his brain turns to mush.

There are far more people on their side than ours, and I'm afraid we might not win if I don't join in the fray.

Dare I expose my electric mage ability?

Calder transforms into his full phoenix form and circles around us, keeping the witches at bay as best he can. He dives low to burn them with his fire, but most of his prey have strong magical shields protecting them.

A blast of magic hits him dead on, and he screeches with rage. He's blocking our mate bond connection to protect me, so I can only hope it's that he's pissed and not hurt, but his movements aren't as smooth as before.

I'm at a loss for what to do to help. My witch powers are passive and seem to be a low-level lust power and mediumship. Not helpful in my current situation. Unless I can somehow seduce ghosts into attacking our enemies. Which doesn't seem very practical, even if I could accomplish the feat.

For now, I'm crouched low to the ground like a coward or damsel in distress. I don't like either label. Maxum's warning echoes in my mind that I can't let anyone know what I can do. Only as a last resort. Yanking souls from bodies with this many witnesses who could escape isn't advisable either.

The ground vibrates under my feet, and I hear a chant droning from a group of witches not actively engaged in the battle.

I quickly glance at Arran and Flint, but I don't see them noticing it. Though I'm uncertain, since my eyeballs are rattling in my head.

"Fuck!" Maxum shouts.

Spinning to see what's happened, he stares at the ground below his feet that's shuddering. "*Nooooooo!*" He turns to see that I'm also affected.

He dives for me. As his body collides with mine, I feel the ground below us give way. Our drop ends quickly, and his huge body crushes me as we land.

The wind is knocked out of me. I suck in a breath before I

YVE VALE

can crack my eyes open. When I do, I see we're in a large, dark, concrete room with no windows. It appears to be empty. No people, no furniture, nothing.

Maxum pushes off me and curses a string of expletives that must come from the bowels of hell and fills me with dread. He slams his body against an invisible wall.

I glance down to understand where the little light in the room is coming from and find there's a glowing red circle with sigils surrounding us. I smell blood in the stale air.

"What *is* this?" I ask, but in my heart, I already know.

Maxum throws his body repeatedly against the invisible barrier that lines up with the outer circle, ignoring me completely.

"Maxum!" I cry, to get him to stop. I can tell he's only hurting himself, not making progress. "What is this?"

"A demon trap!" he snarls and slices at the air again, but his claws skid along the trap's boundary.

"Where are we?" My heart crumbles as I worry about my other mates. "What about the guys? We need to get back to them!"

He spins, eyes wide and feral, and I shiver with his madness. "Do you still feel your bonds?"

My attention drops into my heart, and I can sense the tethers linking my soul to theirs. "Yeah."

"Then they're alive for now." Pointing at the place he was attempting to break through, he then demands, "See if this trap holds you!"

I scramble to my feet. No one is down here, and if this trap doesn't hold me, then I can help us escape. I rush to the edge and smash against what feels like an electric fence. With a yelp, I'm thrown backward and crash into Maxum.

"Dammit!" He catches me as I fall and holds me while my dazed wits come back online. My vision is spinning, and I wonder how he could have bashed against the barrier like he did.

As he presses me close to his massive body, I realize we are both completely naked. "Where the fuck did our clothes go?"

"Part of the demon summoning process. It strips a demon of all possessions, so the summoner is protected from retribution." He snarls, "I'm going to *retribute* their ass."

"But how did they do it?" I shake my head. "Why didn't they do this before?"

Maxum slowly calms his breathing, and some sanity returns to his gaze. He considers my question. "There are only two ways to summon a demon like this. One is to know a demon's true name. Only a few of my family know my secret and it's solely in case of emergencies. Two is to have the demon's blood and a line of sight to cast the ritual. The second option is dangerous for the summoner, since a demon could catch and kill them before it's done."

"I heard witches chanting… that must have been it."

"And they must have found our blood at one of the battles we fought," he grumbles.

"But why target both of us?"

"I assume she was targeting me, and you were just pulled along for the ride. They were likely worried if they captured you that I might track you through our matebond."

"But we haven't mate bonded yet."

"They don't know that. And they wouldn't believe a demon would have waited this long to claim you."

"Uh, Maxum?" I hesitate because it feels wrong to confront him now, but I don't know if I'll ever get an answer. Things aren't looking good for our longevity. "Why haven't you bonded with me? If you don't want to, I'll try to understand, but I feel like I did something to upset you."

"What? No." He clasps my face to make me look into his flaming obsidian eyes. "It's not that I don't want to."

"Tell me what it is, then. This might be our last chance to clear the air."

He sags to the hard floor and sits cross-legged. Then he

invites me to sit, cradled in his embrace. I'd rather have his body as a seat than the cold concrete, so I slip down into his arms and find comfort in his warmth, sitting sideways so I can look up into his beautiful crimson face.

"I'm afraid for you."

"Because of rutting me? I don't believe you'd fuck me enough to kill me."

Maxum studies my face for a long time, deciding what he should confess. Then, with a sigh, he begins. "No. It's about the demon lords. There are so few females. If I mate you, the lords in hell might be alerted to your demon nature. If they come for you, they will kill our pack, use you for power plays, and attempt to breed you."

"Well, shit," I whisper. "Force me to make babies?"

"They'd likely first try to make you amenable to the process, so you weren't overly stressed and unable to impregnate. High-powered demons might try to stake a claim, or they might share you until someone's seed took hold."

"But you're so loving with me. How could they…"

"Most demons aren't as empathetic as I am. I think the decline in female numbers has made the males even more aggressive. Historically, demons often shared a female mate. But the problem has only gotten worse. And it's difficult to find a female outside of our realm who can procreate with us. They are valuable, but a commodity, a possession. It's likely the main reason your mother kept you and herself a secret. If either of you had been discovered, it could have meant you would've been taken to the demon realm until you were of age to take mates."

"Shit on a hellstick," I mutter, barely able to process what he just said. "So, when you found out about my demon blood, you felt you had to pull back in case they found me because of our mating."

"I couldn't be the reason they found you. I'm not… *popular* in the demon realm," Maxum admits with a heavy breath.

"Most of them would have no problem killing me and taking you. Mate matches are so rare that most demons don't even believe in them. They wouldn't respect what we have. They wouldn't understand, or care, that you'd be devastated by losing your bonded mate matches."

"Not that it matters what demons might do to you," a cold, threatening voice of a woman cuts through our conversation and echoes around the large, chilly space. "Your fate is mine to deliver."

# 37

## IT'S A TRAP!

JADE

Galiana slowly steps into the glow of the demon trap and looks like the villain she is as she glares down her nose at us.

Maxum clasps me to his chest while I sit in his lap. He angles away from the witch, hoping to protect me.

"Relax, demon," Galiana says with a dismissive tone. "I'm not going to kill her... yet."

Good to know that it's still on the table.

"Maybe I don't have to kill you at all." She shrugs like it's no big whoop either way.

"Explain," I snarl, wishing I could rip her head from her shoulders and dance as her still-pumping arteries rain blood on me like a fountain. Oh my. That was a bit dark. My demon blood might be kicking in.

"If you give me your power willingly. All of it. Then I won't kill you. And I won't kill your little harem."

I roll my eyes because I wasn't born yesterday.

Maxum captures my chin and speaks directly to me. "There *is* a slim chance your body *might* survive without magic. But she won't spare mercy on our pack."

"I figured."

Galiana slowly paces around our demon circle. "Minerva is going to have so much fun during her reunion with the phoenix."

Maxum and I launch at her in unison, snarling, and we're blasted backward for our efforts by the trap.

She tsks us as though we are poorly behaved children. "I'll let you sit with your options for a bit, and if you deny me, I'll allow Minerva her entertainment. I might join her and rip apart the other males. It'll be a party."

My heart pounds so frantically, I expect it to leap out of my chest and die. The thought of these two witches hurting my mates is too much for me. My breaths come in fast and shallow. The room spins.

Maxum gathers me up in his arms and rubs his warm hand up and down my back. "Slow, deep breaths," he guides me gently. He cups my hands over my mouth to curtail my hyperventilation.

"I'll be back in a few hours for your answer." Galiana smirks evilly. "Be smart. Make this easier on yourself and hand over your power to me." She saunters off and a loud, metal clang signals she has shut the door on us in here.

After several minutes, my breathing slows to a regular pace and my mind whirls with questions that tumble out of me. "I don't understand. Why does she need me to hand over my power?"

Maxum jerks his head in confusion. "That is odd. I was so pissed about us being trapped, I didn't question that."

"Do you think she captured the others?" I ask, fearing he will confirm it.

"As much as I don't want them hurt and killed. You can't decide based on saving them. If she's captured them, then she isn't letting them go, no matter how you negotiate."

I check in with my mate bonds, and I sense they are alive, but not okay. "I feel them, but they're emotionally distraught."

"Of course, they're distraught. Their mate has been taken from them." Maxum kisses my temple in a bid to relax me. "But their distress isn't an indicator of *their* captivity."

Bile rises in my throat, and I hold back the urge to retch. I don't know how to get out of here or how to help them. I just hope they're safe now.

Time for answers…

"How do we break out of a demon trap?" I ask.

"*We* don't." Maxum grumbles. "It has to be broken from the outside."

"Like anyone? Or does it have to be the person who cast it?"

"Anyone who has a touch of magic," Maxum sighs. "But we are warded inside. And I don't expect Galiana to drop it until you agree to comply."

"She must need my cooperation to take my power. That's probably why they didn't just take it before when Rob was dating me."

"Makes sense. From what the magical community understands, it's that *stolen* power fades. But perhaps Galiana found a workaround to keep hold of a willing donation."

"Coerced, not willing," I growl. "She's threatening you."

Maxum allows a smirk to fill his face. "It's sexy when you get protective of us."

I nuzzle into his shoulder. "It might kill me to watch any of you get hurt, especially because of me."

"I don't think she's a witch of her word. I expect she'll kill us as soon as she has what she wants from you."

I bite my lip and curse my luck. We're screwed. This might be our death.

"Why aren't you popular in the hell realm?" I ask, an idea forming in my head… likely a very stupid one.

Maxum blinks at that non sequitur. "Uh, well, I'm a disappointment in their eyes. I don't fit in there. I ran off to help weaker or underprivileged supes and demons. Let's just say that philanthropy and community assistance aren't a priority among demons. Most believe that I'm a traitor."

"Oh." I frown, not because of what he said, but that I hoped he'd have more supporters in hell.

"What are you thinking, my sweet monster?" he asks.

"You mentioned demons might sense if we bond. So what if we did, and they showed up and broke us out of the trap? If we stay here, we're both dead. But maybe we have a shot to survive with your people."

"*Survive*, yeah. But you might not want to survive a life with them as your masters." Maxum caresses my cheek and shakes his head, likely thinking of the worst possible scenario.

"We could escape the demons," I say with hope in my heart, and give him a kiss.

He returns my kiss, deepening it until we're panting with need. We've both been holding back our desire for each other, and it feels like something snaps.

"Fuck it. I don't want to go to my death without claiming you as mine," Maxum growls.

"Yeah, fuck it." I laugh wildly. "Why should we stop living our lives just because we are trapped in a demon circle in an underground witch stronghold who is hell bent on my demise?"

Maxum chuckles against my throat as he kisses down my body. "My teeth ache to claim you, but this is not the romantic setting I was hoping for."

"Hey?" I grasp his horns and make him look me in the eye just as his mouth gets to the swell of my breast. "It will be perfect because it's with you."

Maxum bites down on my tit and growls. "No. You are."

He snaps his gaze up to my eyes, and his are wild with need.

*Oh, my spicy ovaries.*

I've unleashed his true inner demon.

Maxum's claws scrape down my flesh, leaving thin lines behind, but never deep enough to bleed. Not yet, anyway. It's a good thing that I don't have any clothes, because they would have been torn to shreds.

His mouth is everywhere. In a frenzy of passion, he bites me with his sharp teeth and licks the sting away with his forked tongue. Like he's searching for the best place to mark me. He only avoids where Arran's mate bite silver scar glows against my skin and where Calder's talons mark my shoulder blades.

"Jade. I need you," he murmurs over my flesh.

"I'm yours."

It's all the encouragement he needs.

He stands, lifting me as he does. His arms hook under my knees, spreading me wide. Placing his hands around my waist, he lifts me so my pussy is level with his face. He swipes his tongue over my center and then plunges inside.

I grab hold of his horns out of pure instinct, but his bruising grip on me ensures I won't fall.

His tail fondles and prods my entrance. Then it slides alongside his tongue, filling me, stretching me. Something begins to vibrate inside me, and I cry out as my pussy clamps down on him.

I'm seeing stars and swaying as he moves me back down his body, then his cock slides into me.

Maxum powers up into my wet heat in one hard thrust.

I grip onto his neck and cry out as he fills me, hitting all my places to drive me wild. His thrusts are frenzied, and I sense he's on the verge of the rut he warned me about before.

His hand fists in my hair and he pulls my head backward, making me arch my body. He descends on my breasts, biting and sucking.

He's barely holding together his sanity.

"Take all of me," he growls.

His tail wraps around my waist, then slips down to stimulate my clit, then slides inside my channel alongside his cock, making me whimper with the stretch.

He bounces me on his cock and tail with his powerful body, grunting and swearing promises. His massive wings expand, crashing against the demon circle boundary. He's so consumed with claiming me that the electric zap of the magic doesn't seem to faze him. Or perhaps it's only adding to his experience.

My skin buzzes and sparks wherever we make contact. My own magical electricity is dancing with the current flowing through him.

"Fuck yes. Mine! All mine!" he chants as he pistons up into me with a fierce expression, like this is exquisite torture.

I'm thankful for my reinforced bones, because I'm sure he could easily shatter my hipbone with his intensity. My enhanced healing is going to help with the bruising and scrapes, too.

I love every possessive snarl and harsh grasp of my flesh.

"Jade," he breathes out, and I know he's close.

This desperate sound, his need for me, catapults me toward my own release.

"Come with me," he shouts.

And I do. My pussy squeezes, milking his thick cock of his cum.

He sinks his sharp fangs into my neck, opposite to Arran's mark.

I cry out with the enhanced pleasure the link brings.

His forked tongue swirls over the flesh, still pinched between his teeth.

I whimper and moan as his energy ties us together and my soul sings.

Tangled up in each other, we listen as our breathing evens out and our heartbeats return to normal. Such a strange quiet after all the frantic bonding, but I luxuriate in the sensation of his skin on mine.

Maxum releases his bite with a gasp.

We both glance down at his muscular chest. Over his heart, his dark crimson markings shift, creating an intricate knot with six threads.

"My mate," Maxum says in awe. "Look."

Over my heart, my chest now glows with the same symbol, just the size of a quarter, then sets into the same color as Maxum's mark.

The meaning of six is not lost on me.

We are truly a pack, through their bonds with me.

## LOST AND FOUND

JADE

*A*s we catch our breath, still tangled up in Maxum's embrace, a male appears through a portal outside our demon trap. The doorway snaps shut behind him, and his intense gaze lands on me.

A shiver goes down my spine. We've been found. Hopefully, this crazy plan doesn't backfire.

His long, silver hair falls around his broad shoulders. He's strikingly handsome, built, and tall, yet I'm not drawn to him like I am to my guys. Nonetheless, there's an unusual pull to him I don't quite understand. He doesn't look like a demon, but he definitely isn't human. He's likely in a glamour like my guys often wear in public, hiding a supernatural's otherworldly features.

Maxum quickly scans the room to see if anyone else has popped in, and then he stands us up and tucks me behind him protectively.

"Mine," the male whispers, ignoring Maxum completely and staring unblinkingly at me.

"No, mine. *My mate*," Maxum challenges with a low growl.

"Yes, of course." The newcomer waves him off, dismissively. "Jadeana? Is it really you?"

My eyes almost pop out of my head when he says my given name. I glance up at Maxum and find him jerking back in surprise and he pulls me tighter to him.

The male finally focuses on Maxum, and his brows knit in confusion. "Maxumus Drakona?"

Maxum doesn't answer to the name, but asks cautiously, "Do I know you?"

Footsteps echo from outside the room. Someone's coming.

"We don't have time for this," the male says and shucks his coat. "We need to get you both out of here and somewhere safe before other demons arrive or the witches discover me here." He eyes Maxum. "Do not attack me when I bring down this trap."

Maxum peeks down at me. Then he turns his gaze back on our presumed rescuer. "Swear you won't bring her to harm."

"It appears I've already inadvertently done her harm, but I swear on my firstborn's life, I'm here to save your mate from a horrible fate."

I don't like the sound of that. But something tells me to trust him. "Maxum, this is our chance."

"I won't attack unless you put her in harm's way," Maxum promises.

The male's hand glows, and he slaps his palm down on the circle on the floor. A wave of energy flares out, breaking the circle. He throws me his jacket so I can cover up my nakedness. As I do, he opens a portal.

We step out of the circle, but Maxum hesitates when the male waves us to the unknown destination.

The metal door flies open and slams against the concrete

wall. Galiana shrieks when she sees us escaping. A shadow tendril flies out like a whip.

Before it can hit us, an electric bolt shoots out to block it. Another crashes into Galiana, sending her to the floor.

It takes me a half a second to realize it's not my magic that did that. It's this mystery guy.

"Go!" the male orders and grabs my hand, dragging Maxum and me into the portal.

The doorway closes before Galiana can follow.

I glance around. By the magic in the air and the unique colors of the foliage, I deduce we're in a remote location within the fae realm.

"Come. We need to throw off any tracking."

Maxum snarls. "I know the drill."

We run a quarter mile, then pop through into a closed clothing store in a strip mall. The new guy grabs a couple pairs of sweatpants and two t-shirts off some racks and tosses them at Maxum and me.

Maxum doesn't protest, and we quickly put them on. I see a fixture with some flip-flops. Not the best gear, but I tuck my feet into them to protect myself from whatever running we have left to do.

The male tosses some cash on the sales counter and shrugs when we give him a questioning look. "Karma is a bitch. Don't want to test her right now."

"Who *are* you?" I ask.

"Don't you know already?" His face is strained, like he's in pain. "Sense it?"

"Are you... my father?"

He nods slowly.

"Are you Erwald Krathion?" Maxum steps closer, studying his face.

My father gives him a sad grin. "It's been a long time, Maxumus." His skin color darkens to a reddish hue and there's a subtle change in his appearance, but his red is not as deep as Maxum's crimson. His eyes become the palest green I've ever seen. His silver hair remains the same and I realize it's the same as mine.

My jaw drops open. "You two know each other?"

"I suspected Erwald was your father," Maxum confesses. "But didn't think he was still alive. When you mentioned you didn't want to drag him into our problems, I planned on hunting down what happened to him, but only after we eliminated Galiana and Rob."

"I've been incognito since your birth," my flipping *father* says to me.

"The last time I remember seeing you was almost three hundred years ago," Maxum adds.

I'm still in a daze when my father opens a portal for us to keep moving. Maxum clasps my hand and guides me through.

We rush through the protocol I've become familiar with when portal jumping and finally we end up outside a simple house in the mortal realm.

Erwald (it's too weird to think of him as my dad) ushers us inside the quaint cottage. The outside reminds me of a gingerbread house. The inside is painted dark reds, grays, and black and has gothic style furniture and artwork.

I realize he's brought me to his actual home. Although if he's a double spy, he likely has many hidden safe houses.

"I'm sure you have a myriad of questions for me." Erwald stands rigid as if he's facing a firing squad, waiting for what he expects to be a brutal interrogation.

I don't really have questions, not right now. I give him a once over now that we've stopped moving. He's handsome, but that's a common trait in the supernatural realm from what I've seen. If I were to guess his age by appearance alone, I'd guess he was younger than I am, perhaps thirty, but with a blend of confidence and weariness that reveals his true age, which apparently is hundreds of years old.

When I look for similarities to confirm that he's my bio

daddy, I find little, except for our silver hair. Even his eyes are a different shade of green. I'm definitely my mother's daughter in appearance.

"How did you find me?" I ask instead of the thousand other things I could inquire about.

"I was able to pinpoint your location through your mate bond with a demon. I was already on alert after I sensed your concealment spell was broken recently. I have been searching, but I couldn't get a reading on where you were located. I assume some powerful magic was hiding you."

My mind swings back to what I've been worrying about since my pack split up. Sure, it's fine and dandy to meet my father, but I need to address what's really important.

"We need to find the others," I say to Maxum.

"That is unwise." Erwald steps closer, as if to prevent me from leaving.

I glare at him with the force of forty years of abandonment. "I'm sorry. But are *you* telling me how to treat *my* mates?" I ask with a snarky tone, making up for him missing my angsty teenage years. He left his own mate and *me*, his daughter, so no, I'm not taking his fucking advice.

"*Mates?*" His eyes dart to Maxum, then back to me. "You have more?"

"Yes, five total. The last I saw them, they were being attacked by Galiana's main bitch witch. The same asshole who tortured and killed one of them."

"One of your mates is dead?" His tall frame collapses onto an elegant chair with an expression that speaks of his own grief about losing a mate.

We don't have time for catching up, and my tone suggests that as I answer him, "He's a phoenix and not dead, or I hope he's not, but that isn't the point right now. We need to rescue them if they have been captured."

"I'll go see if they retreated to our fallback location," Maxum says and brushes his thumb across my cheek in a goodbye.

I grasp his hand and hold it firmly. "I'm coming with you."

"I won't have you captured again." Maxum presses his body up against me as if it's betraying his idea to separate.

"If you will allow my presence, I can help retrieve your mates," Erwald offers.

Maxum's eyes snap up to take him in, finding him wanting. "I didn't think you'd want to get involved. Don't you like to lurk in the shadows?"

"How dare you?" Erwald growls, standing up from his chair. "You know nothing of what I've been through or what's happened."

"I know enough," Maxum throws back at him. "You didn't take care of your daughter."

"I did the only thing I could do to keep her safe." Erwald takes a few steps forward and I'm pretty sure this is about to devolve into a demon brawl.

"Enough!" I shout, stepping in between them with my hands out. "I need to find my pack. Now! So stop whatever the fuck this is and make me a portal before I zap your asses."

Erwald's eyebrows shoot up to his silver hairline, and he says in a wry tone, "I see you definitely inherited my demon side."

Maxum only smirks at that comment, looking oddly twitterpated with me over that. Then he clears his throat and opens a portal. "We'll drop out a few hundred feet away from the house and assess if there are witches in the area."

Erwald huffs but squares his shoulders and gives us a nod. "I'll stay close to Jadeana so you can focus on our surroundings."

With a grunt, Maxum grabs my hand and we jump through to the fae realm. We land close to the small home we stayed in last, and the portal snaps shut behind us.

Crouching down, we peer through the vibrant foliage but find no one wandering around.

"I sense brainwaves in the cabin." Maxum points toward the house. "But it feels muddled. I can't tell if it's our pack."

"Witch magic, if I had to guess," Erwald adds.

We hear a shout of pain coming from the direction of the house.

In my chest, my bonds yank hard. I bite back a screech of my own agony.

I know it's them inside.

My mates are in pain.

# 39

## DESPERATE TIMES

CALDER

*I* knew this plan would devolve into a shit show, but I had no clue how horrendously this would go.

Our beautiful, loving mate has been ripped away from us.

The sheer terror and rage that pulses within our pack makes it nearly impossible to think. Not that we have time to.

And now?

My torturer and murderer stands before me, and I can only see red.

The evil witch has the gonads to offer me a smug grin. "Miss me?"

I'm so insanely enraged I can't even reply to the taunt.

At my side, Osen snarls. Then he swings a shadow tentacle into *Minerva*. What a fucking name… It's an insult to the Roman goddess of wisdom.

My tormentor sails through the air and crashes against a tree with a loud crack, and Osen's shadow pins her to the ground.

"Go. Kill her," Osen says with a jerk of his chin.

I fly over, lighting my wings ablaze and towering over the witch as she comes to. After a hard blink to shake away her dizziness, she gasps as she catches sight of me. But Osen's shadows gag her and ensnare her wrists before she's able to unleash a spell to harm me.

I remember that fateful day when she had captured me and blocked my magic. The haunting memories fill my mind of how she tortured me and how she shattered my soul.

Thankfully, as I stand before her now, I'm whole again. More than just whole... I'm bonded to an amazingly magical woman and my powerful incubus.

My body lights up with my phoenix fire, making her eyes widen with fear. Good. I'm happy she's witnessing her karma come to pass.

I block out the shouts of battle behind me, trusting Osen will do his best to protect me while I sort out my vengeance.

"Your disgusting plan to permanently break me has failed," I inform her. "I'd love for your soul to experience the torture I faced. I should rip it out and tear it to shreds so you never find peace, even in the afterworld, but I'm not that cruel."

I don't say that it's my mate who could destroy a soul with a thought. If anyone else overheard the nature of her abilities, that would be disastrous.

The heat from my body's fire makes her sweat. Her skin is blistering. Osen's shadows muffle her screams from the intense pain. Thankfully, they are immune to my flames.

I shift my fingers into talons to plow gouges in her flesh. Her eyes finally reflect the dullness of acceptance. She knows that this is her end.

Normally I don't revel in killing, but this is a special case. I lean down and whisper, "I hope the abyss swallows you up and you're never thought of again. That is the final death, when no one thinks of you or mourns your absence. Though I doubt anyone will truly miss you. It will be instantaneous. You'll be snuffed out, and the realms will be better for it."

The increasing vibration of the call of death crashes over me, and I know it's time.

I slash my talons over her throat, and she is silenced forever.

But I cannot stop. I slice over and over until she's a heap of meat, no longer identifiable as once having a human form.

"Calder!" Osen shouts, bringing me back from my crazed killing.

I spin to see Flint on the ground, eyes closed. Arran is stumbling in his berserker form and falls as he swipes to take out another witch.

Osen is on his knees, his shadows flailing wildly. But his magic is dwindling, since it wasn't properly replenished for a battle like this.

He's panting with effort but holding on.

I use my magic to open a portal behind me. Not as fast as Maxum can make, but I'm grateful to have the ability right now, although it's draining what magic I have left.

A warlock holds out his hands over Arran's prone form, threatening. "I'll kill him if you step through."

He expects me to abandon my pack, but I have no intention of leaving them behind.

Osen glances at me and reads my plan from my eyes alone.

I throw a fireball at the warlock and blast him backward.

At the same moment, Osen uses his last bit of magic to snatch up Flint and Arran and fling them through my portal.

I drop my flames and grab Osen, throwing his arm over my shoulders and dragging him through.

As I turn to close the portal door, I find I'm too late to block my enemy's path.

I release my hold of Osen and throw fire at the five witches and warlocks who charge through, but I only take out one of them.

A warlock casts a spell at me, binding me in iron chains. I scream out in blinding pain. I'm hit with another spell, and my world goes black.

When I come to, I find Flint, Arran, and Osen are all bound in irons and passed out around me in the living room of the small house we used recently. Flint looks to be frozen in stone by a curse. Arran and Osen are bloodied and bruised, but still breathing.

This was supposed to be our place to retreat if things went sideways. Now we are fully upside down, asses up, and fucked hard.

I don't know how long we've been unconscious, but it's dark outside.

The witch, Galiana, steps in front of my line of sight and glowers at me. "Your little rat pack has been more trouble than I originally estimated."

"Same goes for your pathetic organization," I sneer back at her.

"Pathetic?" Galiana scoffs. "I was the one who cursed your rabid pet wolf. I gave Minerva the tools to shatter your soul. I've already killed your fuck buddy incubus once. And I'm going to make sure your death sticks this time, along with the rest of your pack."

That shuts me up. She's responsible for Arran's berserker curse? She's behind my soul shattering? This witch was behind almost all our trauma. Jade's mother's death. Osen's. And who knows how many other supes have suffered by her hand?

My jaw tightens to the point I expect to crack a tooth.

This doesn't look good for us. If Jade and Maxum escape whatever situation they found themselves in, they'll come here and get caught as well.

Then it dawns on me why we are still breathing.

Jade *is* free.

We're bait.

Galiana wants her prize—Jade's unique magic.

The bit of hope that glows in my heart with the thought of

Jade being free dies with the realization that she'll risk everything to save her mates.

I have no doubt she'd rather sacrifice herself than allow us to die.

Galiana is without honor and even if Jade negotiates her surrender for our release, the witch wouldn't hesitate to go back on her word and slaughter us all.

I must have faith that Maxum will keep Jade away and safe.

Just as I'm convincing myself he will, I sense my mate is close by. Osen and Arran stir as if they sense her too.

Goddess, no.

Run, my love.

Run and save yourself.

## 40

NOT TODAY, WITCH

JADE

*M*axum grimaces as he stares at me. He's itching to demand I stay behind, but knows I'll refuse.

"We have back up now. And I can help," I argue before he can say anything.

My demon glances up and looks at my father. Then his gaze lands on Amira, Darius, and Raithe. They didn't want to help at first, but when they heard about our odds, they agreed to take down the leader causing the most damage in the Anti-Supernatural Organization.

Amira admits she has her own beef with Galiana from back when she was an active member of the ASO. But the powerful witch on our side no longer uses destructive magic. So she'll be assisting us by laying down a suppressant spell to prevent our enemies from creating an escape portal or leaving the area. No one can come in or out unless Amira dies or releases her heavy-duty ward.

Fortunately, Raithe and Darius have no hangups about using

their magic to attack and kill these asshole witches and warlocks.

We go over our plan one more time, then Maxum gives Erwald a nod to set things into motion.

My father draws his electric magic, wrapping it around his body in what appears to be a shield. It crackles like one of those science globes you find in novelty gift stores.

We all race into position, surrounding the house. Since Maxum insists on staying by my side, we approach together from the opposite direction from my father. Raithe and Darius advance from the other two sides.

I send out a plea to the universe to protect my friends and loved ones.

"*Galiana!*" My father's voice booms, and I suspect he can be heard for miles. "You killed my mate, Patricia Rosethorne. Now, come and meet your end," he challenges.

I'm shaking with nerves. My father is risking himself for me and my mates. If our plan fails, my chance to get to know him might have come and gone in a blink of an eye.

Maxum tugs me closer to his side, sensing my anxiety.

There's a stirring in my bonds, and I reach out with my mind. "*Flint?*"

"*Jade?*" he asks, sounding confused.

"*Hang in there,*" I say. "*We're getting you out.*"

"*No. Leave, Heartstone. It's a trap.*"

"*We know. And it's okay. That's my father outside, calling to Galiana. Raithe and Darius are here too.*"

"*Jade, it isn't worth risking you and the others. Arran and Osen are egregiously injured. They may not make it.*"

The horrific news that my mates are dying takes me to my knees. I clutch my chest and already feel the pain of their loss.

Maxum falls to my side and pulls me into a crushing embrace. "What is it?" he whispers.

"Flint doesn't think they'll live."

"Fuck him. He's being a martyr to make sure you turn

around. To keep you safe." Maxum kisses my forehead. "We're going in."

I nod violently, my tears flying from my cheeks. "Yeah, fuck him. I'm saving his rock-hard ass."

Maxum smiles sadly, then gives me a kiss that feels too much like a goodbye.

"Witch!" Erwald commands with the force of someone who is accustomed to getting their way.

"Lord Erwald Krathion, so good of you to join us," Galiana says with an airy tone, as if he's a delightfully unexpected arrival at a cocktail party. "I'm about to kill off one abomination. Might as well kill off two. I'll finally have the father and daughter in the set."

*Lord?* That's something I'll have to inquire about when this is all over.

Maxum snatches up my hand, and we snake through the brush toward the house.

Arran's mate bond stirs in my heart. He's awake, hurting, and frantic with worry. I desperately wish I had telepathy with him. Instead, I send an emotion—hope—letting him know I'm alive and nearby.

I hear a blast go off at the front of the house, and the air vibrates with magic.

We make it to the outer wall of the house without incident.

Maxum stands up and peeks into the building's back bedroom window. He hovers his hand over the glass. His eyes close to concentrate on disabling the ward. After a moment, he smirks and gives me a wink.

I don't care if his saucy behavior is all false bravado. It helps me keep my wits as he swings open the window and jumps through the opening like a fucking acrobat. He somersaults in and bounces lightly to his feet. Dang. I wish I were half as graceful as I clamor up to the high sill. Maxum gives in to his need to help and pulls me through like I weigh nothing and sets me behind him as he faces the door.

Foot falls coming from the hall reveal our enemies moving about as they chant spells under their breath.

Maxum holds up two fingers to give me a head count. Closing his eyes again, he checks for Darius's and Raithe's brainwaves. Then he gives me the signal that they're in position. Raithe at the kitchen entrance. The hellhound should be waiting by the smaller bedroom.

I frown as I stare at the bed where I first kissed Osen. Will my incubus die again? Will any of us live? I'm under no illusion that the whole harem survives like they do in my romance books. In real life, we lose people we love.

Maxum captures the back of my neck and sweeps me in for a bruising, claiming kiss, and presses his forehead to mine. I can almost feel his words press into my soul. "We got this. Believe."

I want to believe.

I *have* to believe.

I pull back and glare at the door like it's stopping me from my happily ever after.

Maxum waits a beat as our enemies in the hallway move closer. He throws open the door and captures the first witch in his mind melting gaze, gripping her head.

She collapses and the warlock behind her is ready with a spell, but my protective electric magic flares inside me and shoots out of my palms before the asshole can hurt my demon, and the warlock crumples to the floor.

Shouts erupt as the rest of the ASO creeps are alerted to our presence inside the house. Mayhem ensues with magic zipping through the house.

I hear Darius's snarl coming from the other room.

Maxum blocks the way and is blasted with magic. As he moves into the hallway, I try my best to remember he's mostly resistant to witch magic. A powerful spell hits him square in the chest, and he's thrown backward, landing on the floor. He's stunned but appears to be alright.

Arran's howl fills the house with an eerie energy and worry fills me that either he or one of my mates are being injured.

Without a care for myself, I launch into the hallway on my way to save my guys.

Maxum scrambles to his feet behind me, and curses. "Jade, no."

That only spurs me more. What's happened to them that he doesn't want me to see?

Racing into the living room, I discover my guys all bound by toxic iron. Osen doesn't even have his eyes open. Calder's flames are sputtering, unable to light. Flint seems to be half stuck in a freezing spell, struggling to break free of its hold. Arran is in his berserker form and snarling at someone walking in from the kitchen.

With four other witches, Galiana comes into view and grins wickedly at me. "There you are."

The house rumbles with what feels like an earthquake. Flint's affinity is breaking through, even in his weakened state.

The witches stumble but remain standing.

Maxum darts around me, but Galiana is ready for him and, with a spell, he disappears, likely by a demon summoning circle.

"Fuck!" I shout. Hopefully, he's only been transported to a demon trap, and my father can get him out. "Erwald! She sent Maxum away."

I hear his curse and the firefight in front of the house dies off.

Raithe appears in his phoenix bird form, screeching as he snatches one of the witches and drags her away.

With a thunderous roar, Darius charges into the living area from the hall. He's an epic creature that looks more like a feral horse than a hound. His skin crackles with fire as he chases another witch from the house.

It's me against three witches. One of them being Galiana.

She's not to be underestimated. Not only is she powerful in

her own right, she has stolen magic on her side. My magic, and who knows what else.

But will she show off her incubus shadows she uses to kill supes in front of the other witches? Or does she wish to keep that a secret?

The spell she uses to steal magic and souls with my power comes to the front of my mind. I hadn't planned on wielding it against her.

Then I remember the innate power I have. Time to see if I can use it on all three witches at once.

I call upon my soul sucking power and visualize yanking the souls from all three. The two witches by Galiana's side scream. Their eyes widen as they sense their essence being ripped from their bodies.

They fall to the floor. I'm a bit dazed. Did I just kill two people so easily? Without a second thought. Without remorse.

I cannot linger on that. I release their darkened souls to the ether for the universe to do with them as it will.

"Wretched abomination!" Galiana unleashes her power on me in retribution. She unravels my hold on her soul and attempts to do the same to me.

She wanted to take my power from me with my willingness. Likely so she could keep it for a longer duration. But she's given up on my compliance and is going for brute force instead.

We're locked in a standstill, both matched in magical strength. Unless someone comes along to take her out, it will be a battle won by endurance alone. She has practice and experience. I don't.

"Your mother was a traitor and a whore," she taunts.

"You sent her on the mission to seduce my father. What the fuck did you think was going to happen?" I demand, while fighting off her hold on my magic.

Galiana's attention snaps to my mates. I see the glimmer in her eye that shines with the desire for their deaths.

A bolt of electricity shoots out from my body and knocks her backward. Her focus falls back onto me, and she sneers. I've gained a bit of an advantage and I feel her faltering.

Raithe's and Darius's shouts carry from the outside, fighting our enemies.

A warlock slips inside and charges for me.

Fuck. I'll need to divert my magic and I can't afford to do that.

Somehow, bound in iron chains, my berserker gathers enough strength to get to his feet. He tackles the man and clamps his vice-like jaws onto the warlock's throat, ripping it out.

I'm distracted though. Galiana takes advantage, wresting me with her soul stealing power until I fall to my knees.

*"You're stronger than her, Heartstone,"* Flint encourages me through our bond. My heart cracks seeing him still cursed and locked in his stone form.

My eyes slide over to Osen and Calder, barely conscious, but they seem to have been stirred by my presence. In their eyes, I see the echo of what Flint said, as if they've heard him.

I have to beat her, if only to save them.

A wave of power flows into me as if the idea of protection empowers me. Like I'm a momma bear.

Focusing back on Galiana, I tug hard on her soul, and she jerks forward. Her eyes go wide in surprise.

I only wish Erwald was here so he could help me kill her and avenge his mate.

As if being summoned by my thoughts, my father appears behind Galiana, stepping out from a portal. "Patricia and I had something you will never know, Galiana. *Love.*"

She flinches when she hears his voice at her back, and I yank at her soul.

He grasps her by the throat and wrenches her head clean off her shoulders as I simultaneously rip her from her mortal coil.

"That is for my mate and my daughter," he snarls, looking like the demon he is.

I gasp in shock at the pure graphic nature of witnessing something so bloody and violent.

Maxum jumps through my father's portal and gives me a look of relief when he sees I'm okay.

Amira rushes into the house with Raithe and Darius by her sides. Since she, Darius, and Maxum are the only ones who can handle iron, they work my mates out of their bindings.

Osen is first as he's the most affected. When he doesn't stir at all, I fall to his side, place my hands on his chest, and pour healing energy into him.

Calder yells to let him out next. He needs to be next to me, helping me. Yet, I don't know how he can assist.

But when his hands land on my waist and he holds me close, pouring his love into me, I know. My power magnifies, and Osen is coughing and opening his eyes within moments.

"What?" Osen sputters and sees the carnage that surrounds us.

Flint crashes into me next, like a freight train, knocking Calder and me over in his need to be near me.

I wrap my arms around him and kiss his beautifully monstrous face with horns and heavy brow. His tusks scrape against my cheeks roughly as he claims my mouth.

Serky-Arran leaps on top of us and officially makes it a dog pile. The berserker werewolf licks his huge, sloppy tongue over my face, and I shriek.

"*That's* what makes you yell out?" Maxum says with a smirk and a shake of his head. But I see the love and relief in his eyes, knowing his pack is okay.

I wave him over.

He drops to his knees beside me and crushes me to his broad chest. "I'm so happy you're alright, my mate."

"Mate?" Calder then glances at Maxum's chest and sees the new marking over his heart. "Thank goddess. It's about time, brother."

"Perfect timing," I say with a wink at my demon.

"Uh, Jade?" Amira calls out, breaking the moment of our reunion. "We should all leave, just in case Galiana's people send reinforcements."

We untangle ourselves from the ground, and it's clear that my mates are *not* okay.

Before I can race to check on my battered mates, I freeze as a presence presses up against my mind. At first, I panic, thinking it might be Galiana's soul trying to possess me.

But then I recognize the energy. My real mother.

*"May I speak to him before I move on?"* she asks me, sounding far away and so destroyed.

*"You're leaving?"* I ask, blinking back the tears because I thought she'd be a ghost forever, and I could get to know her once my anger at her betrayal dissipated.

*"Yes. I was only tied to the world because I needed to see you safe from Galiana. And now I know you will be happy with your mates."*

*"I didn't know you'd leave so soon. I wouldn't have pushed you away."*

*"I understand. And you were right. I should have been there for both you and your sister, but I didn't know how to be a good mother."*

I don't have a response to that. From what Amira told me before about lust witches is that they didn't have a strong maternal instinct. It wasn't in her nature to be there for me.

*"I know you did what you thought was best. I hope you find peace."* Then I suck in a breath.

"Erwald, my love. Thank you for avenging my death and protecting our precious daughter," she says through me.

My father's eyes widen. He races forward and grasps my shoulders, studying my eyes. "Goddess. With your spirit behind Jade's eyes, it's like seeing you again. She looks so much like you, my love."

"And she has your loving, compassionate heart. She would attempt to heal the realms by sacrificing her life, just as you tried to do," my mother says.

Is that what my father tried to do? There's so much I don't know.

"But I see a passion for experiencing life that you had," my father says.

"I have to go now. My soul is being called."

"No, please stay," he begs, pressing his forehead to mine.

"If I stay any longer, I will become a wisp, an echo."

My father kisses my forehead. *Thankfully*. I don't need that memory of kissing my dad.

"I've never stopped loving you, Patricia."

"Even in death, I've loved you."

A breeze moves through the room, and I whisper to my mother. "I love you."

I feel her embrace around me and the longing of being there for me for forty fucking years slams into me and cuts me down to my knees as I sob with the loss and pain of it.

My father catches me, and after a hug of his own, he hands me over to Maxum.

As my demon lifts me into his arms to carry me, I give my guys a worried glance, taking in their rough condition.

Erwald, Darius, and Raithe help to get my recovering mates through the portal.

By the time we go through protocols of various realm hopping and reach the boundary of Amira's property, we're all exhausted.

Darius has already done his 'hellhound sniff test' of my father, and Erwald's formally allowed inside the sanctuary under the old customs.

We place Osen, Calder, Flint, and Arran in the huge bed and, with their encouragement, I lay over them, giving them my healing energy. I only hope it will hold out and supply them with what they need.

Thankfully, my father is invited to stay on Amira's couch for the night.

With a lingering look, he reluctantly leaves me with my

mates. It's so strange to meet this male who is at the very source of who and what I am, yet I know nothing about him.

When I wake in the mid-afternoon, I grunt with the stiffness and utter fatigue that wracks my body.

Fortunately, my mates seem to be recovering.

Maxum left early this morning with Arran to get intel on Galiana's coven and find out if we have to worry about any more of her followers in the ASO.

They return moments after I wake, and I wonder if it's the mate bond that has me so tuned in that I sense when they are nearby.

"So? What's the verdict?" Calder asks, yawning and combing his hand through his messy auburn hair.

"My hackers and informants tell me that Galiana's faction is decimated," Maxum reports with a satisfied grin. "None of the witches know who did it, either."

"That's good," Osen grunts out and labors to sit up. "We won't have to expect fallout later."

"And that means Jade's secret is safe," Flint adds and squeezes my hand happily.

A knock at the door has all of us tensing, expecting the worst. Maxum is closest and opens the door, revealing my father's grim face. He's returned from his own reconnaissance mission.

"Jade's been summoned to hell," Erwald says in a tone that chills me to my bones.

# 41

# HELL FREEZETH OVER

MAXUM

My worst fears have come true. The lords of hell have discovered Jade's existence.

"I will *not* hand you over to them!" I bellow, all the while glaring at Erwald.

Flint tugs Jade to his chest. His wings unfurl from his back, wrap around them, and he turns to stone.

I'd do that too, if I could.

Jade yelps at the sudden cocoon around her. "Flint, my love, they aren't here to take me away." She pauses, then checks, "Are they, Erwald?"

Her father flinches at her use of his common name instead of a fatherly moniker of endearment. The bastard deserves no more since he abandoned her as a baby. I don't care if he thought it was the right thing to do. I could never imagine walking away from my spawn, who I created with my fated mate.

He should have been training her all these years so she

could protect herself and understand the threats in the realms she would face.

Then I remember if he had been around, Jade might not be the loving woman she is now. I know she had a rough upbringing, but I highly doubt Erwald and Patricia would have been overly loving parents. It isn't in their natures. Jade would have likely grown to be a battle-hardened version of herself.

If they had raised her, Jade definitely wouldn't have fallen for our ragtag pack. She'd have caught on to our true natures long before we got close and never have invited Arran inside her home or gone on a brunch date with me. She would have never let her guard down if she knew about all the dangers ready to destroy her.

We might be cosmic mate matches, but that isn't a guarantee for love or a bond. For all my anger over her parents' abandonment, I'm glad she was innocent enough of the supernatural world to give us a chance.

Flint's wings soften, and he draws them away to reveal our mate. "Don't go," he pleads.

Jade strokes Flint's square jaw, then looks at her father. "Do I *have* to go? Can we hide?"

"I don't think you can hide from them… not forever. Believe me, living on the run and in hiding is not a happy life."

A frown pulls at her lush mouth.

"I will accompany you as your representative and guardian," Erwald states, brushing a hand down his expensive shirt.

"Do you think they'll hear you out?" I demand. "Will they give your voice any more weight than five fated mates?"

"I hope they take it all into consideration," he says in a quiet tone that turns my blood to ice. "I'll give you a few minutes with your mates to decide if you wish to live a hard life on the run or present yourself to the lords for their assessment."

Jade gulps at the thought of meeting the demon lords. After Erwald closes the door behind him, we converge on our mate.

We're all arguing for the case to run. Except for Osen.

I grab his collar and shake him. "Are you insane?"

"Are you?" He knocks my hand away. "You both have to face this, or we'll never be safe or at ease again."

I snarl at him. I didn't even want to return to face the lords. I'm afraid that my presence will only harm Jade's case for freedom.

"We are all mated to Jade," Arran says desperately. "Doesn't that mean anything to them?"

"It means they could kill us all to break any claim on her," I answer and step back, palming my face and wishing Jade didn't have a drop of demon blood.

"I don't sense our deaths," Calder says in a quiet voice. "Not that it's proof of that outcome."

That gives me a bit of hope. "Flint? What do you sense?"

"I can't say since my protection gauge is broken to full strength all the time for her."

There is only one person who can decide. If I don't allow her the choice, then I'm no better than the monsters I left behind all those centuries ago. "Jade, what does your gut say?"

She takes a moment to consider the question. "We go, but be prepared to escape."

"Erwald can portal even into the royal chamber, since he holds the title of a lord," I say. "We have to trust he will help us if it becomes necessary."

We say our goodbyes to Amira, Raithe, and Darius. No matter what happens in hell, this will be our last day to seek shelter here. I've already taken Jade's magical creatures somewhere safe, so they won't be harmed if things go fucking wrong.

Darius escorts us outside of Amira's boundaries. Jade's eyes well with tears for the surly hellhound, and he begrudgingly accepts a goodbye hug from her.

"Are you sure you don't wish me to come along?" Darius asks.

"No, I'd rather not bring any more attention to your coven," I tell him, appreciating his offer. He likes us more than he lets on.

"Thank fuck," he says with a sigh, then a smirk. "Be careful out there. And if you ever need help again, find someone else."

Jade pouts, but then gives him a wink. "I'll send you a Happy Yule card with hellhounds dressed up as reindeer on it."

Darius chuffs at her, then disappears.

We portal to a few places before Erwald turns to Jade and places his hands on her shoulders. "I want to tell you how proud I am of you. I've loved you all these years. I wish I made different choices so I could have been part of your life. Whatever happens when we go to hell, I will do everything in my power to get you out safely, but do not let them know about your unique powers."

"Um, I don't know what to say, but thank you for helping me with Galiana." She bites her lip, then regains her strength. "And I hope I get to know you in the future, if you're interested in that. *If* we get through this next hurdle."

"Of course, it will be my honor to do so."

With that out of the way, Erwald shifts to his demon appearance and Jade sucks in a breath, taking in his revealed horns. Overall, he looks the same as his human glamour, and his eyes are still an unusual green that now contrasts with his red skin, which is a lighter shade than mine.

He opens a portal to hell. My pack surrounds Jade, giving her soft kisses on her head, shoulders, and cheeks.

I step in front of her and give her a searing kiss on the mouth. "No matter what you hear about me in there, know that I love you."

Her eyes widen, and her mouth parts to ask me what I mean, but I grasp her hand and pull her through right after Erwald.

The rest of my pack follows, and we find ourselves in an elegant hall reserved for the high lords of hell. The air is warm with a lingering scent of smoke. The polished walls and floors are carved from black obsidian that shines like glass.

The circular royal meeting chamber is just over one hundred feet in diameter, with large pillars keeping the ceiling of heavy rock from crashing onto us. It's made this way to discourage battles since everyone would be crushed under the weight if they broke.

Well, maybe not Flint if he shifted. But his special gift with rock manipulation doesn't extend into hell and it definitely doesn't work in this room.

Seven dark lords sit on gilded thrones in front of us. Each of them rules their regions of hell with a brutal and ruthless hand. Yet, they like to appear as they are above their base, primal instincts and play aristocrats and kings. Their power is waning just as it is in the other known realms. This farce of ruling with civility is their attempt at control, but we're counting on them to play into it today… for Jade's sake.

Their dark eyes are locked on to my mate. I can practically see the drool from their lustful thoughts as they trail their gaze over her curves. I'm tempted to rip out their eyes for daring to looking at what is mine.

Lord Muldon, the menacing male in the center, makes my stomach turn, because it all hinges on him. I fear he will punish Jade to make me pay for our personal connection. My very existence offends him now.

"High lords, I am here to respond to your summons for myself and my *progeny*." Erwald bows his head, but it isn't deep or long.

Interesting that he didn't use the usual demon descriptor *spawn* but used the term 'progeny' as if to claim her in a more significant way—as his replacement or mentee.

"Come closer." The high lord waves Jade to step forward.

Both Erwald and I stay at her side as we stop ten feet from the lords.

He studies her for a long moment, then slides his gaze over to me. "This cannot be my long-lost Maxumus showing his traitorous horns here?"

I clench my jaw but nod. "Muldon," I say, insulting him by not using his honorific.

"You've finally taken a mate, then?" He smirks like he's a cat that's caught the last canary. "When I last saw you, you were telling me to shove the throne up my ass and that you'd never suffer a needy mate."

"Yes, well, apparently, I didn't know the bliss of finding my mate match who perfectly fit with my *chosen* family."

Muldon's eyes dart up to take in the rest of our party. "Quite a menagerie you have collected. Were you trying to befriend every possible tragic and obscure species?"

I shrug off his insult. "Seems fitting I should find acceptance with them since I never fit in amongst those in hell."

"No, you did not," he says with a weary sigh. "At least your brother proved to be a proper demon."

"Don't rub it in," I growl. "I didn't plan on being the white sheep of the family."

Jade snaps her gaze at me, her brow crinkling in confusion, and then perhaps she's figured out my secret. "Are you two related?"

I press my lips flat, but Muldon speaks before I can confirm. "Jadeana of Erwald, you were raised as a human. Is that correct?"

"Uh, yes," she says with surprise at the topic change.

"But it appears you have mated with five males. That is not common in the mortal realm, is it?"

"No, it's not."

"Were you coerced into bonding with these mercenaries?" he asks, as if he's concerned for her agency. "Did they give you no other choice?"

"No. I chose them on my own, after fate put them on my path. My soul was drawn to each of them and picked them as my mates," Jade says with conviction, allowing no doubt to seep into her voice.

"When you made your choice, you were obviously ignorant to all this realm has to offer a female such as yourself." He smiles, attempting to seem accommodating. "I could have the bonds dissolved, and you would have your pick of demons here to shower you with attention and meet your every need."

Jade cocks her eyebrow and her hip defiantly. "Oh? So you'd kill off my loving, chosen mates just so you can all knock me up with your spawn?"

"I don't *need* to kill them." Muldon waves his hand dismissively. "But yes, we'd like a chance to continue our race with your cooperation and in exchange, we'd keep you well fed and well fucked. And isn't that everything you need?"

Jade narrows her eyes at him, calculating how to deal with this situation. "I wish you luck in finding someone else who would appreciate that offer, but I already have everything with my mates, who offer me more than only food and cocks. Besides, I have no interest in accepting a breeding role in *any* realm."

Muldon clenches his jaw. He never did like the word no, and especially from a female.

"If I may interrupt," Erwald cuts in before Muldon can respond. His voice comes out with a commanding force. I can feel the room bending to his will. I suspect he's more magically powerful than those sitting on the council. "This court owes me a life debt. I claim my progeny, Jadeana, to remain free as that favor. All hellborn will leave her in peace, in all aspects, for however long she lives. Do you understand?"

Muldon's eyes bulge out of his head, and he shakes with rage. "This? This is what you call in your favor for? She could be the answer to the lords' dwindling numbers."

He rushes down off the dais and attempts to grab Jade.

I dart in front of him, and he crashes against my chest. I'd sacrifice myself for Jade's freedom. If I have to fight him, I will. He sees the call for an official challenge written in my eyes and I'm pleased as I see nervousness in his returning gaze.

We growl at each other while I sense Jade being pulled into Flint's arms for protection.

"She is mine!" Erwald snarls and seems to grow twice his size. "And I will not have her used for your power games and passed around like she is nothing but a hole to fuck and incubation chamber."

"Come now. She is obviously not opposed to fucking multiple males!" Muldon shouts and moves to look at her again, trying to circumvent me.

"Her *fated* mates!" Erwald steps closer to Muldon, and the lord shrinks back. "*This* is why demons are cursed. You did not value those offering us love and offspring and now you're paying the price with a dying species. We should have been cherishing and protecting our female counterparts, instead we turned against them and now they choose not to incarnate for your bidding and abuse."

I glance back to check on her, and Jade's eyes are wide with a genuine look of surprise and being impressed by her father's words. Finally, the bastard is some use in her life—first with Galiana and now here.

"And this is why I chose not to stay here in hell and sit on this council under your thumb," I add. "I could not claim a seat with someone who harms our precious females."

My stomach turns as I remember how Muldon abused his mate and when she failed to offer him more spawn, my mother was found dead.

"But now that I *have* a mate, I suppose I could challenge you for a seat on the council. Actually..." I wave my hand over to Erwald and Jade. "They are also of royal lineage, so perhaps they might also decide it would be easier to challenge you than to have you decide Jadeana's fate. Three of us on the seven seats sounds fairly tempting."

Muldon snarls at my comment. He knows we could easily be his end.

He turns to Erwald. "Fine. Keep your spawn. I doubt she could produce quality demons anyway, since she's a fucking mutt." He doesn't wait for us to leave and storms out of the chamber.

Another council member speaks up. "Lord Erwald, never mind his theatrics. Consider Jadeana safe from hellborn via your life debt favor, with the condition that none of you attempt to challenge for a seat on this council. And I hope your reappearance now means you're back to your regular visits and reports of goings on in the realms."

"Yes, it seems that since Jadeana's secret identity has been revealed, there is no reason for me to hide away."

"Since you have claimed her as your progeny, then we expect that to be the case. In the coming years, we expect her to be trained in diplomacy and in spy work. Perhaps because of her unusual blood lines, she can be a bridge to all three from her lineage. We all know magic is dwindling, and it's time we stop blaming and root out the source. I've heard a rumor that the Fae Queen is trying to find a solution. Perhaps Jadeana can be the bridge between the witches, the fae, and the demons, so we may all survive."

I sense Jade's anxiety skyrocket as she feels the implications of what Lord Krall is asking of her. But at least we already have a way in to the Fae Queen's court through me. Krall has always been the most sensible demon on the council, and I can see what he asks will benefit all the realms.

"Can you agree to this?" Krall glances between Jade and Erwald.

Jade glances up at her father, who stares at her proudly and nods. They both respond with a yes.

"Then I will see you soon," the demon lord says.

Hearing our clear dismissal, Erwald portals us out, and we quickly escape before they change their minds about letting us go.

Jade slumps against Arran, and he lifts her bridal style into his arms, clutching her to his chest.

I'm just happy he didn't let loose his berserker during that whole shitshow.

"Does that mean I am free?" Jade asks, fear coating her voice. She isn't ready to believe things are going to work out in our favor.

"Yes, my sweet child," Erwald says, true endearment in his tone. "I can report back any information or progress you make so you don't have to suffer Muldon's hostility."

Her mind is easy enough for me to read now that we're bonded, and she wants to scoff at her father calling her sweet or a child. Though another part of her secretly loves it.

She's been aching for love all her four decades. And that's exactly what I, and her other four mates, intend to give her until the end of her days. And beyond.

# THE ANSWER

JADE

*M*y mind is still spinning with the revelation that Maxum and I are both demon royals. I always knew I could be a royal pain in the ass. Now it's official.

Maxum is a bigger deal in hell than he ever let on. No one in our pack knew. He begrudgingly confessed that he could have had his father's seat on the council if he had challenged him for it. But he didn't want a demon's life, especially one of a ruler.

The guys are being brats about it and calling him *The Prince of Morally Gray*.

All too soon, it's time to part ways with my father. He says he has a few things to take care of to ensure my safety.

"If any demons show up, fight with all you have," my father says, then gives me his secret demon name so I can summon him if I need him and asks Maxum to teach me how to dial-a-demon.

I give my father a shaky hug goodbye and a promise to keep in touch.

Maxum gives him our contact information so we can connect in the future since our pack intends on lying low for a while.

Osen has hinted it's a mating honeymoon.

I'm a bit surprised when Maxum portals us back to his lake house as the sun sets behind the rolling mountains.

"I thought this place was compromised and not safe anymore," I say, taking in the beautiful sight. This house was the first place to truly feel like a home.

"We're free to return now that Galiana and Rob are no longer a threat, and it seems her minions are dead, too," Osen explains.

"Amira also gifted me the secret of her powerful wards so I can create them around the property," Maxum adds.

Happiness bubbles out of me that my pack has their home again. It was always meant to be their permanent retreat. I nuzzle into Calder's chest, and Osen presses behind me and kisses the top of my head.

"Stop hoggin' her." Arran grasps my hand and pulls me free from the love sandwich. He turns to rub it in their face that he now has me and sticks out his tongue.

Flint uses the moment to sneak attack, snatches me up, and runs toward the house. He has the widest grin I've ever seen.

"Hey!" Arran whines and gives chase.

Maxum races ahead like a bullet. It's stunning how powerful they are. My demon prince unlocks the front door and flings it open.

I peek over Flint's massive shoulder to see the others clamoring and shoving to be the next through the door.

Their faces are filled with joy and childlike excitement. My heart glows seeing them drop all their past suffering to play.

Flint slides me down his rock-hard body, but with just enough give in his flesh to remind me what I gifted him during

YVE VALE

our mating. He turns me to face the open plan living area with the attached gourmet kitchen.

The entire place is filled with a hundred fae wildflower arrangements, comprised of species I came to adore during our travels. A few dozen candles light up with magic to romantically illuminate the space. A banner hangs above the glass patio doors, reading "Welcome home, our beautiful mate." The sign is inexpertly hand painted, but I think I love it even more because of its rustic, heartfelt style.

*Home.*

My eyes fill with happy tears as my guys crowd around me.

I have a home, not just a house with my stuff inside it.

My guys are that home. No matter where I go, as long as they are with me, I have all I need.

Something zooms past us, and I jerk back, quickly realizing it's Sage as she does a fun kick in the air and spins like a furry ninja.

"You licked them all!" she says like it's her victory cry.

I bark out a laugh. "Yes, I licked them all. They're mine now."

"About time," Trouble snarks. "What took you so long?"

"Hey!" I argue. "It was pretty fast for human standards."

"Well, you aren't a human, are you?" he huffs.

"Touché." I roll my eyes and mutter. "I have the sassiest familiar ever."

"Believe it or not, I've heard others can be more obnoxious," Arran shrugs.

Maxum leads us to his old bedroom that Arran and I shared with him the last time we were here. When he opens the door, there is a gigantic bed that will fit all six of us. My eye travels around the large room to find various sex furniture like leather chaises for hitting the perfect angle, harness swings, and dungeon apparatus with tie downs.

"Fuck, yes." Osen runs a hand over the leather and grins wickedly. "This is perfect."

And I have to agree. We'll have a lot of fun in here. But I will also want quiet, snuggle time with each of them, and the soft bed looks just as inviting. He shows me the closet full of comfy clothes and sexy underwear and a few costumes for play time.

I give Maxum a hug and look up into his glowing obsidian eyes. "Thank you."

"Jade needs to eat." Flint places a kiss on my cheek and rushes back out to the kitchen to cook. He's such a caretaker, and my heart warms with the realization that this is the first time in all my years that I have not only one person to keep me safe and happy, but five.

We follow Flint into the beautiful spacious kitchen, asking how we can help.

When I study the living room and kitchen, I notice that somehow the damage created by the magical fight with Rob, Floofer, and Galiana has been completely erased. Maxum must have had people repairing our home this whole time.

Maxum puts on some music with a beat, and we burst out in laughter when we recognize the song *Monster Mash*. We have an impromptu dance party as we make dinner. I find myself laughing, grinding, and swaying with all of them at some point.

Flint has some secret dirty moves that have all the guys nodding their approval.

"Dang," Osen says with interest. "I can't wait to watch Flint fuck you. I bet he *rocks* your world."

My face and core heat with that image. "Yes, he does *rock* me hard and makes the *earth* quake," I say with a wink. "But you'll need to ask him if he wants an audience."

Flint lifts my chin so I'm looking up at his bold and masculine face. He sees the flush of my cheeks. "Does that excite you, Heartstone? To have me show them how I take care of your needy little pussy?"

"*Fuuuck*," I hiss and my knees give out. My innocent gargoyle is developing a naughty vocabulary, and I'm here for it. "You can't just blindside me, talking dirty like that, Flint. My heart can't handle it."

He holds me to his bare chest, and his pronounced bulge presses into my stomach through his pants.

"I've been reading your books," he confesses.

I blush, remembering some of the things I've written. Will he recite dialogue and reenact the scenes for me?

"Screw dinner. I want to take care of our mate, and properly anoint this entire house with our mate's orgasms and our cum," Osen announces.

The rest of my mates crowd around me, and I'm overheating with their rapt attention. Dang. It's one thing to write or read this stuff, but it's intimidating as fuck when five insanely hot and large males devour me with a hungry look.

"I don't think I'm going to survive this," my voice pitches high with nervousness.

"My phoenix senses don't foretell a death, so you'll live… happily," Calder says with a wicked grin. "We're going to fuck you until you pass out from bliss and then rouse you again so we can give you another round of pleasure."

Flint lifts me so I'm sitting on the kitchen island, and instantly the other guys clear the surface. He kisses me slowly, pouring his love for me into such a simple act and I feel treasured, like the most precious gem.

Multiple hands caress every inch of my body as they strip off my shirt and bra. I'm guided to lie back against the cool tile and Flint slides my pants off. Claws drag against the rise of my hipbone and then slice through my underwear.

I gasp with the sudden breeze of air against my soaked pussy. He lifts my legs and stretches me open for their viewing. My feet are set out as far as possible on the edge of the counter.

I cover my face, slightly embarrassed at my being on display. I hope I don't look like an uncooked turkey like this.

*May the stuffing commence!*

It's one thing for one or even two of my guys to take a

gander at my nether regions, but when I glance down and see five sets of lust-filled eyes devouring the sight of me, I have the urge to either have one of them inside me or to snap my legs shut. I vote for option one.

Both Osen and Calder lean in and their tongues battle over my folds, spearing me. My back arches off the cool tile with the incredible sensation.

Maxum appears over my head from the other side of the island, leaning down and claiming my mouth with his forked tongue. His warm hands brace the sides of my face and then one hand slips down to clamp over my throat. He squeezes just enough to light my body on fire with need. "I know what I'm craving for dinner."

Arran and Flint massage and suck on my tits, drawing the pebbled nipples into their mouths. Osen's thick fingers slide into my channel, and my clit aches as Calder bites down just enough to make me come undone.

My whole body vibrates. My magic electricity crawls over my flesh. I buck, almost sending me flying if I weren't being grounded by five gorgeous monsters.

Osen places light kisses over my low belly and moves upward to finally place his lips on mine. "Are you ready for us, our shadowflame?"

The combination of their mating nicknames is perfect to represent the love we share.

"Yes," I whisper against his lips. I know he's only asking about sex, but when I answer, it means more than that. I'm ready for all of them, for our lives to truly begin with each other.

His eyes swirl with shadow and the promise of making my fantasies come true.

One of his shadowtendrils brushes up against my tight hole and slides inside.

Then I feel the cool liquid move alongside, using his fingers.

"Where the hell did you get that lube?" Arran asks in confusion.

"What? I keep some in every room," Osen says flippantly, like that's what everyone does.

"You gonna plow my back forty?" I joke, using ranching terminology because I've read a cowboy romance.

Osen teases back. "Nah, I'm going to drill for cum. Pretty sure I'm going to stroke my payload."

I'd chuckle, but I'm being lifted by his shadows and positioned with my back to him. Calder steps in front of me and admires Osen's shadowtendril-rigging as I'm harnessed upright so they can both have their way with me. My legs are spread and Calder's hand cups my mound and he slips two fingers into my cunt. All the while Osen makes me ready to take him in my ass.

Dipping down, Calder licks and nibbles along my neck until he bites my nipple, and I cry out with a delicious mix of pain and pleasure.

That's apparently Osen's cue to place the head of his cock at my back entrance. The slow stretch as he sinks me down onto him has me sweating and moaning.

Once he's fully seated, he stills inside me, and Calder notches his cock and presses inside my pussy.

"So full. I... I... please, move," I beg.

And they do. They both work in tandem like this is some dance. Their hot mouths are on my neck. They kiss each other over my shoulder as I watch and clench around their shafts.

They groan and become frantic in their thrusts, as if this is a race, but we are all going to win. Osen wraps his shadow around Calder's balls and the base of his cock, squeezing and stroking. Another shadow flicks and rubs my clit until I'm fluttering around them.

Calder's wings unfurl and light on fire as he cries out, "I'm coming. Goddess, I love you, Jade, Osen." He bucks into me and spasms.

His hot seed fills me. My orgasm hits me hard, and it prolongs his release. Our pleasure triggers Osen, and he unloads in my ass.

Osen peppers kisses over my neck and shoulder, murmuring his gratefulness for having us in his life.

As soon as they slip out of me, Maxum has me in his arms. I wrap my legs around his waist, but don't have enough strength to keep them there. Arran and Flint come to my rescue, and each holds a leg and supports my back as they lift me high enough so Maxum can fuck me.

Maxum's tail presses in my ass, using Osen's release as a lube. His textured cock rubs against my cum covered pussy, making my toes curl with the wicked sensation. "You will have no doubt who you belong to by the time this night is over."

"And you're all *mine!*" I growl back, feeling every bit the demoness that I am.

"Yes, we are, our beautiful monster fucker," Maxum says with a smirk as he thrusts into me, and I cry out with the invasion. His tail and cock claim me all over again. He fists my hair and tilts my head backward as he clamps his sharp teeth over my delicate throat. If I didn't have complete trust in him, I'd freak out with this move, but I'm turned on. He's part crazed, perhaps just as much or more than Serky like this.

Maxum is ramming into me with such ferocity that if I were a mere human, it would leave bruises. Maybe a broken bone. But I'm no longer fragile. With his rhythmic pounding against my clit and how he's stimulating all the right spots inside me, I scream with the orgasm that hits me like a freight train. He plows into me just like one too as he chases his own bliss. His cum fills me with a groan and a shout from his mouth still around my neck.

I must lose consciousness briefly, because the next thing I know, Flint is carrying me over to the living room. He clutches me to his chest as he places a soft throw on the couch and sets me down gently.

My gargoyle stands and shifts to his huge true form. His pants are still on, but I can see the giant bulge pressing against the fabric.

*"Do you need a break, Heartstone?"* he asks via our mind link.

I shake my head no. I want all of them, and I want them *now*. I need this to remember we survived. We need to celebrate that we are all together.

Digging into my supernatural side, I find the strength to sit. My face is level with his groin, and I stare up at his pale gray eyes that shine with love.

My fingers hook on his waistband, but I don't reveal him. "You don't have to hide. You're perfect and gorgeous. And I wouldn't want you any other way."

The other guys glance at each other with intrigue glinting in their eyes.

Flint sighs and nods for me to pull his pants down.

Once his fully erect double cocks are revealed, there are gasps.

"Go ahead." He mutters, appearing resigned to the ridicule he expects. "Make your jokes now."

"Are you fucking kidding me?" Calder almost shouts his awe. "I'm jealous as hell."

"Me too, and I have shadowcocks," Osen adds, but he knew about Flint from when he was possessing me.

"Yeah, buddy." Maxum pats him on the shoulder. "I expected you were packing, but damn, that's impressive."

"And his cum tastes like candy," Arran grins.

Flint's hunched shoulders straighten, and he smiles shyly. "Jade likes them, and that's all that matters."

"I love everything about you," I correct and lean for to lick over the heads of his two cocks, humming when his sweet taste delights my tongue.

Flint moans. "Suck my cocks like a good girl."

I almost choke at his naughty order. I want to argue that I'm hardly a girl, but fuck, compared to his four hundred years, I am.

Besides, he's owning his sexiness right now, and I encourage it by taking one of his cocks down to the back of my throat, while I stroke the second one.

"I need to be inside you," he growls, the floor below us rumbling with his power. He pulls out of my mouth, drops to his knees. Taking my hips in his firm hands, he draws me to the edge of the couch, my back hitting the cushions with the force of his need. He lines up his cocks with my cunt and ass. Without warning, he plows inside me.

I cry out with the sheer pleasure of feeling him inside me.

Flint is a fucking machine, thrusting with a speed that defies his bulk. The fullness and friction are driving me wild, and I'm thrashing under him. His huge wings expand, but instead of blocking the other guys out, he pulls them all closer.

"Holy shit," Arran whispers. "I'm going to come just watching this."

"Fuck her mouth, Arran," Flint orders.

"Stars and stones, is Flint a secret dom?" Osen squeals with glee. "I might be falling in love."

Calder grabs the back of Osen's head, fists his hair, and kisses the ever-living fuck out of him. "*I'll* dom you. Get on your knees and suck the taste of our mate on my cock."

"Yes, sir." Osen drops to his knees. Like a man possessed himself, he swallows Calder down to the root.

Damn, they are beautiful together.

Half shifted and in a lusty daze, Arran finally registers that Flint gave him an order. He leaps up on the couch and presents his aching cock leaking pre-cum.

I lap up the slippery fluid, and he slips his shaft into my mouth to the flare of his knot.

Flint's consistent motion becomes jerky as he gets closer to falling off the edge of bliss. "You're so gorgeous. Magnificent. A perfect fit for our hearts. You take our cocks so well. Made for us." He grunts out the last words. "I love you, Heartstone."

Our bodies arch together and my pussy and ass squeeze down on his shafts, milking them. His cum fills me, his cocks pulsing inside. I cry out around Arran's cock.

My body is a puddle of noodle limbs, and Arran pulls from my mouth.

A tongue licks the cum from between my thighs and works its way to my tender pussy. When Arran swipes over my clit, I buck into the air and then collapse again.

"Sloppy fifths." Arran smirks and licks his lips. "And it tastes so good."

I stare down between my thighs to watch my werewolf. He's part Serky and part Arran, in a sexy blend of man and monster. Serky's wildness shines in his golden glowing eyes, but I sense Arran feels just as wild with the need to claim me now.

He pulls back and flips me over onto my stomach, and my chest lands on the seat of the couch. Arran leans over my body and wraps his hands around my waist and plunges his cock inside me. His knot slams against my clit and labia. I moan, anticipating the glorious stretch I'm about to experience.

I idly realize why he's last, because his knot will lock inside me and keep me as his for however long his knot remains engorged.

Arran's hand slides down and his clawed fingers drag over my clit. The thrill of danger races up my spine.

Calder shouts, spilling down Osen's throat.

The pure debauchery of the night has me coming on Arran's cock. When he feels my pussy spasming around him, he snarls and pushes his knot all the way inside.

I shout with the overly full feeling, and the sensation cascades into another orgasm on the heels of the first. Arran howls as he releases his load.

All four of my other mates howl with him, and I do too.

It feels like we're a true pack in that moment. Wild and bonded beyond anything I ever believed possible for me.

Everyone collapses onto the couch beside us. Serky doesn't take issue with all of them touching and kissing me as we wait for his knot to empty and deflate. I don't think I've ever been so relaxed and contented in all my life.

Osen breathes out. "I'm officially *dead*."

We all grumble at his horrible joke.

"Too soon?" He laughs as we agree. "Well, I am, because this is heaven."

A smile slides over my face as I understand what he means. I *am* in heaven and heaven is being in the arms of my loves.

# EPILOGUE

 *FEW WEEKS LATER...*

"You're the only monster for me," she whispers over his feline ears.

The ears twitch, but his purring gives away how much he adores her words.

No one else would ever come between them again.

### THE END

In my office chair, I brush my hand over my magic containment pendant, thanking it for allowing me to work on my computer as I write. I stretch, grinning at the screen. I've finally finished my novella just in time to send it to my editor. This isn't exactly the full-length novel I had hoped to give readers, but it should satisfy them for the time being.

My mind is already planning my next series based loosely on my monster mates.

I race out to the living room and find Flint reading my older novels on the couch. I launch myself into his arms.

He reacts supernaturally fast and catches me, easing me into his lap.

"I finished!" I kiss his luscious lips and smile.

My gargoyle squeezes me to his chest. "I'm so proud of you."

"What would you like to do to celebrate?" Osen asks as he saunters into the room. "I have some suggestions."

Calder appears next to him and winks at the incubus. "I suspect most are clothing optional."

In his wolf form, Arran races into the room and crashes into me, knocking me out of Flint's arms. He licks my face like he hasn't seen me in a year.

"Be careful with her!" Maxum shouts as he storms into the room.

Instantly, he shifts into a very naked Arran, pinning me down over Flint's lap. "We missed you."

I roll my eyes. "It was only a three hour writing session."

"An eternity," he whines, then kisses me.

Maxum yanks Arran off and claims me for himself, lifting me into his arms. "I'm happy for you. We should celebrate."

"No reason to make a big deal. It's just a novella." I wave him off.

"Never diminish your victories," he reminds me with a firm voice. This isn't the first time, and I doubt it will be the last time he nails me on this behavior. "You were at it for weeks. And with everything that's happened, I'm surprised you could focus on writing at all."

"All cock access all the time has been mighty *dicks-tracting*," I joke.

Osen slides up behind me, making me the meat in the

Maxum-Osen sandwich. "I haven't been able to focus on anything but our mate bond."

"Poor incubus needs more sexy time?" I coo.

He swats my ass. "And I'm severely deficient in the snuggle department."

"Hug attack!" Like a wild monkey, I jump from Maxum's hold and swing over to grab onto Osen. The guys accommodate my awkward fumbling and help transfer me over so I can crush Osen in a big hug.

He hums in my ear, desperately holding my clinging body flush against his muscular chest. "Never gets old."

"My turn." Calder taps Osen on the shoulder.

Instead of giving me up completely, Osen only allows a three-way hug. But I love it just as much. The love that thrums between us swells in my heart.

Maxum, Arran, and Flint join us, wrapping their arms around me, creating the world's best group hug.

Arran's bite mark tingles happily. Flint's mind caresses mine. Calder's talon marks at my back simmer with his warmth. The shadow and light in my chest stir with Osen's bond. The marking over my heart that represents Maxum's bond pulses with light.

I am exactly where I belong.

There's one tradition I have when I complete a book. I have a drink to celebrate down at my old neighborhood bar.

The guys wanted to go with me, probably to protect me, but there wasn't a threat anymore.

The server, Lora, squeaks when she sees me walk in. "Oh my god, Jade. Where have you been? I've been worried sick."

"Sorry. I had a family emergency and had to leave town."

Not completely untrue...

"Everything okay?"

"It is now. And I managed to get a book done," I say with a grin.

"That's wonderful news!" Lora gives me a hug. "I'll want a copy as soon as you're ready to share." She guides me over to the table I often sit at—the one where I first saw my guys. "I'll bring out your signature drink right away."

It only takes a few moments, and Lora appears with my wild cocktail loaded with fruit on a stick and umbrellas. It's obnoxious as hell, but was created in a pouty moment when I needed something fun to celebrate by myself.

Lora had chatted with me that night years ago for hours. It was nice to share a success with someone, even if she was mostly a stranger.

I catch Lora up on a bit of what's happened, a *normal's* version of events and leaving out my monster harem.

"Wow. That must be so weird finally meeting your father when you're forty."

"Yeah, but he seems like a nice enough guy. We plan to meet up regularly now so he can make amends."

Just then, the door opens and five of the most gorgeous males I've ever seen walk through the door. Their handsome leader looks to Lora and points to the empty corner booth. She nods and then her eyes go wide.

"Holy shit," she hisses at me. "Those are the same hot guys you were drooling over the last time I saw you."

"I believe you're right." I grin ear to ear when Maxum gives me a flirty wink.

I should've known these possessive and protective brats would follow me.

"They keep glancing at you," Lora says excitedly.

"Send them a round of my celebration drinks," I say with a smirk.

Lora runs off giggling and within minutes, delivers my ultra girly drinks to the guys and points to me as the gifter.

They all raise their glasses up and toast me with sassy

smiles. But as they lift the glasses to their divine lips, they are poked and jabbed by the ornamentations. I can't help but snicker at their fumbling. Flint gives me a shy grin as he pulls all the fruit and umbrellas out and guzzles the drink in one go.

Osen crooks his finger to invite me over. Then they all do it. A thrill runs down my spine. I'm so gone for them.

Lora looks like she might pass out from the excitement. To be honest, seeing them here in my old stomping grounds, at the same place and the same booth that I first set eyes on them, makes them all seem like a beautiful dream. Like a story out of my books.

I pick up my drink and saunter over. "Hello," I say with a sultry voice. "Are you enjoying your *cock*-tails?"

"We'd enjoy them more if you'd joined us," Osen says like the smooth player he is.

Flint and Arran stand up so I can slide down the corner booth and sit in the middle. With my huge, hulky mates surrounding me, I glance around the mundane bar and almost laugh that my guys could be seen as anything other than the supernatural gods they are.

We flirt and finish our drinks, pretending this is the first time we've met. A do-over of sorts. Last time, I was an embarrassed mess when they caught me ogling them. Now, they are doting over me.

We get up to leave together, each of them giving me a seductive touch while Lora's eyes nearly pop out.

She pulls me aside. "Are you sure you should go with them?" she asks, concerned as a good friend should be.

"Yeah, I have a good feeling about them," I say, looking back over my shoulder at my perfect mates.

"Are you… going to… with *all* of them?" she gulps.

"It's research for my books." I give her a wink and slide back between my mates.

"Let's make this beautiful woman ours," Arran says loud enough for Lora to hear. Then he whispers, "Again."

*THE END?*

If you enjoyed this book, please consider leaving a review on Amazon. It means so much to me!

Check out my **free extra spicy bonus novella** where Jade checks off some wild fantasies on her monster bucket list.
**Possessing Her Monsters**

# A NOTE FROM JADE

ear Monster Fucker Reader,

I hope you enjoyed the slightly fictionalized story of my life. I've written this under my pen name Yve Vale to conceal my real identity.

The names and places have been changed to protect my harem and all my sweet monsters.

If you'd like to know more about proper monster harem care and handling, you can follow me via Yve Vale's newsletters, Facebook reader group, or even reaching out through email.

I'm available for questions and comments, or if you found an error in paranormal creature representation.

And I hope all of you find the supernatural loves of your lives (whether it's in the books or in real life).

Oh, and please keep an eye out for Amira, Darius, and Raithe's story.

With all my supernatural love,
Juniper Jade

# THANK YOU FOR READING!

I would like to thank my readers, launch team, and fellow
authors for your support.
A big shout out to my PA, Clare, for all your amazing help.
And a shoutout to my helpers who won the *Name the Villain*:
Britt'ny Castor, Donna Stolpestad Zug, Naomi Kerr, Maria
Ristow for all suggesting Minerva!
And to La Pookette, for the last name Marvin.

Check out some of my other books and series:

If you love Maxum, he has an appearance in
**Shadowcraft Academy Completed Series**
*I didn't want magic. I was supposed to escape.*
I'm forced to attend a magic academy with five males
who won't leave me alone—my fated mate dragon,
a dangerous vampire, a protective druid, a seductive incubus,
and a hot professor wolf shifter.
https://books2read.com/ShadowcraftAcademy1

**Fae Hearted Series**
A human servant with a secret.
A scandalous bargain with an Elven prince.
Three elves willing to break all the rules for her…
https://books2read.com/faehearted1

**Chained Fates**: Shadow Myths Book 1:
*Four Demon Warriors. The last Serafim. One dark cell.*

I find myself imprisoned with four gorgeous males
from a violent warrior species.
With their massive size, horns, and tails, I worry they will seek
revenge for my reluctant part in their torment.
When my healing hands wander, their growls turn to purrs.
Will they take me with them if we can escape?
Will they give me what I crave—their touch?
https://books2read.com/chained-fates

**Rebel Fates:** Shadow Myths Book 2
*The Egyptian gods were aliens, and their people still exist...*

I'm done with Earth. The moon base has to be better.
However, my plan didn't go as I had hoped.
I end up on a ship with three intense warrior aliens who look
like gorgeous Egyptian gods—all who I begin to crave. They
have heads of animals and bodies of men. They look like
Anubis, lion man, and a minotaur.
*I'm not out of trouble yet...*
https://books2read.com/rebel-fates

Need bonus content? News on new releases?
https://yvevale.com/newsletter

# ALSO BY YVE VALE

*SHADOWCRAFT ACADEMY:*

(Dark Paranormal Academy Trilogy + Bonus Novella)

**Hexed ~ Jinxed ~ Cursed ~ Blessed**

*BEWITCHING MONSTERS:*

(Grown-Ass Woman & Monsters Trilogy)

**Bewitching Her Monsters**

**Charming Her Monsters**

**Enchanting Her Monsters**

**Possessing Her Monsters**

*SHADOW MYTHS:*

(Science Fantasy Standalones)

**Chained Fates ~ Rebel Fates**

*FAE HEARTED:*

(Fantasy / Shadowcraft Universe Origins Prequel)

**Between Realms**

**Tangled Secrets**

**Chaos Tempted**

**Bonds Eternal**

*GODS ARE HIRING:*

**My Karmic Destiny**

A Why Choose / RH continuation of

**My Instant Karma** by Raven Vale

# ALSO WRITING AS

## WRITING AS RAVEN VALE

### *GODS ARE HIRING:*

M/F PNR Standalones

**My Instant Karma**

**Cupid's Last Arrow**

## WRITING AS JADE VALE

### *CAGE BROTHERS:*

M/F Dark Billionaire Contemporary Interconnected Standalones

**For more book details, visit:**

**ValeRomances.com**

# ABOUT THE AUTHOR

Yve Vale loves spicy romance, fated mates, and redeemable supernatural bad boys who end up as cinnamon roll alphas for their woman.

She writes about strong females and their magical males, all set in paranormal worlds.

She is a lover and a fighter. This is why her books feature a fair amount of action, both in romantic endeavors and in battle.

Stalk me here: https://yvevale.com

www.ingramcontent.com/pod-product-compliance
Lightning Source LLC
Chambersburg PA
CBHW060226030726
47499CB00004B/1204